Safe From the War

Chris Hernandez

TACTI6AL™

Safe From the War
Copyright © 2016 by Chris Hernandez

First Edition

Because of the dynamic nature of the internet, any web address or links contained in this book may have changed since publication and may no longer be valid.

"Safe From the War" is a work of fiction. Names, characters, places, and incidents are the products of the author's imagination, experiences, or are fictitious. Any resemblance to actual events, locales, or persons, living or dead, is entirely coincidental.

The views expressed in this work are solely those of the author and do not necessarily reflect the views of the publisher, and the publisher hereby disclaims any responsibility for them.

Published by Tactical 16, LLC
Colorado Springs, CO

eISBN: 978-1-943226-09-2
ISBN: 978-1-943226-10-8 (hc)
ISBN: 978-1-943226-11-5 (sc)

Printed in the United States of America

For Lucas, my youngest son.
You have a hard fight ahead, and you're going to win.

CHAPTER 1

"North patrol dispatch to 1243."

Jerry Nunez knew what was coming. He had seen the call holding when he checked his patrol car's computer a minute earlier. He hadn't avoided the call, but he hadn't volunteered for it either. He picked up the radio mike, keyed up and sighed, "1243, go ahead."

"Family disturbance, 1803 Hanley, apartment A. Caller reports a woman screaming. I'll get you a backup unit as soon as I have one."

Shit. Another family disturbance I'm not in the mood for. Nunez wasn't familiar with that address, but if it was a family disturbance at an apartment complex in North Houston, it was bullshit. After thirteen years on the street it seemed to Nunez that all the calls, even real calls with guns, knives and dead gangsters, were bullshit.

"That's clear, en route. And don't bother anyone else, I'll advise if I need backup."

Nunez pulled into a parking lot and turned the car around, then shifted side to side to get the duty belt's weight off his hips for a few seconds. Over a decade of wearing a heavy leather belt with Sig Sauer pistol, spare magazines, radio, handcuffs and flashlight had left dark brown spots the size of fists on his hips, and he had begun to worry his wife might find him unattractive because of them. He was thirty-seven, not very tall and not nearly as skinny as he had once been. The stress of facing sudden death or injury for years as a cop, and of twice going to war, showed on his once-unblemished face.

He took his time getting to the call. It was just another low-priority disturbance in the 'hood, one of hundreds across Houston every night. He leisurely drove north, running the license plate of any vehicle he saw, hoping he would find a stolen car or something else to pull him away.

His radio beeped again. "Dispatch to 1243."

"1243, go ahead."

"We received a second call about that disturbance, from a different caller. Are you sure you don't want another unit?"

Nunez thought about it. Generally, you never turned down backup. But patrol had been stretched thin for years, and if he asked for backup dispatch might pull someone from ten miles away and leave some other officer uncovered.

"1243 dispatch, nah, I'm good. I'll advise if I need someone. Thanks for looking out though."

"Dispatch 1243, anytime."

Nunez jumped on the freeway, took the first exit and turned onto Hanley. As he approached a stop sign, the radio beeped again.

"Dispatch 1243, we just received a third call from another witness. This one says a female ran out of the apartment screaming and a male assaulted her and dragged her back inside. Who's available to check by with 1243?" The dispatcher wasn't asking this time, she was getting backup whether Nunez wanted it or not.

"1243 dispatch, got it and I've arrived. I'll let you know if backup can disregard."

Nunez passed the stop sign and saw the little apartment buildings, across the street from an old, shabby-looking church. This was a quiet street, and he didn't remember ever seeing this complex. It was neat and clean, and as he turned into the parking lot he saw that it had only ten apartments. Five connected apartments faced across the parking lot at five identical apartments. One block held apartments A through E, with A on the left as you faced the front doors. A light shined from inside apartment A, but the porch light was off. The lone window, beside the apartment door, had closed Venetian blinds hanging inside.

Nunez parked his car out of the immediate danger area in front of the apartment. He stopped the car and shut the engine and headlights off, but left the parking lights on so backup officers could spot it. He stepped out and looked around.

Behind the car, four gangster-looking Hispanic teenagers slouched on apartment F's front porch. Apartment A was silent, with nothing demanding his immediate attention, so he walked toward the teenage thugs. As he got closer he saw that all had shaved heads and tattoos on their forearms.

"We got a call out here about a disturbance. You guys seen anything?" Nunez asked, expecting to hear the usual *Naw, dog, we just got here.*

"Yeah man, that guy across the way was beating up his girl or something," one answered. "We heard screaming and shit, and she ran out the door, but the guy grabbed her and punched her a buncha times in the stomach and dragged her ass back inside. We was inside looking out the window, and when we got outside they was already back in the house, so we couldn't do nuthin'. I'm the one that called though."

"No shit," Nunez said. "How long ago did this happen?"

"Uh, maybe five minutes ago. Not that long, y'all got here pretty fast."

"What'd they look like?" Nunez asked. "Black, white, Mexican?"

"I don't know. They've been around for a while but they speak some weird shit, like Russian or something. They're both young, maybe in high school. They kinda look Mexican."

"You ever see any guns or anything there?"

"Shit, everyone around here got a gun, man," the spokesman answered. "But I never seen one there."

"Alright, thanks," Nunez said, "Stay here, I might need your name for a report."

The mini-thug nodded. Nunez headed toward apartment A, and dispatch piped up on the radio again.

"Still need a backup unit for 1243."

"1113, I got it. Be there in five."

Nunez groaned silently, hoping he would be able to disregard backup. 1113 was Officer Edward Calhoun, a young, violent, pissed off egomaniac who treated everyone like crap whether they were scumbags or not. He was the kind of officer who could show up to a peaceful scene, turn the calm and cooperative into the angry and combative, and within five minutes twist the scene into a shit festival. Plus, he drove like a fucking idiot. Nunez knew Calhoun was flying ninety miles an hour down quiet residential streets, sending pedestrians fleeing into front yards in panic, sliding through intersections and leaving skid marks at every turn to get to 1803 Hanley.

Nunez had first thought highly of Calhoun since he had been a Marine infantryman before joining the department. He had mad tactical skills and a lot of drive, but his abrasiveness and bad judgment soured the good impression within a month. Nunez figured he better handle this call and wave Calhoun off before he screeched sideways around the corner and started motherfucking everyone in sight.

Nunez approached the door, watching the window closely for shadows against the glass, eyes peering through blinds, anything. He saw and heard nothing. The door had no windows, and dirt was streaked across it at waist level.

Everything else was clean. Dirt on the door didn't fit. Nunez pulled the flashlight from his belt and strobed the door with it.

The streaks were drying blood, not dirt. It looked like someone had reached for the door with bloody fingers, smearing it from their hands as they were pulled inside. Nunez strobed again, looking at the doorstep this time.

Blood. Lots of it. Not in a pool but scattered in large spots, each several inches across. Dozens of smaller drops dotted the doorstep. Red footprints covered the gaps between larger spots of blood. The random pattern of the drops suggested a violent struggle at the doorstep.

Looks like my witness was telling the truth, Nunez thought. *But the suspect was stabbing her, not punching her.*

The blood was dark and thick. Nunez recognized it as venous blood, what most untrained observers thought was arterial blood. Nunez knew from previous experience on the street, and more than one bad incident in Afghanistan, that the girl was hurt bad. He reached for his radio shoulder mike and lifted his eyes from the doorstep.

Fingers were inside the window, separating the cheap Venetian blinds. Dark eyes behind them stared hatefully at Nunez. If the other hand held a gun, Nunez was fucked.

Nunez dropped the flashlight and drew his pistol from its security holster in less than a second. He brought the Sig-Sauer pistol to his chest and thrust the pistol straight toward the eyes in the window. When his arms were fully extended, he hit the rocker switch on the light under the Sig's muzzle.

Light bathed the window. The dark eyes slammed shut. The hand disappeared from the blinds, and a shadow sprinted away. Red smears marked where the hand had been. Nunez was pissed at himself; he missed a threat while looking at the blood. He reached for the shoulder mike again, keeping his pistol on the window.

"1243 dispatch, there's blood all over the place and someone inside the apartment. I think it's a stabbing. Send more than one backup unit, and start EMS." Then he turned to the thuglets at apartment F, hoping they would still be sitting outside. Of course they were, if there was going to be violence they had to have a ringside seat.

"Hey!" Nunez shouted. "Do these apartments have back doors?"

"Um, naw, not in mine."

"Alright, cool." Nunez keyed his mike again. "1243 dispatch, a resident says there are no back doors or windows to these apartments, but I want 1113 or whoever gets here first to make sure."

"1243 clear."

"1331, 32 and me are en route. Gonna be a few." Two more officers coming south from Greenspoint, known to locals as "Gunspoint", the high crime area at the far north edge of the city.

"This is 1113, I'm about three minutes out." Nunez heard the motor racing in the background as Calhoun tore through the streets.

"Clear. Don't kill yourself getting here." Nunez pulled his weapon into his chest and ran sideways past the window toward the left side of the apartment. Because apartment A was at the far left end of the apartment block, the left wall faced 1800 Hanley. If there was a window on that wall, the suspect could escape from it.

Nunez reached the left corner and looked around it. There was an upstairs window, closed and covered by a screen. Nunez posted up at the corner, eyes darting from the front door and window to the side window, prepared to use the corner as cover if someone started shooting at him.

After two minutes of watching the door and window and seeing nothing, Nunez heard an engine and tires screaming. Officer Eddie Calhoun's patrol car screeched from the service road onto Hanley, blew the stop sign, passed Nunez and slid to a stop as it turned into the alley behind the apartment complex. The car's spotlight flicked on for two seconds, then Calhoun spun his tires as he backed out of the alley and turned his car's rear end toward the complex's parking lot. He raced backwards down the street but Nunez stopped him with a radio call.

"1113, stop right there! Light up the second floor window that faces Hanley."

Calhoun's car jerked to a stop. The spotlight turned on and rotated to the window. "Clear. Dispatch, show me arrived," Calhoun said. "Jerry, there's no back door or window."

"Okay," Nunez said into his radio. "1113, leave that light on. I need a sergeant on the air, we have to make entry now. This one can't wait."

Dispatch was on it. "Sergeant on the air for 1243 for forced entry. 204, you there?"

"204, go."

"1243 204, we're about to make forced entry to an apartment," Nunez said. "Looks like a stabbing. I saw a suspect inside, there's blood outside and we have a witness who saw the suspect drag a female into the apartment after assaulting her. I have one backup unit with me and two more on the way."

"Clear. Make entry and find the victim but don't clear the entire apartment until I get there. Dispatch, get us a K9."

"1243 clear." Nunez released the transmit button on the shoulder mike. "Eddie, come to me."

Calhoun crab-walked sideways from the driver's side of his car. He held his pistol in a proper grip, covering the second floor window as he moved. As he reached the corner he put one hand out to make contact with Nunez, to confirm he was in the right spot without moving his eyes from the window. Nunez had to admit that asshole or not, Calhoun was perfect for a situation like this.

Nunez grabbed Calhoun's arm. "We do this quick. You kick the door, I'll cover while you. I'm going in first, to the left, you go right. First priority is the stabbed girl, suspect second. If we find the girl we bring her out and wait for backup and K9. Got it?"

"I'm all over it," Calhoun said, still not looking at him. "Tell me when you're set."

The word *set* jolted Nunez. It wasn't a cop word. It was an infantryman's term, a grunt word that took him back to other places, where he had to clear other houses. What happened inside some of those houses wasn't good.

He let go of Calhoun's arm and moved beside the door. "1243 dispatch,

6

we're about to make entry. Clear the radio." He let go of the mike and said "Set" to Calhoun.

Calhoun pulled his pistol into his chest and delivered a tremendous kick that shattered two feet of door frame. The door exploded inward. Nunez sprang through the doorway.

Calhoun pulled his pistol into a muzzle-down position as Nunez passed in front of him. Nunez went left. His area was clear. He looked right and saw Calhoun scanning high and low for threats. Nobody was in the front room, but a huge pool of blood and bloody footprints were. Smears and drag marks led to the kitchen, and bloody footprints went to the front window and stairwell.

"Eddie, we're going to clear down here, starting with the kitchen. I want you to pie the kitchen off, I'll watch everything behind us."

"Got it. Moving." Calhoun stepped to the left side of the kitchen doorway, which was open with no door. He leaned right, peering into the room from that spot, then moved slightly right so he could see just a little more of the room. He kept repeating that movement, cutting a little more of the pie each time.

As Calhoun moved, Nunez took in details of the apartment. Sparsely furnished, a set of small glass teacups on a coffee table in front of a sofa, several pairs of cheap plastic sandals on a small carpet beside the door, a book with what looked like Arabic writing on the sofa. Nunez swept the room, stopped and assessed, swept the other way, caught sight of something red and green and dismissed it. He swept the room again, then suddenly realized what the red and green object was. He jerked his head back to it, and took a long look at the small Afghanistan flag on a coffee table.

"Jerry, I have feet."

"Laying down, standing up, what?" Nunez asked.

"Laying down," Calhoun said. "Little feet, all bloody. I'm continuing."

Nunez heard him shuffle two steps. He stopped. Several quiet seconds followed.

"It's her. She's dead. No question."

"How do you know she's dead?" Nunez asked.

"Jerry, trust me. She's dead."

"We're going to trade places so I can take a look. On three. One, two, three."

And they quickly switched spots. Nunez looked into the kitchen.

"Yeah, you're right," Nunez sighed. "She's dead."

"Told you so."

Nunez could see the entire length of her body. Ugly slashes stood out on her thighs and arms, intestines protruded from her lower abdomen, and her neck and head were tilted at the wrong angle from her shoulders. Her throat had been cut so deeply she had almost been decapitated. It looked like the suspect had tried to saw her head off.

The pool of blood around her body went past her head and almost to her feet, and reached the walls on both sides of her torso. She was small and thin, and Nunez thought she couldn't have been more than fourteen. But with all the damage and blood it was impossible to tell.

"Fuck," Nunez sighed. "Okay, we'll let the dog do the rest of the work. Start moving to the door."

The radio beeped. "1331 and 32 arriving. Jerry, where do you want us?"

"I need 31 to cover the window on the side of the apartment that faces Hanley. Tell me if it's open or if you see any blood around it. 32, come to the door. We found the girl and we're backing out."

Dispatch jumped on the radio. "Dispatch 1243, I need patient information on the girl."

"1243 dispatch, we just need an ambulance to pronounce her. She's DOA."

Dead On Arrival. Houston street cops usually say DRT, for Dead Right There, often pronounced *dead raht thar* with a Texas twang. But in a case with an actual innocent victim they'll use *DOA* instead, as if that shows respect for the dead.

"We just backed out," Nunez said. "The suspect should still be inside. What's the deal with K9?"

"He's coming from southwest area. Eight minutes or so."

"1243 clear." Nunez and Calhoun backed out and took positions on either side of the doorway as Officer John Mata, unit 1332, approached them. Mata was a young, handsome and healthy officer, less than two years out of the academy, one of the college grads with no military experience the department was trying so hard to recruit.

8

Nunez often expressed his bitterness about the department's lack of respect for veterans by saying *I foolishly wasted my time serving my country in the military, including in combat, when I should have been in college binge drinking, smoking pot, date-raping sorority girls, buying my research papers off the internet and badmouthing America, because* that's *what makes you a good cop.* But then there were officers like John Mata, with his college degree and absolute cluelessness about all things military, coupled with an earnest desire to do a good job and plain good sense on the street. And Nunez had to admit a lot of the college guys were good cops.

"The window's clear, Jerry," Mata said. "It's closed and there's nothing around it."

"Good," Nunez said. "If he tried to come out of there that window would look like a mass murder. That scene is bloody as shit. He's still in there, probably upstairs."

"How bad is it?" Mata asked.

"It's a fucking slaughterhouse in there," Calhoun answered. "Girl got butchered, guts out and head cut off. Fucking suspect was trying to eat her or something. I never seen shit like that before."

Mata looked shocked. "He cut her fucking head off? Seriously?"

Nunez interjected, "No he didn't cut her head off. Eddie, it's bad enough, don't exaggerate." He thought for a moment and added, "But he *damn near* cut her head off."

"Jesus. Fuck that shit man, I'm getting my shotgun." Mata headed back to his car. Nunez heard him tell Officer James Wesley, unit 1331, "Dude, he cut her fucking head off."

"912 to the primary unit on Hanley, orient me." 912 was a K9 officer named Jones, getting close to the scene and looking for information.

"1243 912, we have a murder. Victim is still inside the apartment and I'm pretty sure the suspect is also. I don't have any suspect info, all I saw was a hand and part of the face. The murder was a stabbing, unknown if there are any guns inside. We backed out and we're covering the bottom floor of the apartment from the doorway."

"912 clear. I'm five minutes out."

"204 dispatch, I'm arriving." Sergeant Tillis pulled off of Hanley into the parking lot. He drove low and slow, only in a hurry when an officer was screaming for help. Tillis rolled to a stop behind Nunez's car, popped his door and gracefully swung all his six foot, five inches and 290 pounds out of the driver's seat.

Nunez recognized Tillis walking toward him, then turned his head back into the doorway and said, "Hi, Mel." Mel was not his real name, of course, but there was no other name for an old, tall, fat white guy named Tillis.

"Whatcha got, Jerry?"

"It's a combination stabbing, slashing, attempted decapitation, triple nut cutting and aggravated jaywalking all rolled into one." Nunez kept his eyes inside the apartment as he talked. "All my years of police experience lead me to believe something illegal happened inside the apartment. I'm not good enough to be a detective or anything though, so that's probably wrong."

Tillis laughed quietly. Nunez had been furious when he wasn't selected for Homicide Division several years earlier. "Spare me the whining, tell me facts, Jerry."

"Victim's in the kitchen, slashed and stabbed and head almost cut off," Nunez said. "Little girl, looks like a teenager. I barely got a look at the suspect through the window, I'm pretty sure he's upstairs. Take a look at the blood, there's trails leading to the kitchen and upstairs. The only way he could have gotten out is through the upstairs window, but the screen's still on it and there's no blood around it. He could have gotten into the attic and crossed to another apartment though."

"Hmmm…it's been a while since we had this kind of thing around here," Tillis said. "Maybe we'll get ourselves a serial murderer or something interesting like that."

"Wait til you see her, Sarge," Nunez said. "She's shredded."

"Sounds like it. Hopefully the dog will eat the suspect's ass before we hook him up. Hang on, I'm going to try to call him out."

Nunez waited while Tillis bellowed *Houston Police, come outside now* into the apartment. Nobody on the scene expected the suspect to surrender. But they always had to make the show, just in case it turned into a shooting and some lawyer asked, *Are you sure you did everything you could to avoid a violent confrontation with the suspect?*

Nobody answered. Calhoun said "I hope he fucking offs himself when we find him. Maybe with a twelve gauge. I want to see his head explode."

"Yeah, whatever," Nunez said. "Usual deal Sarge, dog goes in first and we hold what he clears?"

"Sure, unless Jonesy wants something different. He might be worried about his dog getting stabbed," Tillis said.

Calhoun muttered, "Oh yeah, we don't want the dog to get stabbed. I guess we should go in first then, the dog's training and insurance costs more than ours does. I'll just take my vest and gun belt off and go in blindfolded too."

"Eddie, I hope you don't whine that much when we actually go inside," Tillis said. "In fact, you can wait outside and cover the window. We wouldn't want you to get hurt."

Calhoun tensed, but stayed silent. All the night shift officers at North Patrol, including Tillis, considered Calhoun a loudmouth prick. Nunez was probably the only one who would ever choose Calhoun for backup. Other officers thought he was such an asshole they couldn't care less about his tactical proficiency.

Jones pulled into the complex parking lot. Grey haired and black, he got out with his short leash in hand and opened the back door. He hooked the leash onto his big Belgian Malinois before letting him out of the back seat. Nunez and Tillis waved him over. Nunez explained the situation while Tillis stood quietly to the side and Calhoun sulked in silence. Jones asked who was going inside the apartment with him for the search.

"Calhoun, tell Mata to come here so he can cover K9's back," Tillis ordered. "Then keep an eye on the front door after we make entry."

Calhoun holstered his pistol in disgust, gave Tillis a hateful look and walked toward Hanley. Nunez noticed Calhoun had tailored his uniform sleeves, making them tighter to show off his upper arms. A few seconds later Mata jogged to the doorway, smiling and holding his shotgun.

"Boy, you sure pissed Calhoun off, Sarge."

"Aww, darn," Tillis said. "Johnny, you're cover for Jones. Watch his back. We'll be in as soon as he says so."

"Got it, Sarge."

"Here we go," Jones said. "HOUSTON POLICE K9, COME OUTSIDE NOW! HOUSTON POLICE K9, COME OUTSIDE NOW OR MY DOG WILL BITE YOU!"

Jones waited a few seconds, then let his dog bound forward to the end of its leash and followed him inside. Mata entered right on his ass. The dog sniffed the pool of blood, followed the trail toward the kitchen, turned and followed the trail the other way to the stairs. Then it growled and pulled on his leash, trying to go up the stairwell. Jones yanked him back and led him through the kitchen doorway. Mata went in at their backs.

Nunez knew Jones would be carefully maneuvering his dog around the body, searching every possible hiding place while trying not to contaminate the scene. In the near future some asshole defense lawyer might tell a jury, *You all heard the officer admit he contaminated the crime scene by putting his dog in there. Don't you think a dog, a big police dog, drooling all over a crime scene ruins it? Don't you think the dog could have wiped off the real killer's DNA with those big paws? If you agree with me on this, and I know you do, you have no choice but to acquit my client. For god's sake, let this innocent man get back to his family! Hasn't he suffered enough at the hands of the police already?*

And some idiot on the jury would buy it. *That's true. I saw it on CSI once, an animal got into a crime scene and it like made a false DNA match or something.*

After two minutes Jones and Mata exited the kitchen. Jones looked at Tillis and Nunez, raised an eyebrow and shook his head in disbelief. Mata was pale and looked about to puke. Both officers had stepped in blood and along with the dog tracked bloody footprints into the living room. The dog pulled toward the stairwell again, and Jones directed him toward the closet and bathroom. Both were clear.

Nunez and Tillis entered the apartment. Jones looked toward the kitchen and shook his head again.

"Jesus Christ. I hope this sorry fuck is in here. And I hope he has a weapon and refuses to drop it."

Nunez and Tillis nodded in agreement. Mata, still looking like he was holding back a gallon of vomit, kept his mouth shut and his eyes on the stairwell.

"Well, let's do this," Jones said. "Sarge, you two should stay down here until we get to the top of the stairs. No point in having all four of us jammed up in the stairwell if it turns into a shooting."

"Sure thing, Jonesy."

Jones said to Mata, "If he pops up at the top of the stairs with a gun you better not shoot my dog," and then moved into the stairwell. Mata stuck to his right side.

They moved up the stairs slowly, with the dog straining on the leash ahead. Mata had his shotgun in his shoulder, muzzle pointed to the top of the stairwell, thumb on the safety and finger alongside the trigger guard, ready to fire. Bloody footprints marked every step.

Five steps from the top, the dog growled and started pulling toward the second floor. Jones stopped Mata at the top of the stairs and motioned for Nunez and Tillis to come up.

"He's in the room across the hallway," Jones whispered. "I need Mata with me and one of you to cover our backs when we go in."

"I got your backs," Tillis said. He eased into Mata's spot. Nunez looked down at faint bloody footprints leading to the room across the hallway. The door was closed, and blood was smeared around the door handle.

Jones crept across the hallway to the left side of the doorway. He had to strain hard to keep his dog from rushing the door, but to the dog's credit it never barked, just growled and choked itself on its collar. Mata moved to the right side of the doorway and lifted his shotgun to high ready, right hand on the pistol grip and left hand on the pump, muzzle even with his eyes. Nunez crept next to Jones.

Jones whispered to Mata. Mata reached slowly across the door and tried the door handle. It was unlocked. Mata looked at Jones. Jones nodded. Mata turned the door handle all the way and pushed it just enough to make sure it would open. He hesitated again, making sure everyone was ready.

In a flash Mata shoved the door as hard as he could. Before the door could bounce off the wall Jones' dog was in the doorway, barking and spraying saliva through the air, trying to get to a blood-covered figure ahead.

The figure shrieked *"Dog out my house! Dog out my house!"* Jones screamed unintelligibly in Dutch at his dog to keep him from breaking free and charging the suspect. Mata ordered "DROP THE FUCKING KNIFE, MOTHERFUCKER! DROP THE KNIFE!"

The suspect stood at the back wall, almost completely covered in blood. He held his hands away from his body as if he didn't want the blood on his hands to dirty the rest of him. He was young and thin, no more than 5'2" and maybe 110 pounds, with a scratched, bloody baby face topped with a tangle of black, blood-soaked curls. He wore a grey *sharwal kamis,* the traditional Afghan men's outfit that consisted of a long shirt that looked like a night shirt, and large baggy pants underneath.

The boy's clothes were soaked through with blood. Nunez only knew they were grey because a few spots weren't stained dark red. He held a large butcher knife in his right hand. Nunez saw a large slash across his left palm.

The boy had a dark, thin face with thick eyebrows and nearly black eyes. Nunez recognized them as the same ones that had looked at him through the blinds. The suspect screamed, "You shoot me! You shoot me!" at Mata.

"You want me to shoot you, motherfucker?" Mata asked. "COME AT ME, MOTHERFUCKER! WALK AT ME WITH THAT FUCKING KNIFE!"

"Get dog out my house!" the suspect screamed. "You shoot me! Make me for heaven now!"

"Mata, calm down," Tillis ordered. "Talk the knife out of his hands."

Nunez announced "I'll give the commands" and began talking to the suspect. "Drop the knife," Nunez said. "If you don't, the dog's going to bite you."

"You shoot me or I cut your head!" the boy yelled back.

"Fuck you," Mata hissed, not loud enough for the suspect to hear. Jones adjusted his leash and let the dog spring forward three feet. The suspect cringed, threw himself backward into the wall and lifted his right leg into a defensive position. He raised the knife above his head.

Mata's shotgun muzzle abruptly dipped two inches. Nunez knew Mata had almost pulled the trigger, anticipating the recoil and throwing his shoulder forward in the instant before firing.

Jones had his hands full with the dog and Mata had the shotgun, so it would be Nunez's responsibility to cuff the suspect. He holstered his pistol and quietly announced, "I'm gloving up." He kept talking to the suspect as he pulled a pair of rubber surgical gloves from his back pocket.

"Listen kid, if you don't drop that knife you're going to get eaten by this dog. You can't get away. Drop the knife and lay down, you won't get hurt."

"No. You liaring." The suspect had stopped shrieking and spoke at an almost normal volume, but had a thick-as-shit accent Nunez recognized. "You just want kill me because I Muss-lim. I let go knife, you shoot me."

"If you don't put down the knife, you get shot," Nunez said. "Drop the knife and you'll be fine. I promise. Look, I'll even make the dog move back for you."

He tapped Jones' shoulder. Jones yanked the dog back, hard, two feet toward the door. The suspect put his leg down, and slowly lowered the knife.

"Keep dog away me," the boy said, a little calmer now.

"I'll keep the dog away from you, I promise," Nunez lied. If the kid did anything the least bit threatening, fangs would sink into his flesh to the gums in seconds. "Just drop the knife and lay down."

The boy hesitated, thinking it over. "I should not be taken to jailed. I have done nothing wrong. Leave my house."

"Who said you did anything wrong?" Nunez asked. "What's your name, anyway?"

"You cannot say my name," the boy said. "No American say my name rightly."

"Try it, you might be surprised," Nunez said.

"What? I do not understand."

"Tell me your name. I can say it right. I've had practice."

"My name is Mohibullah," the boy said.

"Mo-heeb-oo-lah. Okay Mohibullah, my name is Jerry. How about you drop that knife, so we can talk?"

"I CANNOT TRUST YOU!" the suspect yelled, agitated again. "You lie! You kill Muss-lims!"

"Mohibullah, calm down," Nunez said soothingly. "I haven't killed anyone. If we wanted to kill you, we would have done it already."

Tillis offered his opinion from the hallway, quietly, so the suspect couldn't hear him. "Well Jerry, you've killed Muslims and you're lying to him. Sounds like he has you pretty well figured out."

15

Mata mumbled, talking to the suspect but only loud enough for Nunez and Jones to hear. "The only one here who killed a Muslim today is you, fuckhead."

Nunez almost laughed. He put his head down until the smile passed, raising it only when he had his serious face on again.

"Mohibullah, tell me what you want."

"I want you to out my house."

"We're not going to," Nunez said. "Be smart, Mohibullah. You know we have to figure out what happened to the girl. After that, we can leave. You help us, and we'll be out of here faster."

"What girl?"

"The girl in the kitchen," Nunez answered, annoyed.

"What girl kitchen?"

"The fuckin…the dead girl in the kitchen, Mohibullah."

"You speak for the woman? For my sister?" the boy asked.

"I guess so," Nunez said. "I didn't know she was your sister."

"My sister is a whore."

Nunez paused. Even though Mohibullah had destroyed someone, he had seemed like a little kid. A fucked up little kid, but still a kid. Until he called the sister he had just murdered, just stabbed, slashed and tried to dismember, a whore. That single comment made him seem like a real life, honest to god, cold-blooded murderer.

"Mohibullah, we're not going to wait," Nunez said. "Drop the knife and lay down, or the dog is going to bite you. And it's going to hurt. A lot. You've got ten seconds."

Mohibullah looked at the dog, seemed to ponder his options. "You promise me. I put the, down the knife. Then you let me go and get out my house."

Sure, whatever. "Okay, no problem. Put the knife down, then we'll get out of your house. Just throw the knife in front of you."

Mohibullah stood silent a few seconds, looking at Nunez, and at Mata's eyes behind the shotgun muzzle, and the dog. He swung his hand forward as if to throw the knife, but held on to it and moved it back to his side.

"Mohibullah, come on. Throw the knife in front of you."

Mohibullah took another long look at Nunez, and began mumbling

16

something under his breath. Nunez didn't understand what he was saying, except for *inshallah*: "It is god's will". Nunez knew from experience that some Afghans said that whenever they made decisions. They meant it as "the outcome is in god's hands", but Americans usually interpreted it as "I don't care what happens."

Mohibullah pitched the knife five feet to his front. He stayed against the back wall, fifteen feet from the officers. Mata lowered his shotgun and took a step into the room. Jones yanked his dog back and stepped through the doorway while Nunez walked inside, between the two others officers.

Mohibullah took a step forward.

"Stop, Mohibullah," Nunez ordered. Mohibullah stopped. "Lay down right where you are. You made the right decision, Mohibullah."

Mohibullah took another step.

"Stop, god damn it! Lay down right there."

Mohibullah exploded forward, fell onto the knife and popped back up with it over his head. He charged. Nunez and Jones backpedalled. Nunez went for his pistol.

"STOP!" Jones let go of the leash and the dog started to pounce.

"ALLAHU AKBA-!"

BOOM! Mata's shotgun cracked a few feet from Nunez's head. The blast made Nunez duck as pain stabbed his his right ear. Jones jerked the leash back to protect his dog. Nunez had his weapon out of the holster and onto his target before he realized what he was seeing.

Mata racked a fresh round into the chamber of his shotgun. Nunez rose from the crouched combat stance he had taken. He looked over his sights at the broken corpse before him through a haze of shotgun smoke.

Mohibullah lay on his back with his legs folded, right arm still over his head with the knife clutched tightly in his hand. He had a shocked look on his face, which was odd for a dead person. A two-inch hole marred the middle of his sternum.

His head jerked left. Nunez knew it was just nerves. Mohibullah's eyes and mouth eased halfway closed. He was done. He was completely, unquestionably *Dead Right There.*

17

Nunez heard "Shots fired! Shots fired!" on his radio, coming from Calhoun or Wesley outside. He reached to his shoulder and keyed up.

"1243, we're okay. Suspect is down, no officers hurt. Everything's under control." He looked at Mata as he spoke. Mata was still on the sights, ready to pop another round at a dead man. His hand shook on the pump. Nunez reached out and touched his shoulder.

"Ease up, Mata. It's over."

Mata exhaled. He took his finger slowly off the trigger, waited a couple of seconds, and put the shotgun back on safe. Then he and Nunez both jumped when Tillis spoke up behind them.

"Well, this looks pretty good," he observed, looking over their shoulders. "The knife is still in his hand. This shooting should turn out okay." Then he added, "That was a great shot, Mata."

Nunez holstered his pistol as he breathed in a lungful of gunpowder-tinged air. The four officers stood just inside the room, looking at the tiny body on the floor. A question popped into Nunez's head.

Why did that kid scream Allahu akbar at us?

CHAPTER 2

Nunez walked into the roll call room, just before Sergeant Tillis started calling names. A few minutes later roll call ended amid the usual banter and playful insults bouncing among the men and women in the room. Officers headed for the equipment room to draw their car keys and radios and Tillis said to Nunez, "Hey Jerry, meet me in the sergeant's office a minute."

Nunez nodded and followed him into the communal patrol supervisors' office. As soon as Nunez walked in the door he saw a probationary officer, fresh-faced and young with a perfectly pressed uniform, shiny leather gear and a new haircut. Nunez immediately knew what Tillis wanted.

"Wait Sarge, don't tell me. You're firing me because of my crack addiction."

"You wish. I'm giving you a probationary. He just finished training and wants to work nights til he's off probation."

"Damn. That's what I thought," Nunez said. "Why don't you give him to someone else? Are you trying to convince him to quit or something?"

"Who else should I give him to?" Tillis asked. "The trainers all have rookies, Beal and Jensen already have rookies, Edloe is the laziest fuck on this shift, and you know I'm not about to give him to Perkins or Myer."

Perkins and Myer were the two oldest officers on the shift, having spent their entire careers, over thirty years each, on night shift patrol in north Houston. They were aged, tired, pissed off and would never let anyone ride with them, except when they rode together. They had a funny habit of fighting each other for the radio when they got into something exciting, which fortunately wasn't very often.

1118 dispatch, we got...let go, gimme the damn radio! We got a rolling stolen car, south on 45 approaching Gulf Bank...shut up! I know where we are! I mean, approaching Tidwell! Red Nissan pickup, license plate...leggo of the radio and just drive, dammit!

"You could give him to Calhoun," Nunez said.

19

Tillis snorted and gave a look that said, *Oh come on.*

"Okay, you can't give him to Calhoun," Nunez admitted. "He'd have a good time dodging calls with Edloe though."

"Jerry, get out of my office," Tillis growled. "And take the rookie with you."

"What if he's an idiot and does something stupid like the last couple of guys you gave me?" Nunez asked.

"Then I guess you'll both die. See you later, Jerry."

The probationary officer stood uncomfortably on the wall listening to the conversation about him taking place five feet away as if he wasn't in the room. Tillis leaned back in his *chair*, getting a kick out of the exchange, getting a bigger kick out of the rookie's discomfort.

"Fine," Nunez said. "But I promise he won't enjoy it. And if someone else gets available put him with them. I don't want to get stuck babysitting some fool for the next three months."

"This one's pretty good, Jerry," Tillis said. "He had good trainers and passed everything first try. Olson was his evaluator, and you know he doesn't pass idiots."

"Huh. Was he military?" Nunez asked.

Tillis looked at the rookie. "Were you military?"

"Uh, no Sergeant, I wasn't."

"No he wasn't," Tillis said.

"I don't want him then."

"Jerry...god damn it..."

"Okayfinewhatever." Nunez said. "What's his name?"

"His name is...ask him what his damn name is, he's right here," Tillis said.

Nunez turned to the rookie, who looked really self-conscious at the moment. "What's your name?"

"Michael Woods."

"Alright Woods, go to the equipment room and get the keys to my patrol car. Load your stuff up and meet me at the back door to the station."

"Yessi...Okay, I got it."

Woods walked out of the office, still looking a little perturbed. When the door closed, Nunez smiled and said, "That was kinda fun."

20

"I'm sure the rookie thought so. Don't fuck with him too bad Jerry, he seems like a good one."

"I won't fuck with him, Sarge. But seriously, if someone else is around later, it would probably be better if he rode with them. I'm not nearly as rambunctious as I used to be, most of the time I just want to be left alone. I know you've noticed it."

"I've noticed, ever since you came back from Iraq," Tillis said. "If I can take him off your hands I will. But teach him something, Jerry. Get him into stuff on the street. Turn him into a Mata instead of an Edloe. And keep him away from Calhoun."

"I think you're making the wrong choice putting him with me, but okay, I'll make him work," Nunez said. "Speaking of Mata, you hear from him lately?"

"I called him yesterday, he's okay," Tillis said. "He's still a little intense, but he doesn't sound like he's drinking himself stupid or feeling super guilty about it," Tillis said. Tillis had been in a few shootings and knew the emotional highs and lows Mata would be going through. "You might want to give him a call in the next couple of days."

"I got his number, I'll call him. Later Sarge."

"See ya, Jerry."

Nunez walked out the back door and saw Woods sitting in the driver's seat of the patrol car. Nunez opened the driver's door.

"No driving. I let the last two rookies drive and they both tried to kill me. Trade places."

Woods got out and walked to the passenger side. Nunez logged onto the car's computer while the rookie sat in silence. The computer showed no calls holding in his beat. Nunez turned to Woods and offered his hand.

"I was just fucking with you in there, Woods. Don't get me wrong, I don't go asking for rookies or anything, but that was just an act. Jerry Nunez."

Woods looked at Nunez, seeming unsure if he was being jacked with again. Then he hesitantly put his hand out. Woods looked twenty-five or so, tall and athletic, with sandy blond hair over a thin, angular face surrounding two dark brown eyes. "Uh, okay. Mike Woods."

"Nice to meet you, Mike."

"Nice to meet you too."

Nunez drove to his Jeep, got his carbine and patrol bag out of the back and put them into the patrol car's trunk. Nunez carried a civilian-legal, semiautomatic M4 carbine with six thirty-round magazines. Nunez got back into the driver's seat, stowed his binoculars and recorded his information and the car's mileage on the activity form.

He gave Woods sideways looks as he wrote. Woods didn't look like he had relaxed a bit, even after the friendly little speech. Still writing, Nunez spoke to Woods without looking at him.

"Dude, relax. If you stay all stiff and uptight like Al Gore we're going to have a shitty night."

"Okay, I'll try. Uh, do you need me to bring any of my stuff up front?"

"Nah, unless you want to," Nunez said. "I've got all my forms up here. Now, let's go find something cool to do. You like traffic, calls, chasing dope, what?"

"I liked working traffic with two of my trainers," Woods said. "But that was because they didn't write tickets, they did it to get searches on gangsters and stuff. We made some good arrests that way, but none of us cared to write too many tickets."

"Good man," Nunez said. "Fuck tickets, I only write them when there's no way I can avoid it. I like running calls. I've gotten a lot of good stuff on traffic stops, but it's always the same. Dope, guns and warrants. On calls you get all kinds of different stuff. You never know what you're going to find inside someone's house, or see what kind of weird shit they do in private."

"I haven't had anything really interesting yet," Woods said. "Just a bunch of boring assaults and thefts."

"Hopefully some good calls will drop tonight. It's Thursday, beginning of the weekend, so there should be some action." Then Nunez pronounced, "Let's go get a damn soda."

By the time they walked out of Nunez's favorite gas station twenty minutes later, Woods had relaxed and was asking Nunez questions instead of silently waiting to be spoken to.

"So how many years do you have on, Jerry?"

"Thirteen. Sort of. If you don't count the three years I was away in the military against me."

"Yeah, Olson mentioned you've left a couple times. You went overseas?"

"Yeah, I did."

"Iraq? Afghanistan?" Woods asked.

"Both."

Woods waited for Nunez to offer more information. Nunez stayed silent. Woods changed the subject.

"How long have you been at North station?"

"My whole police life. I trained here after the academy, then got a spot on night shift in the 'hood. I really got to like working nights and decided to stay on this shift instead of going to days and having to deal with heat and traffic and all that shit. I've passed up a couple of day shift spots, and boy did that piss off my wife. She's alright now that I have Sundays and Mondays off though."

"You plan on staying in patrol until you retire?" Woods asked.

"I don't know. I put in for homicide a couple of years back and didn't get picked, but that was my own fault," Nunez said. "I didn't go to any extra training to get ready for it. I don't know if I'll put in for another investigative division or not. I might be another Perkins or Myer. Just an old, pissed off asshole who doesn't know how to do anything but be the real po-lice in the ghetto."

"I've been wondering if I want to stay in patrol or not," Woods said. "In the academy everyone says they're going to SWAT or helicopters or K9 or something, but that sounds unrealistic to me. I mean, isn't everyone trying to get the cool jobs? It can't be that easy. The academy staff was always telling us to 'advance our careers' and stuff, basically to get off the street as soon as possible. But I really looked forward to working the street and think I might want to do it for a while."

"Cool," Nunez answered. "Stay on the street, not many officers decide to do that."

Woods hesitated for a few seconds before he asked the next question. "Uh, sorry to change the subject, but...I heard about the shooting you were in Tuesday night."

"Yeah? What'd you hear?" Nunez asked.

"Heard it was really bad, the suspect cut his sister's head off and an officer named Mata killed him when he came at y'all with a knife.'"

"That was pretty much it," Nunez nodded. "He didn't cut her head off, but it sure as hell looked like he tried."

"Were you there when Mata shot him?"

"Yup. I was standing right next to him."

"Just curious, why didn't you shoot?" Woods asked.

"Didn't have time. I was going to cuff the suspect, so my weapon was in the holster when he charged us. Good thing Mata was ready."

"You mind telling me how it all happened?" Woods asked. "I mean, I heard bits and pieces, but not really the whole story. Unless, uh, you don't want to talk about it or something."

"Nah, no problem. It doesn't bother me, nothing like that," Nunez said.

As they patrolled in random patterns around the beat, Nunez laid out the whole story to Woods, from the first dispatch call to the shotgun blast that killed Mohibullah. Nunez discovered he needed to talk about the shooting, to get everything off his chest. He hadn't talked to his wife about it when he got home, like he normally did after a murder or a good chase or fight. As he spoke to Woods he felt the pressure ease a little.

"So what happened afterward? Did y'all ever find the parents?" Woods asked.

"Yeah, they showed up after the Homicide investigators did. When they showed up the mom was screaming in Pashto and beating herself on the head, just freaking the fuck out. She wouldn't talk to anyone at the scene, not even the female officer who showed up. Then again, I don't know if she even spoke English."

"What about the dad? Was he freaking out also?"

"No, he wasn't," Nunez said. "He was really calm. One of the things I saw in Afghanistan was that Afghans didn't react much when people got killed, I guess because they were so used to it. Except with kids. They went nuts when kids got killed. The dad didn't go nuts though. I've tried to figure that one out, maybe he considered his kids adults and not children."

"How old were they?"

"The son was sixteen and daughter was eighteen. We thought they were a lot younger, they were both real little. Almost like they were malnourished or something. They had only been living here a few years, maybe they were too poor to eat when they were in Afghanistan."

"What did the dad do? Did he speak English, did he talk to anyone?" Woods asked.

"He spoke English," Nunez said. "Not real well, but he did. When he showed up a couple of guys took him to the side and brought the lead Homicide investigator to talk to him. I talked to the Homicide guy later, he said the father kept asking 'Are you sure my son is dead? Can I make sure he's dead?' instead of saying he wanted to see him, or something normal like that. Maybe it was just the language barrier, but it sounded weird. And fucking Calhoun…the dad asked if he could check his son's heartbeat, and Calhoun says, loud enough for the dad to hear, 'We already checked his heart, it's stuck to the wall upstairs.' Fucking asshole."

"No shit. What'd the dad do?"

"According to the investigator, he didn't react at all," Nunez said. "Something else that was super fucked up though, he didn't ask about his daughter. Not one time. He kept asking if we were sure his son was dead, and when the investigator finally said, 'I have more bad news for you, your daughter's dead too,' you know what dad said?"

"No idea. What?"

"'My daughter is a whore.' That was it," Nunez said.

"Damn. That's fucked up."

"Yeah, it is. The investigator was shocked. He's one of the old guys, been in Homicide over twenty years, and said he's never seen a parent react like that. And one other thing, the dad got pissed when he found out a K9 went into the house. Of all the things he could have gotten pissed about, that was it."

"Why? What's the issue with the dog?"

"I don't know a whole lot about it, but when I was in Iraq I heard devout Muslims think dogs are unclean, almost like pigs," Nunez explained. "Supposedly when our guys searched houses with bomb dogs, the people would get so mad about dogs in their houses they would swear allegiance to the insurgency, you know, promise 'death to the American invaders', all that crap. Even in houses where nothing was found and nobody was detained. But like I said, I never saw it personally, I just heard about it."

"That's weird," Woods said. "I've never been around Arabs, I don't really know what they're like."

"The people on Hanley weren't Arabs, they're Pashtuns. Afghans aren't Arabs."

"Is that what you said earlier?" Woods asked. "That the mom was screaming in Pashtun?"

"Pashto. The people are Pashtun, the language is Pashto."

"Did you ever get a motive? I mean, I know the suspect and dad said the girl was a whore, but did you get anything specific?"

"Nope," Nunez said. "They asked the father what she did that was so bad, and he just said, 'She was a whore.' We asked some of the neighbors if they knew the girl, they said she was respectful and seemed real nice. One of them said she didn't know if the girl was Muslim because she never covered her head. Maybe that was it, she refused to cover her head."

"Just that? That's enough to make her a whore?"

"In that culture, maybe so," Nunez said. "I want to know what else the investigators found out, maybe she was screwing somebody at school or something. Hell, she could have just kissed some boy, or maybe one just called her at home. That might be enough. Normal teenage stuff over here would make her a screaming whore over there."

"And they have to kill her if she's a whore?" Woods asked.

"They have to kill her if she's a whore," Nunez answered. "She shames the family, she's dead. They might have picked someone for her to marry and she refused, that would be a major humiliation for them."

"Jerry, would you mind going back to Hanley?" Woods asked. "I'd just like to see the place where the shooting happened. You know, to try to get a better picture of what the situation was actually like."

Nunez took another drink. "Yeah, I guess that's okay. Just curious though, why are you so interested?"

"I think it's because…I've never been in a situation like that. I was never in the military, I never even really shot much until I went to the academy. This whole 'tactical mindset' thing is new to me. Since I started the academy I've been wargaming situations, trying to figure out what I should do if such and such happens. None of the trainers I had were ever in a shooting, they couldn't tell me what it was like. I'd just like to get a better look, to figure out what I would have done."

"We can't get inside where the shooting actually happened, but no problem," Nunez said.

"I know," Woods said. "I'm curious about how you approached the door when you first got there, where you set up the perimeter, all that stuff."

"I understand that. Most rookies have their head completely up their ass when it comes to tactics, it's good you're thinking about it."

Nunez drove toward Hanley, running license plates and hoping to find a stolen car. "You know, I thought I knew my beat pretty well. But I had never seen this place. Turned out the old church across the street from the complex owns it, and it's only for refugees from other countries. It's got families from Afghanistan, Iraq, Kosovo, Central America, a couple other places. I thought the little gangster kid that was our best witness was from Mexico but it turned out he was from El Salvador. The families only pay what they can afford, and they help with upkeep for the complex. It's a pretty cool little community they have there, really. The neighbors said that the only thing that had ever happened there were vehicle burglaries. A murder was completely out of character for that place."

"That sucks," Woods said.

"Yeah, it does. The priest who runs the place showed up after the shooting, and I hear he was really shook up. I didn't talk to him though."

After a few minutes of conversation, they arrived at the murder scene. "We're here," Nunez said. "It's the first apartment on the left, in front of us."

———

Woods looked around, taking in the sight of the darkened apartment complex. There were no lamps in the parking lot and no porch lights on. The only illumination in the complex came from the patrol car's headlights, which were pointed to the side of apartment A. Woods pictured how he would approach this complex on a disturbance, or a shooting, or maybe a man with a gun call.

"Mind if I get out?" Woods asked. "I'd like to just walk around a little."

"No problem, go ahead."

"K. You want me to just walk around by myself, are you going to wait at the car or…?"

"I'm going to look up a report, be there in a little bit," Nunez said.

"Okay, cool," Woods said, and walked into the parking lot. Nunez surprised him by turning the car's headlights off, making it almost impossible to see anything.

Woods looked at apartment A. It had a big picture window. If he was answering a real murder call, it would make sense to approach from the side, not the front. He walked toward apartment F, trying to figure out what he would do if he knew there was an armed suspect inside A.

An accented voice said, "Good evening, officer."

Woods jumped. The voice came from the black space in front of one of the apartments. He peered into the darkness. The burning end of a cigarette swung upward, stopped and brightened before swinging back down. The cigarette was just outside apartment D. Woods walked toward the cigarette, curious.

He turned on his flashlight, keeping the beam pointed at the ground and using the light reflecting upward. He saw a thin, distinguished-looking man in his fifties wearing what he thought were Arab clothes and a small, flat circular hat. The man wore squarish glasses and had a white, neatly trimmed beard. He sat with legs crossed in a plastic lawn *chai*r, letting his left hand with its cigarette hang out of view behind him.

"Is everything well tonight, officer? I have been sitting outside for almost an hour and have seen nothing unusual."

"Yes sir, everything's fine. Just taking a look around."

"I see, very good. I am glad to see a police presence here. Our little apartment complex used to be such a calm and quiet place, but I suppose all things change with time. Tell me officer, were you here two nights ago, the night of the murder?"

"No sir, I wasn't," Woods said. "I heard about it though. Did you know the girl?"

The man stood and reached inside his doorway to turn on the porch light.

"Yes, I knew her well. Her name was Fahima, she was a nice, proper young girl. Very intelligent, a good student, polite and respectful. It was a terrible tragedy, what was done to her."

"Yes, I agree. Did you know her brother also?" Woods asked.

"Yes, I knew him," the man said curtly. Woods thought that probably meant he hadn't liked the boy much.

"Sir, where are you from? Saudi Arabia?"

"No, I am from Afghanistan," the man said. "From Kabul. Do you know it?"

"No, sorry, don't know anything about Afghanistan," Woods answered.

"That's unfortunate, officer. I think if you knew Afghanistan, if you knew my people, you might better understand what happened to Fahima. I think it is likely that the police do not have a very good understanding of why such a thing was done."

Woods' eyebrows rose. "Sir, can you wait here a minute? I need to talk to my partner."

The man smiled. "Of course, officer, I will be right here. I have nowhere to go at this time of night."

Woods hurried back to the patrol car. Nunez sat in the driver's seat with his binoculars in his lap.

"Hey Jerry, that guy-"

"Stop. You better not have told him I'm an Afghanistan vet."

Woods hesitated. "No, I didn't tell him you were in Afghanistan. He's from Afghanistan though, and-"

"Gosh!" Nunez blurted. "No shit? Really? He's from Afghanistan? Is that why he's wearing Afghan clothes and a fucking Afghan hat? Gee, I thought maybe he was from Cleveland or something."

"Yeah, I guess that's why he's wearing Afghan clothes," Woods said, not understanding Nunez's sudden change in demeanor. "Listen, he just mentioned something about the murder. He said it's too bad I didn't know Afghanistan, that I might better understand why that girl was murdered, something like that. He said he didn't think the police understand it real well. I thought, maybe, you know, since you were there and all…"

"Me being there doesn't mean shit. Nothing he says is going to make me say,

'Now I understand why that little girl got murdered! That makes so much sense, go ahead and go kill another one!'"

"That's not what I mean, Jerry," Woods said. "I mean, I don't think that's what he meant." Confused, he said, "Look, you're the one who said you had all these things about the murder that you didn't know, or didn't understand. Maybe this guy can explain it to you. Quit being such a dick and just talk to the guy."

"A dick? Why it gotta be about dicks? I was gonna go talk to him, but now you hurt my feelings."

Woods frowned and looked away. Nunez picked up his soda and sucked the last bit of Dr. Pepper from the cup. "Fine, I'll talk to him. But don't say shit about me being in Afghanistan. Nothing at all, got it? If you tell him, he's going to want us to go inside and drink tea and eat cookies and we'll have to sit there and listen to all the bullshit about why his people or tribe or whatever are the only real Afghans and why they should be in control of the government and how wonderful and powerful and honest they all are. And I don't want to fucking hear it again. So don't give any information away, we're just talking about the murder."

"Yeah, whatever," Woods answered. "I got it. Can we go? He's waiting for us."

"We'll get there when we get there. Why do you care so fucking much about it anyway?" Nunez asked.

Woods took a moment to think it over. "Because I want to know why this girl's brother stabbed her guts out and tried to cut her head off. I can't understand why someone would do that, and I want an answer. I haven't been on the street for years, I haven't worked a million murders, I haven't been to war and seen guys get killed left and right. This is the first murder I've been close to, and I want to know more about it."

Nunez's face tensed. "Who the fuck are you to talk about my friends getting killed around me in the war?"

Woods looked back at Nunez, not sure what to say. Nunez glared angrily at Woods for a few seconds.

"Fine, Kojak. Whatever." Nunez got out of the driver's seat, turning his radio up as he followed Woods to apartment D. "I swear, you better not tell him shit."

The Afghan man was standing outside his door waiting, and as the two officers approached the door he extended his hand to Nunez.

———

"Good evening, officer. My name is Yussuf. I am very happy to meet you."

In as bland a voice as he could muster, Nunez replied, "Yeah, good to meet you too, Yussuf. I'm Officer Nunez."

They shook hands. Yussuf reached up and patted his heart, something all Afghans did when they shook hands with each other. Without thinking, Nunez patted his own heart, a reflex he had learned from shaking hundreds of Afghan hands during his deployment. As soon as he patted his heart he saw Yussuf's eyes light up, realized what he had just done and thought, *Awww, fuck.*

"Officer Nunez! You are familiar with the customs of my people?"

"Uh…just a little."

"Officer Nunez, if you did not have a Spanish last name I would think you are Afghan," the man said, smiling. "You could easily be an Afghan."

Nunez had been told the same thing by Afghan soldiers several times during his deployment. He replied, "Yes, I have been told I look Afghan before."

Yussuf's smile widened. *Fuck!* "I mean…Hispanics are often confused with Arabs, or Pashtuns sometimes." Nunez realized he had reverted to the slow, clear language he used when speaking to Iraqi or Afghan English speakers.

"Ah, you know of the Pashtuns?" the man asked, smiling as if he knew a secret.

God damn it! "I've, uh, heard of the Pashtuns, you know, on the news and stuff."

"Please, Officer Nunez. I think you know a little more about us than you have seen on the television."

Nunez looked at Woods. Woods looked back with an expression that said, *This is your fault, not mine.*

"Well, what the hell," Nunez said. "I guess you caught me. I was in Afghanistan, last year."

"Last year! It has been many years since I was back in my home, you are so

31

lucky to have been there so recently!" Yussuf glowed as he spoke, holding his palms together and shaking them in excitement. "What did you do there, where were you? Were you in my home? In Kabul?"

"I was a soldier, in Kapisa province. In the northeast near Bagram."

"Ah, Kapisa province, I have been there a few times. Many Tajiks in the northern part of Kapisa, my people are in the south. And there are many Pasha'i and Kuchi there, I believe. Did you meet any of the Pasha'i? They are very interesting people, with a language almost nobody else in Afghanistan speaks. Like the Nuristanis."

"I met many Kuchis, and I think I fought Pasha'i Taliban once or twice."

"Pasha'i Taliban? That is very strange, things must have changed since I was last there. But it has been many years since I was there, of course it has changed." Yussuf stroked his beard thoughtfully. "I am sorry, I am not being very hospitable. Come inside, my wife will prepare tea for you." Nunez raised an eyebrow at Woods at the mention of the word *tea*. The man said, "Please, my home is your home."

Inside the apartment Yussuf directed Nunez and Woods to a couch and walked into another room, speaking in a foreign language to his wife. Nunez leaned toward Woods. "If his wife comes out, don't talk to her or offer to shake her hand unless she does it first or he tells you to."

Yussuf walked back into the room. A small woman in what looked like a house dress with her head covered in a shawl quickly walked across the room and disappeared into the kitchen.

"It is so good to have guests, Officer Nunez, Officer Woods. I am very happy to have you here. In Kabul we had guests three or four times per week, it is the need of Afghan people to visit often with their friends and family. I have very much missed that since we left our home."

"We may not be able to stay long, Yussuf, we are on duty and may get a call," Nunez said.

"Yes of course, of course," Yussuf said. "I am happy to have you visit, even if only for five minutes."

Woods asked, "Yussuf, was that Pashto that you were just speaking? I know it's a dumb question, but I've never heard it before."

"It is not a stupid question, Officer Woods. Of course I speak Pashto, but I speak Dari in my home. Dari is a form of Farsi, the Iranian language. In Afghanistan it is usually Tajiks and Hazaras who speak Dari, but Dari is also the language of Kabul. It was my first language."

Yussuf's apartment was very clean, like Mohibullah's had been, but was not so sparse and had much more of a warm, comfortable feel to it. Woods had relaxed almost immediately when they sat down inside, but Nunez sat tense and uncomfortable. Yussuf's wife walked back from the kitchen and placed a small tray of cookies on the coffee table, then went quickly back to the kitchen. She reminded Nunez of Afghan villagers who invited them into their homes, except that it was always men serving food, never women.

Nunez had never really felt comfortable in Afghan homes during his tour. He felt nearly as edgy and nervous now as he had then. He had never hated the Afghan people, and truly liked some of them. But he was discovering he wasn't real happy some were living in Houston, in his beat, near his home.

"So Officer Nunez, you have been to Kabul? You have seen how beautiful my city is?" Yussuf asked.

I heard Kabul was a complete shithole. "No, I never had the chance. I would have liked to have seen the city, I know it is very historic."

Yussuf rocked slightly in his *chair*, obviously enjoying a chance to talk about his homeland. "Oh it is, it is. Not as historic as Kandahar, but it has had a very important place in history." Yussuf stroked his beard and leaned forward, becoming serious. "Tell me Officer Nunez, were you here two nights ago, when the girl was murdered? I am sorry to change the subject so abruptly, but I am very curious to know what you saw if you were here."

"Yes, I was here," Nunez said. "I was the first officer to arrive."

"And you saw the girl, Fahima?"

"Yes I did."

"Ah, that must have been very terrible for you to see," Yussuf said. "I was told how badly she had been, eh, mutilated. Yes, mutilated. And her brother Mohibullah? Were you there when he was killed?"

"Yes Yussuf, I was there. I was in the room when he was shot." Despite Yussuf's friendly demeanor, Nunez half expected him to explode with some bullshit about the unnecessary killing of a poor, misguided young immigrant who had only attempted to decapitate his sister because of an unfortunate cultural misunderstanding.

"Tell me, Officer Nunez. Did Mohibullah say anything before he was shot?" Yussuf asked. "I know he was shot as he attacked police officers with a knife. Did he say anything as he attacked?"

Nunez was surprised at the question. Mohibullah's last words had already been released to the local media, who hadn't widely reported them. Nunez figured it wouldn't hurt to tell Yussuf.

"Yes, he did," Nunez said. "He yelled *Allahu akbar.*"

Yussuf clasped his hands, index fingers extended, touching his lips with them. "Yes, I had been told that, but I did not know if it was true. Tell me, Officer Nunez, do you know what that means?"

"I know what it means."

Woods leaned forward. "I don't know what it means. I've heard guys yelling it on TV, when they're showing news about the Middle East and stuff, but I don't know Pashto. What does it mean?"

"Officer Woods, it is not Pashto, it is Arabic," Yussuf explained. "Arabic has never been the primary language of any of the people in Afghanistan. But Islam has spread much of the language of Mohammed, peace be upon him, throughout all the Muslim lands. *Allahu akbar* means 'god is great.' I find it very strange that a young boy would say such a thing at his death. This may be normal behavior for older men who are facing death as part of their wish to become martyrs, but not for young boys such as Mohibullah who have simply committed a crime."

"Wish to become martyrs? Can you explain what that means?" Woods asked.

"Officer Woods, you know very well that there is a strain of Islam that breeds men who wish to do nothing more than die, supposedly in defense of our faith. The men who attacked your country on eleven September, for example. When they carry out their attacks they call out 'god is great,' to demonstrate their faith in the face of death."

Nunez added, "Woods, if you're ever in a mall and you hear someone yell *'Allahu akbar'*, you better duck. Or start shooting."

Yussuf looked a little offended, but continued in the same even, friendly tone.

"Of course there are valid reasons to pronounce your faith, not for the purposes of conducting immoral attacks on innocent people. Such behavior was not part of Afghan culture when I was your age, Officer Nunez. Nothing like what you saw two nights ago. Kabul in the 1970's was a beautiful city, very western and free, covered in beautiful gardens. You know women often walked the city by themselves, in western clothes, with no *hijab*, no head scarves? Kabul was much like Beirut at the time, a cross between east and west. The Soviet invasion began the changes that have produced the Kabul of today. I still see the beauty of the city, but only because of the beauty of my memories. I believe you would see only danger and poverty if you were to visit my home. I could not expect you to see anything else. You did not have a happy, wonderful childhood there as I did, you did not sit on the terraces with your mother and see kites flying overhead, and hear the music playing at the outdoor restaurants."

Sensing the beginning of a long, Afghan-style monologue, Nunez interrupted with a question. "Yussuf, how did you learn English so well? I don't think I ever met an Afghan who spoke English as well as you do. Not even our interpreters."

"Thank you for the compliment, Officer Nunez." Yussuf's wife walked back into the living room with three teacups and a pot full of steaming tea, plus a silver container with sugar and a small spoon. After laying out the tea, she disappeared into her bedroom. Yussuf watched her leave and laughed softly.

"Ah, my wife. My childhood was not very traditional, Officer Nunez. My mother never behaved as my wife does, she was not very obedient. She gave my father and grandfather fits with her independence and stubbornness. But my wife came from a traditional family, and even after five years in the United States she still insists on covering her head, and refuses to sit with me when I have American guests. Perhaps she will change someday."

He waited until Nunez and Woods filled their cups with steaming green tea, then filled his cup and took a drink. "I met the father of my wife at Kabul University. I will be forever grateful that he thought me worthy to arrange my marriage to his daughter. The University is also where I learned English. During my years there I often made extra money by working as a guide for western tourists, and for a time I worked at both the German and French embassies. Later, just before the Soviet occupation, I was a professor of English at the University."

"You speak German and French also?" Nunez asked.

"Oh yes. And Urdu, and some Hindi. I am fortunate to have inherited my mother's gift for languages." Yussuf swirled the remnants of leaves floating in his tea. "Officer Nunez, why do you think Mohibullah killed his sister? Have you established a motivation? A motivation you believe?"

"Mohibullah told me his sister was a whore," Nunez said. "Sorry, those were his words. His father...I don't know his father's name...told the detective his daughter was a whore. We didn't get a better explanation than that."

"Their father's name is Rahim," Yussuf said. "I know him, though not very well. We are neighbors and attend the same mosque, not far from here, but I do not know him well. I knew Fahima well, and she was not a whore. I do not believe she ever responded to a boy's attention in any way, although I know she received much attention at her school. She was a beautiful young woman, far past ready for marriage by the standards of my culture. But she was not as traditional as her family was. She was very thankful for the freedom that comes with life in America, while her family wished for nothing more than the simple, devout life they lived before they left Pakistan."

"Pakistan?" Woods asked. "I thought they were from Afghanistan."

"They were, Officer Woods," Yussuf said. "They were *Kandaris*, from Kandahar. Fahima told my wife they left Kandahar because the Taliban accused her father of not being sufficiently devout, because he did not wish for Mohibullah to attend training a local Taliban commander ordered all boys to attend. They settled in Pakistan for some time, then were able to come to America as refugees, through the help of the Catholic church. The same church that assisted my family."

Interested, Nunez asked, "So Yussuf, do you think Mohibullah killed Fahima because she wasn't religious?"

Yussuf stroked his beard again. "I think that is the obvious answer they have provided. But I do not know of any sixteen year old Pashtun boy, no matter how devout or traditional, who would be willing to kill his sister and lose his life because his sister lived as Fahima did. Fahima did nothing to bring shame to her family. She would not cover her head, and she had friends at school, but nothing more than this."

"Yussuf, aren't 'honor killings' very common among devout Muslims? I mean, among less educated and devout Muslims?" Nunez asked.

"Officer Nunez, please ask yourself this…"

"Please Yussuf, call me Jerry."

Yussuf smiled. "Thank you, Jerry. Ask yourself, Jerry, when did you ever see such a thing happen in Afghanistan? When did you ever hear of such a thing as a young Pashtun boy killing his own sister over something so frivolous as not covering her head, over having friends at school? If she had lost her virginity before marriage, yes, such a thing is possible. If she had refused her parents' orders to marry. But even killings for reasons such as these are not common. And I ask you to consider this as well. So-called 'honor killings' are not a Muslim phenomenon, they are a cultural phenomenon. Such atrocities are not common to every Muslim nation, they are only found among cultures who carried out such crimes before they adopted Islam. It is unusual, but there have even been such killings committed by non-Muslims also. What this means, Jerry, is that killing one's sister is not done in the name of god. It is done in the name of one's culture, or family. Why, then, would one proclaim *'Allahu akbar'*, a term reserved specifically to express faith, when he has done something that is not part of his Muslim beliefs?"

Nunez thought about it. Although American soldiers told lurid stories of all the horrible things Afghans did to each other, he didn't know of a single confirmed honor killing that happened while he was in Afghanistan. And he could see Yussuf's point. It didn't make sense for Mohibullah to have acted like he was dying as a martyr after killing his sister.

"You're right, Yussuf. I don't know of such a thing happening in Kapisa while I was there. Maybe it was common in other provinces, but I don't know. So if Mohibullah didn't do it for religious reasons, why do you think it happened? What reason can you give me?"

"I can give you no good reason, Jerry," Yussuf said. "No good reason at all. There can be no good reason for the commission of such a crime. I simply ask of you, please do not blindly accept that Mohibullah killed his sister because she shamed the family. Perhaps you should look behind the obvious answer you have been given."

37

Nunez's radio beeped. "Dispatch 1243."

Damn. "1243, go ahead."

"Check your computer for a call. Code three loud noise, no big rush."

"That's clear, I'll put us en route in a few."

Yussuf looked disappointed. "It appears you must go, Jerry. That is unfortunate, I have enjoyed this discussion with you. You will visit on another night, then?"

Nunez stood. "I think I might be able to visit every so often, Yussuf-*khan*." *Khan* was an ancient word that meant "king". When added to a first name it denoted respect, and Nunez's use of it immediately brought a wide smile to Yussuf's face.

"Ah Jerry-*khan*, you make me miss my home so. It has been very good to meet you. I will look forward to your next visit, and I shall pray for your continued safety. For both of you."

"Thank you, Yussuf," Nunez said. "We'll come by and check the apartment complex more often now. You might not see us, but we'll drive through as often as we can."

Woods added, "Yeah, we'll drive by and look around, hopefully every night. Thanks for the tea, Yussuf, and thanks for talking to us. I learned a lot tonight. It was really interesting."

"Thank you, Officer Woods."

"Mike. Call me Mike."

"Mike. I suppose I still love to teach, although it has been many years. Thank you for being an attentive student."

"Anytime, anytime."

Yussuf followed Nunez and Woods outside, shaking their hands again. Woods awkwardly tried to mimic the heart-patting gesture, drawing an appreciative laugh from Yussuf. As they turned to walk back to their patrol car, Yussuf asked, "Officers, might one of you have a number where I can contact you? I assure you I would not be a bother, but it would be a measure of security for me and my wife. In case problems develop in this area again."

Woods answered first. "Sure Yussuf, no problem. I'll write it down for you."

Nunez considered it. Like most cops, Nunez was leery of giving his personal cell number to anyone who wasn't a cop. And if they started friendly contact Yussuf might try to unofficially adopt him into his family, an aggravating consequence of the famed Afghan hospitality. But Yussuf seemed like a genuinely good person, one of the first Nunez had met in what seemed like a long time.

"Mike, give me that paper when you're done. I'll write my number on there too," Nunez said.

Woods handed the paper to Nunez, who wrote his cell number and name on it before handing it to Yussuf. Yussuf took the paper in both hands, bowing slightly to show his gratitude. "Thank you, Jerry, Mike. Have a good day, and I sincerely hope to see you tomorrow night."

"Good night, Yussuf," Nunez said. "And tell your wife, that was great tea. I haven't had hot green *chai* since I was in Kapisa."

"Yes Jerry, of course I will tell her. Our home is always open to you. Good night."

"Good night."

They walked back to the patrol car and got into their seats. Jerry pulled up the information for the loud noise call and hit *en route*, then started the car and drove out of the parking lot. Out of the corner of his eye he saw movement at apartment A. He turned his head and thought he saw the door closing in the darkness.

"That old guy was interesting, Jerry. Did you already know all that stuff that he was talking about?" Woods asked.

"I knew some of it," Nunez answered. "When you go places as a soldier there's always a barrier between you and the locals, so you don't learn what they're really like,. Some soldiers come out of Iraq or Afghanistan with all kinds of fucked up ideas about how the population is, what the locals believe, everything. I like to think I learned about the Afghans while I was there, but Yussuf might have taught me something tonight. Then again, he might be full of shit." Nunez picked up his drink, forgetting he had emptied it before he went into Yussuf's apartment. He took sip of melted ice and said, "I need to get some more soda. We'll stop somewhere on the way to the call. Afterward I want to go by the station and see if there are updates on the murder report."

"Cool. I could use a drink too."

"Alright, sounds like a plan." Nunez turned off Hanley and quickly accelerated. Then he muttered, "And next time I suggest we get out and talk to some nice old guy, don't argue with me about it, just do it. Dick."

CHAPTER 3

"Homicide division," a pleasant female voice said over the phone. "May I help you?"

"Yes ma'am, you can," Nunez said. "I'm looking for Detective Helmers. He was the investigator on the murder case on Hanley a few nights ago. Is he around today?"

"Yes he is. May I ask who's calling?"

"Officer Jerry Nunez, from North patrol. I just needed to talk to him about that Hanley case. It shouldn't take more than a few minutes."

"One second please." The receptionist put Nunez on hold and he listened to the Muzak version of Rod Stewart's *Do You Think I'm Sexy* for a minute before the voice of a gruff older man came on the line.

"This is Helmers."

"Hey, Detective Helmers? I'm Jerry Nunez, the primary patrol officer from that murder call on Hanley."

"Nunez, Nunez...you're the one that loudmouth reporter, the hot one, kept trying to interview, right? I remember you now. That was a pretty good report supplement you wrote for that murder."

"Thanks, I appreciate that." Nunez leaned back at one of his dining table *chair*s, stretching to shake off soreness from the three mile run he had just finished. "Do you have a few minutes? I have something I'd like to talk to you about, about the Hanley murder."

"We're always pretty busy, but I'm sure I can spare a few minutes for a hardworking officer. Whadaya got?"

Nunez wondered if Helmers would think he was wasting his time, especially since Nunez really didn't have any new information. "Well, it's nothing solid, no new evidence or anything like that. A few nights ago my probationary and I were checking out 1803 Hanley and we had a talk with one of the residents out there, another guy from Afghanistan. Nice old guy, seemed real educated. Anyway, he

41

talked to us for a while about Pashtun beliefs and stuff, and he said it didn't make sense for that kid to have killed his sister over her supposedly being a whore. It doesn't fit in with their culture."

"How does he figure it doesn't fit in with their culture?" Helmers asked. "I'm no expert on Arabs, but we hear about honor killings all the time. If they thought she was a whore, like the kid and his dad both said, why wouldn't it make sense?"

Nunez didn't feel like explaining the difference between Arabs and Pashtuns again, so he ignored that comment. "Well, according to this guy we talked to, the daughter wasn't a whore. Not even by Afghan standards."

"Sure, that's what *he* says. But her own family probably knew her better than he did. If the victim did something seriously bad, or at least what they consider seriously bad, I bet they would have kept it to themselves."

"He probably didn't know as much about her as he thought, but that's not all he said," Nunez said. "According to him, it didn't make sense for the suspect to yell *'Allahu akbar'* after he killed his sister, because it doesn't fit with this kind of killing."

"'This kind of killing?' What does that mean?"

"Muslims yell *Allahu akbar* when they're dying to be martyrs," Nunez said. "Not dying to be martyrs, not like 'Gosh, I'm just dying to be a martyr,' I mean, dying in an act of martyrdom, dying for Allah, you know. If that kid had blown himself up to attack Americans, it would make sense that he would yell *Allahu akbar*. Or if he shot up a mall or something, any terrorist attack in the name of Allah. But what he did to his sister wasn't something he did in the name of Allah. It was something else, cultural instead of religious. According to this old man, anyway."

"Huh," Helmers said, sounding unimpressed. "I guess I get his point, but I don't know if what he said about the culture is true. Do you? Really, do you know for sure there isn't something in the Koran or whatever that says you're supposed to kill your sister if she breaks the rules?"

"No, I don't," Nunez said. "This old guys seemed like he knew what he was talking about though. He seemed pretty honest to me."

"Maybe he is honest, maybe he told you what he honestly believed. But is that the same thing that the girl's family believed? Do they belong to the same sect, or branch, whatever the hell they call it in Islam? Even if he thought he was being honest, it could still be wrong. My son was in Afghanistan a couple of years ago, he got wounded by some of those nutjobs over there. Personally, I don't trust a single one of them. I halfway didn't trust anything those kids' dad said to me on the scene."

Nunez shifted in his *chair*, feeling like he wasn't getting his points across real well. Changing the subject, he asked "Your son was wounded in Afghanistan? I was in Afghanistan in the National Guard, last year."

"No kidding? Welcome home. My son's a Marine, got hit pretty bad in an ambush in Helmand. He's a hell of a Marine, that boy of mine. The only good thing to come out of his mother. Took a bullet in the face and kept on fighting for several more hours. He's still in the Corps, crazy bastard is trying to go back to Afghanistan now. Were you down there, in Helmand?"

"Nope, I was in the northeast," Nunez answered. "Little quieter where I was, but still enough action to keep you on your toes. Glad to hear your son made it through that ambush okay. I was in one or two, they aren't much fun."

"Yeah, I'm glad too, believe me," Helmers said. "My ex and I almost lost it when we got the call. But anyway, back to Hanley. I don't mean to cut you off at the knees or anything, but I don't see what we get from what the neighbor said."

Nunez looked at the information through the detective's eyes. Did Yussuf's opinion mean anything? Other than giving Nunez and Woods a lesson in culture, which might or might not be factual, did he tell them anything of value?

"Yeah, I hear you. All I can tell you is, I've got a decent amount of experience on the street. I can usually tell when someone is honest, and when they're full of shit. The neighbor seemed legit to me. And I've been to Iraq, I've been to Afghanistan, I've been around these people before. That doesn't make me an expert either, but what the neighbor said makes sense. It makes me wonder if there's something we missed."

The *call waiting* tone beeped in his ear. Nunez glanced at the phone to see his wife was calling from her office. He ignored it.

"I understand that, and it's good you're looking into it," Helmers said. "But let me ask you this, Nunez. Let's say we find out that there was something else to it. Maybe the brother tried to rape the sister and she fought back, although we didn't find any evidence of sexual assault. Maybe Mohi-whatever was just a sick little bastard who hated women. Who knows, and what difference would it make now? I don't mean to be a smartass, and believe me, up here in Homicide we get way turned on when a patrol officer cares enough about a case to call us. Especially when he's off duty, like I'm sure you are now. But if we dig into this and find out something else about the motive, it won't bring the girl back to life. The suspect is dead and burning in hell, the case is closed. Every single piece of information we had on the scene pointed to the kid being the killer, and the only killer. The blood, the knife, the slash on the kid's palm from when he accidentally cut himself like a lot of knife killers do, the statements he made to you, all of it. Don't get me wrong, I'd like to know the whole story too, not just the little bit the father told me. I don't get why the kid did it, I don't get why the father reacted the way he did, and I really don't understand the overkill, all the hate this kid must have had for his sister. But I've got lots of cases, Nunez. Active cases I need to make an arrest on. I can't take what little time I have and use it to investigate cases that are already closed."

Nunez grudgingly accepted that Helmers' analysis of the situation made way more sense than his own. Still, it felt like there was something important left to be discovered about this murder. "Yeah, I hear you. I hope you know what I was trying to get at though, I just want to make sure nothing gets left unchecked. Hey Detective Helmers, I appreciate your time, thanks for listening."

"No problem, Officer Nunez. And listen, don't get me wrong. I am *not* telling you to stop looking into this murder, if you really think there's something more to it. I'm just saying that as far as I can tell, and I've been doing this a long, long time, nothing will change the basic facts. I could be wrong, god knows I've been wrong plenty of times before. So if you find anything else you think is important, don't think twice about calling me."

"I will, thanks."

"Thanks for calling, Officer. Take care."

"You too." Nunez hung up, not feeling nearly as foolish as he had at about the halfway point in the conversation. He stood and stuck his cell phone into the pocket of his running pants. It started vibrating immediately. He picked it up to see his wife calling back. He thought, *Here it comes.*

"So, finally done wasting family time on the phone to the department, or do you have to call someone else now?" Laura had called earlier and Nunez had cut her off, saying he needed to call Homicide before it got too late.

"I'm done. Laura, do me a favor, don't jack with me right now. I'm trying to figure something out about a murder I worked last week. It's not fun, don't accuse me of having a good time with it."

"What murder? You didn't say anything about a murder."

"Last Tuesday night," Nunez said. "Bad one, worst I've ever seen. Innocent little girl got killed, and I was talking to the investigator in charge of the case."

"Are you talking about that little Arab girl that was stabbed to death, the murder they showed on TV? The one that was killed by her brother? The officer-involved shooting?" As she spoke, Nunez could hear her level of anger rising.

"Yes, that murder. That officer-involved shooting."

"You worked that one? You were in that shooting? And you didn't bother to tell me?" Laura asked.

"I was there, but I didn't shoot. And I didn't want to talk about it."

"Uh huh," she said. "I'm not worth talking to when something important happens."

"God damn it, Laura, lighten up on me. You know that's not how it is." Even though her words aggravated him, he understood her anger. Despite their frequent arguments and flare-ups they were close, and he generally told her everything that happened at work. But for whatever reason he hadn't wanted to talk to her about the murder of the little Afghan girl on Hanley.

"You're worth talking to. That isn't the issue. You know how I laugh off most murders, but I couldn't joke about this one. That little girl could have been Alyssa in ten years, she could have been you before we met. Dark haired little girl, pretty, and people say she was smart too. I saw her school ID, she was just beautiful. I think I've only seen two other actual innocent murder victims. Every other murder victim was doing something stupid that got them killed. Most of them deserved it, especially the gangsters. This was completely different, and it bothered me. I didn't want to talk about it."

"Jerry, I'm your wife," Laura huffed. "If you won't communicate with me about things that bother you, our marriage is seriously flawed."

"Yeah, I guess it is. Sorry."

"'Sorry our marriage is flawed'? That's all you have to say?"

The *call waiting* tone beeped again. Nunez looked at the phone. Alex Wilson, his gunner from Iraq and Afghanistan, was calling. Wilson had volunteered for another Afghanistan deployment, and Nunez knew he was leaving within hours.

"Laura, I need to go. Someone's calling."

"Who is it?" She demanded. "Why is it so important?"

"What difference does it make who it is? I just need to go, I'll call you back."

The phone beeped again. "Jerry, who's on the other line?"

"It's Alex. I have to go."

"Alex? He's always calling and bothering us. Can't you let go of your army friends? Don't answer it."

"Would you just…I'll call you back, I promise. I need to go, Laura."

"Jerry, if you hang up-"

"I'llcallyoubackbye." Nunez switched lines. "Hey Alex! What's up, gangster?"

"Kay pah so, hermano? I thought I was gonna miss this last chance to talk to you, man. We're in line at the terminal, about to get on the bird."

"Going to Kyrgyzstan again, like we did last time? I bet you're looking forward to sitting around for two weeks with nothing to do."

"Rumor is we'll only be there a few days, then on to Bagram, then a few of us head to smaller bases from there," Wilson answered. "I hope I don't get stuck in Bagram, the place is a daycare from what I hear. Millions of officers with no war to fight, so they just sit around making up bullshit rules."

"Well, I hope you do get stuck there," Nunez said. "I hope you never leave the wire and come back fat from always eating junk food. Maybe you'll even bring a pregnant fobbit girlfriend home when this is over."

"Ha! Don't jinx me. I doubt I have to worry about that anyway, I'm pretty sure I'm going to a small combat outpost. I'm keeping my fingers crossed on that one, cause I'll go nuts if I'm sitting around in Bagram with my thumb up my ass."

"I know. But I'm willing to never shake your hand again, if a shitty thumb is all it takes to get you home safe," Nunez said.

"Jerry, you're so full of shit your eyes are brown. We both know that if you were coming with me we'd figure out a way to go to the worst place in Afghanistan. Shit man, the line's moving, we're headed out the door! I'll email as soon as I'm there."

"Alright brother. Stay safe, I'll be waiting to hear from you."

"Okay man, gotta run! Later!"

Wilson hung up. Nunez put his phone in his pocket before getting up to check his emails. Within a minute of sitting down in front of the computer his phone rang again. He pulled the phone out, saw his wife's name, and put it back in his pocket. He'd give himself a few hours of peace and wait until she came home, when they could argue face to face.

The laptop's background picture was him and Laura, taken two years earlier in Cancun. Laura was a beautiful woman, petite and curvy with light skin and dark hair and eyes, an exotic cross between an Irish father and Mexican mother. In the picture they looked happy enough; their smiles didn't give any hint of tension between them.

Their marriage had not started well. When they first met, Laura was married to an evening shift officer named Gary something-or-other who Nunez was vaguely acquainted with. Nunez had bumped into Laura and her then-husband at a party thrown by a mutual friend. Nunez had simply shaken hands with her, said hello while admiring how pretty and shapely she was, and as she walked away he admired her butt until other party guests blocked his view. She hadn't made much of an impression on him, nothing more than admiration for how hot she was and a little envy for Gary.

At that time Nunez's primary focus in life, outside of work and drills in the old, pre-war National Guard, was going clubbing, partying and doing his best to get into the pants of any single, good looking, middle class, decently dressed, non-crazy woman he met. He forgot about Gary's wife, and a year later bumped into Laura at a mall food court. He asked how Gary was, and wound up standing beside her table for twenty minutes while she went on about what an asshole Gary had been. She said she should have listened to friends and family who warned her she was too good to marry a cop, and how she would be smarter the next time she married, which wouldn't happen until all the hate for Gary was out of her system. During her tirade she threw in "But maybe you're not as big of an asshole as other cops," which Nunez figured was as charitable as she could be under the circumstances. He was finally able to break away, just before she almost talked herself into a crying fit, and headed to Victoria's Secret to buy lingerie for the girl he was currently having friendly sex with.

Another year later he ran into her at a downtown bar. Both were a few beers and shots into their evening, and Nunez was surprised to find Laura flirting with him. Within half an hour she was rubbing his leg under the table, within an hour making out with him on the dance floor. They finished the night having sex in the back seat of his pickup in the bar's parking lot, while their sober friends waited uncomfortably for them to hurry up and finish so designated drivers could take them home.

They didn't talk for several days afterward, until Laura called him at the number he had forgotten he gave her. She apologized for her behavior at the club and assured him their tryst was just a consequence of her loneliness since her divorce. Nunez said he understood and apologized for his behavior as well. He assured her he wasn't the kind of guy to have casual sex with random drunk women he met in bars, which was a total lie.

She surprised him by suggesting they meet sometime for lunch, which they did later that week. And again the next day, and then for dinner that weekend, and by the next week they were seeing each other almost every day. After the first time they had clear-headed, sober sex, Nunez thought he should shut this budding relationship down before it really got started. He worried that Laura might still hate her ex, all cops and maybe even all men.

And there was another girl, a nice girl he met after her car was burglarized at a gas station. He had taken her to dinner once, before he and Laura started dating. The other girl was quiet, shy, demure, beautiful, coy and came from a traditional family in Mexico. Placing each woman on the "happy wife, happy life" scale, the other girl was the clear winner. The time Nunez spent with Laura made him worry he'd knock her up and get stuck with her; the other girl made him want to quit being such a tomcat, stop drinking and smoking and start a family, since he was already thirty years old.

48

One afternoon, after talking to the other girl on the phone for over an hour, he made his decision. He was going to call Laura and tell her Gary had been too good a friend of his, which was bullshit, and that he didn't feel right getting involved with her, which wasn't. She called him first, to tell him she was pregnant.

And that ended the debate. Neither of them believed in abortion, Laura because of her Catholic upbringing and Nunez because he was a firm believer in personal responsibility. There was no question the baby would be born, and that he would support it. There was definitely a question, however, as to the nature of the relationship Laura Simpson and Jerry Nunez would share.

Nunez felt like the decision about their relationship seemed to have been made for them, without either of them thinking much about it. After Laura broke the pregnancy news she had gone to his apartment to discuss what they should do, and didn't leave until the next morning. During the night Nunez had laid in bed with Laura curled next to him, warm and soft and naked. When he put his hand on her womb to feel the space where his child grew, he thought, *I could do a lot worse than this woman.*

And he could have done a lot worse, and their marriage could have been a lot worse. Being married to Laura *had* pushed him to stop drinking, smoking and tomcatting around, and it *had* turned him into the family man he thought he should be. And Laura seemed to have grown to love him, or at least depend on him for security and stability. When he spent time with his wife now, he felt love that had developed in his heart while his daughter Alyssa developed in her womb, and he felt respect for her as a woman and mother. But he could never quite lose the feeling she was disappointed with her life and with him, that she felt she settled for something far below what she deserved.

Laura tried to make them what she thought they should be: a happy little family in a nice house in a nice neighborhood, with her husband home every night and weekend. And Nunez screwed that up by working nights because it was his favorite shift, and working holidays because his low seniority meant he had to, and by going to drill and hanging out with his soldier buddies one weekend a month, still hitting the bars with them but now as designated driver instead of designated drunken skirt-chaser.

And then he really screwed it up by deploying to Iraq. Laura plain hated everything about his police work. And how she felt about police work paled in comparison to how she felt about the military.

Laura was not built to be a soldier's wife. During his deployment she was constantly checking emails and waiting for Nunez's calls. She insisted he tell her about every dangerous thing that happened and then burst into tears when he did. When he came home on mid-tour leave she was so relieved to have him home safe she forgot about birth control and wound up pregnant again. She gave birth to their second child, a son this time, a few months after he finished his Iraq tour. They hadn't had much time to reconnect when the deployment was over; he was worried about having enough money to cover the expenses of a second child, so he went back to work early. Straight back to night shift, weekends and holidays.

Laura's relief at having her husband back home turned quickly back to sullen anger and resentment. Two years later, when Nunez was in Afghanistan, she started to feel she'd once again had enough of being a cop's wife, and was way past having enough of being a soldier's wife. Since Nunez's return from Afghanistan their marriage had been on the verge of being on the verge of collapse, and all Nunez could do was hope it got better.

Late that night, after Nunez spent an hour arguing with his wife until he left for work, he and Woods drove slowly around the beat looking for something to do. Nunez yawned and said the most profound thing he had said all night.

"I'm bored as shit."

"Me too. How about Yussuf, want to go check the complex?"

"Sure, why not. Nothing's holding, right?"

Woods checked the call status on the car's computer. "Nope, we're good."

A few minutes later they pulled into the parking lot on Hanley. As they had promised, at least once every night they had checked on Yussuf, although they hadn't seen or talked to him. This time they saw Yussuf again sitting outside his front door, smoking a cigarette and smiling excitedly at them. To Nunez's surprise, Yussuf was wearing black western dress slacks and a white long-sleeved dress shirt. Nunez and Woods got out and greeted Yussuf, who acted as if they were long lost brothers.

"Michael! Jerry! It is good to see you again! Would you like to come inside for tea?"

"Oh no Yussuf," Nunez said, shaking his hand. "I hate to bother your wife again this late. We'll just visit with you out here tonight. So what are you all dressed up for, have you found a second woman you'd like to marry?"

Yussuf laughed. "Ah Jerry, of course you know I could not afford a second wife. And this is not my home, where such a thing is legal. I would prefer to not trade my freedom for a jail again. I am dressed this way because I assisted the professor of Southwest Asian studies at the University of Houston for his evening class, and I have been too busy to change. Besides, should I decide to find a second wife among the many beautiful women at the University, I believe they would prefer to see me in western clothes."

"You have a point Yussuf, they probably would," Nunez said. "So, no more problems here in the last week?"

"No, nothing unusual," Yussuf said. "Perhaps the residents of this complex are still in shock over the murder and shooting, it is unusual to see anyone outside now. I suppose that will change with time."

Woods asked, "Hey Yussuf, I was wondering something. What happened to the girl's parents, do they still live here? Did they move into another apartment?"

Yussuf nodded. "Oh yes, they are still here, in the same apartment. At the moment there are no open apartments they can move to. The church paid for them to spend time in a hotel, and while they were away several of our neighbors cleaned the apartment."

"Did you help? It must have been a mess," Woods said.

"No, I did not think it proper for me to go into their apartment. For the same reason, I stayed inside my home and did not come outside to talk to the police that night. It was not a matter I felt I should be involved in."

Nunez considered that. The night they met, Yussuf practically begged them to talk about the murder and shooting, and tried to get them to reconsider the motive. Yet now he said he didn't think he should be involved.

Nunez remembered something Detective Helmers said. "Yussuf, are you and…what's his name…Rahim, are you and Rahim from the same sect of Islam?"

"Yes, we are both Sunnis," Yussuf said. "In Afghanistan only the Hazaras are still Shia. Our mosque is a Sunni mosque. Are you familiar with the mosque, Jerry? It is in this area so I would think you have seen it before."

"Where is it?" Nunez asked.

"It is on North Shepherd at the intersection of Crosstimbers, no more than fifteen minutes from here."

Nunez knew the intersection, but had never seen a mosque there. The intersection had businesses and warehouse on the east side of the street, and nice old residential homes on the west. Nunez had seen plenty of mosques in the last five years, but he didn't remember seeing anything resembling a mosque where North Shepherd met Crosstimbers.

"I've been there many times, Yussuf," Nunez said. "I've been working this area for years, and I can't remember a mosque there."

Yussuf nodded. "It is understandable that you have not seen it, Jerry. It is simply an old warehouse that we have converted to a mosque until we are able to raise enough money to build a proper house of worship. The mosque has no markings and no minaret, simply a sign at the door. We in the Muslim community know where the mosques are, there is no reason to make advertisements of them. They are simply there for the faithful to gather and pray, not to proclaim to the world who we are. Of course, we would all prefer to have a traditional mosque, but Mohammed, peace be upon him, had no need for a mansion in which to worship god. A simple home or even open desert was sufficient for him to practice his devotion."

Nunez thought about the intersection, trying to place the warehouse Yussuf was talking about. The only warehouse he could remember was on the southeast corner, just north of a shopping center. As Nunez pictured the area, Yussuf continued, "The warehouse is a wonderful building, Jerry, my first look at the wonders of American architecture. I had no idea such a simple structure could be built of walls so thick, and contain so many different rooms. Such wonderful craftsmanship in this country, Jerry, one of the many amazing things I have discovered here! You know the warehouse is composed of two levels? I was not aware when I first saw the building from outside how complex it was. Of course, we use the open, main area of the warehouse to gather and pray, but on the lower level there are small rooms perfect for private study, or for the discussions we often have, the comparisons between different versions of Islam we practice in our own countries. On pleasant evenings we sometimes gather on the roof to drink tea and have the political and religious discussions which so many of us love, discussions which are common in most of our countries. The only concern among some of those who attend the mosque is that the large loading door at the rear is perhaps very simple for a thief to enter. Please, you should join us some evening, Jerry. You might learn much that is of interest to you."

"I'll think about that, Yussuf, but I'm not a very religious person. Thank you for the invitation though."

"Ah, I understand. But perhaps, if the mosque is in your area, you could check on it periodically? There is often activity around the mosque at night."

"We don't work that area, but I'll ask the officers who do if they can keep an eye on it," Nunez said.

"That is very kind of you Jerry, thank you."

Woods spoke up. "Yussuf, you said you knew the boy who killed his sister."

"Mohibullah," Nunez said.

"Right, Mohibullah. I noticed you didn't have much to say about him. What kind of kid was he?"

Yussuf sighed, indicating again he hadn't liked the boy. "Mohibullah was not a bad son to his parents, Michael. But he was not...ah, what is the correct way to say this? Mohibullah was not a...a personable boy. He was unfriendly to many of us. He was not disrespectful, he was simply unfriendly. To non-Muslims he refused to speak at all. My wife and I were always uncomfortable at the manner in which he spoke to his sister, at his seeming belief that she should follow his every command. He had no friends, no outside activities. He detested the school he and Fahima attended, because he believed it to be a den of immorality and evil. He was very devout, Michael, he was a pious Muslim. And that is all he was. Much like his father."

"Huh," Woods said. "So, do you think he killed Fahima because she refused to do what he told her to? I mean, is that part of his culture?"

"Mohibullah and his family are very simple, conservative, rural people, Michael," Yussuf said. "Or perhaps I should say, Mohibullah and Fahima were, and their mother and father still are. But this still does not explain why Mohibullah would kill his sister. Beat her, yes. My culture does produce men who think nothing of beating a woman for failing to immediately obey. But if a man murdered a woman for such a trivial reason, particularly if he mutilated her, the man would be killed himself. So, no, Michael. Any possible disobedience Fahima committed would not be a justification for her murder. Not even in as harsh a culture as the rural Pashtun culture."

"Shit. I mean, shoot. Sorry Yussuf, didn't mean to cuss," Woods said. "I just keep trying to figure out some reason for this murder that makes sense. If it wasn't an honor killing, and he didn't kill her because she refused to do what he told her to, what else could it have been?"

"Yussuf," Nunez said, "I hate to ask this, but do you think Mohibullah was trying to force Fahima to have sex?"

"No, Jerry," Yussuf quickly answered. "No. That is not possible. A boy as devout and pious as Mohibullah would not conceive of such a thing. And in a family such as his, the penalty for such behavior would be death. No, Jerry, there are boundaries that simply will not be crossed. Mohibullah was not trying to force his sister to have intercourse. And I ask you, was there any reason to believe sexual desire was a motivation for this killing? Was there any indication Mohibullah attempted a sexual act with Fahima?"

Nunez shook his head. "No Yussuf, there wasn't. There was nothing at all. But I really don't get this. Last time we spoke, you said I should look behind the reason we were given for the murder, the thing about Fahima being a whore. And we're looking, but nothing fits. I haven't figured out what other reason there could have been. Is there some other motive Mohibullah could have had? I know you don't know either, but what other ideas do you have?"

They heard hinges squeak. The door to apartment A swung open. Rahim stepped out into the dim light, wearing a white *sharwal kamis* and smoking a cigarette. Nunez hadn't expect to see him at the complex again, maybe because Nunez knew he himself couldn't have stayed in the apartment where his two children died.

Looking at Rahim, Yussuf slowly said, "It appears our conversation is disturbing my neighbors. I suppose it is time for me to join my wife inside." He turned toward Nunez and Woods. "Good night, my friends. I have enjoyed our visit. I hope to see you again soon."

"Good night, Yussuf. We'll keep coming by at night."

Yussuf glanced nervously at Rahim. He looked the way Afghan villagers did when their neighbors caught them talking to American troops.

Woods said, "See you later, Yussuf. Have a good night."

"Take care, my friends," Yussuf said, walking in the door. As soon as the door closed behind him, the porch light turned off.

Nunez and Woods got back into their patrol car. Nunez wondered why Yussuf seemed so uncomfortable. Then he saw Rahim glaring hatefully at them as they drove past.

Nunez caught Rahim's eyes for a split second. Two men, roughly the same age, with the shared experience of being a foreigner in the other's homeland, each a husband and one of them still the father of a son and daughter. They even looked similar, with thin bodies, medium dark skin, dark hair and eyes. Each had experienced war, death, and suffering, although Nunez could never comprehend how Rahim felt when his children died horrible, violent deaths.

In the brief instant their eyes met, the two men could have recognized all they had in common. Instead, Nunez only saw the hatred Rahim felt toward the type of men who killed his son. And he knew it hadn't dissipated in the week since Officer Mata blew Mohibullah's life out of his chest.

CHAPTER 4

Nunez walked into the officers' work room to hang out, having arrived early for work. He was drinking a Dr. Pepper from one of the machines in the station, like he always did when he got to work early. A dozen or so evening shift officers were there, along with several night shift probationary officers who arrived early for everything. And Calhoun, because he had no wife, girlfriend or friends and nowhere else to go.

The evening shift officers were mostly hunched over computers that lined the walls, trying to finish reports that had stacked up during their shift. The night shift rookies sat in a tight circle telling stories and trying to outdo each other on who made the most arrests or ran the most dangerous calls, laughing, high-fiving and accusing each other of being full of shit. Calhoun sat by himself, saying nothing to anyone and not being paid attention to by anyone, not even two officers who had been in the academy with him.

Evening shift officer Ray Walker finished his last report, got up from his computer and picked up his Coke, ready to rush out and unload his gear so he could hit the road when his shift was actually supposed to be over. He saw Nunez and his eyes lit up.

"Hey, platoon daddy! What's up?"

"How you been, Jarhead?" Nunez asked, and gave Walker the half handshake, half hug that soldiers, Marines and cops give each other when they're among their own kind.

Nunez and Walker had been in the same brigade in Iraq, but in different battalions in different places and never met each other until Walker showed up at the North station for field training. Walker started his military career in the Marines and joined the Guard later, with the intention of eventually retiring from the service. His experiences in Iraq, however, made him alter his plans. He got out of the Guard when his three year enlistment expired, less than a year after he got home from their deployment, around the same time he got a spot in a

Houston Police academy class. He was finishing his first few years on the street, and had ridden with Nunez a few times while he was on probation. During their first shift together they discovered they had deployed with the same unit and had several mutual friends in the Guard. Although they hadn't ridden together for long and rarely saw each other now, they considered themselves good friends.

"I've been good, real good," Walker said. "I just came back from an Alaskan cruise with Stacy, and we're pretty sure I knocked her up again. I'm hoping for a girl this time, my two boys are tearing the house apart. And work's been good, I've gotten some good turds lately. You hear about that check-cashing store robbery a couple weeks back? I got one of those guys on a traffic stop two days ago. How about you, what's new?"

"Same as always," Nunez answered. "You know how it is, man. The kids are good, Laura's the same. I hate this job but I'm not good for anything else anymore, so I'm counting the days til retirement. Only 48,663 to go."

Walker smiled. "You're such a bad liar, Jerry. You said the same shit when we rode together, and you worked harder than any officer I know. If you really hate the job that bad, get into a few chases and make some good arrests. That'll bring you back."

"Maybe so," Nunez said. "But it's been so many years now, it's like being sick of all this shit is normal and getting excited about the job is weird. I'm just tired of it, bro. Hopefully it'll get back to the way it used to be, but it doesn't feel like it."

Walker nodded. "It'll get back to normal, 'cause no matter how burned out you think you are, you're still a real cop." He glanced at his watch. "Hey dude, I gotta run. Stacy's got dinner going and she'll be pissed if I'm not there when it's done. I better not get on her bad side, there's a limited amount of time before she's too pregnant to have sex with me." Then, lifting his coke, he said, "To Jeff. Semper Fi, Jerry."

Two young officers with high and tight haircuts called out "Semper Fi!" without turning away from their keyboards. One had a long scar across the back of his scalp.

Nunez lifted his Dr. Pepper and touched Walker's Coke with it, returning the toast. "To Jeff."

Walker's smile held a touch of sadness now, and he grabbed and held Nunez's shoulder warmly for a second before leaving the room.

———·———

Woods watched the exchange with interest as he sat with the other rookies. He had met Walker but didn't know him. When he heard the "platoon daddy" comment he got the distinct impression Walker and Nunez had served together, but didn't understand the "To Jeff" thing. He made a mental note to ask Nunez about it.

Out of nowhere Calhoun asked one of his academy classmates, "Hey Gonzalez, why do you Mexicans call your kids 'mommy' and 'daddy'?"

Officer Rob Gonzalez rolled his eyes and swiveled around to face Calhoun, who was leaned way back in his *chair* with arms crossed and a ridiculous smirk. Giving Calhoun a look that said *Eat a dick,* Gonzalez answered, "I don't know, Eddie. Why do you white guys call your kids 'the master race'?"

The room erupted in laughter, from officers of all colors, which drowned out Calhoun's weak "Because they are" response.

Offended, Calhoun said, "Last night I arrested some Mexican for traffic warrants and when I was towing his car his wife was standing by the road telling their kid, 'It's okay daddy, it's okay.' What the fuck is up with that shit?"

Gonzalez said, "Couldn't tell you, Eddie. I guess she said it just to fuck with you. And I told you before, I'm not 'Mexican'. I was born here and my parents were born here. How many traffic warrants did the guy have anyway?"

"Sorry, Mexican-*American*," Calhoun sneered. "He had two warrants, plus his inspection was expired two months."

Gonzalez pursed his lips. "So you arrested him and towed his car over two traffic warrants and a chickenshit ticket, even though his wife and baby were with him?"

Calhoun nodded proudly. "Sure did. She didn't have a license, I wasn't about to let her drive."

"You could have let that little bullshit go. Or you could have let her call someone to come and get the car, asshole. What'd you do with the wife and kid?"

"I couldn't give a fuck less about the wife and kid," Calhoun said. "I told the wife to haul ass. Last I saw her she was carrying the kid down the service road. If her husband didn't want them on the street in the middle of the night, he shouldn't be driving around with expired shit and warrants. But don't get all butt-hurt about it, it's not like I hate you Mexicans as much as I hate Hajis."

Gonzalez rolled his eyes again. "Eddie, you never even left the U.S. when you were in the Marines. You told us that, remember? What reason would you have to hate Arabs? What actual, personal reason would you have?"

"It doesn't matter whether I went anywhere or not," Calhoun retorted. "Lots of my friends got killed by Hajis, just because I wasn't there doesn't mean I can't hate them too."

Gonzalez looked at the other classmate of theirs, who had turned from his computer to watch the exchange. Gonzalez and the other officer shook their heads, then turned back to their computers. Nunez looked at Woods and mouthed *what an asshole*. Then he looked at his watch, finished the last bit of Dr. Pepper and walked to the roll call room.

Roll call went quickly, and the officers were on the street earlier than normal. After leaving the station, Woods asked, "Jerry, why'd you come in so early? I don't remember seeing you in the work room early before."

"You've never been married, right?" Nunez asked.

"Nope. Engaged once, never married."

"If you're ever married you'll get it. There are times it's better if you get out of the house as soon as you can."

Woods wondered exactly what Nunez meant, but decided it wasn't important enough to pursue. Instead he asked, "Um, what did Walker call you in there? It was 'platoon daddy', wasn't it? What's that?"

Looking bored, Nunez answered, "It's a nickname for platoon sergeant. I was a platoon sergeant all the time I was in Iraq and Afghanistan. That's the senior NCO, the senior non-officer in the platoon."

"I see," Woods said. Then, preparing himself for Nunez to cut him off or make a smartass remark, he asked "And what was that 'To Jeff' thing y'all did? Who's Jeff?"

Nunez stayed quiet for a few seconds. Woods felt almost certain he was going to say something sarcastic and tell him to shut up. Instead, Nunez gave a quiet answer.

"Jeff was a friend of ours. He was one of my soldiers, a fire team leader in my platoon before we went to Iraq. Jeff Colin. Good guy, funny as hell. He was smart too, always made the right decision under stress. At least in training, anyway."

Nunez rolled his head on his shoulders and closed his eyes for a few seconds while he drove, making Woods nervous. He opened them and said, "When the Guard picks a unit to send overseas, they strip other units to make sure the deploying unit has everyone it needs. Guard units are always short of people, we never had everyone we were supposed to. My unit got stripped so they could send guys to other battalions that were deploying. I wound up on a convoy escort team in an artillery battalion, Jeff got lucky and went to an infantry battalion. Lucky…huh. Jeff wound up in Walker's platoon. They were good friends."

Nunez got to the service road and headed toward a business park. "Their platoon was on route patrol and Walker's humvee got hit by a roadside bomb. It disabled the humvee, and I guess Jeff thought it was on fire because of all the smoke. Jeff was in the Humvee behind Walker, and he told his guys to stay inside while he went to check on Walker's truck. Before Jeff got there, two secondary IEDs went off. One of them was right next to him, like six feet away. He didn't have a chance. The other IED didn't hit anything. It turned out Walker's humvee just got a wheel blown off and took shrapnel down the driver's side, but that was it. Walker and his guys got their bells rung by the blast, no injuries. When Walker shook it off he got out and found Jeff."

Nunez swiveled his head on his shoulders again. "He never told me how bad Jeff was hit, and I'll never ask him, but I figure Jeff had to have been torn up pretty bad. Probably in pieces. I just hope he didn't…well…I've always wondered if Jeff was still alive, and Walker watched him die."

Woods realized he wasn't paying attention to anything around them. He forced himself to look out the windows, then back at Nunez. Nunez stared straight ahead, speaking as if Woods wasn't there.

"Walker had to put him in a body bag, stick him in the back of their humvee and drive him to a firebase," Nunez said. "This happened toward the end of the deployment, when we only had about six weeks left. Walker got onto the department after that deployment, and we rode together when he was on probation. That's when we found out we both knew Jeff."

Silence followed. Nunez kept driving and staring straight ahead. Woods, waited, then felt he should say something.

"I'm sorry about your friend."

"Don't be," Nunez said. "Jeff was a grown man, he knew what he was doing. He wouldn't have regretted taking care of his buddies, even if it meant he would die. It's a warrior thing, civilians just don't get it. It sounds weird, but sometimes it's better that you die trying to protect your soldiers, instead of living while your friends get killed around you. Jeff knew it. He didn't just talk about it, he lived it. He died living it."

"So Walker just decided to bring him up in the roll call room?" Woods asked.

"No, he didn't decide just then. Every time he sees someone who knew Jeff, he makes a toast to him. A raised glass, handshake, fist bump, high five, whatever. So we never forget."

"Damn," Woods sighed. "That's really…touching, I guess."

Nunez cocked an eyebrow and finally looked at Woods. "Touching? Fag. That's not 'touching', it's just what soldiers do. We don't leave our dead, and we don't forget them."

"Ohhhhkay," Woods said, holding back sarcasm. "Dick. Sorry man, I don't know anything about the military. Except way back in World War Two, I don't think anyone in my family ever served. Hearing all this stuff is new to me."

"Good thing you went to college then," Nunez said. "I'm sure that toughened you up for the street."

"Aw, bite me, Jerry. There are plenty of college guys who are good street cops. You said so yourself."

"Yeah, but that doesn't include you. At least, not yet."

———

Nunez's phone vibrated. He pulled it off his belt. A number he didn't recognize was on the screen. Probably another night shift officer.

"This is Jerry."

"Jerry, my friend, it is good to hear your voice again. I am sorry if I am disturbing you, are you able to speak?"

Nunez silently mouthed *Yussuf* to Woods. "Yussuf, how are you? You had me a little worried when you went in so fast last time we visited, and we hadn't seen or heard from you since. I thought you might be having a problem with Rahim. You looked a little afraid of him."

"Jerry, of course not," Yussuf said. "Please pardon me for saying so, but such talk is foolish. I simply do not wish to have any unpleasant experiences with my neighbors." Then, laughing, he said "Should there ever be any tension between Rahim and me, you know of course I would have no recourse but to avoid him in the manner a rabbit avoids a hawk. I am an academic, not a man of violence like Rahim. I should not like to have physical confrontation with him."

"Man of violence?" Nunez asked. "What do you mean by that?"

"Ah Jerry, remember, I am a citizen of Kabul, which in my youth was a city of western ideals. Those of us fortunate enough to have received an education in Kabul do not display the same tendencies as rural villagers, especially those from Kandahar. You may not know this Jerry, but *Kandaris* are known throughout Afghanistan for their short temper. Rahim is the type of man used to settling disputes with violence. Of course, Rahim has never displayed any hostility toward me or any other residents of our complex, and I do not mean to suggest that he personally is a violent man. It is not likely that Rahim would return to any of the activities he was involved in when he was in Kandahar. I simply would prefer to not provoke any anger, from any of my neighbors."

"Yussuf, what activities are you talking about?" Nunez asked. "What was Rahim involved in?"

"Oh, just such activities as are normal for rural Afghan men, Jerry," Yussuf answered. "I am sure you recall many incidents of violence such as feuds between tribes and families. Such a life is normal for a man such as Rahim, whether or not the man is a member of a militant organization."

"A militant organization, like the Taliban?"

"Yes Jerry, an organization such as the Taliban," Yussuf said.

"Was Rahim Taliban?" Nunez asked. "I'll go over there and shoot him in the head right now if he was a Talib."

Yussuf laughed again. "Please do not, Jerry, I would prefer to not see more death around my home. No, I don't believe Rahim was a Talib, I believe he angered the Taliban by refusing to heed their orders. I think you are perhaps too fixated on the Taliban, Jerry. There were many such extremist organizations before the Taliban, and there are many more today. You need not go far to find such an organization, Jerry. They are not hidden."

"In that case, it's a good thing we met, Yussuf," Nunez said. "Make sure you tell me if there are organizations like that around here."

"Yes, Jerry, of course I will. Perhaps that is the purpose God orchestrated our meeting."

Nunez looked at Woods with an expression that said, *What the hell did that mean?* Woods returned the look and mouthed *What?* Nunez held up one finger, signaling for Woods to stand by.

"Yussuf, are you busy?" Nunez asked. "Do you want us to visit? I'd like to talk to you about Rahim."

"I am sorry Jerry, it is very late and I do not wish to disturb my wife," Yussuf said. "Please accept my apologies for being so inhospitable, my friend. I would very much like to entertain you and Michael as guests, but I am afraid it would not be wise for me to have you here tonight. Perhaps another time. I believe I must end the call now, my wife is getting annoyed at my absence."

"Okay Yussuf, maybe we can visit tomorrow. Hey Yussuf, is everything okay? You sound like something's been bothering you lately."

"Nothing is bothering me, Jerry. Thank you for inquiring as to my safety, but I am fine. There is no danger to my life, nothing for you to worry about. Even if something should happen, it would simply be God's will."

Nunez gave Woods the same confused look as before. "Well, okay, Yussuf. Let me know if there are any problems, alright?"

"Of course, Jerry. Thank you for your concern, and good night. Please give my regards to Michael."

"I will, Yussuf-*khan*. Good night."

"Good night, Jerry-*khan*."

Yussuf hung up. Nunez put his phone away. Woods stared at him with curiosity. "Damn, that guy keeps fucking with my head," Nunez said. "Sometimes I just can't figure out what the hell he's saying to me."

"Yeah, he confuses me too," Woods said. "But that's usually because I don't know shit about Afghanistan or Islam. What'd he say that messed you up?"

"I asked him if he got scared the other night when Rahim walked out of his apartment, and he said no, he just doesn't want any problems with his neighbors. Then he says he wouldn't want to face a 'man of violence' like Rahim. I asked him what he meant, and he teaches me another cultural lesson about guys like Rahim being used to violence, but says not to worry, he doesn't do anything like that here. It just sounded kinda odd, you know?"

Woods nodded. "So, what, you think he was lying? He really is scared of Rahim for some reason?"

"Yeah I do, but that wasn't all of it. He said a few things about the Taliban, and about other groups like them, and then he said something about not having to look too hard to find one of those groups."

"No shit," Woods said. "You think he knows of some extremist group in Houston?"

"Anyone who pays attention knows of groups like that in Houston. Supposedly there are a lot of them here, guys with connections to extremists in Saudi Arabia, Syria, all over the place. At least that's what we've been told by Criminal Intelligence."

Woods asked, "You think a harmless old man like Yussuf is part of some evil terrorist group?"

Nunez shook his head. "No, I don't think so. He's too nice of a guy, and he's a complete pussy. He's scared shitless of Rahim. He did say one other weird thing that got me thinking though. I asked him if something was bothering him, and right away he says something like, 'Don't worry about me, there's no danger to my safety and if there is it's just God's will anyway.' Just brought up something about danger, out of nowhere. Maybe it's the language barrier, even though he speaks English real well I don't think he always gets what I'm saying."

"Yeah, that does sound weird. What did he say when you asked if we could go over? I know he said no, but what was his reason?"

"He said it would bother his wife too much," Nunez said. "But he sends you his regards."

"Tell him I said thanks. Want to check out Hanley again, just in case…?"

Nunez nodded to Woods. "Yeah. That's probably a good idea."

———

A few minutes later they pulled into the parking lot of 1803 Hanley. Yussuf's apartment was dark inside and out, but Nunez was surprised to see a light on inside apartment A. A well-kept blue Dodge was parked in front of it.

Woods asked, "You ever see a car at Rahim's apartment before?"

"Nope," Nunez said. "I know there wasn't one here the night of the murder, or the nights we hung out with Yussuf."

Woods ran the license plate. "2012 Dodge four door, registered to a, uh, an Abdul Al….Al Tay…Tay something."

Nunez looked at the computer screen. "Al-Taymiyyah. Abdul Al-Taymiyyah. Lives on Rossey, in the Inwood area.'"

"Abdul Al-Taymiyyah…what kind of name is that? Is it Afghan?"

Nunez squinted, trying to recall the Arab culture familiarization classes he had been forced to sit through before going to Iraq. "It's not an Afghan name. Don't have a clue where the guy is from, but I think it's Arab, not Afghan. I remember the name Abdul when I was in Afghanistan, but I don't remember an Al-anything."

"Interesting," Woods said. "Think he's just visiting, or what?"

"How the fuck should I know?" Nunez asked. "What, do I look like the 'Arab Whisperer' or something?"

"Alright, dick, so we don't know why he's here," Woods said. "I'm going to write the info down and run the name later."

"Good deal. See anything else interesting around here?"

Woods looked around. "Nope, nothing. Other than the mysterious Arab car and the light inside the scary Afghan guy's apartment, it's quiet as a cemetery in this place."

"A cemetery," Nunez said. "How appropriate. Yeah, you're right, this place is dead. Let's jet."

The rest of the shift passed uneventfully. North Houston was as quiet and safe as a cemetery.

CHAPTER 5

Nunez's phone vibrated on the nightstand. He grunted in exasperation. Now wasn't the time for an interruption.

Nunez and Laura lay in bed naked, facing each other. Her face was pressed against his neck, his arms wrapped around her, one of his legs rested between her thighs and the other lay over her hip. It was Tuesday afternoon, the end of Nunez's weekend, and Laura had taken the day off so they could have time alone while the kids were at school. Whenever they had the day together they invariably wound up in bed naked, usually just cuddling instead of actually having sex. Even if they had both slept well the night before they would find a way to fall asleep together.

They often argued and needed to get away from each other, but just as often they needed the intimacy of being together. Nunez had worked nights, weekends and holidays for most of his career, and the deployments had taken years from their marriage. Laura jealously guarded their alone time and hated when anything intruded on it. Especially phone calls.

Nunez rolled over and reached for the cell phone on his nightstand. The call came from a number he didn't recognize.

"Who is it?" Laura asked, cuddling closer to his chest.

"I don't know. I better answer it, maybe it's the FBI calling to tell me I'm being investigated for denying teenage sister-murderers their civil rights." He answered, "This is Jerry."

"Jerry! What's up man?"

Nunez recognized his friend Alex Wilson's voice. He turned slightly away from Laura to speak, as if that would keep her from getting pissed at him for wasting valuable couple time talking to army buddies. "Hey Alex, good to hear from you! It's been what, three weeks? You in Afghanistan yet?"

Laura groaned. Nunez turned to see her giving him a dirty look.

"We got to Afghanistan a week after I last called. But it looks like I won't be

69

making any more trips. I'm pretty sure I'm stuck here in Bagram."

"Oh yeah? What happened to you going to a smaller outpost?" Nunez asked.

"Blow me. You won. I'm stuck here in fobbit paradise. I started patrolling a few days ago and we're going to start running convoys pretty soon. But I'm going to be here the whole deployment."

Nunez laughed. "I'm crushed."

"You should be, you dick," Wilson said. "Save me, bro. I can't stay here, it's retardation city. There are unemployed colonels and sergeant majors out the ass over here, with nothing to do. I mean, literally nothing to do. Every time we go into a chow hall officers and NCOs wander around the tables busting people for wearing paracord bracelets, having their cuffs folded back, not having their pants bloused to exactly the right length, all kinds of bullshit. It's fucking pathetic, Jerry. Hard to find a real leader around here anymore, especially since you were too scared to come with me this time."

"Too scared?" Nunez asked. "Fuck yes I'm too scared. I pissed my pants twice just listening to you talk about Afghanistan. It sounds like there was a perfectly good war going on over there and then garrison broke out. And that's scary. Dude, I'm done with that shit, my job is being a husband and daddy, and sometimes to make money I pretend to be a cop. Two deployments was enough, man. I'm done. Maybe when the war on terror ends I'll get back in the Guard and finish my twenty so I can get a retirement. I figure the war'll be over right around 2099 or so, I'll just wait til then."

Wilson said, "If you were here, this bullshit would make you quit again."

"Then I'm glad I'm not there. And I'll be really glad when you leave. So sit at the FOB and hide in your room all day. It's the best thing to do."

"Good idea, that might be the only way to keep me from suck-starting my pistol," Wilson said. "Hey bro, I gotta run, I still need to call my parents and I only have about twenty minutes on this morale phone."

"Okay, Alex. Take it easy, no stupid chances this time. You used up eight of your nine lives on the last two deployments, you don't come back to life if you get hit over there this time."

"Jerry, you're such a hypocrite," Wilson laughed. "Remember when you charged that compound during the ambush in Kapisa?"

70

Nunez cringed, hoping Laura hadn't heard Wilson. He had never told her about that, and didn't think she needed to find out now. He looked to see if she had heard. She had the same annoyed look on her face as before, not the look of horror that would be there if she found out about that day.

Wilson added, "You didn't exactly play it safe in Afghanistan, or over here, so don't preach to me, reverend. I'll be okay man, don't worry about me. Later man, I'll call you again in a week or so."

"You better. Later homie, stay safe."

Wilson hung up. Nunez put the phone down before turning toward Laura and snuggling his face into her breasts. She put her leg over him and asked, "What was that about?"

"Nothing. Alex got to Afghanistan a couple weeks ago. I hope he gets stuck on base this time."

"But if he gets stuck there, won't that mean he gets to use the phone whenever he wants?" she asked. "Then he'll call and bother us all the time."

Nunez lightly bit Laura's breast, drawing a playful "Ouch!"

"Laura, give the guy a break. Did you know that every single mission in Iraq and Afghanistan, every single one, Alex was with me? I know he gets on your nerves, but he had my back in a lot of bad situations. There aren't many people who would rather die than let me get hurt. Alex is one of them."

"Fine," she said. "I understand. That doesn't mean I have to like him bothering us all the time. It just bugs me that you're always preoccupied with the war, and your army friends. Half the time we're together, you're off somewhere else. You're not a soldier anymore, you're safe from the war now. I just want you to myself. I don't think it's unfair of me to ask that."

Nunez pressed his face further into Laura's soft, full breasts and nodded in agreement. Even though he didn't agree, even though he wouldn't tell Wilson to call less often and had no intention of breaking ties with people he served beside in combat. Laura made more comments about how often Nunez's army friends interfered in their lives, Nunez murmured and nodded, agreeing with whatever she said until they were both asleep.

As usual, Tuesday night started off boring and slow, no calls holding and not much going on. Nunez and Woods wandered around the beat after they burned over an hour hanging out in two different gas stations. Then Nunez remembered something he had meant to ask Woods several days before.

"Mike, I completely forgot about that Abdul guy's car on Hanley. Did you run it, was there anything on the guy?"

"I ran it, and I didn't find shit," Woods said. "The guy's never been arrested here, or been a suspect in a report, or been a victim or witness. Near as I can tell, he's completely clean."

"Well, that sucks," Nunez said. "Not that we had any reason to suspect anything on him, but it would have been nice to find a warrant for crimes against humanity or something."

"Yeah," Woods agreed. "Maybe next time. You hear anything from Yussuf during the weekend?"

"Nope. Maybe Rahim kicked his ass and told him to stop calling us."

Nunez turned down a dark and narrow residential street. Two middle aged black men in shabby jeans and t-shirts riding bicycles down the street turned and looked at the patrol car. One stuck his hand in his pocket, which would have looked nonchalant except that people usually don't ride bicycles with their hands in their pockets.

They passed the slowly-pedaling bicyclist, who kept his eyes on the patrol car and his hand tensed in his pocket. Ahead, a young couple argued in front of a tiny house that would have looked abandoned if not for the single light on above the front door. The house had been white but most of the paint had deteriorated, leaving weather-beaten wood exposed. The front windows were broken, and the entire house leaned to the right. Trash littered the overgrown front yard and a broken down Chrysler New Yorker sat on four flats in the driveway.

The male half of the couple, a black man in his early twenties, wore baggy black jeans pulled down so low the crotch was between his knees. Baby blue boxer shorts were exposed over the top of his pants. The woman he was yelling at was tall and thin, with long braids and skintight white clothes that displayed a four or five month baby bump. The young woman stood stoically as the man screamed and waved his arms in anger.

Neither of them noticed the patrol car until it was less than two houses away. The young man looked up, and without a moment's hesitation sprinted toward the far side of the house, disappearing into a wooded area in seconds. The woman stood in the same spot, not looking at the car, acting as if running at the sight of a police car was the most normal thing in the world.

"You know what I love about my job?" Nunez asked Woods. "Everyone in my beat is so fitness minded. It doesn't matter what time of night it is, there are always people out taking a walk or riding bicycles. Sometimes people see us and decide it's time for a quick jog. It's so nice to be around people who care so much about their health."

Woods asked, "Why don't you ever bother running after them? That guy could be wanted for murder or something. And that old crackhead on the bike might have had a gun. Why didn't we stop and check him out?"

"The guy on the bike had a crack pipe or a rock in his pocket. Crackheads don't hang on to guns. They're valuable, so they trade them for crack as soon as they can. If we had stopped him, he would have pulled a pipe or rock out and thrown it and we'd have never found it. Maybe he would have run and we could have had a foot pursuit through the ghetto and gotten hurt jumping a fence, or been bit by a pit bull or 'rockwilder' in someone's backyard. When I was younger and twice as stupid I used to get all excited about chasing people over bullshit like that. Now, I don't see why I should risk my fucking life over anything crack-related. And do *you* think you could have chased down the Carl Lewis of north Houston when he ran from us back there? *I* couldn't have. Tell you what, next time someone runs from us you go ahead and charge after him. I'll just take a nap until you come back."

Nunez pulled into the driveway of an abandoned house to turn around. A group of older men and women sat on the house's front step. All but one got up and walked away in different directions. The one who stayed was a rail-thin woman in ragged pants and t-shirt with stringy white hair over a scarred and scabbed face, who looked like she was in the process of being slowly beaten to death. She started shrieking unintelligible gibberish.

Woods turned to Nunez. "You hear that?"

"She's fine," Nunez said as he backed out of the driveway. "She was probably afraid we were going to jack her up and find her dope or pipe, and she's too old and fucked up to run, so she's pretending to freak out to keep us from arresting her. It's an old trick that doesn't work so well anymore, but some of the hardcore old crack hoes still try it every once in a while. I guess she can chalk it up as a win tonight."

Woods muttered, "Is *everything* out here related to crack?"

"Yes. Well...no, not everything. I think once there was a crime out here that wasn't crack related. Like maybe...no, that murder was over crack...and so was that kidnapping last month." Nunez frowned, then lit up. "But the murder on Hanley wasn't crack related! Whoopee!"

Woods said "You need help."

"Good idea."

Woods looked at Nunez in confusion. "What are you talking about?"

"Our Afghan brother," Nunez said. "We should go check on him and see if he needs help. No, wait, I want to go look at the mosque again."

"Ya wanna? You almost got us in trouble last time, when we got that robbery call and we were out of our beat."

"Yeah whatever," Nunez said. "I'll let dispatch know we're checking a place that's just outside our area. She'll give us a heads up if something's coming."

Nunez turned onto North Shepherd drive and headed south toward Crosstimbers. North Shepherd showcased one thing that made Houston unique; because Houston has no zoning laws, Shepherd held a mix of homes, apartment complexes and businesses of all types. For most of its length the road was packed with businesses on both sides, but closer to Crosstimbers the businesses on the west side gave way to the residential Garden Oaks area. Garden Oaks was full of older, well-maintained, very expensive homes.

They reached the intersection and stopped at the light. Across the intersection, on the southeast corner, stood the mosque. Neither one of them would have had the slightest idea it was a mosque if Yussuf hadn't told them; there was nothing about the mid-size, single story, plain grey, square warehouse to suggest what it was being used as. The first time they checked it, they had parked their car in front of it and walked to the door. There was in fact a sign proclaiming *Masjid* on the front door.

Every time Nunez and Woods had checked the warehouse they hadn't seen anything. The mosque always had a few cars parked outside, all registered to people with Arab-sounding names and no apparent criminal history or ties to any crime reports. But Nunez and Woods never saw people around it.

The warehouse had a bare front wall with a single, solid-looking front door to the right of a plate glass window. The plate glass was embedded with reinforcing wire, easy to crack but not easy to get through. The building looked slightly taller than one story, with brick-size openings at regular intervals all the way around the roof. Nunez figured the roof had a raised lip around it. The entire warehouse sat on a three foot high concrete foundation. The front door could only be reached by a small stairway rising from the parking lot. The loading bay door at the rear that Yussuf had mentioned, just a big metal garage door, was at the top of a two-car-wide ramp. Another solidly built door, the same as the front door, was to the left of the loading bay, also at the top of a small concrete staircase. The warehouse had no other doors.

Nunez had a hard time believing the warehouse/mosque actually had a lower level; Houston was notorious for its high water table and constant drainage problems. A good rain lasting longer than an hour put roads under water, and a few rainy hours later cars would float around flooded underpasses. The warehouse had to have an outstanding drainage system to keep the lower floor from flooding.

The warehouse was square, maybe sixty feet on each side. A small front parking lot was able to hold no more than twenty cars and the rear parking lot had spaces for maybe another twenty, but the rear lot adjoined the parking lot of a small grocery store. A small shopping center was immediately south of the mosque. To the north was Crosstimbers road. Across Crosstimbers was a small two story building, an auto parts showroom with a fenced-in junkyard behind it.

Nunez and Woods slowly drove beside the building, looking for suspicious activity. As usual, nothing was going on. Nunez drove past the building to get a look at the back door.

Woods jerked upright in his seat. "Jerry, the loading bay door's open."

"Is it a burglary? What do you see?" Nunez made a quick turn into the back parking lot and reached to shut off the patrol car's headlights.

"There's a van in the bay, plus a couple of guys inside wearing Arab clothes. It doesn't *look* like a burglary, but…"

Nunez had made a tight turn so he could get a view of the loading bay. The bay door was raised and a white cargo van was all the way inside. The van looked beat up and old, not like the newer, nicer cars they had seen in the parking lot at night. The back doors stood open and the bare interior of the van was illuminated by a light on the ceiling. Three men in Arab man-dresses stood outside the van, having what looked like a normal conversation. They noticed the police car and looked at it as they spoke. They didn't set off any danger signals in Nunez's head, although he wondered why they were in the loading bay at nearly midnight.

Nunez slowed and turned the car slightly away from the building. He picked up his binoculars and said to Woods, "Lean back in your seat so I can take a look. And wave."

Woods leaned back as told, gave a goofy smile and waved at the three men. The men smiled and waved back. Nunez peered through his binoculars and called out a license plate, which Woods entered into the computer as Nunez drove out of the parking lot.

Woods said, "1998 GMC utility vehicle, registered to a Ruben Arredondo on Mykawa. That's southeast area, right?"

"Yeah, it is, and Arredondo isn't a very Arab name. Registration current? Maybe one of these guys just bought it."

"The owner just renewed it," Woods said. "Think maybe it's one of those overnight cleaning crews?"

"Could be," Nunez said. "I wish we had seen the van on the street, it might have a business name or something on the sides."

Nunez circled back around in the parking lot, stopping the car so that it didn't quite face the warehouse and was far enough away that it didn't look like they were watching the building.

"Mike, do a query on the license plate, see what comes back."

Woods typed in the proper command and hit enter. The returns that came back in seconds surprised them both.

"Damn," Nunez said, scrolling through the first page. "Prisoner vehicle May 2009, prisoner vehicle November 2009, prisoner vehicle...several times in 2010, suspect vehicle 2010, prisoner vehicle 2011. This guy's a turd. Hang on...there's nothing from mid-2011 until 2013. Write all the incident numbers down so we can see what he keeps getting popped for."

"Okay...2013 incident...suspect vehicle in a criminal mischief report," Woods said.

"That's it? Hmmm...know what I'm thinking?"

"You want to set up on this place, hide in the dark and wait until the van leaves so we can get a stop on it?" Woods asked hopefully.

"Exactly," Nunez said. "We go back to the station and run the vehicle and this Arredondo guy. I want to know what he's about. I'd set up on the van but we could be here hours waiting for it to roll, and we're out of our beat already. Let's go."

"Alright, let's go."

"No, wait!" Nunez exclaimed. "That's a great idea, Sherlock, let's call Yussuf! Maybe he can tell us something about the van."

"Really? You think you should call him this late?"

"He's called us later than this, why not?"

Nunez pulled out his phone, looked through his contact list and called the number, then handed the phone to Woods as it started to ring.

Woods pushed it away. "Why are you giving it to me? I don't want to wake him up. You talk to him, it's your idea."

Nunez dropped the phone in Woods' lap, put the car in drive and started rolling slowly toward the back of the warehouse. "I'm driving, you talk to him. If he gets pissed off at you, tell him I told you not to call but you did it anyway. Don't tell him about the van in the bay, just ask him if they have a cleaning crew at the mosque at night."

Just as Yussuf answered the phone Woods called Nunez a dick. Yussuf fumbled about in confusion.

"Jerry, did you call me Dick? Have you unintentionally called the wrong number?"

"No, Yussuf," Woods stammered. "Sorry, it's Mike Woods, I'm calling you from Jerry's phone and, uh, I was saying bye to my friend Dick on another phone. Are you awake, can you talk?"

Yussuf sounded fatigued and bleary. "Yes Michael, of course I can speak to you. Thank you for calling me. Is everything alright, is there a problem?"

"No, not at all, I was just wondering if…" Woods looked at Nunez, who motioned for him to go on. "If a cleaning crew comes to the mosque at night. I mean, do you hire people to clean the mosque? Is it normal for someone to be there in the middle of the night?"

Nunez looked sharply at Woods, silently mouthing the words *Don't. Say. Too. Much.*

Woods covered the mouthpiece and whispered "Well then *you* fucking talk to him."

"No Michael, we do not hire anyone to clean the mosque. That work is performed by several of the wives and daughters. Tell me Michael, why do you ask? I am certain you did not call me at this hour simply to inquire as to how we maintain our mosque."

Woods looked to Nunez for guidance. Nunez was watching the back of the warehouse. The bay door was closed. Nunez said, "Tell him we saw a white van stopped there and thought it might be the cleaning crew. Has he seen a white van around here before?"

"Yeah, Yussuf, we just saw a white van stopped here, a Mexican guy's van." Nunez turned sharply to Woods again, taking his hands off the wheel and lifting them briefly in a *what the fuck* gesture. Woods glared back at Nunez for a second, flipped him off and continued. "The van wasn't doing anything weird, we just hadn't seen it around here before. You know it? You know the white van?"

"Perhaps, I may know it, Michael," Yussuf said. "There is a member of the mosque who drives a white van, an older one. I do not know him well, he is often out of town. I am told he travels frequently between Houston and Mexico for business. That is the only van I am aware of."

Woods raised an eyebrow and looked sideways at Nunez. "He goes to Mexico? Is he Mexican?"

"He is Hispanic, Michael, but I do not know if he is from Mexico. As I said,

I do not know him well, I have only spoken with him on a few occasions."

"Do you know his name?" Woods asked.

"I believe his name is Ruben. I cannot recall his family name, it was an unusual name which I had difficulty pronouncing."

"Okay, Ruben something. Is he a bad guy? Did he seem like a troublemaker to you?"

"Oh, I cannot say, Michael," Yussuf said. "We have only spoken a few times, and then only briefly. He was polite and respectful, and showed the eagerness to learn that most new converts do. But I was not chosen to educate him, others claimed that responsibility."

"So he's a convert?" Woods asked. "How long has he been going to the mosque?"

"Ah, I would have to say it's been a year, Michael, or perhaps slightly less than a year. I should not be so shallow, but I was put off by the man's tattoos and did not wish to speak to him very much."

"Why's that? What was with his tattoos?"

"It was nothing important. The tattoos were not a serious matter, and as a Muslim I know I should accept others as they are. But this man, Ruben, he had many tattoos on his arms and hands, one on his neck, and even two on his face. Perhaps I am being a purist, but I do not see why a man would mark himself in such a way."

"Uh-huh," Woods said. "Did the tattoos say anything?"

"I did not understand them, they were of various symbols and words, I believe. But they were, ah…I do not know the word. Altered? I cannot explain to you correctly what I mean, I am afraid. There were words, but they were not, not normal. I am sorry, I wish I could describe the tattoos in a way that you would understand."

As Yussuf spoke, Woods held the phone slightly away from his ear to make sure Nunez could hear. Nunez leaned over to listen as they crept through the mosque parking lot.

"What was the tattoo on Ruben's face, Yussuf? Do you remember?"

"I believe…I am certain one was a small teardrop, at the edge of one of his eyes. The other was a number, between his eyebrows. I cannot remember what number, I am afraid."

Both Woods and Nunez raised their eyebrows at this last statement. Nunez mouthed *thirteen*. Woods started to ask another question, but Yussuf spoke first. "Michael, my apologies, but it is very late and our conversation is disturbing my wife's rest. Would it be *possible* for you to call me tomorrow morning?"

"Sure, Yussuf. Sorry I woke you up, thanks for the information."

"Of course, of course. Please give my regards to Jerry. And Michael, I ask that you assure me on this subject…you are being careful as you investigate the area of the mosque, yes?"

"Of course, Yussuf, we're always careful. We have to be, it's our job."

"Yes, of course you are always careful. But I mean to ask, are you being more careful than normal when you are there? I have asked you to check the mosque, and I would experience horrible guilt if you were hurt or killed performing the task I have asked of you. All I ask, Michael, is that you, my two friends, that you please keep yourself safe when you check the mosque. That is all."

"Uh, yeah, no problem, Yussuf," Woods said. "Why do you ask? Is there something we should worry about over here?"

Yussuf stayed silent for several seconds. Nunez and Woods also stayed silent, waiting for him to speak.

"Michael…perhaps there is," Yussuf said. "Perhaps the area around the mosque is more dangerous than areas you normally patrol. I cannot say for certain. I simply ask that you be more careful than normal when you are in that area. I am sorry, Michael, but I must go now. Good night, my friend."

"Okay, good night, Yussuf," Woods said. "Thanks."

"Hang on!" Nunez blurted. "Gimme the God damn phone!"

Woods handed Nunez the phone and he threw it to his ear. "Yussuf, wait a minute! I need you to tell me what the hell is going on. You told us there's more to the murder, you asked us to check on the mosque, you tell us about this Mexican scumbag who's going there, and then you say we need to be careful around the mosque. I'm no genius, but I think there's something you're not saying."

Yussuf stayed quiet. Nunez hit the speaker button, waited ten seconds for a response and asked, "Yussuf? Are you still there?"

"Yes Jerry, I am still here."

"Look, Yussuf, I'm not trying to piss you off. To make you angry, I mean. But you're driving me nuts with all the stuff you're telling me, and especially with all the stuff you're not telling me."

"Jerry, please," Yussuf pleaded. "You are not a stupid man. It is for this reason that I have chosen to speak with you, to request that you look further, that you investigate, what happened to Fahima. The night of the murder, you were handed a very easy explanation for why she was murdered, were you not? You did not have to dig very deeply, perhaps you did not have to dig at all. You were simply given a reason, a reason you believed to be plausible. Jerry, did you think that possibly the explanation was too easy, too simple for such a complex situation as a murder of a young girl by her brother?

"There is something you should know, Jerry. The night we met, I had been seated outside my home, hoping an officer would come to the apartment complex so I could speak with him. In truth, I had been sitting outside my home every night since the murder, asking God for this, for an opportunity to speak to someone of importance. And then you arrived, Jerry. Not just a random officer, not a, a normal American who knows nothing of other cultures, but instead an officer who had been in my homeland, who knew something of my people, who I knew would listen to me. An officer who knows and understands Afghanistan, and hate and war, and death. Tell me, Officer Nunez, is there another officer with your understanding of such things, anywhere in this city? I beseeched Allah for his blessing, for his intercession in this matter. And he sent you, Jerry. Only God could have answered my prayers so quickly and so perfectly."

Nunez and Woods stared hard at each other over the phone. Woods started to speak, but Nunez shushed him with a finger to his own lips.

"Jerry, I truly wish I could speak to you about everything you should know. And if the situation involved only me, I assure you I would. But we both know this is not the case."

Nunez waited an extra few seconds before responding. "Yussuf, I need you to be real honest, okay? Is there something you can't say because it would put your life in danger?"

Yussuf laughed softly. "Please Jerry, I believe you do not know me as well as you think. I have faced mortal danger many times, it is not a concern. After the

Soviet invasion I found myself often threatened with death. Do you recall that I told you I have been imprisoned before?"

Nunez and Woods looked at each other. Nunez shook his head. Woods thought a moment, and his face lit up.

"Oh yeah, you said you wouldn't take a second wife because you didn't want to be in jail again! Yeah, I remember that."

"That is correct," Yussuf replied. "I was jailed by the Soviets because I had worked for western embassies, then I was jailed by the mujahedin because they suspected I had collaborated with the Soviets in prison, then I was jailed by the Taliban for the crime of not being a pious enough Muslim. I was beaten, not simply beaten but tortured, each time I was jailed. But during the time just before the Taliban, I was able to send my wife and children to safety in Pakistan. After my family was safe, nothing inflicted on me was more than a trifling matter.

"We are grown men, Jerry. We must be willing to stand in defense of what we believe, even to death. I am certain you have already done so, in your duties as a soldier. But would you have acted in the same manner, had your family been with you in Afghanistan? If your service there had not been of a predetermined length? Do not take this as an insult, but bravery is a far less complicated matter when you have no fears for your family, when you can see your own war's end in a short amount of time. I do not have this luxury, Jerry. My actions, and my words, affect more than only myself. And there is no set date for the end of what I must face."

Nunez nodded. Yussuf had hit several nails, square on the head. Nunez had never considered his actions in Iraq or Afghanistan to have been particularly brave. He had done his duty, and more. But if it had been his home the war was revolving around, if it had been his family hiding in his house as rounds slammed into the walls, if he hadn't known he only had to survive to a set date… any desire to be brave would have been filtered through the lenses of his wife's safety, his children's futures, and the possibility of his own life's endless misery.

"You're right, Yussuf," Nunez said. "Whatever it is you know, if you tell us, it doesn't just affect you. It wouldn't be as easy for you as it was for me when I went to war. So what can I do to make you and your family safe? There are things we can do, help we can give you if you need it. Just tell me what needs to happen to make you feel safe enough to talk."

"Jerry," Yussuf said. "This is my honest answer. I do not know. I do not know if there is any truth to what I suspect. I do not know if there is any help you can provide, if there is any way you could truly protect those close to me. I hope you have never doubted this fact, but I am a devout Muslim. I believe all must be as God wills it. I believe he will reveal what is truth and what is falsehood, and will guide my actions and words when the time is right. But the time is not yet right. If my suspicions are shown to be indisputable facts, this will be communicated to you, either by me or by another whom God chooses. But make no mistake, Jerry. The men whom I suspect are certain God guides their hands also. And should I waver from the path that God shows me, should I speak before the certainty of their future actions is revealed, they will follow me to the furthest reaches of the earth for revenge. Revenge on me, and my family.

"Please, Jerry. Let this matter rest, at least for the moment. There is no reason to take hasty actions. Even if I am right, there is time to wait, and watch, and prepare."

"Yussuf...alright, I'll wait, for a while," Nunez said. "Like, a real short while. But you have to promise, when you know something for certain, you'll tell me. Not a day after you find out, not hours later, but right when you get the information. Okay?"

"Yes, of course. There could be no other option. I could not sit in silence, holding such information at the cost of the lives of others. Such an action would be an unforgivable sin. I must go now, please. I will speak to you within a few days."

"Okay, Yussuf. No more than two days and you call me, whether you know anything or not. Deal?"

"It is a deal. Good night, Jerry."

"Good night, Yussuf."

Yussuf hung up. Woods and Nunez looked at each other in silence.

Several seconds later Woods asked, "What the fuck does all that mean?"

"I guess...well, it could mean a couple of things," Nunez answered. "It could mean there's something seriously bad going on in this mosque, and whatever it is has something to do with that little girl's murder, and maybe a Mexican shithead driving a white van. Or," Nunez said, rubbing his hand over his face again, "maybe Yussuf is a crazy old man who's got an overactive imagination and likes to bark at shadows. Maybe he gets his rocks off pretending to be an informant in his own little James Bond movie. Maybe he's getting us all worked up over nothing."

"You think so?" Woods asked. "You think he's yanking our *chain*?"

"Brother," Nunez said, thoughtfully, "my instincts are screaming so much different crap right now it ain't even funny. On one hand, I think we need to call in everyone who might be able to help on this. Criminal Intelligence, Homicide, the FBI, everyone. On the other hand, and this is more likely than there being some horrible monster living in the mosque...I think when Yussuf said 'I'm not sure what's going on, but I think there's something', however it was he said it... that might have been a sign from Allah that Yussuf is completely full of shit."

"Maybe he is, but we still need to go to the station and read all these incident reports. I want to know what this Ruben guy is about."

"Word," Nunez said, pulling onto the street. "Let's go."

———————

"Oh, wow," Woods said. "You have to read this one, Jerry."

Nunez walked to Woods' computer. "I hope it's good, all I've found so far is that Arredondo was a major dope dealer and prison gangster."

"You'll like this," Woods said. "Remember the criminal mischief report that Arredondo's a suspect in? Arredondo went into a convenience store and started getting friendly with an Arab guy working the register. He greeted the guy in Arabic, then in English asked what type of Islam he practiced. The clerk said he wasn't a Muslim, he was a Lebanese Christian. In the report, the Lebanese guy said there wasn't an argument or anything, he just told him he wasn't Muslim. Arredondo told the complainant he was going to hell and deserved death for rejecting Islam, knocked a bunch of stuff off the counter, kicked over some displays, threw his soda across the store and left. The patrol officer took the report and the complainant cleaned the place up. No damage, Arredondo just made a mess."

Nunez rubbed his chin. "What I found was that he's got arrests for dope, robbery, regular theft, auto theft, simple assault, aggravated assault, everything. There was one report that he got stopped by Narcotics because they had information he was coming from the Mexican border to deliver dope to a house. But when they stopped him he had already made the delivery, all he had were empty duffel bags that reeked of weed. He had a little baggie of weed on him too, he went to jail on that charge that night. So we know he runs drugs from the border, or at least he did several years ago. He's also been busted for weed several times and for having trace amounts of coke. Five years ago he got busted for kicking his girlfriend's ass, and when they searched him at the jail they found a bag of rocks hidden in his asscrack. He did a year in state jail on that one. But there hasn't been anything since he got out, except for that criminal mischief report."

"This guy converted to Islam in prison, didn't he?" Woods asked

"Sounds like it," Nunez answered.

They remained silent for a few seconds, then Nunez spoke up.

"There's a drug runner turned devout Muslim making trips to Mexico and going to the mosque in the middle of the night. That's not something Yussuf is making up. We need to talk to someone about this."

CHAPTER 6

Nunez checked his watch again. 8:14 a.m. He had come home after what turned out to be a boring second half of his shift, saw Laura off to work and the kids to school and day care, then waited for eight o'clock so he could call Criminal Intelligence.

He got tired of waiting and called at 7:55. Voicemail. He tried again at eight sharp. Voicemail again. He got the same response at 8:05, and 8:10. He spent five more fitful minutes sitting in front of his computer, then dialed again.

"Criminal Intelligence, this is Officer Delisle."

"Officer Delisle? This is Officer Jerry Nunez from North Patrol. You have a few minutes for me to run something by you?"

"Sure thing. Hope it's interesting, it's been slow lately."

"It's interesting," Nunez said. "Y'all have any information on a mosque at North Shepherd and Crosstimbers? Or on a murder on Hanley street? Or a Mexican Mafia scumbag in a white van? Or the possibility the three are related?"

That got Delisle's interest. Nunez ran the story down as Delisle looked up every report on Ruben Arredondo. But there was nothing in Intelligence's database about the mosque, and other than his criminal history there was nothing intelligence-related on Arredondo either. He was just a normal scumbag. A member or maybe former member of the Mexican Mafia to be sure, but nobody special.

"Damn, Nunez," Delisle said. "That's a hell of a story, and it sounds like there could be something to it. But there's nothing we can act on. I wish your informant hadn't been so mysterious. You're the one talking to him, what do you think this is about?"

"I've been asking myself that, and I don't know," Nunez said. "Every time there's anything weird going on around a mosque the first thing anyone thinks about is terrorism. But I don't see what that has to do with Afghan girl's murder, or the Mexican Mafia guy. My gut reaction is some immigrants are doing something involving drugs at the mosque. I'd guess that Arredondo is their connection to the dope trade. He's got the knowledge and experience, and the conversion to Islam would have probably given him some discipline, made him less of a dumbass. Which would explain why he hasn't been arrested since he last got out of prison. That would make him worth a lot to them, if they really are trying to launch a dope dealing ring."

"Yeaaaaahhhh," Delisle said. "That accounts for Arredondo, but what does it have to do with the murder? And what about the stuff that's supposed to happen in the future?"

"You had to fuck up my neat answer, Delisle," Nunez said. "I don't know what the murder was about. Maybe....no, that doesn't work. I was going to say that maybe the murderer or the victim were high, but the autopsy would have shown that. Maybe the brother killed his sister because he thought she was selling, something like that?"

"Sounds pretty unrealistic to me, but who knows," Delisle said. "I don't see why this kid would kill his sister over dope-dealing. Dope use maybe, but like you said, the autopsy would have shown that. He could have killed her because he was dealing and thought she was going to rat him out or something, but then why kill her inside the apartment and not even try to hide it? Or maybe he found her drugs and got so pissed he decided to kill her in the name of Allah...I don't even know if that makes sense. I don't know the first thing about Arabs, I really couldn't tell you what fits and what doesn't. And what about the 'future events' your guy was talking about?"

"You tell me," Nunez answered. "Like I said, my first thought is terrorism. But I would think there'd be some other evidence pointing to that. Weird events around the mosque, phone traffic intercepted by the feds and shared with you guys, something. But my guy says something bad involving people getting killed is going to happen in the future. So what else could he be talking about? Maybe saying that the drugs are going to kill people? Hell, what he actually said was 'I couldn't keep that information to myself, at the cost of other peoples' lives', something like that. Does that mean people are going to get killed, or just fuck their lives up? I don't know. I was hoping you could throw down some of your intel expertise and solve this mystery in seconds."

"Within seconds?" Delisle laughed. "Hey man, you want it solved within seconds, call Scooby Doo. I'm just a cop, I don't solve mysteries real well. You've convinced me the dope thing is possible, even though at first I couldn't see it at all. I'll have to turn this one around a little, talk to the other guys in the office about it. And I'll put a notation in the database, so any new reports about the mosque or 1803 Hanley get routed to us. You work today?"

"Yup, night shift," Nunez said.

"Alright, I would highly suggest you write a report on this. That'll put it on everyone's radar up here. And call me if you think something serious is about to happen. Other than that, I don't see what else we can do. We can't get surveillance started, not with just this. Right now we can't even classify this as an 'investigation', it's more like 'suspicion'."

"Crap," Nunez said. "Should I call the FBI and let them in on it?"

In the background Nunez heard a voice say, "Tell that officer it's not his job to call the FBI about shit. It's our job and we'll do it *if* we need to."

The phone made a noise as Delisle picked up the handset, and Nunez realized he had been on speaker the entire time.

"No Nunez, don't do that," Delisle said. "We'll make that call, if we get enough to act on. If we drop this on the FBI, it'll just be more crap for them to analyze. And they're in overload already."

"I guess someone in your office thinks that's a bad idea," Nunez muttered.

"It's not exactly a bad idea, it would just be wrong procedure to jump the *chai*n like that," Delisle said. "Trust me, we deal with the FBI all the time. If we go to them we need all the information gaps filled, and that's going to take time. Unfortunately, or maybe fortunately, right now we don't have anything to really react to."

"Okay, that's cool," Nunez said. "I'll get that report out tonight, and stay in touch with you. I'm going to keep on my supposed 'informant' for more information. Anything else I need to do?"

"Bro, you want my opinion?" Delisle asked. "First, make sure you let all the officers know about that mosque so nobody gets blindsided. Second, wear your vest and carry a carbine whenever you're anywhere near the place. But keep it quiet, don't have the roll call sergeant announce it to everyone. You know how cops talk, some officer with a big mouth might say something to some guy working at a convenience store, and he tells his buddy, and he tells his priest who preaches at the mosque, and the whole thing gets blown. Know what I mean?"

"Gotcha, I'll spread the word on the down low. Thanks for your help, Delisle, I'll keep you posted," Nunez said.

"Great, thanks for letting me know about this. Take it easy, and call me."

"Okay, later." Nunez hung up, got up from the computer and walked to his bedroom. He took off his uniform pants, hung them in his closet and got into bed. With sunlight flooding the bedroom, he closed his eyes and tried to sleep.

Years of night shift had completely screwed his sleep schedule; he couldn't sleep during his nights off. He was only home two nights a week, and on those nights Laura was constantly frustrated with his need to get out of bed in the middle of the night. He could usually sleep after work, but this morning he tossed and turned for almost an hour. He didn't think of Afghanistan, like he normally did every morning and every night. What kept him awake this morning was his curiosity about whether or not Yussuf really knew anything, what it could be, and what if anything Nunez could do about it.

CHAPTER 7

"Shut the fuck up, asshole! I'll tell you when you can fucking talk! Got that, motherfucker?"

Nunez and Woods stood quietly twenty feet away as Calhoun yelled at the man who had called the police. Nunez refused to do anything except make sure nothing got out of control, and Woods followed Nunez's lead.

The call had been simple, just a minor complaint at an apartment complex about a neighbor parking his truck in the wrong spot. Calhoun responded and within minutes was on the radio shouting for backup over the neighbors' screams. Nunez and Woods had been closest. When they arrived they found exactly what Nunez expected: Calhoun had pissed everyone off so badly that the incident was now on the verge of turning into a mini riot.

"Officer, you best check yo' self. I fixin' to get fed up wit' how you talkin' to me," the caller said. He was a heavyset black man in his forties, facing Calhoun in a bladed fighting stance. His neighbor, a thug-life looking white kid in his mid-twenties, skinny with a ragged goatee, stood to Calhoun's side, assessing whether or not he could take the muscular officer in a fight.

"'Fixin' to get fed up wit' me?' Fo' real? Think I give a fuck, asshole?" Calhoun yelled at the man, spawning angry murmurs among the twenty or so young black men and women who had come outside to watch. Calhoun turned to the white neighbor and realized that he was being sized up.

"You wanna try me, motherfucker?" Calhoun yelled as he stepped forward. "Do it! Jump, bitch!"

"Uh oh," Nunez said to Woods. "Check out the bruthah in the green 'do rag, in the back of the crowd. He pulled his pants up, he's tightening his belt, and I bet…yup, he just put his hood on. I doubt he'll actually try it with us here, but he's getting ready to fight. Keep an eye on him."

"Got it," Woods said. "He's talking to another guy, they're both checking us out. Think we should step in now and break this up before we all get our asses kicked?"

"I'll shoot everyone here before I let anyone kick my ass," Nunez grumbled. "But fuck Calhoun. He does this shit all the time. I think he calls for backup just so he can talk shit to people without worrying about getting his ass beat, 'cause he's got us here to protect him. So I'll just wait until someone's ready to pop him one before I do a fucking thing to help."

"So when do you step in?" Woods asked. "You've got two pissed off guys standing within a few feet of him, plus a group of pissed off people watching, plus two guys in the audience planning a move. It looks like the right time for action to me."

"Mike, I will never, ever, stand by and let a cop get his ass kicked. But if I ever did, Calhoun would be that cop. He deserves it. But we let him get beat, then these guys think they can take every cop they come across. And next time it's me, or you."

"Understood," Woods said. "Tell me when to move."

The white man suddenly bounced backward on his toes, yanked his shirt off to expose a torso and arms covered in Aryan prison gang tattoos, and assumed a street fighter stance.

"I'm about to punk you out, bitch! Come on!"

Calhoun pulled his baton from his belt and stepped toward the white guy. Behind him, the black neighbor took a step closer. Nunez saw the man with the hood and his backup move quickly to the front of the crowd. Nunez slapped Woods on the arm. "Time to move. Watch those two in the audience, I'll get the other ones off Calhoun."

Woods went toward the two men in the crowd and Nunez walked behind the white neighbor yelling "Hey dude, over here!" The two men in the audience immediately backed into the crowd, and Woods was smart enough to not go after them. The white man spun around angrily to face Nunez, who calmly called him over.

"Hey man, relax. Come over here and talk to me. Everything's cool, we'll get this straightened out."

The white neighbor backed away from Calhoun, pointing at him and saying "You're lucky, punk motherfucker!"

"Turn around!" Nunez yelled. "Forget about him, talk to me."

The man turned away from Calhoun, sneering. Behind him, Calhoun told the black complainant "Yeah, and you get the fuck over here with me, asshole."

"Hey, sir!" Nunez yelled past the white neighbor to the black man. "Come on over here also, let's have a talk."

The black man abruptly walked toward Nunez. Infuriated, Calhoun reached for his arm. Nunez yelled to Calhoun, "Eddie! I got this! Just gimme a minute, let me talk to these guys. Get with Woods, he might need help."

Calhoun hesitated, gave a disgusted look, then turned and walked toward Woods. He yelled to the crowd, "What the fuck are you assholes looking at? Never seen a fucking cop before?"

Nunez stopped the black and white neighbors when they were about five feet away. "Let's get this straightened out. What's the deal, who called?"

"I called, offisuh," the black man said. "This boy been parking in my space, I jus' need him to move his truck. There weren't no need for all this mess, all I wanted was fo' that officer to talk to this boy and tell him to move his truck so I can park there like I'm suppose to."

"That's no problem at all," Nunez said. "How'd all this bullshit happen, what's with all the screaming?"

"That guy's a fucking dick, that's what happened," the white man said. "He pounded on my door and when I answered he pulled me out and started motherfucking me. I didn't even know what the fuck he wanted. Then this guy," the white neighbor said, motioning to the black neighbor, "he told the cop to calm down and the cop went nuts even worse. He's lucky you two got here, I was getting ready to violate my parole, man. I'm only going to take so much shit from that motherfucker, cop or not."

"I get that," Nunez said. Then he asked the black man, "You got anything to add, or was that pretty much it?"

"That was it, offisuh, it wasn't nuthin' real impo'tant, I jus' wanted him to talk to my neighbor, I didn't want none o' this mess. This jus' don't make no *sense!* And this boy right, that cop lucky you and yo' friend showed up, 'cuz I wasn't goin' let that muthafuckah talk to me that way in front my family."

Nunez looked at the crowd. The two men who were preparing to attack

Calhoun were probably the black neighbor's sons or nephews. Woods and Calhoun were talking in front of the crowd and nobody was screaming, everything seemed under control.

"So just making sure, you two aren't pissed off at each other at all?"

"Offisuh, I ain't got no problem with this boy, except that he got his truck in my space. That all," the black man said.

"And I ain't got no problem with him either," the white guy said. Then, to the black man, he said "Man, all you had to do was ask me, I would've moved the damn truck. Someone else has had a car broken down in my space for months, I didn't think anyone paid attention to those assigned parking spaces."

Nunez asked the black man, "Why didn't you just ask him to move his truck, instead of calling the cops?"

"Shit, offisuh, look at him," the black man said. "Me and this boy ain't never had no problems, but I know white prison gang tattoos when I see 'em. I didn't know what he would do if I came knockin' on his door at night, I just thought it would be better if I let the laws handle it."

"Whoa, whoa, hang on!" the white man said. "I was a dumbass a few years ago and did some time, but what I was in there stayed in there. Come on, man," he said to the black man, "that's just how it is inside, you need to run with someone or you get run over. And look at where I live. There's ten thousand black people and ten white dudes in this complex, I would be a fucking idiot to pull any stupid shit out here. That's why I just go to work, come home and stay inside."

"Dat true," the black man said. "You stays real quiet, we almost never sees you at all."

"So as soon as we're done here, you move your truck and it's all done with," Nunez said. "No issues, right?"

"No issues, offisuh," said the black neighbor.

"Man, no problem at all," the white guy said.

"Okay. You two hang here while I talk to your favorite cop. You may as well get your ID's out, we'll have to run you before we go," Nunez said.

"Oh shit," the white guy said. "Hey officer, I think…man, I know I got warrants. Most of them are just for traffic tickets, but I got one for a bad check.

I'm trying like hell to pay them off, and if I go to jail I lose my job. Can you please let them slide? Please?"

"We'll see what we can do. What's your name?"

"Richard Holman."

"Alright, let me check it out, Richard," Nunez said. "And you, what's your name?"

"Louis Stevens, offisuh."

"No warrants or anything, Mr. Stevens?"

"Not a thing, offisuh. I ain't never had any kind of trouble wit' the law, you can check me all week long an' twice on Sunday. Here my license, I just got 'em renewed."

"Cool," Nunez said as he took Louis' license. "Richard, go ahead and give me your license too, then just wait and chill out. If it's just a few warrants, I think we can cut you a break."

Then an idea hit him. "Richard, you might have to do something you don't like, but it's the best way to get that second chance. How do you feel about apologizing to Officer Friendly over there?"

Richard's face scrunched in anger. "That motherfucker... damn. Five minutes ago I was ready to punch him and go back to prison, but I'll apologize to that cocksucker if I have to."

"I ain't got nuthin' to apologize for, offisuh," Louis said.

"No, you don't, Louis. I think you're good. Stay here, I'll be right back."

Nunez walked to Calhoun and Woods, who were still standing in front of the now-smaller crowd. The two men who had been conspiring to jump Calhoun had disappeared, along with several others. Calhoun was muttering insults about the crowd but not to it, so everything was calm.

"Eddie, let's talk," Nunez said. Still muttering, Calhoun walked to Nunez. Woods followed. As soon as he turned from the crowd, several more people walked away.

"What the fuck, Noon-ez," Calhoun said angrily. "I had this, you didn't need to jump in and fuck this up. It's my fucking call, right?"

"Yeah it's your call, and you couldn't handle it, which is why you had to call us, isn't it? Don't talk shit to me, Edward. If we hadn't been here at least four guys would have beat you senseless. Your caller and his neighbor are all calmed down, I'm going to run them and then I say we all walk away."

"Fuck that!" Calhoun exclaimed. "That white cocksucker threatened me, he's going to jail for assault by threat. The old black dude can walk, I don't give a fuck. But nobody punks me out and gets away with it."

"Nobody punks you out?" Nunez asked. "Eddie, you talked shit to these two guys, you punked *them* out in front of everyone, probably for no reason. They're not pissed at each other, the original problem is handled and none of this bullshit was necessary. Why don't you just talk to them? The white guy even wants to apologize. Let the guy tell you how sorry he is, then let it go. Mike, do me a favor and run these guys."

Woods took the two driver's licenses from Nunez's hand. Nunez leaned in, saying quietly, "If you find warrants, *do not* confirm them. Just let me know what they are."

"Gotcha," Woods said as he walked to the patrol car.

"That ex-con piece of shit goes to jail, Jerry," Calhoun said. "I don't know what the fuck you're trying to prove. You were there, you saw him threaten me."

"Yeah, and I saw you talk shit first. 'Jump, bitch,' you remember that? I do, and I bet everyone else does too. If that guy's got a brain, he pleads not guilty and asks for a jury trial, and then you get to tell everyone in the jury that you asked the fucking guy to hit you before he threatened you. Either that, or you lie to everyone. Or you avoid the entire problem, and walk away. Don't turn this into something personal, Eddie. It's handled, just let it go."

"Whatever. It doesn't matter what you say, he rides," Calhoun said.

"You sure are a tough motherfucker, Eddie. If you arrest that guy, you do it alone. I'm not here to make sure you get to talk shit to everyone, and I'm sick of having to fix the scenes you fuck up. You make this stupid arrest, forget about having me for backup anymore. Next time you call for help, you better be dead when I get there."

Calhoun was taken aback. His view of police work consisted of one principle: whatever another cop does, you back him up.

"You going to do that, Jerry?" Calhoun asked. "You'll let me get whacked even though you could have done something about it?"

"Nice try, Eddie. Your guilt trip doesn't work. I'm doing something about it right now. I'm telling you, you're a prick. Everyone thinks so. Not just the people who live out here, but every cop at the station. You don't have to treat all people like shit all the time, Eddie. You keep fucking with decent people, for no reason, nobody's going to back you up."

"Decent people?" Calhoun said, flabbergasted. "Who the fuck are you trying to kid? Look at that white guy, he's got 'prison Nazi' written all over him. You calling him a decent person? You taking his side over mine?"

"I'm not taking his side," Nunez said. "He's not a nice guy. But what did he do to you, personally, before you motherfucked him?"

"Jerry, all these people out here saw that guy threaten a cop. What happens if they see him get away with it?" Calhoun asked. "Next time, one of these guys thinks he can do it because that guy did it, and maybe the cop gets his ass kicked, or gets killed. We can't let these motherfuckers get away with that shit, and you know it."

"Here's what I know, Eddie. These people understand what goes around comes around, the law of the jungle, whatever you want to call it. They know if they hit a cop, they get their ass kicked. They know that if they fuck up and get caught, it's their ass. But if a cop does something wrong and kicks a guy's ass, it ain't fair. When we're not being fair, we get attacked.

"I'm the closest thing you have to a friend, Eddie. I'm the only cop who would want you on a scene with me, and that's just because I know how good you are tactically. But nobody else cares about that. Nobody. They'd rather have a rookie like Woods backing them up, no matter how good you are. The way you treat people makes it more likely an officer will get killed out here. Because you make people hate us."

Woods walked back with the licenses in his hand. He said quietly to Nunez, "Three traffic warrants and a bad check warrant on the white guy, black guy's clear."

"What's the level of offense on the check warrant?" Nunez asked, just as quietly.

"I think it's just city level."

"What'd you say?" Calhoun asked Woods sharply. "Why you whispering?"

"He didn't say anything important, Eddie. I asked him what kind of criminal history the white guy had. What was it again, Mike?"

"Burglary, and, uh, auto theft. I think that was all," Woods said.

"No warrants?" Calhoun asked.

"No warrants," Nunez said, before Woods could answer.

"Fuck," Calhoun said, disappointed. "So you really think I should let this slide, huh?"

"Yeah, you should," Nunez said. "Let the guy apologize, then walk away. Everyone out here will see him begging you for mercy, so you don't lose any pride over it. Then it's all handled, nobody gets hurt or complained on. Stay here a second, I'll talk to the guy first and call you over."

Nunez walked back to the two neighbors. "Richard, listen. When the officer comes over, just tell him you're sorry and lost your temper because of something else. Marriage problems, your job, health, whatever, just make something up. And whatever you do, don't say a fucking word about having warrants. Cool?"

"No problem, officer," the man said, nodding enthusiastically. "Whatever it takes, no problem."

Nunez motioned Woods and Calhoun over. As soon as they were face to face with Richard Holman he apologized profusely, wisely heeding Nunez's advice to not mention the warrants. His neighbor Louis Stevens turned and walked away.

"Hey officer, I'm really sorry," Richard said, eyes downcast. "I mean, I just lost my temper. My mom's been sick, and I've been worried about getting laid off and stuff. It don't excuse anything, but I've just been real stressed lately. I mean it, man, I know I fucked up and I appreciate you letting it slide. Really officer, thanks."

"Yeah, you did fuck up," Calhoun said. "I coulda beaten the shit out of you and thrown your ass in jail for that. Next time you lose your temper and want to get stupid, think about how bad this almost turned out for you. And I'll be patrolling through here, looking for you. Don't let me catch you again. Got it?"

Richard looked up, trying and almost succeeding in getting the *fuck you* look out of his eyes. "Yes sir, I understand. You won't catch me doing anything out here, I promise."

"Good. Get the fuck inside." Calhoun ordered.

Nunez gave Holman his license back and he shook Nunez's hand, saying, "I owe you one, big time," before going back inside. Calhoun turned and walked away without a word, leaving Nunez and Woods to saunter back to their patrol car and drive away from the scene.

"That was. . . interesting," Woods said. "Why didn't you want to take that guy in?"

"That was a bullshit call to begin with, and after Calhoun freaked out it would have made everything worse to arrest that guy. He was white, so the crowd wouldn't have jumped in, but if Calhoun tried to arrest the black guy it would have turned into a riot. And Calhoun was going that direction. Besides, do you care that the white dude's got four city warrants? I don't. I wouldn't want anyone to write me a bad check, and he needs to pay it back. But if he goes to jail and loses his job he can't pay back shit. So it's better for everyone if we let him slide."

"That makes sense," Woods said. "Is Calhoun always like that?"

"All the damn time," Nunez said with disgust. "He's gotten a lot of officers complained on and almost gotten himself fired. I don't know any officer who would ignore a cop screaming for help, but nobody backs Calhoun up until it's an emergency. Except me, and it's only because I respect all the Marines I've ever known. Except him."

Nunez's phone vibrated on his belt. He picked it up, seeing the same Virginia number Wilson had called from several days earlier. He was near highway 45, a short block from a 24 hour gas station on the service road. Nunez pulled into an abandoned adult bookstore parking lot, which the previous owner had thoughtfully surrounded with thick hedges for his customers' privacy.

"Yussuf?" Woods asked.

"Buddy in Afghanistan," Nunez said quickly, before saying into the phone, "Hey Alex! What's shakin'?"

The phone was silent for several seconds.

"Alex, you there?"

"Uh, Sergeant First Class Nunez?" a shaky voice answered.

"This is Jerry Nunez, former Sergeant First Class. Who's this?"

"This is Sergeant Joseph Hollis. I'm...I was Sergeant Wilson's squad leader."

Not "I am Wilson's squad leader." I *was*.

"Oh, shit," Nunez said. He knew what was coming next. "Tell me what happened."

"Sergeant, I can't give you all the details yet. Wilson's family has been notified, but not about everything."

"I'm Jerry Nunez, not sergeant Nunez. Just Jerry, got it?" Nunez almost yelled. "Just tell me what happened."

"I'm sorry, Mister Nunez. Sergeant Wilson was killed by an IED on a patrol, near Camp Phoenix. You know where I'm talking about, sir?"

"What does it fucking matter if I know where you're talking about?" Nunez asked. Then he felt anger at himself, for taking his pain out on someone he knew was just trying to do a difficult, painful job. He calmed himself and asked, "When did it happen?"

"Two days ago, Mister Nunez. Sergeant Wilson gave me your number when we first got here and told me to call you if anything happened. I'm sorry, I couldn't call earlier. Not until his family had been notified."

"God damn it," Nunez said, covering his face. "Was it, was it quick? Did he suffer?"

"No sir, he didn't suffer. It was a large buried IED. It killed him instantly."

"Don't lie to me, man," Nunez said, trying to keep his voice from cracking. "Did he die right away or not?"

"He died right away, sir. The IED went off right under him, he...he really didn't have a chance. His driver lived for almost a day, he died in Germany. The gunner and dismounts made it out okay."

Nunez took note of those two words, "his driver". That probably meant that Wilson had been in command of the vehicle, that he'd finally gotten his own troops to lead.

"Was it his truck? Was he the commander?" Nunez asked.

"Yes sir, he was."

"Who was his driver?"

"PFC Sylvester Owens, sir."

"Okay," Nunez said, not recognizing the name. "Did y'all kill the triggerman?"

"Man, I wish. Sorry, I mean, it was a remote control device. We never found the triggerman."

"What else do you know? When does he come home?"

"Sir, I don't know any of that. The best thing to do is call our battalion headquarters, they should know. Do you know the number, sir?"

"I can find it," Nunez said.

"Then I guess that's it, Mister Nunez. I'm really sorry I had to tell you this. Sergeant Wilson was a great guy, a great leader. He volunteered for everything, always wanted to get out on missions. I know y'all were good friends, so this is a lot harder on you than us. But trust me, we got to be pretty good friends too. We're going to miss him, he was a great guy."

"Yeah," Nunez said quietly. "He was."

"Okay sir," Sergeant Hollis said. "I'm going to go now. Please, call our battalion HQ, they'll give you the funeral details. And sir, you take care. Okay?"

"Yeah, okay," Nunez said. "Hey, don't worry about me, Sergeant. You stay safe over there, take care of your platoon."

"I will, sir. Good night."

Nunez hung up and put his cell into its case. He leaned back against the headrest, closed his eyes, clasped his hands in front of his face and tapped his upper lip with his knuckles. Woods watched him in silence. A tear ran from the corner of Nunez's right eye down his face, and slowly dripped onto his collar.

Woods had figured out, more or less, what the call was about. He thought the best thing to do was sit silently and wait. He should probably suggest that Nunez take the rest of the shift off. The desk sergeant wouldn't hassle him about it.

"I just talked to him," Nunez said. "Less than a week ago. He was fine." He shuddered once, unable to hold back a sob. "I told him not go out," he mumbled. "I told him not to run missions anymore."

Woods watched Nunez shake again as a second sob escaped, then a third. Then Nunez couldn't hold it anymore. He leaned forward, covered his face with his hands, and exploded into tears.

Woods stayed frozen. *Should I say something? Or reach out and touch him?* He held back, unsure how Nunez would react.

Nunez cried openly for no more than a minute before getting himself back under control, choking off sobs and wiping tears from his eyes. He leaned back against the headrest and covered his face, saying something into his hands that Woods couldn't make out.

Through his barely opened window, Woods heard glass breaking. He looked outside, unable to see past the overgrown brush that bordered the parking lot. A short distance away he could see the lights and roof of the gas station, but brush blocked his view of the station itself. He couldn't tell if the sound had come from there, or from the old porn shop they were parked next to.

Woods looked at Nunez again. He was still leaned back in the seat with his face in his hands. Woods lowered his window the rest of the way.

A gunshot rang out from the gas station. Woods jerked upright in his seat. He looked toward the station in alarm, unable to see a thing. Nunez didn't react at all.

Bang! Bang! Two more shots from the station. Nunez sighed. Woods looked at him. Nunez uncovered his face but held his forehead in his hands and grimaced like he had a headache.

"Jerry…" Woods began.

"I don't care," Nunez replied.

Bang! Bang! Bang! Three more shots. Followed less than two seconds later by another two. A woman's shrill scream cut the night air.

"Jerry, something's going on at the gas station!"

"I don't give a fuck!" Nunez exploded.

BANGBANGBANGBANGBANGBANG! The gunshots were more rapid and much louder, like a large-caliber semi-auto rifle fired at max rate.

"Shit Jerry, come on!"

Nunez threw the car into drive and peeled out of the parking lot, blazing toward the highway as he wiped tears from his eyes. As Woods rolled up his window he heard tires screeching, then saw a cloud of black smoke as the gas station came into view. A burgundy Chevy Tahoe tore out of the parking lot, fishtailed over a curb onto the service road and headed north. Woods saw bullet holes in the gas station windows and people lying flat near the gas pumps.

Nunez flew around the corner, raced north and grabbed the radio. "1243 dispatch, emergency traffic. In pursuit of a burgundy Chevy Tahoe heading north on the 45 service road from West Gulf Bank. Suspect fired shots at the gas station on the service road. Break."

The patrol car burst through the burned-rubber smoke on the service road. Woods saw the Tahoe two hundred yards ahead, passing other cars in the left lane.

"I need backup units," Nunez continued. "And someone with spikes. Send a unit to the gas station and see if anyone's been shot, we think he's got an assault rifle. Dispatch, start Fox and K9."

Nunez tossed the mike to Woods. "Call it." Woods reached for the overhead lights and siren switches. Nunez stopped him.

"Not yet. He might not know we're here, wait til we get on him."

Their Ford Crown Victoria's engine revved to a high pitch as they accelerated to over a hundred miles per hour, slowly catching up to the Tahoe.

"Oh shit, oh shit," Woods said, his voice high. "What if he shoots at us?"

The Tahoe swerved to the far right lane, then shot left across the service road and hit the freeway entrance ramp. The service road was dark but the highway well lit. If the suspect didn't know police were behind him, he was about to find out.

Nunez already had the car floored, and continued accelerating as they shot up the ramp. Houston's traffic, even at one a.m. on a Sunday morning, was as heavy as some smaller cities' traffic at rush hour. The Tahoe weaved around cars blocking its path as the driver pushed it to the fast lane.

"Tell them we just got on the freeway north of Gulf Bank," Nunez ordered.

"1243 dispatch, we just got onto the service road! I mean onto the highway, headed north from Gulf Bank!"

"1243, do you have a plate?" dispatch asked.

Woods moved his head side to side, illogically trying to read the plate on a speeding vehicle darting in and out of traffic several car lengths ahead.

"Negative dispatch, we can't see it yet," Woods said, trying to keep his voice calm. "It's got a big Texas A&M sticker in the back window."

"If he shoots at us, shoot back," Nunez said, not looking at Woods.

"Got it," Woods said. He drew his weapon.

"Put your fucking pistol away!" Nunez barked. "If we get into a wreck you'll lose it. Tell dispatch we're about to pass West road."

Woods quickly reholstered the pistol while he spoke into the mike. "Still north on 45, passing West road!"

Nunez caught up to the Tahoe in the far left lane. He stayed about two car lengths back and straddled the stripe dividing the far left lane from the lane beside it, giving himself time to react in case the driver suddenly swerved hard right to exit the freeway. The Tahoe, which had been doing about 110, sped up to over 120.

"Shit. They know we're here, hit the lights and siren."

Woods hit the switches. The overheads flashed to life, strobing everything around them with red, white and blue flashes. The siren screamed out a warning, which most drivers on the highway would only hear as or after the patrol car passed them.

Woods keyed the radio and called out the Tahoe's plate, easily visible now. The Tahoe's driver jerked it one lane to the right and almost sideswiped a Honda. Nunez glanced sideways and swerved behind the Tahoe. Ahead, Woods saw a patrol car charge north on the service road with its overheads on, about to jump into the pursuit.

"Dispatch 1243, that vehicle was taken in an aggravated robbery in South Central's area during evening shift. Suspects were armed and shot at the complainant. Do you copy?"

Nunez nodded. Woods said, "We copy. Any word on Fox yet?" Fox was the call sign for the department's helicopter division.

"Fox is en route from Northeast's area. Also, we're receiving calls about a robbery with shots fired at Gulf Bank and 45," dispatch said.

"Find out a suspect description, how many suspects, weapons, anything," Nunez said to Woods.

The Tahoe suddenly shot to the right again, cut across three lanes, drove over the shoulder and flew over a patch of grass before bouncing back onto the service road, just as the backup patrol car veered onto the entrance ramp ahead of it.

"Fuck!" Nunez yelled. He took a tenth of a second to make sure they were clear before shooting across the highway and flying off the curb onto the service road behind the Tahoe. Woods tensed and his head bounced off Nunez's shoulder as they banked almost sideways in front of traffic coming at them at seventy-plus miles per hour. He closed his eyes, sure they were about to get nailed on the passenger door. The patrol car hit the service road at an angle, slid almost into the far curb and forced a pickup to slam on the brakes behind them.

"Tell dispatch he just got back on the service road, northbound approaching the Beltway!"

"1243 dispatch, he's back on the service road, northbound toward the Beltway! He just drove off the side of the highway!" Woods yelled.

"Calm down and quit yelling on the radio," Nunez said as he straightened out the car. "She can't understand if you scream."

The Beltway is a huge loop around the city. The Tahoe veered into the right lane as it approached the large, busy intersection of the Beltway and 45. Vehicles were stopped in each of the three lanes of the service road, their drivers waiting for a green light. The Tahoe braked as it neared the intersection and hit the right side curb.

"He's about to go over the curb and drive around the stopped cars," Nunez said. "I think he's gonna make a right on the Beltway service road."

Woods held the microphone to his lips, waiting to tell everyone where the suspect vehicle was going. The Tahoe drove halfway onto the grass, straddled the curb and rear ended a Dodge Charger in the right lane, knocking it into a pickup. The Tahoe slowed but didn't stop. It drove past the wreck, then surprised Woods by making a sharp left. The Tahoe drove on the wrong side of the road until it reached the other side of the freeway, then made a left turn and sped south on the service road.

"1243 dispatch, he just hit a car at the 45 and Beltway service roads!" Woods yelled into the mike, forgetting what Nunez had just told him about keeping calm on the radio. Cars approaching the intersection slammed on the brakes as Nunez turned left from the center lane.

"Oh shit!" Woods winced and threw his hand up in defense as two patrol cars flew southbound on the freeway service road toward him. Their brakes screeched and they slid almost to a stop when the Tahoe and patrol car turned in front of them.

Woods exclaimed, "Someone's gonna get killed in this fucking chase!"

"Yeah, maybe. Tell them where we're at," Nunez said.

"1243, he's headed back south on the 45 service road now!"

"1331 and 1332 are with 1243, dispatch," Mata said calmly on the radio, from one of the patrol cars now behind them.

"1331 and 1332 with 1243, clear. Fox is on the way, guys," dispatch said.

The Tahoe didn't seem to have serious damage from the accident, and was back up to nearly a hundred within seconds. The patrol cars caught up as it approached the intersection of 45 and Aldine Bender, where two cars were stopped at a red light. The Tahoe suddenly shot to the left across the service road and entered the turnaround.

"1243 dispatch, he's turning around at Aldine Bender, about to head north again," Woods said, much calmer than before.

At the end of the turnaround the Tahoe unexpectedly turned the wrong way on the service road, then made the quick left turn east in the westbound lanes of Aldine Bender.

"God damn it," Nunez said, hitting the gas to get off the service road before someone nailed them head on.

"1332 dispatch, suspect vehicle juked us. He's eastbound on Aldine Bender in the westbound lanes," Mata called out on the radio.

Several cars swerved out of the Tahoe's way. A primer grey, beat up Chevy Corsica came to a stop, right in the Tahoe's path. The Tahoe's driver tried to slow down, way too late, and slammed head-on into the Corsica.

Glass and plastic sprayed the pavement. The Corsica spun away. As they passed it Woods saw a large dark object spill off its hood and flop onto the pavement, just before the smoking car rolled to a stop.

The Tahoe's driver tried to speed up again, but he had damaged the engine this time. The vehicle jumped forward in fits and starts before picking up any speed. Aldine Bender was a long straight road, and Woods saw the overhead lights of two more patrol cars blazing toward them from almost a mile away.

"1243 dispatch, suspect vehicle just hit another vehicle on Aldine Bender east of Airline road!" Woods shouted.

"1110 1243, coming toward you with spikes," an officer Woods didn't know said on the radio.

The hollow spikes are on an expanding frame attached to a cord. Officers throw the spikes into the road to puncture the suspect vehicle's tires, then jerk them back out of the road before anyone else hits them. In theory, a suspect will stop once his tires are flat and he realizes all is lost. In reality the spikes were rarely pulled back in time, and one or two cops always got their tires punctured along with the suspect. Besides that, the suspect vehicles always seemed to keep rolling, even if they were on four bare rims.

"Tell him to set up the spikes right there," Nunez told Woods.

"1110, set the spikes up right there!"

"Damn it, Mike, calm down on the radio."

As if the suspect heard them, he jammed on the brakes and made a U-turn. Nunez flipped the car around in an easy turn behind it while Woods called out the direction change. As the Tahoe turned around, the rear driver's side door opened. A rifle barrel poked out toward the police cars.

"Shit! He's getting ready to shoot!" Nunez yelled.

Woods reached for his pistol and keyed the mike, yelling "The suspect is about to shoot from the Tahoe!"

Nunez yanked his pistol from the holster and jammed the muzzle into the windshield. Woods did the same thing, waiting for Nunez to shoot before he pulled his own trigger.

Oh, shit, Woods thought. *I'm about to get into a shooting. I can't believe this is happening.*

The suspect threw the rifle from the Tahoe. Woods watched it flip end over end as the Tahoe's door slammed shut. The driver tried to accelerate south, with smoke trailing from the engine compartment. Nunez holstered his weapon as Woods fumbled to holster his own pistol. Nunez grabbed the mike away.

"1243 dispatch, suspect is southbound on Airline. He just threw out a rifle on Airline just south of Aldine Bender. AK or SKS, someone needs to pick it up."

"1110 I got it. Y'all stay on him."

Nunez closed the gap between the vehicles. The best the suspect could do was about eighty now. The Tahoe was smoking badly, and the driver finally turned the vehicle's headlights off, something most pursuit suspects knew to do as if by instinct.

"Suspect just shut his headlights off," Woods said into the mike.

"42 Fox, I'm thirty seconds away."

"1243 Fox, that's clear. We're still south on Airline approaching West road," Woods said, calm and professional now.

"1110, I got the rifle, I got the rifle."

"1136 1243, I'm with you now."

The suspect was in bad shape. Four police cars were on him with a fifth just seconds behind. A helicopter was about to arrive, drastically cutting down his chances of escape. As the suspect neared West road a blue and white Houston Police K9 unit stopped a hundred yards from the intersection, waiting to see what direction the chase would go.

Ahead, two oblivious drivers prepared to make a left turn, right in front of the pursuit.

Nunez muttered, "Jesus fucking Christ, come on. Don't make that turn."

The first car made the turn. The second car followed close behind. Woods hit the air horn, hoping the two cars would jam on the gas and clear the intersection before the Tahoe was on them. The Tahoe stayed on the same course. Nunez eased back.

The first car made it. The Tahoe hit the second car, an old Ford Escort with plastic spinner rims, square on the right front quarter panel. The Escort threw off broken glass and plastic as it whirled into the median. Nunez swerved away from the wreck. Woods watched Wesley clip the back end of the spinning Escort. The Tahoe swerved toward the center of the road on flat tires.

A huge spotlight lit the Tahoe as Fox arrived overhead.

The Tahoe slowed to a crawl and the front doors popped open. Nunez raced toward the driver's side. Behind them, the K9 unit screamed around the corner onto Airline.

Before the Tahoe rolled to a stop, a young black male in baggy pants and red t-shirt bailed out of the driver's seat. He ran eastbound across Airline, and a truck barely missed him. Nunez drove over the median toward the fleeing driver.

"This is Fox. The driver's eastbound across Airline and one passenger's running south. Several units are on the passenger, us and one unit are on the driver."

The driver pulled his t-shirt off as he sprinted across the road. He ran into the parking lot of a closed gas station, looked over his shoulder and reached toward the front of his waistband. Nunez accelerated across the northbound lanes of Airline and into the station's parking lot, closing on the terrified driver.

The gas station was bordered on two sides by a large open field, which itself was bordered by a thick treeline. The driver ran into the field, headed for the woods. Nunez drove into the field, four-wheeling through grass and brush.

The driver looked back, eyes wide. He tried to speed up, but was starting to burn out from the exertion. He was still almost twenty yards ahead of them, trying to make the treeline before the car caught up.

Fox's spotlight flashed across the field and caught the driver when he was about halfway to the trees. He kept running, arms and legs flying. He wasn't far from the trees and possible freedom.

Mata's voice came over the radio, huffing as he sprinted after the passenger. "Black male, *huh, huh,* running south on the west side of Airline, *huh, huh,* trying to get over a fence!"

"Turn off the siren and get ready to bail, Mike," Nunez said, taking off his seat belt. Woods popped his belt, hit the siren switch and put his hand on the door handle. Above them Fox cruised over the field, no more than a hundred feet off the ground.

The driver stepped into a hole and went down, then popped back up in seconds. He was limping.

Nunez yelled "Let's go!" He threw the car into park, in a flash turned off the ignition, yanked the key out and hit the door lock as soon as both doors were open. They were out in an instant and charging toward the driver. Woods was shocked to hear the loud *whumpwhumpwhump* of the helicopter, close above them. It was almost sensory overload.

They were about thirty yards from the treeline, the driver about twenty, when he flung a bright silver object into the field.

"Passenger in custody, passenger in custody! He's got a gunshot wound, not from us!" Mata called on the radio. In the background a voice screamed, *"You hurtin' me! You hurtin' me!"*

"42 Fox, the driver just threw a gun."

The driver was slowing from fatigue and the leg injury, but he made it to the treeline. Fox's spotlight followed him as he ran a few feet into the woods. He ran headfirst into a tree trunk as he crashed through brush. Nunez and Woods entered the trees close behind him.

"Stop, you motherfucker!" Woods yelled as the driver tried to force his way between two trees. The driver, bathed in the broken rays of a spotlight shimmering through tree branches, saw the two furious officers no more than five yards away. He turned and looked for a way out. There was nowhere to go.

He faced Nunez and Woods, held both hands to his front and screamed, *"I didn't do anything!"*

Woods drew his weapon and yelled, "Get the fuck on the ground, motherfucker! Now!"

"But I ain't did nuthin'!"

Woods stopped, covering the suspect with his weapon. Now he and Nunez could make a contact/cover arrest, one officer covering the suspect and the other going hands on. Just like Woods had been taught in the academy.

Nunez charged the driver and elbowed him hard in the upper chest. The driver slammed flat onto his back, shrieked in terror and feebly threw his hands up in defense. He sat up and Nunez dropped his knee onto his chest, forcing him back down.

The driver kept shrieking, reached up and tried to force Nunez off. Nunez grabbed his right wrist, twisted it hard and rolled the driver onto his stomach. Woods wavered, trying to figure out what to do, then holstered his weapon and ran in to help. Woods saw that the driver was no older than eighteen, skinny with homemade tattoos on his neck and back. His hands were under his stomach.

"Git off me dawg! I ain't did shit!"

"FUCK YOU!" Nunez bellowed, and kneed the suspect's left thigh. Woods yanked his handcuff case open and pulled cuffs out as he grabbed the driver's arm. He yanked as hard as he could, hoping the driver wouldn't pull a gun from his waistband. They had seen him throw a pistol, but that didn't mean he didn't

have another one.

"42 Fox to the officers on the driver, we can't see you, tell me what you got."

Nunez ignored the radio. Woods yelled, "1243, we're getting the driver in custody now!" Nunez screamed "Get your fucking hand out from under you or I'm gonna fucking kill you!" The driver shrieked like a girl and forced his arm further under his torso. Woods pulled on the driver's arm but couldn't move it. He gave up and threw one cuff onto the wrist that Nunez was holding. Nunez dropped his knee onto the driver's back and put all his weight on it.

"Get your fucking arm out from under you, you piece of shit!"

"Okay, dawg! Back off!"

The driver lifted his midsection off the ground and threw his hand out. It was empty.

Woods quickly cuffed the second wrist. Nunez stayed on the driver's back, breathing heavily, holding one wrist in a death grip. Woods heard him mumble unintelligibly. He couldn't make out the words, but heard anger in them.

"1243 dispatch, driver is in custody," Woods said nervously, watching Nunez.

Nunez finally eased up. He straddled the driver and flipped him, then stood over him.

"1110 dispatch, any other suspects on the ground?" the unknown officer asked.

"All suspects in custody," Mata answered.

"Clear. The driver of the car the suspect vehicle hit on Aldine Bender is dead. We need an ambulance to pronounce him, and an accident unit."

Nunez looked down at the driver. He squinted back, panting, almost blinded by the helicopter's spotlight filtering through the trees.

"You hear that, you piece of shit?" Nunez asked. "You killed that guy on Aldine Bender."

"That wasn't me! I wasn't drivin'!"

Nunez tensed. He reached down, drew his pistol and held it by his thigh. Woods froze. The look on Nunez's face was pure hatred and fury. The driver screamed, "Don't kill me dawg, don't kill me!"

Fox's spotlight suddenly turned off. The wooded area around them went

111

black.

Woods could hear Nunez's heavy but even breathing, and the driver's ragged, terrified gasps and pants. Then he heard a metallic click.

Oh god, Woods thought. *He just cocked the hammer. He's about to shoot this asshole.*

"42 Fox I copied, all suspects in custody. I'm gone, back to Hobby Airport for fuel."

Shit. What do I do now?

"Hey Jerry," Woods pleaded quietly. "Come on man, let's get this guy back to the car."

Several more seconds passed. Woods pulled his flashlight from his belt, took a breath and turned the light on.

Nunez didn't move when Woods' flashlight lit him up. Woods looked at Nunez's weapon. The hammer wasn't cocked. The suspect twisted a little and Woods heard the metallic click again, as the handcuffs tightened another notch from his body weight pressing down on them.

Nunez closed his eyes, sighed, and put his pistol back in its holster. Woods grabbed the driver's arm, yanked him to his feet and searched him. No weapons.

They walked him back out to the patrol car, and on the way found the chrome revolver he had thrown as he ran into the trees. Nunez roughly shoved him into the back seat and slammed the door hard behind him. They bounced back through the field to the Tahoe.

Several more patrol cars, including one driven by Sergeant Tillis, had arrived. The second suspect, another teenage black kid, shirtless like the driver but scraped and bloody, sat crying in the back seat of Mata's car. The driver of the Escort the Tahoe hit was laying on his back next to his car, either hurt or acting like he had spinal injuries so he could file a lawsuit. One officer was with him, writing down the Escort's plate and identification number.

"Hey, Jerry!" Wesley said. "Good fucking catch, brother! Two turds down for aggravated robbery and evading. Fucking awesome!"

"Yeah, awesome," Nunez said. "And one innocent bystander killed in the chase. Anyone else get hurt?"

"Naw, man, everyone else is good, as far as I know. Except for our robber with the little bullet hole in his leg."

"I saw people laying all over the parking lot of the gas station when we passed it," Woods said to Wesley. "Nobody there got hit?"

"Nope. Sarge has been on the phone with Lorenzo, he went to the gas station while we were on the chase. Lorenzo said one of these turds went inside to rob the gas station and fired two shots just to show off, so some customer with a concealed handgun permit pulled his Glock and shot his ass. They had a little gunfight inside the gas station, then the robber ran outside and jumped into the Tahoe. Then homie number two opened up with the AK, but didn't hit anyone. Fucking idiots."

Wesley stepped toward Nunez and held his palm up. "High five, Jerry. If you hadn't stayed so tight on them they might have bailed and shot it out with us. But you kept your brothers alive tonight."

Nunez stepped back. Woods saw his eyes water. He turned around. Wesley lowered his hand in confusion.

"I can't do this," Nunez whispered. "Not now."

He walked toward the patrol car, wiping his eyes. Woods knew he had started crying again.

"What the fuck?" Wesley asked Woods. "What's with Jerry tonight?"

"He got some really bad news earlier," Woods replied. Then he thought better of sharing Nunez's personal tragedy. "That's all. Just some bad news."

"Man, he needs to get his shit together," Wesley said. "Y'all have a lot of work to do. This is probably gonna keep you at the station til ten a.m."

"Yeaaaahhh. . . I need to talk to Sergeant Tillis, I'll be right back," Woods said.

Tillis was on the phone when Woods approached. Tillis held up a finger as a signal to wait while he finished up his conversation.

"Just hold that scene until we get the suspects there for witnesses to ID. What? Tell that guy to relax, the only thing we'd arrest him for is not shooting the robber twice. I'll be there to talk to him as soon as I can. Good job, Lorenzo, I'll see you in a few."

Tillis hung up, smiling at Woods as he put his phone away. "Hi there Mikey, good job you and Jerry did on this one. Where is Jerry anyway?"

"Sarge, I need to talk to you about Jerry. I don't think he can handle working this tonight."

Tillis frowned. "What's the problem?"

Woods explained the phone call from Afghanistan, Nunez's breakdown, everything. "If we hadn't gotten caught up in this, Jerry probably would have gone home already."

Tillis nodded. "Alright, Woods. Nunez goes home, you stay here. I'll partner you up with someone to help you get this shit sorted out. Come with me."

Woods followed Tillis to the patrol car. Tillis knocked on the window. Nunez opened the door and said, "I'm coming out Sarge, I just needed a minute. I'll handle my scene now." Nunez wiped tears from his eyes as he spoke. In the back seat the Tahoe's driver sat in silence, head hanging.

"Don't worry about it, Jerry," Tillis said. "Mata and Wesley can handle this. Why don't you let Woods get his gear from the car, he'll ride with Mata for the rest of the night. You just go home."

Nunez looked at Tillis through red, swollen eyes. "It's my scene, Mel. I can handle it."

Tillis squatted in the open doorway, his old man knees popping from the strain. "Jerry, I know what happened tonight, with your friend. You've done enough police work for one night. Mike can write the report. Go home, curl up with your woman, and get some sleep, Jerry. You need to."

Nunez closed his eyes, then ran his hand through his hair, stopping at the end to squeeze the back of his neck. "Okay, I'll go home. Thanks, Mel."

"No problem, Jerry," Tillis said. "I'll let Mata know what's up."

Woods transferred his gear and the prisoner to Mata's car while Tillis explained to Mata that he was now primary officer. If Mata was pissed about everything being dropped on him, he let it go when Tillis explained why.

Nunez left a few minutes later. Several officers who didn't know the situation asked aloud why he wasn't handling his own arrests. Woods, Mata and Tillis kept the reason to themselves.

As Wesley had predicted, handling the robbery, shooting and accidents took Woods and Mata until after ten a.m. Before Woods finally left the station, several day shift officers asked why he and Mata were doing Nunez's work. Woods didn't tell them the truth. He didn't think it was his place.

CHAPTER 8

Some people pretend they're just not there, some drink themselves stupid, some find the right mix of drugs and chemicals and live in a haze nothing can penetrate. Some run from everything, changing jobs, cities and spouses the moment anyone gets too close. Some talk to friends, family and professionals, and learn the right way to deal with it. Which method one chooses depends on character, circumstance, and what one carried into the war, not just what they carried out.

Some people literally run. They put on jogging shoes, turn on music and hit the pavement in an attempt to get their minds off it. It doesn't work. The memories keep pace and stay at your back, they don't stand quietly at your door and await your return. But Nunez had tried it again, all weekend, even though it never worked and he knew it never would.

The comfortable houses along his route turned into mud-brick compounds, picket fences transformed into rock walls, exhaust from passing cars became gunsmoke, quiet intersections transformed into ambush kill zones. Remembered explosions, screams and gunfire forced their way through his headphones. As he ran he relived it, not flashbacks but memories, bits and pieces of the warrior life he and Wilson once lived.

Nunez's house was a few blocks away, the finish line for a three mile run. He had run every day since he learned of Wilson's death, hoping to focus on the physical effort. He only managed to give himself more time to dwell on memories.

Nunez was fighting the nagging thought that Wilson's death was a waste. There was no other word for it. The Afghanistan war was winding down. Wilson hadn't been allowed to actually fight, he'd simply been there to keep the peace as the American mission faded into the sunset. As a result, he'd been killed by a coward hiding on the side of a highway holding wires to a car battery. His killer was probably a teenager who had run away laughing, but would have cried, pissed himself, denied his involvement and begged for forgiveness if he'd been caught.

Wilson had been a soldier, a warrior. At the very least, he deserved to have been killed by a warrior. Not by a coward.

So many times they had faced death together, heard bullets scream over their heads, and come back to the firebase without a scratch. Now Wilson was dead and gone, just a memory. And in his shadow Nunez jogged down a street in his neighborhood, crying over lost friends, nursing a marriage and hating the job he had once loved, wishing desperately he could be back in the fight, hoping Wilson and the others hadn't died for nothing.

Nunez arrived at his house. It was empty during the day, and Nunez had a while to get ready for work. He had signed up for an overtime evening shift, and during the weekend he was so preoccupied with Wilson's death he hadn't asked anyone else to cover it. He figured he may as well get back to work. Sitting at home wasn't helping.

Nunez went to his bedroom. On the wall above his bed was a picture of ten soldiers from his platoon, the day before a major operation in Afghanistan. They were posing in front of an armored vehicle, holding a Texas flag. Wilson and Nunez stood next to each other, Wilson's arm around Nunez's shoulders, like they always were in group pictures.

Nunez looked at the picture, allowing himself to tear up. He kept telling himself he was done crying, then some memory would prove him wrong. Wilson smiled at him from the photo, full of life, eager to get into the fight that would kill Eli Gore, another of their friends. The fight that would make Wilson go back to Afghanistan in the hopes of getting into more just like it.

Nunez put his hand on the wall under the picture and wiped his eyes with the other. He reached up and tapped the picture frame with his fist, giving a soldier's farewell to his brother. Then he turned and started to get ready for work.

He saw the red light flashing on his cell phone as soon as he stepped out of the shower. He dried off and shaved, then got his uniform halfway on before picking the phone. The screen displayed a single line, from Yussuf.

You must act.

Nunez looked at his phone for several seconds, then texted back.

Give me details, fast.

Nunez put his phone down and rushed to put his uniform on. As soon as he had his duty belt on, he checked his phone again. No new texts. He thought about it. Yussuf could be in the middle of whatever was happening at the mosque. A phone call now might burn him.

Nunez decided it was worth the risk. The call went to voicemail. He hung up, walked out the door to his jeep, threw his bag and carbine in the back, got in and drove out of the neighborhood toward the North station, thirty minutes away.

As soon as he was out of his subdivision, he called Criminal Intelligence to tell Officer Delisle about the text. Delisle was busy in a meeting, and the officer who answered wasn't too worked up about it. He promised to pass the information on.

Disappointed, Nunez hung up. Maybe he was making too big an issue of Yussuf's text. Or maybe Intelligence wasn't making it a big enough issue.

As soon as he stuck the phone back into its case it vibrated again. He quickly pulled it out to see another text from Yussuf.

There is very little time.

"God damn it," Nunez said, hitting the *talk* button even though he was sure Yussuf wouldn't answer. He was right, the call went straight to voicemail this time. He waited for a few moments, thinking about trying Delisle again. Instead, as he got onto the highway he called Woods.

"Hello? Jerry?"

"Mike, have you heard from Yussuf?" Nunez asked. "Has he called you?"

"No, I haven't heard anything at all. What's up?"

"I don't know. He sent me a text saying 'there is very little time', and then didn't respond to my text or answer my call," Nunez said. "Then a minute ago he texted 'you must act soon.' He still won't answer the phone."

"Have you called Intelligence?" Woods asked.

"Yeah, but Delisle wasn't there, and the guy who answered today wasn't too wound up about it. I'm not sure if I should start screaming to everyone, or stay quiet and wait for more information." Frustrated, Nunez said, "I wish Yussuf wasn't trying to be such a mysterious bastard."

"Yeah, me too," Woods said. "Uh, think I should come in today? Just in case something happens?"

"No, I don't think so," Nunez said. "Unless you feel like donating some free time to the city."

"Alright, I'll hang out here," Woods said. "But call me if anything happens."

"Word," Nunez said. "Later."

As soon as he hung up with Woods, Nunez called Criminal Intelligence again. The same officer as before answered, and when Nunez told him about the second text he seemed about as interested as he had been in the first one. He promised to talk to Delisle as soon as the meeting was over, which he said should be within the hour.

Nunez gave a perfunctory thanks and hung up. Maybe Delisle would have blown him off too, but at least he would have seemed interested.

Nunez arrived five minutes before the three p.m. roll call. The roll call room was full of the usual characters who worked overtime every chance they got: desk officers, academy staff, investigators who usually worked plainclothes but got into uniform once or twice a week for extra money, and a scattering of officers like Nunez who wanted to work overtime before their regular shift. Calhoun slouched in a *chair* on one side of the room. He gave Nunez an uninterested glance, then turned away.

Nunez pulled his phone from his belt as he settled into a *chair*. No new messages. An ancient evening shift sergeant was conducting roll call, lounging at the podium and looking at his watch. He spoke slowly, called a few names, greeted old friends and playfully poked fun at others, just killing time while waiting for latecomers.

Nunez grumbled, turned the phone over in his hands several times, then started to send Yussuf another text. A new message from Yussuf popped up.

Goodbye, Jerry.

Nunez blurted, "Son of a bitch!"

The roll call sergeant stopped speaking. Everyone looked at Nunez in silence. Nunez stared back at all the eyes on him.

"Um. . . sorry."

Nunez shrank into his seat. The desk sergeant began to slowly read names again, made more jokes, forgot where he was on the list and started over, asked if anyone knew when latecomers would arrive, joked some more, took a long drink from a soda, then started reading names again. He plodded through the roll call list, stopping several times as officers walked in, talking and gossiping with some of them. Nunez looked at his watch, fidgeted in his seat like a first grader, tapped his fingers on the desk, pulled his pen from his pocket and clicked it a few times, then finally jerked up from his *chair.*

"Sarge I gotta go! I have to follow up something I'm working. I'll be in my beat as soon as I'm done."

The sergeant nodded absentmindedly and droned on with his list of names and assignments. Nunez rushed to the equipment room and waited for the slow-as-molasses equipment officer to give him a radio and keys to an available car. He urgently wandered the parking lot for several minutes until he found the car, an old piece of crap that looked like it hadn't been driven in years. He tried to start the engine. It was so dead the dash display didn't even turn on. He ran back to the equipment room, threw the key across the desk to the equipment officer and told him he needed a different car, fast.

The equipment officer took a few seconds to pause the movie he was watching on his laptop computer, took another bite from his sandwich, then slowly picked up the key Nunez had thrown to him and walked to the back of the room. Nunez stood by the equipment room counter, tapping his foot on the floor and his finger on the counter, checking his phone to see if he had missed another message. Nothing.

The equipment officer ambled back to the desk, got onto his work computer to change the status showing which car had been issued to which officer, and tossed a key to Nunez. Nunez grabbed it and took off out the door, calling Yussuf again as he looked for the car. No answer. He found the car after several more minutes, parked in the wrong spot, far from where it was supposed to be. He jumped in and turned the key.

It worked. But, of course, the officer who had last driven it hadn't bothered to fuel it up at the end of his shift. The tank was nearly empty.

Nunez rushed to the station's gas pumps, then had to wait for officers who were already there to fill their cars. Over five minutes later he finally had the car fueled, then sped to his Jeep and loaded the patrol car's trunk with his gear. He flew toward 1803 Hanley, frustrated when he caught a red light or got behind a slow vehicle. It seemed like everyone slowed down when they saw his cop car behind them.

He reached the freeway and headed north, dialing Yussuf as he weaved through traffic. He made three calls, getting Yussuf's voicemail every time. A few minutes later he was there.

1803 Hanley was as quiet as usual. Only a few cars were in the parking lot, maybe half as many as in the middle of the night. The parking spaces in front of Rahim's and Yussuf's apartments were empty. Nunez drove past Yussuf's apartment, slowing to take a close look. No activity, nothing unusual.

Nunez parked and cautiously walked to Yussuf's door. He looked at the window, door, porch, walls, everything. Nothing attracted his attention. The Venetian blinds in the window were closed. Nunez stood to the side of the door and put his ear against it. Nothing. He stepped across the door and put his ear to the window. Still nothing.

He knocked softly on the door, not pounding on it like cops normally do. No answer. He waited a minute and knocked again, a little harder. No answer. He pounded on the door, cop style.

"Yussuf! It's Jerry! Open the door!"

Still no answer. Nunez pounded on the door again so hard his fist hurt.

"Yussuf! Open the god damn door!"

Still no answer, but the door to apartment E opened and an angry-looking Arab with a huge grey beard stepped out. He saw Nunez and jumped back into his apartment.

"Hey! Wait up!"

Nunez ran to apartment E. The man slammed the door just before Nunez got there. Nunez pounded on his door. "I just need to ask you something! Did you see Yussuf today? Open the door, I need to talk to you!"

A gruff, accented voice answered, "I have seen nothing. Go away."

Nunez muttered "Fuck!", hit the door again and walked back to Yussuf's door. As soon as he reached the window he banged on the glass.

"Yussuf!"

Still no answer. Nunez pulled his phone from his belt and dialed Yussuf again, saying "Answer the damn phone, answer the damn phone," as he put the phone to his ear.

A ringtone faintly sounded inside the apartment.

Nunez jerked his head up and looked into the window. He held his phone away from his ear and moved closer to the glass. The ringtone, which sounded like music Nunez heard once at a Mediterranean restaurant, still played somewhere in the apartment.

Nunez hit *end*. The ringtone stopped. Nunez called Yussuf back. The ringtone played again.

"Motherfucker," Nunez said as he put his phone away. He wasn't sure what to do. He could call a supervisor and run the situation down to him, but the supervisor would probably just tell him to try again later. Or he could call the fire department for forced entry. And tell them. . . what? The guy who lived in the apartment had sort of given him a little bit of what might be information about something bad that might happen somewhere, and then had sent him some text messages that sounded bad but didn't really tell him anything, and then wouldn't answer the phone that was ringing inside his apartment? Oh, and that he had given Nunez this semi-information because Allah had arranged for the two of them to meet. Yeah, that would work.

Nunez could just make up a story about the whole thing, claim that Yussuf had called him in a panic because he was having a heart attack or something. The fire department wouldn't question him about it, they'd just break the door down. But if they damaged the hell out of the apartment and found nothing inside, he'd have a lot of explaining to do.

Nunez looked at the window. The edge of the window was pretty close to the door handle, probably close enough for him to reach in and unlock the door. The window was made of several small square panes; if he broke out the pane closest to the door, opened the door and discovered nothing was going on inside the apartment, it wouldn't be that big of a deal. But if that didn't work, he'd have to break more glass and go in through the window.

Whatever he did, he'd look like a complete dumbass if he was wrong.

Nunez looked around. Nobody was outside the apartments or looking out the windows. Feeling a little like a burglar, he pulled his flashlight off his belt, turned it around and hit the window pane. Not full force, just testing it. The glass flexed, but held. He backed the flashlight off and hit the window again. Same result. He finally gave it a good hit, and the flashlight still bounced off. He looked around again, then held the flashlight as far away as he could before swinging it hard at the window pane.

The pane shattered. Nunez used the flashlight to knock all the glass from the edges, then reached in and felt for the doorknob. His fingers brushed it, then he got a solid grip. The handle wouldn't turn. He felt around on the face of the handle, looking for the lock. He found a small horizontal tab, turned it vertical and tried the doorknob again. The door opened six inches and creaked to a stop.

He reached into the doorway and felt the edge of the door lock, searching for a deadbolt. It was there, above the handle, but hadn't been locked. That could mean someone who didn't have a key had left the apartment, locking only the handle behind him.

Nunez gently pushed the door open. Only the front room and kitchen were visible. Both were clear.

He knocked on the open door. "Yussuf, it's Jerry! You in there? Come on man, I need to talk to you."

No answer. He took another look around the apartment complex. Still no people, no activity. He drew his weapon and stepped into the apartment, keeping the pistol tight against his chest in a combat-ready hold.

And he saw it. Yussuf's phone, on the dining table beside the kitchen.

Yussuf's apartment was small. A hallway led to the single bedroom. Two closed doors were in the hallway, one on each wall. Nunez looked on the floor, doors and walls. He half expected to find bloody footprints like at Rahim's apartment the night of the murder, but there was nothing. Nothing but a faint smell, like a mix of shit and copper.

Nunez moved down the hall to the door on the left side of the hallway. He kept his muzzle pointing into the room and opened the door. It was an empty bathroom. He turned to the door across the hallway, twisted the doorknob to confirm it was unlocked, and pushed it open.

The smell of fresh death intensified. Nunez saw Yussuf's wife face down alongside the bed's footboard. Her head scarf was soaked in blood. The light was off in the bedroom, and Nunez flicked on a flashlight. A dark black and red hole was centered on the back of her skull.

Nunez's heart sank. He pied off the room, taking in a little piece at a time, strobing with his flashlight as he moved. On his third step, he saw what he first thought was a crumpled body on the bed. But when he looked closer he realized it was a pile of bloody clothes and towels, beside several empty plastic water bottles and two pairs of plastic sandals. He kept going until he saw feet on the floor next to the bed. He stepped into the room, knowing he was going to find Yussuf shot in the back of the head as well.

It was Yussuf. He hadn't been shot. He had been decapitated. His head sat upright in the center of his back, face turned to the rear. Nunez found himself looking into Yussuf's dull, barely open eyes.

The corner of the room where he lay was drenched in blood, the carpet soaked red with bodily fluid so thick it looked like liver. Yussuf's hands were unbound and laying limply by his sides, as if he hadn't fought back at all.

Nunez wondered if Yussuf would have resisted anyway. He had seemed so peaceful, not the kind of guy who would have gone kicking and screaming to his death. But what about his wife, dead a few feet from him? Wouldn't Yussuf have done something, anything, to protect her from being murdered?

Maybe Yussuf agreed not to resist, accepted death by decapitation, in exchange for a painless shot to the back of the head for his wife.

Nunez reached to the wall and flipped the light switch. The light hit Yussuf's blood-streaked face. Even though his eyes were barely open, the pupils stared straight into Nunez's. Nunez returned Yussuf's accusing stare.

Why didn't I get up from roll call as soon as I got his text? Why didn't I just take off without worrying about fueling the damn car? It had to have had enough gas to get here. Why didn't I call the desk sergeant and tell him I was going to stop here on my way to the station? Why didn't I just get on the desk radio and ask a fucking patrol officer to go check on him? He was trying to let me know something bad was going to happen, and I didn't react fast enough.

Nunez felt his face flush with anger, at Yussuf and himself. If Yussuf knew he was about to be murdered, why didn't he call 911? Why wasn't there forced entry? Had he actually let the murderers into the apartment, after taking the time to send a text message saying goodbye? Nunez looked for a logical answer, but the only thing that made any sense was that Yussuf had cooperated with his killers, just to get the smallest measure of mercy for his wife.

Nunez walked out of the room carefully, so as not to step on any evidence. But there wasn't anything outside the bedroom, not a speck of blood anywhere. Whoever had committed these murders had gone to great lengths to not leave a trail of blood, even bringing towels, water to clean up and a change of clothes. But the fact that they left the clothes and towels on the bed had to mean they weren't worried about leaving evidence. They just didn't want the murders to be immediately discovered.

Nunez walked out of the apartment, stopped just outside and looked around. *Where the hell is everyone now? Where were they when Yussuf's head was sawed off and his wife was shot in the back of the head?* If the Arab with the bad attitude stepped out now, Nunez would probably knock his teeth out.

He reached for his mike. He knew over the next few hours he was going to have to explain a lot to a lot of people.

"1243 dispatch."

"Dispatch 1243, go ahead."

Nunez sighed, looking around the complex again. Still no people, no activity. "I have two DOAs, 1803 Hanley, apartment D. They're both murders. I need officers with crime scene tape to secure the scene. I also need an ambulance to pronounce the victims, and you might as well let Homicide know. And get a crime scene unit out here."

"Dispatch clear. Any chance there's a suspect still around?"

"I don't think so, dispatch. It's empty except for the victims."

Dispatch acknowledged, and several officers jumped on the radio volunteering to check by. Nunez walked toward his car, changed his mind and walked back toward Yussuf's door, then changed his mind again and just stood there. He knew he had to start making calls, to get the word out about whatever Yussuf had been trying to tell him. He didn't know if Yussuf's messages had been about whatever was going on at the mosque, or about his own impending murder. But now Nunez had to take a minute to clear his head and try to figure out what the hell was going on.

———

Nunez stood outside the apartment door talking to Sergeant Bush from Greenspoint Patrol. Bush was a new sergeant Nunez had met once or twice before, a veteran of ten years patrolling some of the worst neighborhoods of the city in Northeast Station's area. He had arrived first, before Delisle from Intelligence and well before Detective Helmers from Homicide, the same Detective Helmers who had been primary on Fahima's murder in October. Helmers had been meeting with a prosecutor on another case and rushed to Hanley as soon as he heard the news.

Patrol officers had taped off the parking lot, allowing only the crime scene unit and a Houston Fire Department ambulance to come in. The ambulance was gone, the paramedics having only stayed long enough to officially pronounce Yussuf and his wife dead. A local news channel's media truck had arrived and was being kept on the street. They would stay until the bodies were moved, which wouldn't be for hours, so they could have something to put on the news at 10:00. The team was also trying to interview any officer who would go near them, but so far had only gotten a "no comment yet" from Sergeant Bush. Calhoun had swung by, talked to the patrolmen blocking the parking lot but not to Nunez, and left within minutes. Nunez didn't know where he went or what he was doing, and didn't care.

Nunez had called Woods to tell him about the murders. Woods was shocked, and asked again if he should come to work. Nunez answered, "Probably not. It seems like everyone who gets near me lately winds up dead."

Nunez ran the whole thing down to the Sergeant Bush when he arrived, then to Delisle when he arrived and then to Helmers when he arrived. Each time he told the story he left out nothing. He admitted his policy violations when he forced entry into the apartment and searched it without backup. If he got suspended for discovering this murder and telling the entire department about a possible plot of some kind at the mosque, then so be it.

"So that's it," Nunez said after he finished going over it for the third time. "That's the whole thing. "I don't know what else to tell y'all. Now I think we need to call someone and do something."

"What's your idea of 'something'?" Sergeant Bush asked.

"Yeah, that's my question too," Helmers said. This 'evil plot' shit is out of my lane, but I think Nunez is right. Something needs to be done. I wish I knew what that something was, though."

Delisle spoke up. "I think the best we can do right now is set surveillance on the mosque. Maybe we can also put someone here after we clear the scene to see what Rahim is up to, but that might be hard to pull off because I'd bet that all the residents here know what cars should be here and what cars shouldn't. Other than that, I don't know what we can do."

"Let's think this out," Sergeant Bush said. "The text messages were either about this supposed thing going on at the mosque, or about the fact that your friend was about to be murdered, right? If the messages were about the mosque, then what use is it to only put surveillance there? It would make more sense to have someone out there that can react to what they see, instead of just sending surveillance officers who can only report it."

"So if not surveillance, then what?" Delisle asked. "Send patrol officers over there to hang out and see what happens?"

"No, that wouldn't work," Nunez said. "If there are marked units all over the place, whatever they're planning probably won't happen. They'll sit tight and wait for the units to disappear, since we can't keep patrol there forever. What if we send SWAT in their unmarked cars? That keeps it low profile, plus it puts people on the scene who can do something if the shit hits the fan."

"And if whatever's supposedly being planned at the mosque isn't actually going to take place at the mosque?" Bush asked.

Nunez said, "We don't have anything pointing us in any other direction than the mosque. If it's somewhere else, well…I guess we'll find out when the 911 calls start rolling in."

The sergeant nodded. "Gotcha. I'll call the lieutenant and he can call the captain, then it's up to someone at department headquarters. What do y'all think?"

"I think it's a good idea," Helmers said.

Delisle said, "I concur."

"You know my vote already," Nunez answered.

"Alright, I'll be right back, gimme a few minutes," Sergeant Bush said, walking to a quiet spot.

Over an hour had passed since Nunez had first arrived on Hanley. If the lieutenant agreed with his patrol sergeant about calling out SWAT, if the captain agreed with the lieutenant, if whoever answered the call at headquarters decided to make the callout, it could take who knew how long. And if SWAT didn't get rolling soon, they'd get caught in rush hour traffic.

Nunez had been a harsh critic of the department for his entire career. He hoped that this one time, the higher-ups he complained about would make the right call.

———————

Captain English cursed as he rolled to a stop in his black Ford Taurus. He was on Crosstimbers just west of North Shepherd, parked along the curb in front of a house, looking through the building traffic on Shepherd toward a nondescript warehouse. Less than twenty minutes earlier he had received the near-frantic call from some assistant chief's secretary, telling him to get every SWAT officer available to a mosque at Shepherd and Crosstimbers. When English asked what the situation was so he could brief his team leaders, he got a weird response: "I don't know. A patrol sergeant from North station called y'all out, but I don't know why. I'll call back as soon as I know something. Get your people out there, but stay in your cars and just watch the place."

English geared up and responded as quickly as he could, drove through the intersection several times but didn't see anything remotely resembling a mosque. He called the assistant chief's secretary and told him there wasn't a mosque at that intersection. The secretary smugly assured him there was. Instead of driving around aimlessly, English decided to sit at the intersection until the secretary figured out what he was talking about.

Houston SWAT didn't roll to the scene in a big delivery van like on TV. When they got a callout they arrived in ones and twos in unmarked cars, to a scene usually held by patrol officers. Normally, SWAT officers could scribble a rough sketch of the objective, assign responsibilities to different teams and sections, find a good spot for their snipers, coordinate with the patrol units to get a suspect description and rundown of events, take time to plan. The secretary probably thought his "just sit there and wait" order was simple enough. But without information Captain English couldn't get his team together to make a plan, and on top of that still didn't know why he was there.

Only one other officer had arrived, just before English. That officer was in the grocery store parking lot behind the warehouse, telling English he couldn't see a mosque either. Several SWAT officers had been training at the range and others had been training another agency just outside Houston. English had been forced to call those officers in, ruining important events that had been scheduled for months. Other officers were fighting the rapidly building rush hour traffic to get to the intersection from home. When they bumped the captain on the radio to ask if they needed to pick up special equipment or stage somewhere to plan, the captain had to give them a big fat "I don't have a clue", making him seem like a total dumbass.

A SWAT officer called the captain on SWAT's frequency. "Sam 22 this is Sam 118. Me and Sam 113 are here, in the same car. Where do you want us at?"

"Ed, set up in the shopping center just south of the intersection. Me and Sam 162 have the east and west covered. I still haven't heard crap about what's going on, and we haven't seen a mosque out here. I'm going to switch to North's channel for a minute on my car radio, but I'll monitor my portable. If someone else shows up, have them set up to the north."

"Clear."

English switched to North patrol's frequency. "Sam 22 to North patrol dispatch, we've been called out here by a patrol supervisor. Do you have anyone on the air who can tell me what's going on?"

Sergeant Bush spoke up. "209 to Sam 22, sending you my cell number in one minute," the sergeant answered.

English sat in his car, cursing the morons who had sent SWAT out in this bullshit way. His computer beeped, and he saw a phone number on the screen. He dialed it and got an immediate answer.

"This is Bush."

"Is this 209? This is Sam 22, Captain English from SWAT."

"Yup, thanks for calling. Are you at the mosque?"

"There isn't any damn mosque," English grumbled. "I'm here at Shepherd and Crosstimbers with three of my guys and I've got several more coming, for no reason I know of. You want to tell me what we're doing out here so we can make, oh, maybe, some kind of plan? Did we get sent to the wrong place, or what?"

English heard the sergeant say to someone away from the phone, "He says there's no mosque at that intersection." A voice answered, "The warehouse is the mosque, I told y'all that three times already."

"Oh yeah," Bush said. "The mosque is that grey warehouse, on the southeast corner of the intersection."

"That's the mosque? Damn it…hang on."

English keyed his portable radio and said, "SWAT units, the mosque is this grey warehouse on the southeast corner of the intersection. Make sure you can get eyes on it."

His officers acknowledged, and English got back on his phone. "Alright, it would have been nice to know about that before we got here. So why are we out here anyway?"

"Captain, we explained everything to headquarters, they swore it would be passed on to you," Sergeant Bush said. "Did they tell you anything at all?"

"They didn't tell us shit. Why did you call us out?"

"Alright captain, here's the deal. It's a long story, so give me a minute to explain it. I'm making it as short as possible," Bush said.

Bush laid it out. When he got to "Nunez came over here to check on the informant and found him in his apartment decapitated, and his wife shot in the back of the head," English replied, "Yeah, I guess that's significant." Then English asked, "What else is there?"

"That's it," Bush said. "That was enough for us to call SWAT, in case the messages meant something's being planned at the mosque and is about to go down."

"You don't have anything else?" English asked. "No real information on what's supposedly about to happen, no names, no idea on weapons, no layout of the mosque? Nothing else?"

"Nope."

"So we got sent out here for just this," English asked. "Just a hunch?"

"Yup."

"Jesus Christ. Is the primary officer there on the scene?"

"Yeah, he is," Bush said. "Hang on."

There was noise and mumbling, then a new voice picked up. "This is Officer Nunez."

"Nunez, this is Captain English from SWAT. Can you tell me anything else about what's going on out here?"

"Sergeant Bush pretty much covered it, Captain. I'm not sure what other information I have that would help," Nunez said.

"What about numbers? Did your guy ever tell you how many people might be in the mosque?"

"Nothing I can remember," Nunez said. "He said they hang out there all night sometimes. And I think...hang on. He did say the mosque has real thick walls, and they sit on the roof so there must be a stairwell. I think the roof has a raised edge around it. And...he also said they were worried burglars could get in through the bay door at the back. Me and my partner drove past there one night and saw the inside of the bay door, it's about two cars wide and two cars deep. I think."

"Okay, that's good," English said. Two more of his units arrived, and he told Nunez to hang on while he set them up. "What else can you tell me, Nunez?"

"Uh. . . he said there's a lower level to the mosque, it's full of rooms they use for meetings. And he said the main floor where they pray is mostly open."

While English repeated the information back to him, Nunez thought about the innocent conversation he and Yussuf had one night, when Yussuf praised the construction of the warehouse. The old man had actually given him details he didn't realize were important until now.

Yussuf-khan, you crafty old bastard, Nunez thought. *I'll miss you.*

"Nunez, can you meet me face to face?" English asked. "I want to go over everything with you, and I want you to draw a sketch of the mosque."

Nunez checked with Bush and Helmers. "No problem, Captain. You're on Crosstimbers, right? I can meet you a couple blocks west of Shepherd, out of view of the mosque. I have your cell number, as soon as I find a good spot I'll call you. If you need me before then bump me on the radio. My unit number is 1243."

"That'll work," English said. "How long will it take for you to get here?"

Nunez thought about it. Hanley was maybe eight miles north of the mosque. On night shift that would be nothing. On evening shift, at rush hour, it might take a while.

He checked his watch. 5:23 p.m., rush hour was about to be in full swing. But the heaviest traffic would flow northbound out of the city. Southbound should be smooth sailing, although traffic sometimes jammed up at the huge West Little York overpass.

"Give me fifteen minutes, Captain," Nunez said.

"Okay. Nunez, you have any tactical background?" English asked. "There's only six of us here, if we make entry we might need you to watch our backs."

Nunez answered, "I was infantry, Iraq and Afghanistan."

"Outstanding. You have a carbine?"

"Yes sir."

"Great. All my guys are geared up with their carbines up front. You might want to put yours up front too," English said.

"Got it, I'll have it ready."

"Okay, see you in a few minutes."

English hung up. Nunez jogged to his car, popped the trunk and pulled his M4 carbine out of its case. He slapped the magazine in the magazine well and pulled the charging handle to load a round into the chamber. He pulled his "bail out bag" from his other gear, making sure it had all five of his other magazines, plus a tourniquet and medical trauma kit. Since Iraq he carried ammunition and medical gear in a bag so he could just grab it and run toward a fight.

Nunez threw the bag and carbine onto the passenger seat, then jumped behind the wheel and headed out.

As soon as English hung up on Nunez, one of his officers, Sam 111, called to let him know he had arrived in a black Chevy Tahoe with three other officers. English told him to park in the grocery store parking lot just east of the mosque.

English pulled out a notepad and drew a diagram of where his units were. So far ten SWAT officers had arrived at the intersection, with several more on the way. None of the SWAT officers there reported any activity at the mosque.

Officer Karl Rivera, Sam 125, called English to let him know he had arrived. English directed Gevers to park just in front of him on Crosstimbers.

English thought eleven SWAT officers plus Nunez should be plenty. And if the shit really hit the fan, patrolmen would come from everywhere to help. Some might be undertrained and unprepared, but they'd come in anyway. That's just what Houston cops do.

English wondered if this was serious, or was bullshit from a cop with an overactive imagination. The story Sergeant Bush told him was suspicion-provoking, but nothing screamed, "Something's about to happen. This shit is *real*." Still, English understood why SWAT had been called out, and why department headquarters had been so concerned. He assumed the department was in communication with the FBI and Homeland Security, putting things in motion bigger than what he and his team were doing.

He looked at the cars scattered around the small parking lot in front of the mosque, wondered who and how many people were inside, and what they were doing. There were no more than fifteen cars total at the mosque, front and back. People had to be inside, but how many? Were there exactly fifteen people, or did five people show up in each car? Were some of the cars just parked there all the time? If they had to make entry, would they find ten people inside, or over a hundred?

English looked at the mosque through binoculars. He saw nothing out of the ordinary, nothing to suggest what if anything was happening inside. For the moment he could do nothing but wait.

———

Inside the mosque, Abdul Al-Taymiyyah stood in the open worship room, pacing before the gathered faithful. Twenty-five men from all corners of the Muslim world plus one convert from Houston, all sitting on the floor, engrossed in the words of their *imam*.

Al-Taymiyyah had worked hard to select and assemble them, had sifted through hundreds of local Muslims who attended the mosque regularly or semi-regularly, determining which among them were devout, which were simply going through the motions to please their parents or wives, which were willing to risk their lives to prove their devotion, and which were willing to go deliberately to their deaths. After months and hundreds of individual meetings with certain followers, he had found the men he needed. The men who sat before him now.

Some were from sub-Saharan Africa, some from north Africa, some Indonesian, many from Pakistan, a few from Afghanistan, a few Saudis like Al-Taymiyyah, one Kosovar Albanian, and one Chechen. Most had come to the United States as refugees, wondering how the country they had publically professed deep hatred for in their homelands could blindly accept them as prospective citizens. Most were amazed at the ease with which they could meet others like them, the absolute lack of attention paid to them as they plotted, conspired, stockpiled necessities and communicated their intentions to those who needed to know.

Many left their homelands because heretical governments that falsely professed to be Muslim persecuted them. American freedoms allowed them to worship God as they truly should; such freedom wasn't something they respected and felt thankful for, it was simply evidence that Americans were stupid, weak fools who deserved to be smashed into submission to God's will, as all humanity someday would be.

Not all the men before Al-Taymiyyah were dedicated to the point of asking for death, and Al-Taymiyyah did not need them all to be. Twenty were "American" enough to desire life over martyrdom. They wouldn't be required to die, not yet. Perhaps after the day's events set an unstoppable *chain* of secondary events in motion they would find themselves faced with no choice other than death as martyrs, and would be ready to embrace it. For now they simply had to possess the will to act decisively in the name of Allah and Mohammed his messenger, peace be upon him, even if their will to act was tainted by a belief they would survive another day, or week, or month afterward. No matter. God would call them to martyrdom when he was ready.

Four of the men in the small crowd were easily distinguishable from the others. They were simply more intense, with darker eyes and focused, creased faces, standing out even as they sat quietly together. The other followers looked to them often, faces full of admiration, as if the men had a visible aura bestowed on them by God. Al-Taymiyyah thought that even if he closed his eyes he would still be able to see the four men, their piety and passion burned so bright.

These men had received the blessing of selection and recognition by Allah, communicated through his faithful slave Abdul Al-Taymiyyah. They had made their final videotaped testaments to family and friends, had shaved their bodies and bathed in rosewater. They wore large dark jackets, much too heavy for the moderate Houston weather. Under their jackets were cheap Chinese chest rigs with three AK-47 magazines, plus three magazines in their jackets. Each would have another in his weapon, giving them seven thirty-round magazines to complete their mission. Their weapons were semi-automatic instead of fully automatic like they were accustomed to using in their native countries, so the limited ammunition they carried would be more than sufficient.

The other twenty, those willing to act but who wished to survive to fight another day, were armed with pistols hidden in their western clothing. Some carried an extra magazine, but most had chosen to only carry the magazine that was inside their pistol. Their work would be done up close, at ranges where they could not miss, against targets who they knew would stand still and not resist.

Americans were cowards. The men in the mosque knew that an American's first impulse when confronted with violence was to call for help, to timidly submit and wait for rescue. Such cowardice had enabled nineteen heroes of Islam to bring down the great American towers in New York years earlier, and the Americans had learned nothing in the time since then. Brave Muslim men stood on streets in America and Western Europe, proclaiming with voices, signs and banners their desire to destroy western values, western democracy, western religion, western life. And every time they did so, the very targets of their rage just as loudly proclaimed the Muslims demonstrators did not mean what they said, were simply misguided or were solitary voices in a sea of what they insisted was Muslim moderation. Americans simply refused to see what was in front of their eyes, refused to believe the thousands of voices who spoke for hundreds of millions of others.

True Muslims despised America. True Muslims rejected American democracy, because any system of government not based on God's law was false. True Muslims knew women were not the equal of men, and any society that claimed so was unforgivably weak. True believers would destroy this worthless, immoral country, by infiltration and subversion. God would not let them fail.

Al-Taymiyyah knew that even after his goals had been achieved this day, even after Americans lay dead in piles in their streets and homes, other Americans would not try to remove the insurgents who lived openly within their own country. Any who attempted to fight the growing insurgency would be denounced as extremists by their own countrymen, would be shouted down by others who were desperate to demonstrate they were free of the unforgivable sin of racism. Americans were undeniably stupid and weak, pathetic creatures who had become far too powerful than destiny and logic should have allowed. Whether in his own lifetime or the lifetimes of his sons and grandsons, Al-Taymiyyah knew this error of history would be corrected.

Al-Taymiyyah looked at the clock on the wall. Less than five minutes until start time. He had assembled the men, God's tools to bring forth unavoidable destiny, hours earlier so that he could speak to them at length, gauge their states of mind, ensure none were wavering. God was guiding their actions, assuring the success of their mission.

Nothing had gone wrong, nobody had shown himself to be unworthy of their task and glory. Not until one of their number, an Indonesian, spoke to Yussuf in front of Rahim's apartment. The Indonesian had not revealed crucial details, but what he said to Yussuf had been enough.

The Indonesian had been sent to pick up Rahim, and had parked his car outside the apartment to wait while Rahim said goodbye to his wife. Yussuf approached him and began a friendly conversation, saying everything a pious

Muslim should say to another pious Muslim. And the Indonesian had been deceived.

He told Yussuf this was a great day for Islam, that great events would take place before sundown, that the followers of Mohammed, peace be upon him, would today begin the destruction of the *kuffar* in Houston. Yussuf acted as if he was overjoyed, and pried more information while he casually fiddled with his phone. He was coaxing more information from the Indonesian when Rahim came outside.

The Indonesian invited Rahim to join in the joyous conversation. He didn't see the look of terror in Yussuf's eyes. Rahim did, and right away, he knew. So he had taken the necessary steps.

They all knew, or should have known, that Yussuf was speaking to the police. They suspected Yussuf had betrayed the faithful. And he had paid the price for his betrayal. Along with his wife, who failed in her duty to God to report Yussuf's traitorous communications. They received just punishment. Rahim took meticulous care to avoid leaving obvious signs of the murders outside the apartment.

Rahim reported everything to Al-Taymiyyah when he and the Indonesian arrived at the mosque. Yussuf had quietly gone to his death in order to spare his wife unnecessary pain. Rahim allowed Yussuf the small courtesy of allowing him to purge himself of waste in the bathroom prior to his death, but that had been the only mercy shown to him. He died with less dignity than the goats Rahim used to butcher in his village near Kandahar. After Yussuf's death Rahim had briefly examined Yussuf's phone, then simply wiped his fingerprints off and left it on the dining table.

The Indonesian had nearly broken down with guilt in front of Al-Taymiyyah at his failed judgment, begging for a chance to redeem himself through martyrdom. Al-Taymiyyah assured him he was forgiven, that the killings of Yussuf and his wife were a welcome gift from God that had not been expected but were to be considered another blessing. Police had discovered the bodies sooner than expected, but that was of little consequence. If anyone knew who bore responsibility for the killings, they would be too terrified to speak.

And, of course, there had been Fahima. Such a shame, such a waste of a young woman. A prospective wife for one of the believers, a woman who could have borne many sons to continue the fight for Islam. The plans for the attack were something of an open secret at the mosque, not shared with those not chosen to participate but not totally hidden. True believers could be trusted to say nothing of the planned events, even if they had no wish to take part themselves.

Sometimes those who would take part in the mission spoke out loud of their involvement. One young believer told Fahima about his part on the operation, trying to impress her with his bravery and dedication. Fahima had not been the most pious or devout, but Al-Taymiyyah did not believe she would betray them.

Mohibullah was enraged that she knew. He and his father insisted Fahima could not be trusted, that she had become far too westernized to keep the plan secret. They convinced Al-Taymiyyah to allow them to eliminate her, and along with her the possibility that she might speak out. Al-Taymiyyah reluctantly agreed. But he didn't know that part of the plan for her death included Mohibullah's martyrdom.

Mohibullah, their first martyr. And his father, a man so devout he was willing to sacrifice both his children in the name of Islam. Al-Taymiyyah could not have been blessed with better servants to bring about God's wishes.

Nothing else had marred their preparations. The weapons had been purchased with ease through legal means. The ammunition was available on the internet, or at hundreds of retail stores. The small personal radios were bought at several different locations at different times to avoid suspicion, although that had not been necessary. Nobody was watching, nobody paying attention.

There was no need to tempt fate by using explosives. Far too many others had been brought down when they attempted to purchase explosives, or components to make them. All the tools they needed for their missions were easily available. For future planned missions, however, certain risks had been taken. Al-Taymiyyah would never have considered taking such risks, had Allah not unexpectedly delivered a servant unto him with the knowledge and experience needed to gain important tools.

Ruben Arredondo had been guided to the mosque by God's own hand. There could be no other explanation. Arredondo had simply knocked on the door of the mosque one day, saying he had recently converted and was in search of a place to worship. Al-Taymiyyah had been hesitant at first, but as Arredondo's connections became known and the apparent earnestness of his belief displayed, Al-Taymiyyah embraced him. And he returned their acceptance by taking risks that could put him back in prison, buying items that could be found on the Mexican border for the right price.

He had risked his life meeting with men who could easily have killed him for the money he carried. But Allah had protected him, and he bought what was needed. He brought the first item back one day, the ammunition to feed it in ones and twos on others days. The prize, along with twelve rounds, was now downstairs in one of the small meeting rooms with the other weapons and ammunition. The Chechen had inspected it and pronounced it functional, although they of course could not test it. God would ensure it worked when needed.

Ruben Arredondo would not take part in the missions. His ability to procure items nobody else could was simply too valuable to risk. The Chechen likewise would not take part. He was too well trained and experienced at conducting ambushes and sniper attacks, setting explosives and torturing prisoners to extract information. His skills would prove very valuable in the near future. Despite his sincere desire to become a martyr, he understood that God had a different plan for him.

Arredondo had expressed disappointment at being denied permission to take part, but Al-Taymiyyah understood it had been an act. Arredondo had no wish to take such risks, and there was no reason to make him. His importance came from the support he could give those who would take action, not by taking the actions themselves.

Al-Taymiyyah stopped pacing and turned toward the faithful, staring each of them in the eyes. They stared back, tense and ready, coiled springs ready to unleash their stored power at his command. Another minute had passed since he looked at the clock.

"My brothers," he said, in English, their only common language. "Are you prepared? Are your hearts pure, empty of everything other than the desire to carry out God's will?"

The men nodded, some of them whispering words of assent. Al-Taymiyyah had stressed to them the need to control their emotions, and they were doing so even now, minutes before the start of the operation. There were times to strike with fury, other times to strike with cunning and deliberation. For success, this operation required the latter.

"Today is the day, and the hour is nearly upon us," he continued. "As you go about your tasks today, I ask you to think of your families, your homelands, your faith. Has the enemy not attempted to destroy all three? Has anyone in this room been spared the brutality of the crusaders, has anyone not lost family to the guns and bombs of the infidels, the *kuffar*? Who here has not suffered for his faith?"

No hands rose. Even Arredondo stayed silent, even though everyone in the room knew his faith had cost him nothing.

"Today is your opportunity to take back what has been taken from you. To strike back at the enemy for their arrogance, their imperialism, their lack of respect for God and our prophet Mohammed, peace be upon him. This is a mission we cannot fail to undertake. Our wives, our children, our mothers and fathers all implore us to reclaim their stolen honor, to punish the enemy for invading our homes. For sending their filthy, whoring soldiers to the land our prophet claimed as Islam's homeland. The enemy must be humbled, must be made to quake at the power of the faithful."

The men in the room nodded with enthusiasm. A few said *Allahu akbar* quietly, heeding Al-Taymiyyah's extortions to keep their feelings under tight control.

"Hundreds of millions of faithful look to you today, my brothers. Hundreds of millions who have been beaten into near-defeat, near-submission at the hands of American criminals and thieves. Hundreds of millions injured and desperate but not defeated. Because they know, they know they can rely on you to lift them back into God's light. You can be their saviors, my brothers. You can reverse what has been done to them, you can make them victors standing over the broken bodies of the infidels. You can bring the pain of death to the Americans, and to the Jewish sons of pigs and dogs who control them."

The men nodded again, many of them glancing at the clock on the wall. They were supposed to be in the loading bay already, sending the first men to their targets. Al-Taymiyyah kept them a little longer, using their anxiety to coil the springs tighter.

"Today the fourth largest city of this filth-ridden country will feel the power of the faithful. Today we begin to restore the caliphate. For thousands of years, the faithful will know where the struggle to establish Islam over the West truly began, and who truly began it. Some of you will sleep tonight in your beds, feeling the warmth of your weapons and knowing you have done great things for God. And some among you, four of you, you special few will sleep tonight in the arms of the most beautiful virgins your minds can imagine, clothed in the finest robes, eating the most pleasing food, sleeping on the softest beds. Paradise awaits you four, my brothers. You have my respect, and my envy. I will join you there soon. But not now, not until God wills it."

Several of the men yelled *Allahu akbar!* now, unable to hold it in any longer. The four martyrs smiled but stayed quiet.

Looking at Rahim, Al-Taymiyyah said "When you reach paradise, my brothers, greet Mohibullah for me, for us all. Greet our first martyr, the young boy who became the man we all aspire to be."

Several of the men looked at Rahim, and two near him touched his arm. He smiled proudly at the special attention and honor Al-Taymiyyah was bestowing on his son.

"Strength, faith, and dedication, my brothers. Our missions will succeed today, if our hearts are pure. Please, brothers, stand and join me in a last farewell to the most fortunate among us. To our martyrs."

The men stood and gathered around the four martyrs, hugging them warmly and shaking their hands. As they did so, Al-Taymiyyah said loudly "Brothers, it is time! Allahu akbar!"

"Allahu akbar!" they roared back in unison, moving as one toward the loading bay. Al-Taymiyyah followed them silently. No more words were needed.

The men walked through to the loading bay, squeezing themselves around the four cars parked in two lines inside. The cars had been staged in a precise manner. Those of the first two martyrs were backed into the loading bay facing the door; when the door opened they could drive straight down the ramp toward Crosstimbers and the freeway. The cars of the second two martyrs were backed in behind the first two. The four chosen men were hugged and patted on their backs for nearly a full minute in the loading bay, proudly receiving kisses on the cheeks from others who would not follow them.

Only the chosen martyrs would leave now. The first two men in two cars would leave the mosque and head toward Highway 45 on Crosstimbers, turn north onto the highway and drive side by side in the heavy traffic until they reached the overpass above West Little York. There they would swerve and hit the cars next to them, then hit each other, creating an instant traffic jam. After that, it would be a simple matter to get out with their weapons and massacre the fat American cows who would do nothing but sit inside their cars, shriek in terror and beg for rescue but not lift a finger to defend themselves.

The second two martyrs in their two vehicles would leave seconds later, head to the other side of Highway 45 and make their way to the Northside mall. As the carnage on the highway unfolded, the two martyrs would park together near one of the mall entrances, then walk in and kill every American coward they saw.

Al-Taymiyyah believed his four martyrs would kill at least a hundred Americans in the two attacks. Police would flood the highway and mall in response. Some of the police would undoubtedly die too, hopefully dozens. But the four men would eventually be surrounded and killed, would receive the honor and glory of death for Allah. Police would ignore the rest of the city, focus everything on the mall and highway while raging at the deaths of their supposedly innocent citizens.

And exactly one hour after the first two attacks, twenty more believers, two men in each of ten cars, would leave the mosque and head into neighborhoods miles to the west. Neighborhoods that would be left totally uncovered by the police.

The believers would split apart and knock on doors at random houses or apartments. The residents inside would look through their peepholes and see nicely dressed men smiling in a friendly way, and would open their doors. And the nice young men would pull pistols and shoot them twice in the head, then calmly go back to their cars and drive away.

Al-Taymiyyah's instructions were clear: "Unless it is obviously a Muslim, whoever answers the door, whether man, woman or child, shoot them twice in the head and calmly leave. Do not run, do not yell, do not jump in your car and speed away. Then go back to your homes and park your cars where they cannot be seen from the street. God will ensure you are not caught."

Al-Taymiyyah's heart jumped at the thought of the attack's success. One hundred American pigs dead in the first attacks, twenty more in the second. A nation of frightened women who would be paralyzed with fear, refuse to travel highways or answer doors. Who would demand their pathetic government do something, anything, to make them feel safe. Pathetic, shameful creatures who would do nothing to defend themselves from future attacks, who would simply hide and pray to their false god for protection that would not come.

If only it were possible to kill more, he thought. Today the Americans would feel the barest taste of the pain inflicted by the Jews on the Palestinians, of the horror unleashed by the American military against the Iraqis and Afghans. Today they would be the horrified victim, as they deserved. As God demanded.

It pained Al-Taymiyyah to wait to conduct more attacks, but he could not squander all his assets in one day. The war would continue, there would be time for more strikes soon. The next strikes would be smaller in scale, but hopefully richer in rewards. The special item Arredondo had brought, combined with the Chechen's skill, could have a spectacular impact. The future held such promise.

One of the faithful hit the button that opened the loading bay door. The electric motor whirred, slowly raising the metal door, letting in the afternoon light. The four martyrs received their last hugs, sat in their cars and started the engines. One of them got back out for a moment, to give Al-Taymiyyah one last hug.

The man's AK was on the passenger seat with the sling hanging onto the driver's floorboard. The man accidentally snagged the sling with his foot when he got out of the car and pulled it off the seat. After hugging his *imam* for the last time, he lifted the AK and slid it back onto the passenger seat before sitting down behind the wheel.

East of the mosque, an unmarked black SWAT Taurus was parked next to an unmarked black Chevy Tahoe. They were at the edge of the grocery store parking lot, less than a hundred yards from the loading bay door. The Taurus' driver, Harlan Quarles, was bullshitting with Rafael Elizondo, in the front passenger seat of the Tahoe. So far they had bitched about the callout, bitched about the North patrol sergeant who had called them and bitched about the lack of a plan, but Quarles hoped there was something to this. SWAT officers want action as much as infantry soldiers do.

Henry Watson sat in the driver's seat of the Tahoe, occasionally throwing a comment into Quarles' and Elizondo's conversation. The two officers in the back seat of the Tahoe, Jason Erikson and Kent Parker, couldn't see anything and had fallen asleep from boredom.

Quarles asked, "How long you think this will go on? Think it'll be a good amount of overtime?"

"I hope so. I'm asking for comp time, I need time off more than I need money."

"Eyes front, guys," Watson said, lifting a pair of binoculars. "The bay door is opening."

Quarles quickly lifted his binos, looking into the crowded loading bay. It looked like a party was going on in there, with at least twenty men hugging and slapping each other on the back. Four cars were inside, facing outward from the bay.

The two snoozing officers in the back woke up as Watson reported, "Sam 117 to Sam 22, we have activity. The back bay door just opened. About twenty people in there milling around four cars."

"Clear. Let me know what else you got," English answered.

The hugs went on for about thirty seconds. Two men in black jackets opened the doors to the first two cars and got into the driver's seats. Quarles caught a glance of something olive drab on one of the men's chests as his jacket flopped open.

Quarles said to Elizondo, "I swear one of the two guys who just got into the cars had a green chest rig under his jacket."

"Did you see a chest rig?" Elizondo asked Watson.

"I don't think so, but those jackets look really fucking big to me," Watson responded.

145

The driver of one of the cars got back out and gave an emotional embrace to a tall man in dress pants and dress shirt. Quarles said, "That guy right there! Look real close, his jacket is open and he's got something green under there. It looked like one of those shitty Chinese AK rigs."

"I don't see it," Watson said, looking through his binos. Quarles picked up his radio and called English. "Sam 162 to Sam 22, two guys are loading up in two cars and getting ready to take off. What do you want us to do?"

"Can you read the plates?" English asked.

The man who had gotten out of the car started to get back in, then reached down and moved something. He lifted an object briefly before getting back into the driver's seat. "What was that he just picked up?" Quarles asked.

Watson jerked forward, almost hitting the windshield with the binos.

"Oh, shit," Watson blurted. "Something really fucking bad is about to happen. He's got an AK."

CHAPTER 9

"Say again!" English yelled into the radio. "Did you say one of the drivers has an AK?"

"Clear. They probably both do," Watson answered.

"Shit! Are they leaving?"

"They're rolling, right now."

The first two cars rolled down the ramp. At the bottom of the ramp they veered to their left, toward Crosstimbers.

"They're at the exit to Crosstimbers now," Watson said.

"Which way are they going?"

"Their turn signals are on to go east. What do you want us to do? We need to know, quick."

English cursed his options. He had one vehicle with four officers next to another vehicle with a single officer, watching the two suspect vehicles. None of the other vehicles could leave where they were to follow the two cars; traffic was too heavy, the only officers who could get on them and stay on them were the officers watching the bay door. And he had to leave one of those units in place.

If he sent the four officers in the Tahoe, that left one SWAT officer to watch the bay door. One man with no backup, against who knew how many people up to who knew what. But if he sent the one officer alone, that officer could find himself facing two nut jobs with AK-47s. And if the suspect cars immediately split up, then what would SWAT do?

"Quarles, you go after the two cars," English said. "I want you to hang back a little and get some patrol units to make stops on those cars. Got that?"

"Moving now," Quarles said. "The cars are leaving the parking lot heading east."

"Clear. Don't get hurt, Harlan."

"I'm bulletproof Captain, it's all good," Quarles responded, rushing to catch the two cars. He turned onto Crosstimbers just after three other vehicles passed, getting between him and the two suspects. Quarles punched it to catch up.

———·———

They all saw it. The cheering and waving abruptly stopped. The *imam* lowered his hand, watching the black Taurus with dark tinted windows jump from its spot and speed out of the grocery store parking lot. The martyrs' cars were quickly lost in the traffic, the black Taurus disappearing after them. Next to the spot where the Taurus had been parked, a black SUV sat with its nose pointed at them. Al-Taymiyyah couldn't see through the vehicle's windshield, but it looked new and very clean, like the black car had been. Al-Taymiyyah motioned to the Chechen to come to him, and reached for a radio. The Chechen put it in his hand.

The four martyrs had small personal radios, with a range of a mile or two, just to communicate with their partners. The martyrs had been prohibited from carrying mobile phones to the attacks, ensuring they would leave no electronic traces of their communication to each other.

"Brothers, look into your mirrors," Al-Taymiyyah said into the radio. "You are being followed."

A few seconds later a response came back, the speaker carefully avoiding the use of any names. "I see several cars, my brother. Which one is it?"

"The black one, the new-looking Ford. It looks like a police car. Do you see it?"

A few moments passed. "I see it. Shall we adjust our plan?"

Al-Taymiyyah considered the options. But the answer was obvious: he shouldn't alter the plan. God would do whatever was needed to ensure the mission's success.

"No. Do not adjust the plan. When the time to act arrives, make those following you your first target. Hit them quickly, before they can react. Do you understand?"

"Yes brother, I understand," the martyr said, his voice now garbled from the distance. "The blessings of God are upon us, these *kuffar* cannot stop the faithful."

Al-Taymiyyah didn't respond. He looked at his followers, searching for the face he trusted more than any other.

"You," he said, to the Chechen. "Go to the roof, search for any more of the enemy who are watching. Hurry." Behind him, the second two martyrs sat uncertainly in their cars. They had heard the radio traffic. Both had their cars in drive and feet on the brakes, waiting for the order to move.

Al-Taymiyyah turned and looked at them, then looked out from the loading bay. He was almost certain he should send the second two martyrs. Almost. He wasn't sure the black car truly was following the first martyrs. And he had no reason to think the SUV was enemy, other than his instinct.

Both cars could be full of enemies. Maybe. But he could send the second two martyrs anyway, with the same instructions he had given the first. Carry out God's will, make anyone following you the first to die.

And he couldn't stop what had been set in motion, not now. The operation would go forward, whether the next two martyrs were committed or not. There was no reason to hold the second two men back from their mission, to rob them of their destined paradise.

Al-Taymiyyah turned abruptly and faced the two men, motioning them toward the parking lot.

"Go! Carry out God's will!"

The two men smiled broadly and rolled out of the loading bay. One of them reached out his window to shake hands with two men as he drove past. Tonight he would be in paradise.

As they hit the bottom of the ramp and veered toward Crosstimbers, the black SUV jumped from its spot and accelerated toward them.

"Captain, the other two cars are rolling," Watson said into the radio.

"Were the drivers of those two cars armed also?" English asked.

"Don't know, but they both had big jackets like the first two. Probably armed," Watson answered.

Fuck! English was out of options. If he sent Watson's Tahoe after the two cars, the back of the mosque would be uncovered. And he had to keep it covered, now that they were almost certain something was going on in there.

He didn't like the obvious answer: his officers had to take the two cars down in the back parking lot of the mosque, right in front of everyone in the loading bay. If they didn't, they'd have at least four suspects armed with AKs in four separate cars going to maybe four separate locations. And they'd still have to deal whatever might happen at the mosque.

English needed patrol to back up his officers. SWAT officers with bulky rifle-protective body armor and carbines couldn't go hands on with suspects as easily as patrol officers could. But as far as English knew, the situation unfolding at the mosque was known only to SWAT, some of the department command downtown, and the few officers at the murder scene on Hanley.

"Watson, take the two cars down in the parking lot," English said. "And keep an eye on those fucks in the loading bay. I'm calling North patrol to get patrol officers out here. Moreno, you and Guthrie back them up."

"Watson clear."

Edward Moreno keyed the mike to say quickly "Moreno clear." English heard the car's engine racing in the background as Moreno and Shelton Guthrie sped out of their parking space in the shopping center south of the mosque.

———

Watson shot forward from his parking space and cut off the two vehicles before they hit Crosstimbers. His carbine was laid across his lap but his responsibility right now was just to drive, to block the suspects before they could haul ass. In the back seat Erikson and Parker lifted their carbines to their chests with the muzzles pointing out the window. Elizondo lifted his muzzle to eye level, prepared to either thrust it out the window or jam it against the windshield and fire through the glass. To their left, Moreno's Taurus weaved through the shopping center parking lot, making its way to the back of the mosque.

The two martyrs saw them coming, in fact had already been watching the Tahoe before it moved. The first instinct of the martyr in the lead vehicle was to charge out of the parking lot. He was picking up his radio when the *imam* called out an order, making them both jam on the brakes before they reached the exit.

———

Al-Taymiyyah was furious. He had already suspected the Tahoe was a police vehicle. Now he was watching it fly toward his two martyrs, and knew what would come next. The martyrs would be arrested or killed, the mosque entered and searched. Al-Taymiyyah had to face the inescapable truth; they had been betrayed, their plot discovered. It would be no use to tell the martyrs to run, to try to get to their target. The police would follow them, would probably be waiting for them at the mall when they arrived. The twenty believers prepared to carry out the third part of the attack would be unable to do it now, they couldn't leave the mosque if it was under surveillance.

Yussuf. God damn him, he had to be the cause of the failure. The plan had been so perfect, its execution promised to be flawless. It could not have gone wrong so quickly, not without an enormous betrayal of the faithful. So much effort had gone into the preparation, so much time, so much dedication and faith. Why was God allowing them to fail now, when their plan was already in motion, when they were so close to doing his own work?

The realization dropped onto Al-Taymiyyah from heaven. God was not leading them to failure, he was giving them a wonderful opportunity. Martyrdom would not only be the reward of the four chosen believers, it would be the reward for them all.

In a flash he put the radio to his lips and keyed the microphone. His eyes were wide and his heart pounding as he yelled his orders to the two men, the men who would be the first to draw the blood of the unfaithful that day.

"Kill them! Kill the *kuffar!* God be with you!"

———

The two cars abruptly stopped, one behind the other, less than ten feet from the exit to Crosstimbers. The driver of the lead vehicle lunged toward his weapon, struggling to get the rifle into firing position. The Tahoe was coming from his right side, creating an awkward angle for him. He pulled the stock into the center of his chest, straining to get his left arm onto the wooden foregrip to steady his aim. He reached to the right side of the receiver to flip the safety downward.

The front passenger side window exploded as Erikson put seven rounds through it, into the driver's head and upper torso. The driver felt a tremendous impact to his face as part of his upper jaw burst apart, followed an instant later by intensely hot pinpricks on the right side of his rib cage. By the time his body flopped against the driver's door he was dead. His car began rolling slowly forward as his foot went limp on the brake. The man's body shuddered slightly as Watson put two more shots into his chest.

The driver of the second vehicle threw his door open and fell onto the pavement, dragging his rifle behind him. The officers in the Tahoe lost sight of him until he popped up from the side of his car, sprinting toward the loading bay door and holding his rifle by the magazine. Erikson put the red dot of his holographic sight onto the running suspect. Police aren't supposed to shoot at fleeing felons unless they present a threat to an officer or other innocent person; Erikson had seconds to decide whether or not to shoot at the running man.

One of the men inside the loading bay made the decision for him. He drew a pistol and fired wildly toward the Tahoe. Watson and Erikson ducked. On the passenger side of the Tahoe Elizondo and Kent Parker bailed out and went toward the wheels, looking for ballistic cover. Watson spotted the shooter first, at the left edge of the bay doorway, standing next to a thick wall that could stop rifle rounds. He wasn't using the wall for cover like a trained person would. Behind him most of the other men were sprinting toward a single door out of the loading bay.

Watson opened up on the shooter. He hit the wall with his first two shots and shifted right. One round tore through the man's thigh. The man half fell, half jumped behind cover.

The driver of the second vehicle running toward the bay made an unbelievably stupid mistake. He raised his weapon and turned his upper body to fire on the Tahoe behind him. Erikson centered his dot on the man's back and pulled the trigger. The man's weapon fell to the pavement. His momentum carried him far enough to drop him onto his face in a bloody pile at the foot of the loading bay ramp.

Tires screeched on Crosstimbers as cars slammed on their brakes and swerved away from the noise of gunfire. Erikson kept his weapon on the dead man lying and Watson kept his weapon trained on the area where the pistol shooter had been, making sure he didn't pop back into view and open fire again.

The *imam* watched from the right edge of the loading bay. He had seen the horrified look on the martyr's face as bullets punched through his back and burst from his chest, pulling gobs of blood and flecks of tissue with them. Another faithful innocent, another devout Muslim murdered by the infidels for his beliefs. Al-Taymiyyah trusted that God would allow him into paradise, even though he had not killed any *kuffar* that day.

Al-Taymiyyah screamed, "Close the loading bay door!"

The motor whirred and the door began to descend. Officer Moreno yelled "Shots fired by the loading bay!" as he rolled to a stop.

"What's going on?" English shouted into his radio. "Is anyone hit?"

"Hey!" Elizondo yelled at Watson and Erikson. "Are you guys okay? Are you hit?"

They yelled back "We're good!" without moving their heads or weapons, keeping the bay covered as the door closed. Elizondo keyed his radio. "We're all good, two suspects down and no officers hit. One suspect inside the mosque shot at us, the bay door is closed now. That's all we got."

"Clear. Back your vehicles away," English replied. "Don't worry about the DOA's, we'll handle them when patrol gets here. Right now it's a barricaded suspect scene. Copy?"

Elizondo and Moreno acknowledged. Officers and vehicles bounded back to cover. Elizondo set up behind an old truck and Parker tucked in behind a dumpster.

"Sam 117 to Sam 22, we're set in decent positions," Watson said on the radio. "We'll have to come up with something better if they have AKs inside, but for now we're alright."

A head appeared above the edge of the roof. Not a complete head, just a face from the eyes up. The head was visible for no more than two seconds, then dropped out of sight.

"We have someone on the roof, east side of the mosque. Didn't see a weapon," Parker said into his radio.

Seconds later Guthrie keyed up. "I just saw him too, head came up for a couple seconds."

"Clear," English answered. "I saw him too. Keep an eye on the roof." Then he called Quarles, the officer following the first two cars. "Sam 162, what's your location?"

———

Quarles had done his best to stay back from the two cars, but with the heavy traffic on Crosstimbers he had to get almost on their bumpers to make sure he didn't lose them. He hoped the one car between them was enough to keep them from getting suspicious.

Quarles was less than a mile from the mosque when He heard the traffic between Watson and Captain English. He felt a little let down. Watson and his guys would take their suspects down right there while Quarles was stuck following these other two cars. And even if he called patrol to stop them he would probably only have a backup role in the arrests. It was frustrating. He wanted to put hands on them himself.

He was too far away to hear the gunfire, but when he heard Moreno scream "Shots fired!", his heart sank. He had missed what must have been a close range shootout with possible terrorists. He wasn't worried about the officers. He couldn't believe his friends would be hurt. They were too well trained and too smart. He knew no officers were down before Elizondo said no officers were down.

He flipped the radio to North station's channel. He needed to get patrol on these two fast, before they split up and he lost one of them. He hoped these drivers also wanted to shoot it out, because he knew what the outcome would be. Two more dead suspects, no officers hurt.

"Sam 162 to North patrol dispatch."

"Sam 162, go ahead."

"I'm eastbound on Crosstimbers, following two suspect vehicles that just left Crosstimbers and Shepherd. Other officers were just in a shooting with two other suspects from this same group at that intersection. You copy?"

The dispatcher answered with obvious surprise. "Sam 162, this is the first I've heard of it. Are any officers hurt?"

"Negative, two suspects down and no officers hurt," Quarles said, as the car between him and the second suspect vehicle changed lanes. He pulled up closer, to discourage anyone from getting between him and the suspect vehicles. The driver of the car in front of him was talking on what looked like a phone, maybe receiving instructions from someone.

"Don't send any patrol units to Shepherd and Crosstimbers yet. Sam 22 is on the scene and will let you know when he needs them. Right now I need patrol units with me to stop two vehicles eastbound on Crosstimbers. The drivers are probably armed with AK-47s."

"Sam 162 clear, what's your cross street?"

"We're a little east of Shepherd. I'm not familiar with this area, let me get you that cross street."

Quarles turned his head to the side, trying to read the small side street signs. He passed two before he was able to read *N. Ingleside.* He keyed the mike and turned his eyes forward again.

"Sam 162 to North dispatch, cross str....*oh shit!*"

The driver of the second vehicle was turned in his seat, holding an AK with one hand and pointing it at Quarles.

Quarles dropped the mike and jerked the wheel left. Rounds blew out the back window of the suspect vehicle, punched into the Taurus' hood and traveled through the dash into the cab. Quarles gripped the Glock in his thigh holster. A bullet tore through his lower right arm, breaking both forearm bones and nearly tearing his arm apart below the elbow. He screamed as another round blasted through the windshield and hit just under the lip of the heavy ceramic plate in his chest armor. The impact broke one of his ribs and almost knocked him unconscious.

Quarles thought he had been shot through the chest. He reflexively reached up to protect himself with his right arm. His forearm just flopped at the elbow, spraying blood all over him and the front seats.

He made a hard left and floored the accelerator, bouncing over the median into oncoming traffic. He heard the last few shots the driver fired at him, shots that missed. Cars slid to a halt as he rocked and fishtailed across their lanes, stopping when his front tires banged into the curb. He groped for the door handle with his left hand. The door popped open and he fell hard onto the pavement, pushing away from the car he thought was still being shot at.

Cars in the westbound lanes honked as he clawed his way onto the sidewalk, desperately trying to get away from his car. Barely conscious, he got to his feet and took two steps before tripping over a trash can next to a bus stop. He landed on his mangled arm and screamed as unimaginable pain shot through his body.

He knew the bleeding was probably bad enough to hill him within minutes. He needed to get his tourniquet off his body armor and onto his arm quickly, or he would die. But he was still being shot at. He had to get to cover before he could worry about anything else.

He couldn't see. His vision blurred, he couldn't make out anything other than the bus stop next to him. He didn't know where the nearest cover was. He couldn't even recognize his car anymore. He wiped his eyes, managing only to smear blood into them. He had to get to his feet and move somewhere, anywhere. He couldn't stay in the open.

He tried to get up again. Hands forced him back down. He panicked. The two men in the cars were on him already, and he couldn't see them. He screamed and reached for the holster on his right thigh with his left hand. Hands pulled it away. He went for his combat knife on his body armor. A hand jerked his fingers from the knife.

Quarles screamed again. He felt arms on him and tried to push them away. He felt so tired, so weak. He couldn't move the arms, they were holding him down now. His scream weakened, the sound dwindling and useless. He swallowed and breathed in hard, trying to suck energy into his body. He had to fight back, to get these people off of him. He couldn't just give up and die.

The terrorists holding him down yelled back. Their words took a few seconds to penetrate the haze.

"Damn it officer, stop fighting me! I'm trying to help you! You're bleeding, bad!"

In his earpiece, Quarles heard his captain ask *Quarles, where are you?*

Quarles got it. Nobody was shooting. A citizen was helping him, the suspects had to be gone. He whispered to the voice above him, "...radio...tell them on the radio...I need help."

"Which radio?" the voice asked. "This one? This one that's on you, or the one in the car?"

Quarles tried to force a complete thought through his head. The radio that was on him had a throat microphone and a small transmit button on a wire. He reached for the transmit button. It wasn't there, he couldn't find it. He whispered, "...the car...get in the car."

"Okay, I'll be right back." The man let go. Quarles couldn't see him, couldn't tell where he was anymore. A few seconds later he heard someone yelling, "Hello, hello? There's a cop shot on Crosstimbers in front of the Beverly Place apartments! Hello? Can anyone hear me? Hello?"

Quarles reached for the tourniquet on his body armor, tried to grip the nylon band sticking out from his left shoulder strap. His fingers slipped off. He tried again. He couldn't feel the strap anymore. He tried one last time. By the time the stranger returned from the car to say, "I don't think the radio works, there were no lights on it or anything," Quarles was unconscious in a spreading pool of blood, his motionless fingers less than an inch from the tourniquet.

———

Nunez heard the radio call from Sam 162 and swore out loud. Two suspects had just been shot at the mosque, two more were rolling east on Crosstimbers. And Nunez was stuck behind traffic crawling south on the freeway.

It had taken him forever just to get through the heavy northbound traffic on the service road to the turnaround and head south. Then the southbound traffic which he expected to be light wound up being heavy and slow. He was taking way too long. It had only been a few minutes since he talked to the SWAT captain, and things were already breaking loose at the mosque. He turned his radio up, waiting for the SWAT officer following the suspects on Crosstimbers to give them a cross street.

Nunez weaved left onto the narrow shoulder to pass the traffic and turned on his lights and siren. The shoulder was barely wide enough for his car, he couldn't just go flying past other cars without risking a sideswipe. A lot of the cars in front of him wouldn't hear the siren at all, especially if they had their stereos blaring. And even if they did hear the siren, cars locked in bumper to bumper traffic didn't have anywhere to go anyway.

It was going to take a while to get to either the mosque or the SWAT officer on Crosstimbers. Crosstimbers was way south, almost to Loop 610, the highway that circled the downtown area. There was no way Nunez would be first to back up the SWAT officer.

Up ahead Nunez saw a minor accident. Two drivers were stopped in the fast lane talking on cell phones…on the other side of the highway. The traffic backed up on the southbound side was caused by dipshits slowing down to look at the accident on the other side of the freeway. Fucking Houston drivers.

The radio blared, "Sam 162 to North dispatch, cross str….*oh shit!*"

Nunez jerked upright in his seat. The dispatcher quickly responded, "Sam 162, what's your location and status? Sam 162, talk to me."

No response. The *oh shit* could mean the SWAT officer just wrecked, or had a near wreck. Or just got shot at.

The dispatcher called again. Still no response. Patrol officers got on the radio to tell dispatch they'd check all of Crosstimbers west of the freeway. Nunez wished he had SWAT's frequency on his radio so he could find out if they had any more information from their officer.

Traffic in front of Nunez opened up as he passed the minor wreck on the northbound side. He swerved off the shoulder into the fast lane and sped up, just as Captain English jumped onto North's channel.

"Sam 22 to North dispatch, emergency traffic."

"North dispatch to Sam 22, go ahead."

"We just had shots fired at Shepherd and Crosstimbers," English said, his voice calm. "No officers hurt, two suspects DOA. There's at least one more suspect inside a warehouse at the intersection who shot at officers. I need patrol units out here, but they need to stage away from the intersection and let me tell them where to go. Copy?"

"Sam 22, I copy. Do you have communication with Sam 162?"

"Negative, I was about to ask you the same thing," English said.

"Sam 22, he just called us and said he was following two vehicles from that intersection, then he said…then his traffic was cut off. It sounded like something happened."

"That's clear," English said. "We can't reach him either. This scene is under control, I need you to send patrol units to check by with him first. We'll try to get him on the cell phone, I'll let you know."

"That's clear. Patrol units are already on the way."

"Good. I'll keep monitoring this channel," English said. His voice was still controlled, but anyone who knew how cops sound under stress could hear the concern behind the calm.

Ahead of Nunez was West Mount Houston Road. Traffic on the freeway was still heavy but not terrible. Cars ahead took their time getting out of his way, but if he got right on their asses and hit the air horn they would eventually move over. By forcing his way through he could make it to Crosstimbers in less than ten minutes.

Dispatch came back on the radio in a breathless rush. "All units, we're receiving calls reporting shots fired and an officer down at Crosstimbers and Ingleside! Assist the officer at Crosstimbers and Ingleside!"

———

The Chechen ran downstairs to the main floor, excited but calm as he searched for the *imam*. He found him and others gathered around two men lying on the floor in the open prayer area. One screamed and clutched his thigh, trying to stop the blood spurting from between his fingers. The other had a single bullet hole just below the solar plexus, shot as he ran behind the man with the leg wound. There wasn't much blood, but the Chechen could tell the man was dead.

"*Imam*," the Chechen said. "There are more of the black cars, on all sides of our mosque. The *kuffar* have surrounded us."

Al-Taymiyyah looked down at the two young men side by side on the floor. One dead, one soon to be. Four of the faithful murdered, without having destroyed a single *kuffar*. He prayed that the first two martyrs had begun their mission on the highway. But he could not count on the martyrs alone to do God's work that day. God demanded they join in the struggle, that they fight unto death and destroy as many *kuffar* as possible before they died. The infidels held so many advantages now, but the believers held what the infidels did not. They held faith, in the one true God, and such faith could not be defeated.

He looked the Chechen in his dark eyes, admiring the serious look on the man's face, the long dark beard, the honor, courage and faith the man possessed. Al-Taymiyyah was an educated, faithful man, but he was not a military leader. He had fought apostates who claimed to be true Muslims, but he had never fought the *kuffar* like the Chechen had. Al-Taymiyyah led the believers spiritually, but he could not lead them militarily. The fight that was to follow would be commanded by the Chechen.

"My brother," he said, gently placing his hand on the man's shoulder. "You are the bearer of special gifts, of talents and abilities I do not possess. I place my faith and belief in you, to command the faithful in this struggle. They are yours. Lead them to victory, and to paradise."

The Chechen took Al-Taymiyyah's hand. He looked back at him, then said simply, *"Allahu akbar."*

"Allahu akbar, brother."

The Chechen let go and stepped into the crowd around the two gunshot men. He grabbed men by the arms and shoulders.

"Brothers, come with me!"

Not all followed. Some pretended not to hear, some started to follow but turned back. By the time the Chechen reached the stairwell and turned around, only eight of the fourteen men he had ordered to follow were behind him.

He was surprised to see Arredondo still with him. But about the others who had not followed, the Chechen didn't care. He didn't want anyone who wasn't committed to a fight.

He led them down the stairs, into the hallway on the lower level. The second door on the right side of the hallway was the only locked room, secured by a hasp with a combination padlock. He and Al-Taymiyyah were the only two in the mosque who knew the combination. He opened the door, told the eight men to wait in the hallway and turned on the light in the small room. AK-47 rifles in racks lined the walls. He handed them to the waiting men.

When he had given each a weapon and a handful of magazines, he picked up his personal weapon. His Romanian PSL sniper rifle was a close copy of the Dragunov he had become expert with during both huge battles for Grozny, Chechnya's capital, when he was just a teenager. He had taken the PSL to the range many times, zeroed it at 200 yards and never bothered to fire it at any longer distance. In Grozny he had killed scores of Russian soldiers with his Dragunov at less than 200 yards. He had killed several more up close, prisoners he tortured and beheaded with a knife.

From the roof he would be able to kill many of the police; the stupid fools were sitting in the open, exposing much of their bodies or sitting still in their cars. He knew the men in the black cars were the enemy, and thought he had seen many more cars like theirs in different spots around the mosque. He would kill the people in those cars as well, just to be sure. If they weren't police, it made no difference to him.

He slung the rifle across his back, grabbed seven ten-round magazines and stuck them into his pants and jacket pockets. Then he grabbed the big rounds for the other weapon, the special one Arredondo brought from the Mexican border. He handed all the big rounds but one to the men in the hallway, inserted the last round into the weapon and strode purposefully from the room. The other men fell in behind him as he started back up the stairs to the roof. He made a mental count of the men as he walked, then turned around to look at them again.

Arredondo wasn't there. He hadn't gone into the weapons room, so he must have walked into one of the other unlocked rooms in the hallway.

Coward, the Chechen thought. The *imam* had been wrong to trust anyone who had been raised in the west, as a Christian. When the Chechen arrived in paradise, he wouldn't be surprised if he discovered Arredondo had betrayed them.

When they reached the door to the roof, he turned and faced the men behind him. They were terrified. He knew they were not warriors, they were not well trained or experienced. Over the past months he had taught them the basics of marksmanship, although he didn't trust any to hit a target further than a hundred yards away. That made no difference either. As long as the men could spray rounds toward the police, they would do what he needed them to do: keep the enemies' heads down so he could kill them, one at a time with the rifle and handfuls at a time with the other weapon.

"Listen to me," the Chechen said to the wide-eyed young men. "Do exactly as I say. When we walk onto the roof, spread out and stay very low. Make sure there is at least one of you on each wall, and two of you on the wall above the loading bay. Everybody outside the mosque is enemy. If you shoot someone who is not a police, it does not matter. Kill anyone you can see. But do not raise your heads until I tell you to do so. I will fire the first shot. Do you understand?"

The men nodded nervously, murmuring empty words of agreement. The Chechen did not think they really understood what he wanted from them, and did not expect them to perform well in the following minutes. He didn't expect many to be alive after the first hour of fighting. He trusted that Allah would provide worthy replacements from the rest of the believers inside the mosque. They would find the courage and strength to join the battle before the *kuffar* forced their way into the holy mosque and murdered them all.

The Chechen opened the door to the roof. The door was set halfway below roof level, so the men had to climb a half flight of steps to get onto the flat roof. They mimicked the Chechen's crabwalk, staying below the edge of the low wall. The Chechen moved east first, looking through one of the small apertures that were spaced evenly along the entire wall. The apertures were only the size of one brick, large enough to stick a rifle barrel through but not big enough to use the sights. The Chechen would only use the rectangular openings to view the areas around the mosque, not to shoot from.

He looked out of one of the openings to the east. He saw the Tahoe, and two heads sticking up from vehicles on its sides. He popped his head above the wall briefly, getting another look east. After another second of searching he saw another enemy, taking cover behind a dumpster. He hadn't seen that one when he had run to the roof before.

He ducked back down. He wouldn't be able to begin the attack from the east side, it was too well covered. He saw that the other seven men had done as he told them, spreading out to all sides of the roof. He scuttled to the west side, popping his head up to look across the intersection. Two black cars were still parked there, one behind the other facing the mosque. The distance to the first car was no more than seventy-five yards, an easy shot. He ducked back down, pulled the sniper rifle off his back and laid it against the wall, ready for use.

He had learned in Grozny to initiate an ambush with the most powerful weapon he and his fighters had. There was no reason to open fire with a pistol when his men could destroy a tank with a mine in the first second of the attack. He checked the special weapon again, ensuring it was ready to fire. Then he yelled to the men on the wall, "After I fire, find targets and shoot until I tell you to stop! Do not waste all your ammunition! *Allahu akbar!*"

The men shouted back in unison, *"Allahu akbar!"* with fists raised. The Chechen smiled. Maybe they would prove themselves to be worthy warriors for God after all.

He moved sideways ten feet from where he had just stuck his head up, swung the special weapon over his shoulder, quickly rose to his knees and aimed in on the first black vehicle across the street.

Karl Rivera sat in his car on Crosstimbers in front of Captain English, looking east across Shepherd toward the mosque. He didn't like sitting still, especially inside a vehicle. But English ordered them to maintain positions until patrol arrived, then SWAT would pull off and get organized. The people in the mosque apparently hadn't "made" all their cars, hadn't recognized who and where all the police were. Watson's Tahoe and Moreno's Taurus had been made, but hopefully the rest of the cars weren't.

Civilians around the mosque hadn't reacted much to the gunfire behind the mosque. The stopped traffic on Shepherd hadn't been affected at all. The suspects died out of view and the mosque blocked some of the sound. A few drivers on Crosstimbers right next to the mosque had freaked a little, but within seconds drivers who had witnessed the shooting were far down the road, and the drivers that passed them right afterward had no idea what had happened. Those who saw the shot-up car in the parking lot, or the dead man and AK, either didn't believe what they saw or were smart enough to accelerate away. Several people who had been in the grocery store or shopping center parking lots had run back inside when the firing started, but a few people were walking around now. Some people refused to believe they had seen and heard what they had just seen and heard.

Rivera wished they could shut the intersection down and get all the civilians out of the area. But there was no way to do it until tons of patrol officers showed up. And even then, the patrolmen would have to set up well away from the mosque, leaving side streets uncovered that unsuspecting civilians would use to get right back into the danger area. It would take a lot of officers to block off every possible side street around the mosque, and the traffic jam they'd cause would make it harder for SWAT to get into the area.

Rivera saw a black dot pop up from the roof, then drop back down. He raised his mike, but English was already on it.

"Sam 22 to all units, someone's on the roof again, west side of the mosque. Still don't see a weapon."

Rivera picked up his binoculars, looking to the spot where the head had appeared. Several seconds later the head came up again. It wasn't where he expected it to be, this time it was barely within the view of his binoculars to the right. The head came all the way up along with some of the man's upper body. Something long and dark was on the man's right shoulder, pointing toward him.

Rivera's eyes widened and his heart rate doubled as adrenaline flooded his body. He dropped his binoculars and popped the door, scrambling to get out. English was on the radio yelling "He's got a rifle! He's got a rifle!" as Rivera lurched halfway onto the street.

A tremendous explosion blasted from the roof. Less than a second later Rivera's body was blown to pieces by the detonation of a Rocket Propelled Grenade on the hood of his car, just forward of the windshield.

———

English ducked as Rivera's car exploded, blasting debris in all directions. When he jerked his head back up he saw something semi-human in form, blackened and hanging out of the driver's door, small flames visible on it in the settling dust.

He threw his car into reverse and hit the gas without looking in his rear view mirror. Gunfire rattled across the street. On the radio someone screamed "RPG! RPG!" as English shot backward as fast as he could.

He hopped the curb on his right, smashed into a truck in someone's driveway, threw his door open and rolled out. Furious gunfire sounded above screeching tires and *bangs* of cars crashing into each other on Shepherd. He reached into the door to grab his carbine and sprinted around the back of his car. Rounds zipped through tree branches over his head. He charged toward the front of the nearest house and moved toward the mosque.

More gunfire rang out, what sounded like ten rifles firing from the roof. He heard the sound of other rifles firing, from his officers on the ground. As he reached the front of the house nearest the mosque he heard panicked screaming. Drivers who had abandoned their cars ran from the intersection west down Crosstimbers. Rounds kicked up asphalt around them and they almost trampled Rivera's smoking corpse.

English yelled "Get over here! Get the fuck out of the middle of the street!"

A few heard him and changed direction, most heard nothing but gunfire and their own screams. Those who stayed in the street were bunched up when the rifle bullets found them. The rounds punched two women lifeless to the street and blew a man's head halfway off. The man staggered a few steps, dropped to his knees and grabbed the gaping, ragged space where the right side of his skull had been, then toppled over without a sound. English stared in horror and keyed his radio.

"Fire on the god damn roof! They're killing civilians!"

Watson answered back, gunfire loud in the background. "We're firing on the fucking roof, we've got multiple suspects with AKs firing down at us! There's civilians down all over the place! Were those explosions RPGs or what?"

"It was an RPG! It took out Rivera!" English yelled, trying like hell to stay calm. "Stay behind cover and put fire on the roof, I'm switching to North to get some backup out here!"

English turned his radio knob to North's channel. The civilians who had run toward him crowded around, some crying hysterically and grabbing him as they pleaded for help. He shoved one sobbing man roughly to the west.

165

"Go that way, stay close to the fucking houses! Keep running until you find someone to let you in!"

He looked through the brush onto Shepherd. Dozens of cars were stopped and at least ten people were down in the street. Most looked dead, but a few clutched wounds and screamed in pain and terror. English keyed his radio, panting and out of breath. He needed patrol units, helicopters, ambulances, everything. And he needed them fast, before this massacre got worse than it already was.

———

"Bring your car next to mine," the older of the two martyrs ordered over the radio. "Keep it exactly in that spot until we are ready to begin the battle."

"I understand."

The younger man accelerated and swerved into the lane to the older man's right, pulling his car even. They occupied the middle two lanes now, with their target overpass only minutes away. The younger man had been worried that someone would take notice of his shattered back window, but he had not received so much as a second look. They had seen several police cars speeding south on the other side of the highway, but nothing on the northbound side.

They passed Tidwell road. Little York was two overpasses away, the time almost upon them. The older man keyed his radio again, saying "Watch me, brother. When I hit the car next to mine, you do the same."

"I understand. Peace be upon you, brother."

"Peace be upon us both."

They passed Parker road. Little York was ahead, they were near the base of the overpass. The older man men slowed to well below the speed limit and the younger one immediately followed his lead, making cars behind them honk and drive up close to their back bumpers. The martyrs looked to their weapons, felt for their magazines, made sure everything was where it should be.

They began to ascend the overpass. Only seconds left.

As the crest leveled below their wheels the older man suddenly jerked his steering wheel hard left, striking a Ford F-250 in the fast lane. The younger man immediately mirrored the move, swerving hard right to hit a minivan. Both vehicles that had been hit slammed on their brakes. The truck fishtailed and screeched to a halt in the fast lane, the minivan pulled partway onto the right shoulder. Several small accidents occurred as other cars swerved and slid behind them, trying to avoid smashing into the stopped vehicles.

The two martyrs rolled a short distance forward, then the older man swerved hard left again and then back to the right, stopping his car in a position to block the two left lanes. The younger man did the same, stopping with the bumper of his car almost touching the bumper of the older man's car. Within seconds the traffic jam behind them was hundreds of yards long, within a minute it would be over a mile. All the lanes were blocked except the far right lane, which cars could still crawl through.

Drivers got out cursing and slamming doors, about to get into the faces of the dipshits who had been texting or reading behind the wheel, or who just flat out couldn't drive. Several reached for their insurance cards or cell phones before getting out, dialing spouses, lawyers or the police.

The older man got out of his car, his movements slow and deliberate. The younger man did the same, ignoring the shouted insults from other drivers, waiting until the older man reached into his car for his rifle before grabbing his own weapon.

When the two martyrs stood with their rifles, everyone around them simply stopped talking and moving. A group of people stood silently, looking at two men holding AK-47s. Nobody moved. Nobody seemed to believe what was about to happen, even though they were looking right at it. They got out of their cars thinking "car accident", and suddenly were faced with this. It just didn't fit, their minds couldn't immediately grasp it.

The driver of the F-250 was a twenty-two year old girl whose boyfriend was a country boy. She was driving his truck. Her boyfriend had a lot of guns. When they started dating he took her shooting, showing her what he liked to do on weekends. She enjoyed shooting, which surprised her, considering her city-girl, urban liberal upbringing. She had enjoyed firing his AR-15 and AK-47. She knew what those rifles could do to beer cans, water jugs and deer. She had a good idea of what an AK-47 would do to a person.

Without a word she turned and sprinted south away from the two men. She

167

cut between cars just as the older man jerked his rifle to his shoulder and opened fire. Rounds blasted through her boyfriend's truck, riddled the car behind her and killed its driver but missed her. She kept running as hard as she could, not looking back, not screaming. Behind her two voices bellowed *"ALLAHU AKBAR!"*

The other drivers at the head of the traffic jam fled, screaming as they desperately lunged for cover. The minivan's driver had her three children inside, and made a valiant effort to get back into the driver's seat to drive them away. The younger man shot her twice in the back just as she got the driver's door open. As she sunk to the ground he fired another five rounds through the van's passenger compartment. Then he stepped between the lanes and fired at everyone he saw.

Panicked drivers and passengers flung open doors and spilled onto the street, trying to get away from the rounds ripping through their cars. The younger man watched with satisfaction as five dropped onto the pavement, dead or dying. The older man fired into the F250 in case anyone was still inside. The rounds punched all the way through.

One of the rounds fired by the older man went through the door of a Lincoln Navigator across the highway on the southbound side. It hit the driver just under his ribs. He swerved across two lanes, hit a concrete barrier and flipped onto his passenger door. Cars skidded to a halt, creating an instant traffic jam on the southbound side.

The older man walked between lanes, methodically firing into each car he passed. Some drivers had fled, others sat screaming behind steering wheels. He fired into their faces and moved on.

The younger man stood near the minivan's dead driver for several seconds, firing into any cars that caught his interest. His weapon clicked on an empty chamber, the magazine expended. He pulled a fresh magazine from his jacket pocket and replaced it as rapidly as he could, the way the Chechen had shown him. As he charged the weapon he saw the punctured side door of the minivan pop open and slide slowly to the rear, pushed on its track by a small and bloody hand.

"Mommy!" a tiny voice cried out. "Mommy! Help me! It hurts!"

The younger man saw an outline of a little body buckled into a booster seat, a blond mop of hair over a blood-smeared face. He stuck his rifle into the open door, fired, wiped his face to clear what had blown back, and moved forward. He didn't register the wail of the approaching sirens over the sound of his own gunfire.

———————

Nunez's radio screamed, "Sam 22 to North dispatch, shots fired, shots fired!" In the background Nunez heard heavy fire, so much that it brought back memories of Afghanistan. "Automatic weapons and RPG fire, coming from the roof of the mosque! One SWAT officer and several civilians DOA! I need everyone you can get, especially officers with long guns! Citywide assist, send everyone we've got!"

Nunez exclaimed, "Motherfucker!" *How the fuck did they get an RPG?* He hoped it was a mistake, a misidentification by an overexcited officer. But he didn't think so. And they had lost an officer already. He had to get down there.

He punched it, urgently hitting the air horn to get people out of his way. Up ahead another patrol car flew south on the service road. The driver swerved over the curb to get onto the highway instead of waiting to find an entrance ramp.

Traffic was still heavy, and as he approached West Gulf Bank it seemed to slow more. He kept pushing forward. The patrol car in front of him did the same thing. As they neared Little York he noticed that northbound traffic had disappeared, as if it had been diverted from the highway.

Cars passing over Little York slammed on the brakes and scattered wildly. A sudden dust cloud erupted as an SUV rolled over a few hundred yards ahead. Cars were stopped in the northbound lanes on top of the overpass, and he thought he saw one person lying on the pavement. He jammed on his brakes as the cars around him did the same, and suddenly he was in the middle of a traffic jam.

Some asshole was looking at the wreck on the other side of the highway and rolled his SUV. Son of a bitch, not now.

He hit the air horn and inched closer to the car in front of him, trying to force it forward. It had nowhere to go but the shoulder. He swerved into the shoulder himself as the patrol car ahead of him did the same.

Drivers abandoned their cars and ran north, away from the overpass. Some were screaming. A few went straight for the concrete barrier at the edge of the overpass, climbed over and scrambled down the embankment.

Nunez had a sudden, sick feeling. *Something is seriously wrong. This isn't an accident.* He shut his siren off and popped his door.

He heard gunshots. Further south, maybe just over the crest of the overpass. The AK sound was unmistakable, and it was definitely more than one.

What the fuck is happening out here today?

The police car in front of Nunez had stopped and the officer was trying to get out. He was close to the concrete barrier to his left and had to squeeze himself between the driver's door and the body of the car. He was heavyset, an older guy with grey hair and a silver revolver on his left hip.

Nunez threw his car in park, grabbed his carbine and bail-out bag before forcing his way out of the driver's seat. As soon as he was out of the car he threw the bag over his shoulder, tossed his carbine sling over his head and started a hunched-over sprint toward the overpass.

Officers were all over the radio: patrol officers asking where to set up, sergeants screaming at people to get off the air and use their computers instead, someone asking for helicopters, English yelling over gunfire that he needed patrol units to try to get into the auto parts building north of the mosque and put fire onto the roof. As he ran up the overpass past the screaming, fleeing crowd Nunez tried to tell dispatch about the shooting on the highway. But there was never an open second for him to broadcast.

The old officer in front of him ran surprisingly fast. Nunez yelled, "Wait!" But the officer didn't hear him, he just kept running with his revolver in his hand.

Nunez slowed as he approached the crest. A few bodies were scattered around the wreck on the northbound side of the freeway. The gunshots were further ahead, among the jammed-up cars to the south.

The older officer stopped running, planted his feet and took two shots at something Nunez couldn't see. He then quickly jerked his muzzle in the air, as if trying to get his weapon off something he didn't want to shoot. His head swiveled left, he frantically lowered his weapon onto something else and pulled the trigger as fast as he could. He stood straight up exposing his entire upper body, not using the concrete barrier in front of him for cover.

Nunez was fifty yards away when AK rounds blew through the officer's protective vest and exited his back, dropping him like a sack of rocks. Nunez dove onto his stomach. He listened for more shots, then got to his feet and ran forward again, trying to keep his head below the edge of the concrete barrier.

He stopped twenty-five yards from the downed officer. The man's eyes were open and mouth slack. Nunez wasn't sure if he was alive or dead. But it didn't matter; he couldn't take the time to treat him even if he was alive. His focus right now had to be on whoever was shooting on the highway.

Sirens from two patrol cars screamed down Little York, under the overpass. Nunez felt a fleeting second of hope that they were there for him. But they kept going west, toward the mosque.

The radio traffic cleared. Nunez's hand flashed to his shoulder mike. "1243 dispatch, shots fired on the North freeway over Little York! I've got one officer down and multiple suspects with rifles!"

A furious voice responded, "The shots are being fired at Crosstimbers and Shepherd and we already know about the downed officer! Stay off the damn radio!"

Before Nunez could key up, the radio was a sea of competing transmissions again.

He lifted his head to look over the barrier. The traffic pileup on the northbound side was almost directly across from him. A woman lay dead beside a minivan on the far side of the highway. He couldn't see anything else, there were too many cars jumbled together. The shooting sounded like it was forty or so yards down the highway.

He looked south down the carpool lane in the center of the freeway, checking to see if anyone was still driving on it. He would feel like a total dumbass if he got run over trying to cross it. There was no traffic; several hundred yards south cars were stopped, their drivers having run off like everyone else.

He went over the barrier, keeping his body low as he slid into the carpool lane. He quickly threw himself against the barrier on the other side of the lane, then lifted his head and looked around. He still couldn't see anyone. But he heard firing, and distant screaming.

He needed to move. He slid over the second barrier into the northbound lanes and looked down the shoulder. No shooters, just a few bodies. He sidestepped into the mess of wrecked cars and still saw no shooters. Just bodies, most of them hanging from car doors. He moved across to the next lane, trying to localize where the gunfire was coming from.

As he moved past a punctured and smoking car, he saw what looked like the remains of a man folded over onto the center console. The interior of the car splattered with gore. He moved to the left edge of the car and looked between the lanes.

Sixty yards away, a young man stepped over bodies and fired into cars with an AK. Nunez felt queasy at the sight. In the distance toward the mosque twin booms sounded, the signature of an RPG hitting a target at close range. Immediately after the booms he heard intense small arms fire.

Nunez would have to make a left-handed shot around the car. He threw his carbine to his left shoulder, but his sling wasn't long enough to get a good position. He pulled the sling off and tried again. He felt his hands shake, the same way they had sometimes shaken when bullets flew at him back in Afghanistan. He struggled to put his red dot sight onto the torso of the man with the AK. The stock of his carbine slipped from its "sweet spot" in his shoulder, and Nunez forced it back into the right place.

Hurry the fuck up, man.

He swung the dot past the man's body and brought it back. The man wasn't looking around at all, was completely oblivious to anything that wasn't right in front of his rifle. Nunez's heart pounded as he flipped the safety off and squeezed the trigger, just after the man fired into a Ford Focus.

The first round hit the man in the stomach. He shrieked and staggered backward but didn't fall. He held his rifle with one hand and grabbed his punctured torso with the other. Nunez fired again and hit him sideways through both thighs, dropping him to a sitting position with his back against a car. The man still had his AK in his hand and his mouth was open as if screaming, but Nunez couldn't hear any sound. Nunez put five more rounds into him, until his face went slack and he sagged forward onto the concrete.

Nunez kept his sight on the man for a few seconds, checking for movement. Nothing. He moved up. More firing was somewhere down the highway to his right. He looked over cars' roofs, trying to find whoever else was firing so he could kill them. He didn't think about making an arrest, didn't think about the law, didn't think about being sued. All he thought about was finding the other shooters and killing them.

———

Kent Parker yanked his head back as rounds slammed into the dumpster he was using as cover. Watson was next to him, looking around the other side of the dumpster, occasionally firing one or two aimed shots toward the roof. Parker looked at the cars scattered haphazardly on Crosstimbers next to the mosque. He couldn't tell if any of the dozen or so people laid out on the street were still alive. A black Suburban was in flames, the roof punctured, glass gone and doors blown open. He was sure whoever had been inside when the RPG hit was still there, dead and burning.

Watson had thrown his Tahoe into reverse as soon as the first RPG round was fired, knocking two cars out of his way as he got his vehicle out of the line of fire. Then he sprinted to join Parker at the dumpster. He couldn't see where Elizondo and Erikson were, but he heard them firing somewhere to his left.

Moreno and Guthrie had pulled back, as had other SWAT officers. Every SWAT officer on the scene was reporting civilians down, on all four sides of the mosque. English was behind thick trees across the street from the mosque, trying to keep the suspects on the roof from firing into the mass of cars and civilians on Shepherd. Crosstimbers west of Shepherd was empty of everything but a few bodies and Rivera's burning car.

The gunfire had slowed. In the first few seconds of the attack, the suspects on the roof fired a few rounds at SWAT but emptied entire magazines into stopped cars. Now they were only sticking their heads up long enough to fire a round or two at a time, sometimes just pushing their rifles over the wall and blindly shooting into the street below.

A few minutes earlier the suspects fired an RPG at the black Suburban. Parker thought they must have mistaken it for a police vehicle. There was no other reason it would have been singled out among all the other cars.

Sirens wailed on Shepherd as the first patrol units arrived. Parker expected the sound to stop coming as the patrol car stopped far from the mosque, but the sound kept getting louder. Gunfire from the roof increased as someone uselessly yelled over the radio on SWAT's frequency.

"Patrol, don't approach the fucking mosque!"

Parker heard tires screech. The patrol car slid to a stop at the edge of the traffic jam. It wasn't stopping because of the radio call; patrol didn't have SWAT's frequency on their car radios. The driver's door flew open as AK rounds punched through the roof and hood.

The driver didn't get out. His car rolled slowly forward, stopping when it bumped another car. Delacroix and Vickers, two SWAT officers, fired back from the corner of the auto parts warehouse, trying to protect the officer inside the car. Just after the patrol car came to rest another explosion blasted the air above the mosque's roof. A moment later the patrol car was shattered by the ear-splitting detonation of another RPG round.

"Fuck!" Parker yelled in impotent fury. He still couldn't see a single target on the roof to shoot at. He spun his head to the side. Watson fired around his corner toward the mosque, just trying to keep the suspects on the roof pinned down.

"Watson!" Parker yelled. "I'm switching to North, I need to tell patrol not to get close!"

"Do it!" Watson yelled back, still firing toward the mosque.

Parker pulled his radio off his vest and rotated the knob to North patrol's channel. There was chaos on the net, officers screaming back and forth, stepping all over each other's traffic. Apparently several officers had already arrived in the area of the mosque, but Parker didn't have a clue where they were. He waited for break in the radio traffic, listening to officers and supervisors trying to figure out what was going on.

"1741, dammit, I just told everyone not to go near the mosque! One unit just got blown up!"

"306, 306, everyone meet up at-"

"Break! This is 1611, I need to know where to set up, I have a carbine and ammo!"

"1508, I'm set up south of the mosque, suspects visible on the roof, rounds are-"

"We need to get the officer out of the intersection! Who's forming the rescue team?"

There was a two-second gap in radio traffic. Parker keyed his radio.

"Sam 115 to North dispatch," he said calmly. "I'm one of the SWAT units at the mosque. Clear the air so I can explain what's happening out here."

"North dispatch to all units, clear the air, clear the air! Sam 115, go."

"Sam 115, SWAT is covering each side of the mosque. There are maybe ten suspects on the roof with AKs, plus one with an RPG. Break...The RPG gunner has killed two officers already, west of the mosque. Break...Civilians are down everywhere. Suspects are firing at everyone, in every direction. Patrol, do not come within view of the mosque with your vehicles. Stop a block away and approach on foot, and stay behind cover. Copy?"

"North dispatch to Sam 115, we're clear. All units, stay clear of the mosque, approach the mosque on foot and stay behind cover."

Parker rubbed his face as supervisors acknowledged. He looked around the edge of the dumpster again, scanning the roof. A rifle jutted over the edge of the wall, rounds spraying wildly from the muzzle. He raised his carbine and fired toward the rifle. The rifle jerked back over the wall. Parker couldn't tell if he had hit anything.

"Watson!" he said. "This is bullshit! We have to get snipers into the building across the street or get our asses into that mosque."

"Don't I know it," Watson said back. "I don't know where our snipers are, and English hasn't said a word about setting them up. You have any ideas, let me know."

"We get patrol to replace Delacroix and Vickers, then those two get onto the roof of that building. What do you think?"

"Sounds good. You still on North's channel? Get some patrol units to that building, I'll talk to our guys."

175

The Chechen looked at the squatting, cringing man next to him on the wall, disgusted with his display of fear. Bullets zipped through the air above as he angrily asked, "Why are you not firing?"

"I have no more bullets!" the man nervously yelled back.

"Have you asked for more ammunition from other fighters?" the Chechen asked, knowing the answer.

"No, brother, I have not. Should I?"

The Chechen slapped him hard, nearly knocking him off his feet. The man didn't resist, he just put one hand in front of his face in case the Chechen hit him again.

"Fool! Coward!" the Chechen yelled. "Get another magazine from another fighter! Hurry! And do not waste all your shots, aim when you fire!"

The man started to crawl away, and the Chechen had a different idea. He grabbed the man and said "Stop. Can I trust you? Will you stay by my side and continue to fight, or will you run away?"

"I will stay by your side," the man said. "I swear it."

"Go back to the weapons room and bring more ammunition, as much as you can carry. Try to bring more believers back with you, there are more rifles in the room for them. And tell the *imam* we have killed many of the *kuffar*."

The man nodded, moved quickly down the steps to the door and disappeared. The Chechen looked at the other fighters on the roof. They at least were doing what he had told them. All were staying low behind the wall, raising their heads to fire a few rounds and ducking down. Some were even mimicking the Chechen, moving to a different spot every time they fired.

A few fired blindly. That was alright, as long as they didn't waste all their ammunition. Such a tactic would have been useless against his fighters in his homeland. But the Americans' cowardice would not permit them to advance through ineffective fire, as a true warrior would.

The Chechen looked to the building across the street to the north. It was a two story building, taller than the mosque by far, built of brick and mirrored plate glass windows. He did not understand why the *kuffar* had not taken the roof already, as he would have. There was no other spot close enough that could give the enemy the advantage.

The Chechen recognized the threat the building held. He had recognized it the first time he stood on the mosque's roof, drinking tea with the *imam* and discussing the possibility of a martyrdom operation. He said then that if they ever had to fight from the mosque, they should also take control of the building across the street.

But they couldn't do it, not now. That avenue had been cut off, the moment police arrived outside the mosque. The building was a tremendous threat, a threat he could do nothing about at the moment. He accepted it. If the *kuffar* took the building, he would deal with it then.

The Chechen felt frustrated. He had only fired three RPG rounds, only hit three police vehicles. The police had pulled several black cars backward out of view, but left many others. His fighters had shot those vehicles, then shot every other vehicle they could, and shot down many cowards who had run from them.

Most of the dead *kuffar* were lying in the street in ones and twos. One was burning next to the black Suburban he hit with a rocket propelled grenade. He knew he had killed at least four police so far; one in the black car, two in the Suburban, and the one stupid enough to drive right into the intersection. Perhaps twenty or twenty-five other dead surrounded the mosque. He hoped more police were among them.

Wounded men and women hid behind cars. Dozens of them. If they were left in the street long enough, they would probably die.

Other police were still watching and firing at them. He had no suitable targets for his RPG launcher anymore, the visible police vehicles were either burning or shot to pieces. None of his fighters had been hit so far, the enemy's fire was not as accurate as he expected. Perhaps if he switched to his rifle, he could safely raise his head long enough to hit pick off the enemy one by one.

He moved to his rifle, dropped the RPG launcher and crawled to the north edge of the roof. He looked through an opening in the wall. Below, at the building across the street, a policeman peered around a corner. The Chechen dropped the rifle, crawled back to the RPG and dragged it back so he'd have both weapons.

The Chechen checked his rifle to ensure it was loaded, then laid the RPG by his side. He checked the aperture in the wall, ensuring he could see the corner through the opening. The angle was correct. He put his rifle to his shoulder and set the selector to fire.

The Chechen knew how the enemy would react when he shot one of them with his rifle. They would try to rescue him, to save him from death. And that would lead to the deaths of many more of them, if the Chechen was fast enough.

———

Nunez crept down the right shoulder of the highway, staying low and trying to spot the other shooters. There was at least one more, somewhere on the highway. But all he saw were dead people, blown apart in their cars and on the road.

"Bekim, where are you?" an accented voice yelled ahead.

Nunez froze. The voice was dead calm, not like a panicked civilian trying to run for his life. It had to have come from another shooter, who must have noticed the lack of gunfire from his fellow murderer. He'd be alert now, which meant Nunez wouldn't be able sneak up and shoot him in the back.

Nunez stopped next to a shredded Ford Taurus and tried to spot the yelling man. Too many cars were in the way. He started to move again, then glanced through the Taurus' windows. A man and woman were butchered in the front seats. The man lay crumpled against the driver's door and the woman sat straight up. Her head stopped at her lower jaw, only the jagged back half of her empty skull was still in place. The inside of the car was covered with pieces of her head. Long hair hung down from her scalp, which was stuck to the roof.

Nunez started to move past the car, and was startled to see a face looking at him through the back passenger window. He stopped. A man in a business suit, covered in blood and bits of brain matter, locked eyes with him. The man shook and clenched tense fists over his lips.

Nunez couldn't tell if the man had been shot, and couldn't take time to check. Nunez lifted his hand and waved slowly, then motioned to the man to lie down. After a few seconds the man complied.

From down the highway, much closer now, the voice yelled again.

"Bekim!"

Nunez jerked his carbine toward the voice. All he could see were rows of shattered vehicles.

Nunez had to move toward the voice. The thought scared him shitless, but he had to do it. The man could start killing people again at any time.

Nunez moved between cars and looked down the jammed lanes. He saw nothing but bodies. He moved toward the next lane, and was surprised to see the terrorist he had killed laying nearby. Nunez hadn't realized he had moved that far south.

He looked to the Ford Focus the man had shot just before Nunez killed him. Its windows were shattered and doors punctured. Nunez couldn't see anyone inside.

He looked south again. Nothing. He dashed out from between two cars and stopped behind the Ford Focus. He still couldn't see anyone. He crept forward so he could look between the lanes. Nothing. He backed up.

Something snagged his pant leg. He looked down. A bloody, pale, feminine hand gripped the hem. The woman's body was out of view on the other side of the car, he could only see her hand and forearm. He jerked his leg back softly, but the woman wouldn't let go. He took another look around, knelt and grabbed the woman's wrist to break her grip. She held on. He knelt lower, scanned with his carbine briefly, then turned to the woman.

She was on her back alongside the Focus, her head next to the left rear wheel, legs halfway under the car. She wore a short dress, pulled up to reveal horrible thigh wounds. Exposed bone on one, blood spurting from the other. One of her hands held Nunez's pant leg, the other clutched an infant covered by a blood-soaked blanket.

Nunez looked south again. The other shooter had to be somewhere close, and if Nunez let this woman distract him he might get shot in the back. He saw a few people hundreds of yards away, standing behind cars and looking his direction. Some held phones in the air, videotaping.

He looked back at the woman. Her baby twitched and threw its head back slightly, mouth open and tongue protruding. Agonal breathing, the last movement made by a dying body as the brain gives last-ditch orders to suck in oxygen.

The woman looked at him with wide, expectant eyes, blinking away blood.

She said nothing, silently pleading for help.

He leaned in close and whispered, "Ma'am, let go."

"Don't leave us here," the woman whispered back.

"I'll come back for you, I promise," he whispered urgently. "Let go, I need to find the shooter."

A little louder, she said, "You have to help my baby. Please, help her."

Nunez realized this was his fault. He had taken too much time to find the first suspect, then took forever to put him down. He had shot the man just after he fired into this woman's car. If he had just been faster, if he hadn't been so scared, if he had been steadier, she wouldn't be lying there holding a dying baby.

But it couldn't be helped now. Nunez had to get away from her and find the other suspects. Nunez pulled on her wrist again, harder this time.

The woman tightened her grip and twisted her fist to hang on. Tears rolled down her face, making trails in the blood. She said out loud, "Please don't leave us here, they'll come back and kill us."

"Lady, be quiet," Nunez whispered. "I swear I'll come back for you, but if I stay here we'll all get killed. Let go." He rose and let go of her wrist, prepared to jerk his leg free.

"Help me!" she shrieked. *"Help my baby! Don't leave me here!"*

Nunez jerked his pant leg out of her grasp. He had to get away from her, before the other shooters used her voice to zero in on him. He looked around before hooking left and moving three cars south, to put distance between himself and her scream.

He could still hear the woman sobbing. He looked down, bit his lip and moved again. Ten feet later he stopped by the right front wheel of an SUV, breathing heavily for a few seconds, listening for the suspects. He heard nothing but distant gunfire at the mosque.

He stuck his head and weapon over the SUV's hood. Through several windows, maybe three cars down and in the next lane, Nunez thought he saw a man standing next to a VW Beetle. He shifted his head around, trying to get a better view through the curved and distorting glass.

A woman shrieked. Rapid gunfire exploded near the Beetle. Nunez ducked but kept his eyes just over the hood. Bullets blasted through the Beetle's passenger door and window. He couldn't see the man next to the car anymore. He slid to his right toward the front of the SUV, using the engine for cover.

Just next to the Beetle, barely visible in a narrow gap between cars, Nunez saw a man standing still and relaxed, calmly doing something to an AK. Nunez's heart raced, his fingers felt numb. He raised his weapon, put the red dot on the man's chest, and pulled the trigger.

Several patrol officers had already reached Vickers and Delacroix next to the two story building across the street from the mosque. All of them save one carried carbines, but only two had extra magazines. One was nearly hyperventilating after running four blocks to get to the mosque. Vickers and Delacroix stood by the corner, deciding what they were going to do with them. Sporadic gunfire rang out from the mosque as they spoke.

Delacroix said to Vickers, "Let's set up patrol at this corner so they can lay down cover fire. Me and you break a window to get into this building and find our way to the roof."

"Cool. I'll let the captain know, you get these guys set up."

Delacroix ran to the patrol officers. "Listen up! I'm going to set you up on this corner closest to the mosque. Poke your heads around the corner a few times a minute and fire toward the roof of the mosque, so that asshole with the RPG can't get a good shot on anyone. Me and my partner are going into this building so we can get onto the roof. We need one patrolman with us. You," Delacroix said, pointing to the officer without a carbine, "since you don't have a long gun. Stay with us and we'll tell you what to do. Got it?"

All nodded, except one. "Isn't it dangerous using that same corner over and over? Haven't they seen you there already?"

"We've been using it, it's not a bad corner," Delacroix said. "Check this out." He leaned out and fired four rounds, then jerked back behind the corner.

"See? Now trade places."

The four patrolmen crept closer to the corner. The officer in the lead, who looked young and confident, slapped Delacroix on the back. "We got this, you go ahead."

Delacroix rolled away from the corner and ran to the front door. The lead patrol officer took a deep breath, raised his carbine toward the roof, then leaned away from the corner to look at the mosque.

———

The Chechen saw a dark-uniformed officer lean out and fire at the mosque. He almost jumped up to fire, but the officer quickly disappeared. The Chechen waited, watching the corner. Then he saw a different officer wearing a sky blue shirt slowly lean away from the corner, pointing a rifle toward the mosque.

The Chechen rose above the wall. The officer in the sky blue shirt jerked his head, startled. He panic-fired at the Chechen, missing by feet. The Chechen found the man in the rifle's scope and fired one round. The man shuddered and spun halfway before falling.

Three officers in blue shirts exposed themselves to grab the wounded officer, but the Chechen didn't see them. He was already behind the wall dropping his rifle and hefting the RPG onto his shoulder. He took a leaping sidestep, rose, aimed at the officers dragging the wounded man behind the corner, and pulled the trigger.

Backblast shook the roof. The other fighters flinched. The Chechen dropped below the wall as the RPG round hit six inches from the corner, blasting a half-moon shaped crater and showering the four officers with cement and shrapnel. Two officers fell next to the one who had been shot, the last one ran.

The Chechen shouted "You! Fire!" to the fighter on the north wall. The man immediately jumped up, too high, and sprayed rounds toward the officers below. The Chechen lurched to the aperture in the wall to see rounds impacting around the three officers lying by the corner.

Return fire caught the young fighter in the head. The back of his skull exploded and he plopped onto the roof, dead before he hit the ground. A death worthy of a martyr.

The Chechen ran to the west wall and rose high enough to look down Shepherd. In the distance, he saw several police cars in the street with officers taking cover behind them. Rounds snapped past him as he found one of the officers in his scope, held his breath and fired.

The officer's hands flew to his chest before he dropped behind his car. The Chechen ducked and ran to the south wall, lifting his head for a second to find another target. He saw no policemen, but in the street a crying man sat against the front bumper of a car, his arms tightly folded over his stomach. The Chechen readied himself, rose above the wall, aimed and fired. The man's body jerked and he fell sideways.

The Chechen ran back to the other side of the roof, put his rifle down and picked up his RPG launcher.

_____

Delacroix knew he had hit the guy on the roof. When the corner of the building exploded and three officers went down, Vickers ran to help get them behind cover. But Delacroix stepped into the open and returned fire. He saw one man in a cloud of dust, firing from the roof. He fired, and smiled with satisfaction when the man's head jerked back and he fell.

Another man had popped up a second later, holding what Delacroix immediately recognized as a Dragunov rifle. That man stayed much lower than the first man had, and Delacroix fired two rounds that must have both missed before his magazine ran dry. He jerked behind cover and reloaded.

All three patrol officers who had been hit had been dragged behind cover. More patrolmen had arrived and most of them huddled around the three men on the ground, doing what they could to help. One of the three was coughing and trying to get up, but other officers held him down. Another was obviously dead, but an officer was still tearing the man's shirt and vest off, trying to get to his wounds. Delacroix couldn't see the third man, too many cops were around him.

The officer who had run from the corner after the RPG strike was still on his feet, bleeding from a dozen small wounds, cursing and spitting blood. Far behind them on Shepherd, Delacroix heard someone yell "Sniper! Sniper!" He turned to see officers running toward the east side of the road, getting away from cars they had thought were good cover.

Delacroix keyed his radio. "Sam 130, we just had another RPG impact north of the mosque. Officers down, probably at least one DOA. Officers north of Crosstimbers on Shepherd are taking sniper fire."

Moreno replied, "Sam 118, a sniper just killed a wounded civilian on the south side."

English knelt behind a thick tree listening to the radio traffic, furious at himself. He had seen the RPG explode on the corner of the auto parts showroom, fired ineffectively at the mosque as the three officers who fell were raked by gunfire. Nothing was working, nothing was stopping the suspects on the roof from hitting whoever they wanted.

English had been trying to make everyone hold a perimeter around the mosque while he waited for more resources and some kind of direction from his supervisors. Nothing seemed to be coming. He tried to tally up the numbers, counting how many they had lost. Several officers down, two of those definitely dead and several more probably dead, plus at least twenty civilians killed. He couldn't get to any of the wounded civilians in the street. Now the wounded were being deliberately targeted, and he couldn't do anything about it.

English jumped on the radio. "Sam 22, that's enough of this shit. Delacroix and Vickers, get inside that damn building north of the mosque. Watson, get your people together and breach that bay door. I don't give a fuck how you do it, just do it. Nobody worry about notifying patrol, they'll do what they need to do. Once the mosque is breached, everybody but Del and Vickers head inside. Copy?"

Behind the dumpster Watson and Parker looked at each other in silence. Getting into the mosque wouldn't be easy, and being inside would suck. But English was right, they had to get in there. Sitting outside wasn't doing any good.

"Any ideas on how to breach that door?" Parker asked, motioning toward the single door beside the loading bay.

"We could shotgun breach, but we might get shot from the roof while we're doing it," Watson said. "I'll leave you here to cover the roof while we breach, then you get inside as soon as you can. Whadaya think?"

Parker didn't like the idea, but no other options jumped at him. He was going to tell Watson he agreed, but before he spoke there was a flurry of gunfire from the left, where Elizondo and Erikson had taken cover. Parker spun around to get his weapon back onto the mosque.

An explosion rang out from the roof. The dumpster erupted with a loud metallic clang and a volcano of smoke and sparks. Parker screamed and covered his face as he was blown several feet from the dumpster. When he opened his eyes and looked back toward Watson, he only saw black smoke and dust. Bits of paper and plastic fluttered to earth.

Nearing panic, he got to his feet and lunged back behind the dumpster. He heard Watson yell "Motherfucker! Son of a bitch!" just before he ran through the smoke toward Parker. Parker figured it out; an RPG round had hit the dumpster and exploded through the thin steel wall between him and Watson. Neither had been hit, the RPG's shrapnel had blown straight forward instead of to the sides when it detonated.

"Fuck this!" Watson yelled, his face beet red behind black dust. He keyed his radio and said "Elizondo, Erikson, meet me at the Tahoe, now!"

"What are you going to do?" Parker asked.

"We're breaching the bay door! Stay here and cover, then come in after us!"

"Copy!" Parker yelled, then turned and covered the roof again.

Watson ran off. Parker keyed his radio to let English know the other men were about to breach the door. English acknowledged.

A minute passed. Nobody appeared on the roof. He heard gunfire from the other sides of the mosque. Once he saw a rifle rise over the edge of the wall. He fired three quick rounds and the rifle dropped back down.

Behind him he heard an engine racing. He glanced backward. Watson's Tahoe flew from the other side of the grocery store through the parking lot. He snapped his eyes to the mosque, firing toward the roof to discourage anyone from even attempting to shoot at the Tahoe. He tried to remember how many rounds he had in his magazine; he'd have to lay down a lot of fire to cover the three officers as they blew the door open with a shotgun.

The Tahoe hauled ass toward the loading bay. Parker waited for Watson to slam on the brakes and slide to a stop by the door next to the bay. As soon as the officers bailed out, he'd fire on the roof. He reached to his chest for a fresh magazine, prepared for a quick reload.

Watson ran over the dead man at the base of the ramp. The Tahoe's undercarriage scraped concrete and bounced upward as it shot toward the loading bay. Parker was stunned to see the Tahoe slam straight into the bay door, tear it from its tracks and carry it to the far wall of the loading bay.

CHAPTER 10

Officer Ray Walker and his partner sped past stopped cars on Shepherd. Walker was angry. He had wasted way too much time at the station booking some guy on a minor traffic warrant, less than fifteen minutes before the shit hit the fan.

He and his partner, a probationary named Tonisha Nelms, had been at the station when the officer down call came over the radio. Instead of hauling ass, they had to sit there while their prisoner was booked by a jail officer who refused to work any faster than he ever did. The officer assured Walker he didn't have to worry about it, other cops would take care of the problem long before he reached the scene. Then when the fight started around the mosque, the desk sergeant tried to make Walker stay at the front desk so everyone else could go. Walker argued, then just ignored the sergeant and ran to his car.

The radio traffic was insane. Automatic weapons, fucking *RPG* fire, multiple officers down, dozens of civilians dead around the mosque. Sergeants were trying to get officers to stay back and set a cordon around the mosque, but it sounded like most were heading straight into the fight. One officer from another station apparently hadn't switched to North's channel; he drove his car into the intersection and was killed within seconds by an RPG.

Walker was still a new officer, in his first couple of years on the street. His experience as a Marine and as a soldier in Iraq would hopefully get him through this, because his police experience wouldn't count for much. His partner was just off the field training program. He'd be lucky if she wasn't an anchor.

He was three blocks north of the mosque when he saw ten patrol cars in a clump, blocking Shepherd. Several officers stood around the cars, and an older sergeant waved at Walker. He held a Houston key map, a book with maps of every part of the city organized into a quick reference system.

Walker stopped near the sergeant. He and Nelms jumped out, and Walker grabbed his carbine and spare magazines. The sergeant called him over, scowled and pointed at Walker's carbine.

"Put that damn thing away before you hurt yourself with it," he grumbled. "SWAT's got the scene under control, they just need us to block intersections around the mosque. I want you here," the sergeant said, pointing at the map, "to stop all traffic going east. Get there right now."

In the distance rifles fired back and forth across the intersection, and officers screamed orders and information. Cars were scattered around the intersection, some of them smoking. What looked like clumps of rags surrounded the cars.

"Sarge, it doesn't look like SWAT's got this under control," Walker said. "I'm a combat vet, I can do more good down there than I can blocking traffic."

The sergeant sneered. "Yeah, you and every other rookie out here with enough money to buy one of those toy guns thinks the same thing. You'll just rush right in there and save everyone, won't you? I just told you what I need you to do, officer. Get to that intersection, now."

Twin explosions followed by a burst of gunfire rocked the intersection. Everyone ducked. On the east side of Shepherd a cloud of smoke spread rapidly from a building close to the street. Walker saw figures in sky blue and black scurry through the haze. On the radio someone screamed, "RPG, RPG! Multiple officers down across the street from the mosque!"

A block south two officers, one male and one a young female, stood beside their patrol car looking toward the mosque. The male officer suddenly jerked and grabbed his chest before dropping onto the street. The female officer screamed, dropped beside him and shook him violently. Six or seven other officers behind cars on Shepherd ran out of the street as someone screamed "Sniper! Sniper!"

Walker didn't say a word. He hauled ass southward. Behind him the sergeant yelled "Officer! You better stop!"

Walker sprinted toward the left side of the road, away from the sniper's kill zone. He looked back. Nelms was right on his ass.

A hysterical voice on his radio shrieked, *My partner's been shot, oh god, help us, help us! He's in the street, and, and, they're shooting, there's dead people! Oh god! He's got blood, it's, it's, he's hurt, oh my god, we need help! And, and.....*

Walker saw the female officer squatting next to her partner, crying and babbling into her radio. She was very young, probably still in training, and in complete panic. Her partner sat back against the patrol car, pressing both hands to his chest and clenching his teeth. As Walker passed he saw the male officer reach to the female's belt and turn her radio off. She kept screaming, not realizing she wasn't transmitting anymore.

They couldn't stop to help the officer. If they did they'd probably just get hit by the sniper, adding more downed officers to the problem. They reached the sidewalk on the east side of Shepherd and kept running toward the mosque.

Twin explosions rang out from the intersection, a sound he recognized as an RPG being fired and exploding against a nearby target. Walker reflexively ducked but kept running. He passed officers backed against stores and restaurants, unsure if they should move forward or stay in place. The gunfire ahead grew louder as he reached the building that had just been hit. A crowd of officers was urgently dragging three limp officers to the north, away from the jagged, smoking corner of the building.

Walker finally stopped, panting like mad and leaning against a wall. Ahead of him two SWAT officers used the stocks of their carbines to smash out a plate glass window. Inside the building an alarm klaxon shrieked. One of the SWAT officers yelled, "Someone get the fuck over here and help us into this window!"

Walker sprinted over and boosted them over the window ledge. Walker heard "Ow!" as the second officer lost his balance and fell to the floor inside the building. Neither SWAT officer said a word to the patrolmen, as soon as they were on their feet they were gone.

Walker ran to the back of the building. A fifteen foot high wrought-iron fence topped with concertina wire encircled the building's parking lot. A huge *chain* and padlock secured the gate's double doors. Nobody was getting through that without heavy-duty tools.

He ran to the front of the building. Rounds hit the street and whirred north. Police officers behind cars, trees and lamp posts fired back, hitting nobody. Walker looked into the street. Seven or eight abandoned cars were sprawled around a smashed and smoking police car, surrounded by seven or eight motionless men and women in contorted positions. One of them wore a slashed, bloody, burned, sky-blue Houston police uniform shirt.

Walker heard rifle fire from behind the mosque. The pace of the shots accelerated, accompanied by the sounds of an engine racing and tires squealing. There was a loud crash and screech of tearing metal. Fire from the roof suddenly stopped. Walker sidestepped to his right and leaned out, getting a flash picture of what was around the corner in the two seconds before he stepped back behind cover.

A patrol sergeant's calm voice sounded over the radio.

"219 to all units, SWAT just breached the back of the mosque. Patrol units on Crosstimbers east of Shepherd, move closer to the mosque."

Walker heard an intense barrage of gunfire at the back of the mosque. He couldn't tell, but maybe it was actually inside the building. Officers were inside, and were probably getting the shit shot out of them. Walker had to get inside with them.

He turned around. Nelms stared at him, scared shitless. He said, "I'm gonna try to get into the mosque. Stay here."

Her eyes widened. "What should I do?"

"I don't know. Help somebody or something."

Walker stepped toward an officer he didn't know and slapped him on the back.

"Hey man, I'm going to the back of the mosque. Cover me."

The officer gave Walker a cold look. Blood ran down his face from his scalp.

"I know you just showed up and all, but the last guy who tried that got shot by a sniper and then blown up with an RPG. It's probably not a good idea."

Walker said "Fine, I'll cover you and you run across then."

The officer wiped blood from his head, looked at his hand, then looked back at Walker.

"Stay low. I'll be firing over your head."

"Got it. Tell me when you're ready."

The other officer moved toward the corner, hunched low. He turned and yelled, "Everyone get back! I'm going to fire toward the mosque so this guy can run across the street!"

Other officers backed off. Walker realized they didn't want to be anywhere around when the next RPG round hit the corner. He breathed deeply and steadied himself.

The cover officer set up at the corner, pressed his back against the building and readied his carbine. He edged as close to the blasted corner as he could, looked at Walker and called out, "Ready?"

Walker planted his feet, bent at the waist and pulled his carbine in close. "Ready!"

"Okay. Haul ass when I start shooting."

The officer closed his eyes and took a breath. He started to bring his carbine up, stopped, reached across his body and made the sign of the cross. Properly prepared, he gripped his weapon, leaned away from the corner and fired at the roof as fast as he could.

"Go!"

Walker charged under the cover officer's weapon, wincing at the sound of the muzzle blasts right over his head. Cars blocked his path and he weaved around them, keeping one eye on the roof. Nothing there.

He nearly tripped over the median, recovered his balance, flew across the street, jumped over the curb and veered onto the sidewalk. Gear and ammo bounced on his hips as he pounded down the pavement. Nobody shot at him.

He reached the northeast corner of the mosque, nearly falling as he stopped himself from running into the open. The back end of a black Tahoe stuck out from the loading bay. Gunfire banged and echoed inside. Walker couldn't see shit, didn't know who was shooting at what. He knew the Tahoe had to belong to SWAT, but that was it.

Five feet around the corner was a big concrete loading ramp, a mangled corpse, an AK and scattered magazines. Walker had to move, he didn't know if anyone was still covering him. He ducked around the corner and dove for the base of the loading ramp. Then he got to his knees, braced himself, and lifted his head to look into the loading bay.

Something heavy fell onto him, flattening him to the pavement. He stifled a scream and tried to push whatever it was off his back. The weight lifted on its own. Walker snapped his head back to see an officer in a black SWAT uniform trying to get to his feet, blood streaming from his face onto his gear.

The man's carbine swung loosely from a clip on his shoulder, and Walker saw that the magazine was empty, bolt locked to the rear. The officer was almost standing when he lost his footing, cried out in pain and fell on Walker again. Walker shoved him away so he could get to his own knees, then helped the officer sit up. The man tried to look at Walker through the blood running into his eyes.

"Who are you?"

"Ray Walker, North patrol. Who are you?"

The SWAT officer ignored the question. "Ray, my partners are down. Help me, I need to get back in there."

"Hold on," Walker said. "Reload your carbine, it's empty."

The man looked at his carbine in surprise. He pulled out a magazine to reload. The magazine had been hit by a bullet and was nearly sheared in half, spring protruding and rounds falling out. He dropped it and pulled out another one.

Walker turned and looked into the loading bay. The shooting inside had stopped, and he saw what looked like a collapsed wall on the driver's side of the Tahoe. He caught motion to the right and shifted his head, trying to look under the Tahoe around the rear tires.

Black police boots with toes sticking straight up disappeared around the edge of the collapsed wall. A SWAT cop was being dragged into the mosque.

"Oh fuck!" Walker blurted. He hopped sideways to get a better view. He could only see the wall, the boots were gone. Then he heard incoherent yelling and footsteps pounding toward the bay. He bobbed his head, trying to get his eyes on whoever was coming toward him.

Two sets of feet popped into view, frantically shuffling and hopping next to the left rear tire of the Tahoe. A voice yelled, "Bring him out, quickly!"

The feet were in and out of view, moving around on the other side of the tire. Walker knew what they were doing. They were trying to pull another officer out of the Tahoe. He squared his red dot a foot and pulled the trigger.

An ankle exploded. One of the men dropped, shrieking in a language Walker didn't understand. Walker kept firing, cutting off the cries in mid-scream. The second man fell onto his back, the right side of his body almost fully visible to Walker. The man wailed and waved a pistol.

Walker emptied half his magazine into the man, watching his body jerk and shudder with every round. Gunfire rang out from officers to the east. Several more rounds hit the dead man, the back of the Tahoe and the wall beside the bay. Walker ducked below the edge of the ramp, afraid to get hit by friendly fire.

A hand slapped him on the shoulder. "Let's get in there! Stay on the passenger side of the Tahoe, we'll use the engine for cover!"

Walker turned to answer the SWAT officer, but found himself facing the officer who had covered him when he sprinted across Crosstimbers. The SWAT officer was down and unconscious. A female patrol officer knelt beside him, looking his helmetless head. Walker couldn't tell if the jagged tear on the officer's temple was a bullet wound or not. His helmet rested upright beside him. "Elizondo" was stenciled on the back of the helmet.

Walker dug into his ammo bag, pulled a fresh magazine, then thought better of it and put it away. He pointed at the SWAT officer and said, "Give me two of his magazines."

The female officer dug two mags out of the pouches on the SWAT officer's chest and handed them to Walker. Walker dropped his mag and put the fresh one in. He handed the other mag to the officer who had covered him.

"Here, reload."

The other officer reloaded. Walker looked over the edge of the ramp again, searching for more activity. Nothing. He couldn't hear any fire from inside the mosque, but rounds still hammered out from other sides of the roof. He asked the other officer, "What's your name?"

"Anthony. Miller."

"You ready, Anthony?" Walker asked.

"Yup."

"Okay. Follow me."

Walker took a last look, then vaulted onto the ramp. He squeezed around the edge of the Tahoe and was inside the loading bay, ducking along the passenger side and trying not to notice the exit holes in the doors. He stepped on tiny pieces of shattered glass, pushed the front passenger door closed and dropped behind the right front wheel, looking into the open area of the mosque beyond the collapsed wall. Miller was with him seconds later.

They panted and looked over their sights for targets. They saw two men lying dead near the corner of the open room, but nobody else. He looked into the back seat of the Tahoe and couldn't see anyone, but knew there was an officer down inside.

He keyed up on the radio, trying several times before he broke through the traffic. "We're inside the mosque, we're inside the mosque! One SWAT officer got dragged into the mosque, say again, one SWAT officer was dragged inside the mosque from the loading bay!"

The Tahoe had hit a sheetrock wall on the driver's side and knocked most of it down. Walker and Miller could look into one corner of the mosque, but that was all. The wall that had collapsed looked cheap and flimsy. It sure as hell wouldn't stop bullets. If anyone got smart and started firing through the wall at them, they were pretty much fucked.

For the moment Walker couldn't worry about it. He had huge tactical problems to deal with, and didn't know how they'd recover the captured SWAT officer. But he was inside the mosque, with backup beside him and more officers outside. Cops were in the enemy's house. It would be a different fight from now on.

As soon as Walker ducked under the cover officer's rifle and ran across the street, his partner Tonisha Nelms backed up against the building. She watched other officers running around, trying to figure out what to do. The other officers seemed confused, but Nelms felt absolutely clueless.

She was thirty years old, a married mother of two kids, just four months out of the academy. She had applied for the department in a fit of early-onset midlife crisis when she was twenty-nine, dreading the thought of making her career in copy machine sales and service the sum of her life's work.

She and her husband had fought like cats and dogs about it. Her husband insisted police work was too dangerous and full of sex-crazed men; Nelms argued against the first point, just sort of ignored the second. Nobody had really hit on her in the academy or on the street thus far, so the second point hadn't been anything to worry about. About the job being too dangerous, well… now that she was in the middle of a huge firefight, hugging a building for cover while two officers who looked dead lay ten feet away, she had to admit her husband was right.

Nelms had never been in the military, never had to think tactically, had never even fired a weapon before she went to the police academy. Other officers were milling around with machine guns screaming orders and stalking around like they were green berets or something. Nelms didn't know how she was supposed to act, didn't know how to look like she knew what she was doing. She didn't even bother to draw her pistol, there was nothing she could do with it anyway.

The downed policemen were being tended to by officers who were screaming at each other and jamming torn socks and t-shirts onto bullet holes and shrapnel wounds. Nelms didn't know how to do anything medically. She was CPR certified from the academy but didn't think she could breathe anyone back to life now. She couldn't remember how many breaths to give versus how many chest compressions. She just felt useless.

Before he ran toward the mosque, Walker had told her to help people. In the street she saw a dozen or so people scattered around cars. There had to be more she couldn't see.

She wouldn't do any good if she picked up a carbine from a downed officer and used it to shoot at the mosque. She didn't know how to fire one. She couldn't apply first aid to anyone because she didn't really know how. She couldn't do anything worthwhile, except maybe one thing.

Nelms had always been athletic. She had run track and played basketball in high school and college, stayed in shape afterward, met her husband at a gym, and worked out like crazy after her children's' births to get back in shape. She whipped most of the males in the academy at physical training and defensive tactics. She wasn't skinny, but most of her weight was muscle. She was a strong woman, maybe she could do something with that strength.

Two other officers had run across the street after Walker. Another officer stood at the corner pointing his weapon at the mosque while six or seven others frantically tried to revive two officers who looked dead. Someone bandaged another who had woken up screaming in pain. Nelms had to do something.

She ran to the corner and tapped the officer there on the shoulder. Without turning his head from the mosque he asked angrily, "What?"

"Um…can you shoot at the mosque so I can get some of those people out of the street? Please?"

The officer turned to her with his brow furrowed, looking at her like she had two heads. He turned back to the mosque and muttered, "You're fuckin' insane."

"I'm serious," she pleaded. "There's nothing else for me to do out here. Shoot at the mosque so I can do something."

The officer snapped his head back and looked at her again. "Alright, whatever." He turned away and announced, "You better be real fucking quick, and I'd only try to get the closest person. Tell me when you're ready."

"Okay," she said weakly, wondering what she was trying to prove. She saw another officer give her a strange look as he reloaded his carbine. She leaned back against the wall, thinking about the pressure she thought she felt during track meets in school. That pressure was a pathetic joke compared to what she felt now. She breathed deeply, trying to calm down, and took a minute to look for the right person to rescue.

"Hey!" the cover officer yelled. "Are you gonna do this, or what?"

Nelms nodded, which didn't make sense since the cover officer wasn't looking at her. She swallowed and felt how dry her throat was, then looked at her hands. They were shaking. For a second she thought she might pee her pants.

"Yes," she said quietly. "I'm ready."

"What?" the officer yelled. "I can't fucking hear you!"

"I'm ready!" she said back, sounding more sure of herself than she actually was.

"Alright, I'm gonna shoot!"

Nelms bent forward and set her feet for the sprint. She picked her target, a woman hanging out of the front passenger seat of an SUV. She didn't look too heavy.

The cover officer opened fire. Nelms stayed where she was, trying to work up the courage to move, her heart pounding under her vest. She made a false start and then just stood there, her courage fading.

I don't know if I can do this.

The officer who had given her the strange look screamed "Hurry the fuck up!" before running to the corner and opening fire. Startled, Nelms sprinted across the open concrete toward the woman hanging out of the car. She was across the first lane in a flash, struggling to arrest her forward momentum as she closed on the woman. She grabbed the woman's shirt and yanked her onto the concrete. The woman flopped onto her side like she had no bones. Nelms grabbed her dress to pull her to the sidewalk, and the woman rolled onto her back.

Her face was a blob of blood, bone and exposed membranes. Nelms stopped pulling, horrified by the sight. She let go of the woman and ran around the SUV, further into the street, looking for someone else. A man was slumped over the median with his head on the street. Too big, he would be too heavy to carry.

She cut right and jumped the median, hearing something suck air as it passed over her head. A small woman was flattened out between two cars. Her shirt, face and hair were a mass of blood but her eyes were wide, looking at Nelms. Nelms dove and grabbed the woman's arm, yanking her hard to her feet.

The woman's legs were limp, she dropped back to the street. Nelms picked her up again, screaming "Get up, get up!" The woman didn't say a word. She just looked back with same wide-eyed expression, completely in shock.

Gunfire from the corner behind Nelms intensified and she heard more shooting from a different spot, somewhere on the west side of Shepherd. Another unseen object hissed by her head, making her duck. She grabbed the woman under her arms and threw her upper body into the air, then lunged forward to get her right shoulder into the woman's abdomen.

She jumped up with the woman in a fireman's carry and turned around. Officers screamed "Hurry up, get out of the fucking street!" The woman started sliding down her right shoulder as Nelms sprinted back to cover.

She was almost to the sidewalk when two explosions ripped the air. The first was on the mosque's roof and the second behind her. A wave of heat and ear-splitting noise washed around her. She felt small, hot needles all over the back of her right leg, from calf to ass.

She reached the sidewalk. Four officers by the side of the building frantically motioned her in. The gunfire subsided as the officers grabbed the wounded woman from Nelms and laid her onto the concrete. Nelms turned and dropped

197

onto her butt, looking back to see a truck on fire in a cloud of dark smoke.

An officer was suddenly by her side. "You alright? That was real close, are you okay?"

In the background gunfire started up again. Someone yelled, "Cover that guy! What the fuck is he doing?"

Nelms' vision was blurry and her eyes stung. She couldn't see around the other officers and had no idea what they were talking about.

"I think I got shot in the back of my leg," she said, suddenly aware she was shaking.

The officer grabbed her shoulder and turned her toward the ground, not forcefully but not gently either. "Lay down on your stomach, let me check you."

She rolled onto her face, scared out of her mind. He was going to tell her she had been shot, she was bleeding to death, there was no hope. She felt his hands on the back of her leg and on her right buttock. Her right pant leg tightened and she looked back to see the officer pulling up a knife.

She realized he had just cut her pants open. Seconds later he cut her granny panties to expose her right ass cheek. She didn't feel the slightest bit embarrassed about having a strange man cutting her clothes off, she was too worried about dying from blood loss.

The officer slapped her on the back of her vest. "You're fine. I'm no doctor or anything, but I think you just got a bunch of little pieces of shrapnel or glass or something all over the back of your leg. The holes are small, and none of them are bleeding bad. You're good."

Nelms looked into his eyes in disbelief. She almost started to blubber but held it in. She reached to the back of her thigh and pulled her hand back to see blood. There was less than she expected.

Suddenly self-conscious of her semi-bare ass, she flipped onto her back. Her butt and leg stung from the pressure, but the pain was bearable. She saw other officers huddled around the woman she had carried in from the street.

"You're sure I'm okay?" she asked the officer who checked her.

"You're fine," he said. "You almost got shot before you almost got blown up. Rounds were landing all around you."

"They were?" she asked. "I didn't know."

"They were. Don't do that again, they'll be waiting for you."

The officer looked back at the civilian woman. She was crying in pain now. He turned back to Nelms, glancing at her nametag. "You know what, Nelms? What you just did was badass. The rest of us have looking at all those people in the street, and not one of us tried to save anyone. Good fucking job."

"It was just one," Nelms replied, her voice small and weak.

"Yeah, it was just one," the other officer said. "But she gets to go home to her family. That's a big deal."

The officer lightly thumped her left leg with his fist, then got up and jogged to the corner to confer with other officers. Two were looking at the mosque, not ducking behind cover anymore.

Nelms pushed herself to the building and sat back. She thought going to look for an ambulance, to get some bandages onto her leg. Then she looked back into the street and at the officers around her.

I'm not hurt bad, I can still help someone if I have to.

She remembered that Walker was at the back of the mosque or maybe inside, and she knew better than to go anywhere without him. That settled it. She wasn't leaving, at least not until her partner came back from wherever he had gone.

———

Eddie Calhoun put the front bumper of his car against an old Pontiac, accelerating to force the car out of his way. The old lady behind the wheel looked at him with terrified eyes and frantically turned the steering wheel back and forth. Calhoun bulldozed her out of the way.

Calhoun had been driving east in the westbound lanes on Crosstimbers, weaving around the few cars that were on the road and making good progress until this stupid old lady came to a dead stop right beside some other asshole and blocked both lanes. The other vehicle was a big Chevy pickup, so he chose the old lady in the Pontiac. She looked like she was having a heart attack as he forced her backward, turned her car into the curb and drove around her.

Just as he passed her he heard a sergeant say on the radio, "219 to all units, SWAT just breached the back of the mosque. Patrol units on Crosstimbers east of Shepherd, move closer to the mosque."

Calhoun was pissed. He needed to get to the mosque, officers were inside and he could help them. He had spent the last ten minutes hauling ass all around the mosque, trying to find a place where he could get close to the firefight. He had been coming from downtown when the shit hit the fan, and by the time he got onto 45 northbound traffic was at less than a crawl, going nowhere. He had scraped two cars as he forced his way onto the shoulder and then drove over grass onto the service road, but the traffic there was just as bad. He finally reached a side street heading east, away from the fight, and made a big circle so he could come back south on Shepherd toward the mosque. Then some chickenshit sergeant stopped him at a roadblock and ordered him to direct traffic. He ignored the sergeant and sped away on a side street, then headed south and finally managed to reach Crosstimbers, several blocks from the mosque.

He made it to a cross street two blocks from the mosque before he ran into another roadblock, with two officers standing outside waving him off. He drove over the curb into a yard to get around their cars, ignored the officers' shouts, hit a truck parked in the driveway and kept driving toward the mosque. He didn't slow until he heard gunfire and saw a black Taurus at an angle in a front yard, resting against a pickup.

Gunfire rang out from the intersection. Calhoun sped up. Ahead near Shepherd another Taurus was smoking and shattered. Something red, black, twisted and vaguely human-looking hung out the driver's door. More bodies were strewn in the road. It was time to get out on foot.

Calhoun hit the trunk release, threw his door open and rushed to get his carbine and chest rig. He had no wife, no kids, a paid-for car, lived in a cheap apartment, had no expensive hobbies other than shooting. He had spent thousands of dollars on a top-of-the-line M4 outfitted with a rail system, expensive red dot sight and powerful tactical flashlight. All his magazines were high quality polymer, his chest rig thick black nylon.

Other officers laughed at him for wearing the chest rig to the carbine qualification range, but he blew them off. If they wouldn't train for the terrorist shit they all knew was coming, fuck them. Calhoun would spend the money on the right weapon and gear for a worst-case scenario, and he'd train with it. He wasn't going to buy a carbine and stick it in the trunk of his car until the one time a year he had to qualify with it. He wouldn't put ten magazines loose in his duty bag, not thinking about how he was going to carry them if he needed to move away from his car. He'd learn how to clear malfunctions. He wouldn't fumble simple magazine changes. Calhoun was going to arm, equip and train himself the way he should. The way he needed to for a situation like the one unfolding today.

He threw the chest rig over his head and secured the clips. The rig had four vertical pouches that could each hold two M4 magazines, but the far right pouch held an Israeli bandage and a tourniquet. He pulled the charging handle on his carbine, threw the sling over his head and sprinted toward the nearest house.

A thick stand of trees lined the edge of the yard next to Shepherd. He looked for the thickest tree to use as cover. He was within fifty yards of the trees before he saw a SWAT officer ducked behind them. The SWAT officer waved frantically.

"Over here! Hurry up!"

Calhoun sprinted over and dropped to a knee, switching his carbine to his left shoulder so he could fire around the left side of the trunk. "English" was printed on the back of the SWAT officer's vest. Calhoun looked over the mosque and intersection. Wrecked cars burned on Shepherd, surrounded by scattered bodies. Diagonally across the intersection a gaggle of officers milled around in front of another building, north of the mosque. Calhoun looked closely and saw the edge of the mosque's roof pockmarked with bullet impacts. The front door and window of the mosque were untouched, it didn't look like anything had hit them at all.

English had four empty magazines at his knees and dozens of spent shells in a wide circle to his right rear. He asked Calhoun, "Are you the only one here? Is anyone else with you?"

"It's just me," Calhoun said. "What do we do?"

"God damn it," English said. "I've been asking for other officers since this thing started. Why'd it take so fucking long for you to get here? And why'd you come alone?"

"I didn't hear shit about you calling for more officers. Two cops back there are blocking traffic from coming this direction, maybe you should talk to them."

English shook his head. Calhoun barely heard him mutter, "That fucking figures."

Calhoun pulled a magazine from his chest rig and tapped him with it. "Here, take this."

English looked at the magazine, then quickly took and and stuck it in his chest rig.

North patrol dispatch broke through on Calhoun's radio. "All units, I need a supervisor to answer me right now! We have multiple reports of a mass shooting, 45 at Little York!"

A sarcastic voice answered. "219, we're sorta busy. Send units from Northeast."

"What did the dispatcher just say?" English asked.

"There's a mass shooting at 45 and Little York."

"Jesus Christ," English said, shaking his head. "That's all we fucking need."

"So what do we do?" Calhoun asked.

"I guess you stay here and cover me," English said. Calhoun thought he looked beaten down, exasperated at the situation. "My SWAT officers just got into the back of the mosque, I'm going to them. After I leave, stay real low. I don't think they've seen me, and they haven't shot at me yet. If the guy with the RPG points it at you, you better haul ass before he blows you away."

"Fuck that," Calhoun said. "I'm not going to sit here and do nothing. I'm going into the mosque too."

"No, I need you here," English said. "Someone has to cover this side in case they come out the front door, and if that that crazy fuck with the RPG pops up again. That asshole's good, he stays real low and ducks right after he shoots. I haven't gotten a clean shot at him yet."

"Stay here and keep shooting at him then," Calhoun said. "I'm crossing the street."

English glared at him, then opened his mouth to say something. Gunfire erupted from across the street. Someone yelled, "Hurry the fuck up!" Calhoun saw a female officer charge into the street.

English blurted, "What the fuck is she doing?"

Calhoun mumbled, "Crazy bitch," and lifted his carbine. He saw a head pop up on the roof, high enough to expose shoulders and a rifle pointing toward the street. The man on the roof stood, giving Calhoun and English a perfect profile shot. They both opened up as he fired at the female officer. The man dropped back below the edge of the wall, then rose a second later and dumped more rounds downward.

Calhoun and English fired again. The man on the roof shuddered and violently arched his back, his rifle went almost vertical. He dropped out of sight below the wall.

Ten feet left of where the man fell, the RPG gunner popped up. Calhoun and the gunner fired at the same time. The gunner dropped the RPG launcher off his shoulder and ducked. Calhoun thought the man had reached up to grab his left shoulder as he fell, but wasn't sure. And the man didn't fall, he ducked. Calhoun was sure the RPG gunner wasn't dead.

The RPG hit a pickup in the street. Calhoun thought the female officer had to be dead, then he saw her run from a dust cloud with a civilian over her shoulder. He lifted his eyes back to the roof and fired several rounds. But there was nothing shoot at anymore.

Calhoun rose to his feet, prepared to rush across the street. Captain English yelled at him, "Get down! Stay here!"

Calhoun said, "I'm going. I don't care what you do."

"Officer, I gave you a fucking order!" English said, face red and eyes full of anger. "I'm a captain, do what I tell you!"

Calhoun thought about how this would affect his chances to get into SWAT someday. Every hardcore, well trained, highly motivated, tactically proficient young officer hoped to get into SWAT. If Calhoun pissed off English, any chance he had was gone.

But if he stayed there, he'd miss out on the biggest fight any police department had ever been involved in, anywhere in America. He was a Marine, his place was inside the mosque, shooting it out with terrorists at knife-fighting distance. Not sitting across the street by himself.

Calhoun answered, "I don't work for you." Then he broke through the trees and ran across the street.

The man dropped out of sight, next to the Volkswagen Beetle. Nunez wasn't sure if he had hit him or not. He had been close, only three cars lengths away. Nunez had hit targets that close thousands of times in training, no sweat. But only a small part of the man had been visible, and Nunez had been in such a rush to shoot he might have jerked the trigger and pulled his muzzle off target. He held his position for a few seconds, hoping the man would stand with hands raised. That wasn't likely, and Nunez was so high on adrenaline he'd probably shoot the guy anyway.

Nunez caught a flash of black below the Beetle's driver side mirror, moving toward the front of the car. He popped a handful of rounds toward the top of the hood, hoping he'd get some through the metal into the man. Then he yanked his carbine the SUV hood he had taken cover behind and sprinted south. When the suspect shot back at him he needed to be somewhere else.

He didn't know how many rounds he had fired, but he thought it was more than half his magazine. He pulled a fresh magazine from his bag, dropping the one in his weapon to the concrete.

Gunfire exploded behind him, near the Beetle he had shot at. He flung himself to the street and flipped to his back, pointing his weapon toward the noise. The SUV he had used as cover shattered into a storm of glass and metal as AK rounds sliced through it. The shooter was somewhere near the Beetle, firing at the spot Nunez had been moments before.

Dammit, he thought. He'd lost the element of surprise. The confrontation with the first suspect had been a shooting, but this one would be a shootout.

Nunez looked under cars, hoping to see the shooter's feet. Too much shit in the way, too many tires and dead bodies. He scrambled to push off the concrete and move south again, trying to put distance between himself and the shooter. Loud bangs hammered the air. He looked back to see another car's windows disintegrate from gunfire.

He cut right, dropping to his knees between a van and a pickup. Neither was cover, but at least they gave him concealment. He breathed in and out slowly, trying to bring his heart rate down, and peered around the corner of the van.

He put his left hand on the bumper to steady himself and saw that he was still holding the full magazine. His carbine had no magazine in it, just one round in the chamber.

He cursed himself and put the magazine in, slapping the base as quietly as possible to make sure it was seated. Then he leaned out again and peered between cars, searching for the shooter.

Nothing. He hopped to his right and looked around the corner. Nothing but bodies. He shifted left and looked again, but there were still no live people. He tried not to look toward the Ford Focus. He didn't want to see the woman still there, pleading and holding her dying baby.

He thought briefly about staying there and waiting for the shooter to move. The prospect of waiting in one spot with threat areas literally all around him gave him the willies. He sat still for a second, trying to figure out where to go next.

He heard more gunfire, five or six rounds from directly ahead. He realized the shooter was somewhere in the same lane with him. Nunez looked around the right side of the van, seeing a car in the lane to the right being blasted apart by gunfire. He dropped down to the concrete just as the shooting stopped. He looked under the van and down the row of cars, searching between tires for the shooter.

Seven or eight cars down he saw feet, barely visible among everything else. An AK magazine dropped to the street next to them. The shooter was changing magazines.

Nunez jammed his carbine under the van. The space he was in was narrow, and he realized he couldn't get his eyes onto his sights unless he laid flat on the concrete, with his legs sticking out in the open. He wasn't about to do that. He stuck his face as close to his sights as possible, flipped the safety off and pulled the trigger.

The rounds sounded like they were hitting everything but the shooter. Two tires between Nunez and the shooter hissed and started to flatten, the shooter's feet beyond them bounced as if standing on coals. They hopped forward, to Nunez's right. Nunez pulled his carbine from the street, jammed it around the corner of the van and fired blind. When he got his eyes were around the corner, he saw nobody. Just dust and smoke.

Glass exploded from the windows of a truck ahead in the next lane. Nunez ducked and sent rounds back toward the truck. He recognized metallic slaps beside him, rounds from the shooter's AK punching through the van he was hiding behind. He lurched to the next lane and ran into another truck, then backedpedalled away as the vehicles he had been using for cover were hammered with bullets.

Adrenaline shot through him as he backed into two open doors and pushed them closed with his elbow. Then he tripped over a dead man, landing on his back four cars away from where he had been. The shooting stopped. He frantically rolled sideways and threw himself behind a random car's back bumper. Breathing heavily, heart about to explode, he leaned right to look around the car.

The shooter was maybe ten cars north, kneeling and looking over his sights, his head high. A delivery van side mirror obstructed his face. Nunez shook as he pulled behind cover, brought his carbine up, put it into his shoulder and prepared to shoot. He breathed in, exhaled, and leaned out to fire.

Taking his eyes off the man had been a mistake. The man hadn't seen him before, but as Nunez leaned around the corner the man looked in his direction. He saw Nunez and spun hard toward him. Nunez fired just as the man hurriedly raised his AK.

Nunez saw his first rounds hit the pavement in front of the man. The man fired back wildly as Nunez tried to shift his aim. Rounds screamed past and hit the car he was behind. Nunez ignored them and kept pulling the trigger. The man suddenly folded at the waist, still firing as he threw himself sideways between two vehicles.

Nunez fired into the car the man was using for cover. After only two rounds his bolt locked to the rear, magazine empty. He jerked behind cover and dropped his magazine, quickly pulling another one from the bag on his hip.

Nunez heard several loud bangs as the shooter fired again. He felt a sudden burn as a round slashed across the top of his left boot, blowing open the laces.

"Fuuuuck!"

Nunez dropped the full mag as he hopped backward on one foot. He spun and sprinted toward another two vehicles, clipped a tow hitch and gashed his knee before falling onto his face. He staggered to his feet, dug into his bag for another magazine, and stumbled south while he slammed the fresh mag into his weapon and slapped the bolt release. His left foot burned like a motherfucker, but he could stand if he kept most of the weight on his right leg. The gash in his knee hurt but hadn't slowed him down yet.

He cut between two cars, turned right and dropped behind a Chrysler. He searched for the shooter, ignoring the pain creeping up his left leg. He was sure he had hit him, but couldn't see him. He sidestepped left, looking for the man who should be somewhere between the cars one lane over.

He stepped over bodies, staying as low as possible, only sticking his head up when he had intact glass to look through. Nothing. He kept going, spending only a few seconds at each car. Open car doors forced him to veer into the street. He skirted the doors and tightened in close to the cars, ignoring the punctured and torn bodies inside some of them.

Through a car window Nunez saw the man's feet, sticking out from behind a car. Nunez immediately stopped, aiming at the feet through the window. The feet didn't move. He thought about firing from right there, through the glass and the trunk of the car the shooter was concealed by. But he didn't know if all the obstacles in the way would deflect the rounds, and if they did it would just give him away. He eased left, very slowly, keeping his weapon off safe, his finger on the trigger and his red dot on the area where he thought the suspect's torso would be.

He cleared of the windows of the car he was behind. If the suspect shot at him now, there was nothing between him and the shooter that would stop an AK round. The trunk of the car in the next lane just barely concealed the man's upper body now.

He was almost positive that the feet belonged to the shooter. Almost. These feet might be attached to some innocent guy's legs who had fallen in a bad spot. If Nunez shot him, he might kill one of the people he was supposed to be trying to protect.

Nunez decided to put a round into one of the man's ankles. That was a shitty option, but he didn't see what else to do. If it was the suspect the round would cripple him, letting Nunez circle around and finish him off. If it was an innocent citizen, hopefully he'd survive.

Nunez aimed and pulled the trigger. The man's ankle erupted in a geyser of blood and the legs above it spasmed. Nunez aimed in again.

AK rounds blasted back at Nunez, tearing through the car he was using as cover.

———————

Two more SWAT officers had arrived and taken positions beside the ramp. Walker and the officer next to him, Miller, yelled to the SWAT guys, filling them in on what they could see from the loading bay. The SWAT officers nearly shit when Walker told them he had seen an officer being dragged into the mosque.

The other officer in the Tahoe was dead. Miller had opened the back door and checked on him. The SWAT officer had been hit repeatedly in the chest and head. Some AK rounds had been stopped by the armor plate on his chest, some had gone over it or to its side. One round had penetrated straight through his helmet, front to back. Miller took the dead SWAT officer's carbine and two remaining magazines but left the body there. There was no reason to risk anyone's life to get him out right then.

When Miller crawled back out of the Tahoe to tell the two SWAT officers the man in the back seat was dead, one of them asked him what color his hair was. Miller said it was hard to tell with all the blood, but it looked blond.

The two SWAT officers looked at each other. Then one of them said on the radio, "Sam 113 to all Sam units, Erikson is DOA. Watson is inside the mosque."

Another RPG round was fired from the other side of the mosque, making them all duck in unison. An additional SWAT officer showed up and took a position on the other side of the ramp. He said he couldn't see anything but bodies.

Two patrol officers ran up and smacked into the wall beside the loading bay. Walker, Miller and the three SWAT officers quietly debated how to get inside the mosque. Walker looked east, toward the grocery store. The parking lot was filling with officers in sky blue shirts, taking cover behind anything they could find. There hadn't been any more fire toward the store for a while. Walker figured it was too dangerous for the suspects on the roof to expose themselves, there were too many guns on them now.

Eddie Calhoun suddenly flew around the corner and dropped to his knee beside the ramp, next to the two SWAT officers.

"When are we going inside?" he huffed. "Are we ready?"

"Not yet," one of the SWAT officers responded. "We need to figure out how to get in there without getting massacred first."

Walker didn't know Calhoun well, but didn't like him at all. Former Marine or not, the guy was a prick. But as long as he was there and willing to risk his ass like everyone else, Walker supposed that was all that mattered.

"Eddie, listen," Walker said. "There's like twenty armed guys inside the mosque. We don't rush into this one. We need to be real careful or we're going to get a bunch of officers killed, and probably get the SWAT officer who got dragged inside killed also."

Calhoun's eyes widened. "A fucking cop got dragged inside there? And y'all are still out here?"

"Yeah we're still out here, dumbass," Walker answered. "We're putting a plan together, just calm down."

Calhoun muttered something under his breath and moved quickly around the ramp toward the driver's side. The SWAT officer on the driver's side of the ramp watched him with a *what the hell are you doing?* expression. Calhoun lunged past him up the ramp, moved quickly along the driver's side of the Tahoe and looked into the mosque. On the other side of the Tahoe Walker and Miller stood in silent astonishment. Walker expected Calhoun to get blown away any second.

Calhoun stopped at the jagged, broken edge of the collapsed wall. He shifted his carbine to his left hand and quickly leaned away from the wall. As soon as he leaned over he opened fire. The officers behind him ducked.

"Move up!" Calhoun yelled. "They're running to the right!"

The SWAT officer jumped onto the ramp, dropped to his knees beside Calhoun and opened up. Walker and Miller scrambled across the Tahoe's hood as the two SWAT officers beside the ramp charged in. The SWAT officer behind Calhoun jerked his carbine away when Calhoun charged forward through his line of fire, then jumped up and went in after him.

Walker hit the edge of the wall and hooked around it. He saw two dead men in the corner of the mosque and another two dead where Calhoun and the SWAT officer had been firing. Several other cops charged in behind Walker.

Walker stopped to look around. He saw Calhoun and the SWAT officer who had gone in with him standing on either side of a hallway entrance. Both officers poured rounds down the hallway. Return fire banged away at them. Walker moved up. He heard rounds snapping through the air between the two officers, heading into the open area of the mosque.

The other two SWAT officers rushed past Walker to back up their teammate at the corner. Calhoun stepped back from the corner, yelling "Cover!" as he dropped an empty magazine from his carbine and pulled a fresh one from his chest rig. On the near corner, all three SWAT officers forced their way onto the same spot on the wall. One laid prone and fired past the feet of the other two, one fired from his knees and one stood. Walker looked back to see patrol officers hanging back, trying to figure out what to do.

Calhoun changed magazines and stuck his weapon back around the corner. He didn't fire. The SWAT officers stopped firing and called out to each other over the echo of deafening gunfire.

"Anyone have a target?"

"Not anymore!"

"Nothing!"

One yelled to Calhoun, "You, across the hallway! Do you have a target?"

"Two down in the doorway on your side!" Calhoun answered. "I don't have any more targets!"

"One or two down in the second doorway on your side," the SWAT officer responded. "And I have a blood trail leading into the first doorway, maybe that's where they took Watson!"

The SWAT officer who seemed to be in charge turned around. He and Walker looked at each other.

"You want to get across this hallway to your buddy so we can get two sets of eyes from that angle?"

"Got it," Walker said. "I'm ready. You covering?"

"You're covered. Move."

Walker charged across the hallway. Something dark registered in his peripheral vision. He jerked his head to look down the hall. Something that felt like an anvil falling from the sky hit his cheek. He recognized the sound of intense gunfire and tasted blood. The floor punched him in the face.

A hand gripped his ankle and yanked. He slid out of the open. His face burned and his head pounded. He tried to focus and couldn't. He pushed himself up but his hand slipped. He went down on his face again, the impact almost making him scream in agony.

Hands jerked him from the floor. Suddenly he was on his feet, seeing nothing but a blur. He knew he was facing the loading bay because all the shooting was behind him. He put his hand to his face and felt shattered teeth where the flesh of his left cheek should have been. He looked down to see blood pour onto his chest from his face, and took one wobbly step toward the back of the loading bay.

Someone yelled in his ear "Are you okay? Can you make it out by yourself?"

Walker nodded and waved the man off. He inched his way back to the ramp as officers behind him dumped what sounded like hundreds of rounds down the hallway.

His vision cleared a bit. He kept moving. At the ramp he tripped over one of the men he had killed. He fell, and this time actually screamed in pain instead of just thinking about it. More patrol officers ran into the loading bay. A sergeant was suddenly in his face, telling him to stay there, someone would take care of him. He nodded and tried to talk. Pain shot through his mouth and he gave up.

Instead of staying at the ramp he staggered back toward the building north of the mosque. That had to be the safest spot. As soon as he turned the corner gunfire erupted from the building to the north. He hoped it was cover fire, for him.

Someone yelled "Hurry! Over here, over here!" But he couldn't run, every step hurt his head and he could barely see. Gunfire rang out from the roof above him. Something whacked into the ground by his feet. He kept going, trying to focus on the next building. He heard glass shatter on the concrete. Then a brief shriek rang out above him, just before a long metal object dropped to the sidewalk two feet away. He recognized the shape of an AK-47 and wondered if he was hallucinating.

He nearly tripped over it, then fell again when he stepped off the sidewalk onto the street. He was getting to his feet when a pair of hands grabbed his belt and yanked him up. Then he was in the air, gripping the back of someone's shirt and waving his other arm for balance as he was carried to the building. The person carrying him staggered as they went over the median, between stopped cars and finally made it around the corner.

Hands pulled him down. He looked up to see Nelm's face as she lowered him off her shoulder. Faraway voices asked if he was okay. He nodded, not wanting to speak. He was surprised to see fire department paramedics appear over him. He hadn't seen ambulances near the scene, the paramedics must have run in from wherever they had parked.

There was another burst of fire at the corner. The mosque was rocked by the noise of an RPG launch. The building they were next to shuddered from a detonation. The two explosions were so close they sounded like one long blast. Officers and paramedics ducked at the sound. Several cursed and looked through windows to see what had been hit. Nelms spun around to look toward the mosque, then turned back and knelt beside Walker. He waved her closer.

"Hey, Thonisha," he whispered.

She leaned in. "What, Ray?"

"Nithe athss," he said, just before a paramedic pushed a bandage onto his face.

———

Nothing was working. The Chechen had ordered one man to get more ammunition and bring reinforcements, but the man hadn't returned. Two of the seven remaining men on the roof had been killed, then the Chechen himself caught a round through his arm as he fired an RPG at a policewoman. His arm wasn't injured badly but he missed the woman, and one of his men had been killed shooting his rifle at her. Now the five fighters who remained were almost unable to shoot at all. If one exposed himself even the slightest bit he faced a deadly barrage of fire. The Chechen knew they were facing many officers now.

The four fighters left with him were cowering behind the wall, nearly out of ammunition. The Chechen took ammunition from the dead and passed it around, but it wasn't enough. He was about to get more ammunition and fighters himself when he heard a huge crash and felt the building shudder. He risked a split-second look over the wall. The mosque had been invaded, the bay door destroyed by a police vehicle. Police were inside and more police were advancing on them.

The Chechen knew it was almost over. He would be dead soon. He had accepted death as a martyr many years before, he had no problem with it. But he did have a problem dying among cowards who refused to fight for their god and cause.

He heard intense gunfire inside the loading bay when the police first entered, then more a minute later, and now heard massive amounts. Not in the loading bay, but in the mosque itself. He hoped his fellow warriors were giving a good account of themselves, slaughtering as many of the unbelievers as they could before they went to paradise.

More bullets split the air, coming from the building across the street. The Chechen looked through an aperture in the wall and saw police firing toward the roof from the same corner he had hit with the RPG before. He was amazed at their stupidity, that they'd use a spot they knew was an easy target for his RPG and sniper rifle. But more than that, he was frustrated at his inability to exploit it. Every time Russians made that mistake in Grozny he made them pay with their lives. But he couldn't do it now, not without brave men to assist him.

He heard frantic voices below, police yelling "Hurry! Over here, over here!" He knew what it meant. Someone was in the street, someone who could be shot down from the roof if proper tactics were used.

One believer was ducked below the edge of the wall on the north side. The Chechen yelled at him, "Get up and fire your weapon over the wall! A police is walking in the street!"

The man looked at him with fearful eyes, then lifted his weapon, stuck it over the wall and fired a few shots downward. Return fire hit the edge of the wall and zinged over the man's head. He yanked his weapon back over the wall and dropped flat.

The Chechen ran in a crouch to the man and yelled, "Stand up so you can see! Shoot him!"

The man looked more afraid of the Chechen than he was of the police.

He swallowed hard, then stood and stuck his rifle over the wall. The Chechen readied his RPG launcher, hoping to hit a mass of men who would go to the aid of whoever was in the street.

A plate glass window on the second floor of the building across the street disintegrated. The Chechen didn't see it but heard glass shatter on the sidewalk below. He knew what that meant.

The Chechen jerked his head up, just in time to hear gunfire explode from inside the shattered window. The man he had ordered to fire shuddered as bullets punched through his upper chest. He dropped his rifle over the wall and collapsed without a sound.

The remaining three fighters were spread out, one on each of the other three walls. When they saw their fellow jihadist fall dead they abandoned their positions and fled toward the Chechen in panic. Now that police were finally in the building across the street and able to fire onto the roof, only the wall facing that building provided any cover.

The Chechen ducked behind the wall. Now he had to decide what to do about the men in the building. He had three men, and an RPG ready to go. If he could get all three men to fire over the edge of the wall at the same time, he might be able to fire an RPG at the broken window across the street. The three men wouldn't even have to expose themselves, they simply had to put their weapons over the wall and fire straight across. Such a tactic would have been easy with the fighters the Chechen had led in Grozny. But with these men, it might be impossible.

"Listen to me!" he ordered. "When I tell you, put your rifles over the wall and fire into the building across the street! Then I will kill the men inside with the RPG! Do you understand?"

Two of them nodded, their faces masks of fear. The third one did nothing but shake. It didn't matter, he would act when the other two did. If not, he wouldn't be needed anyway.

The Chechen crawled to the northeast corner of the roof, getting well away from the three fighters. He didn't want to be close when the police returned fire on them. He wanted his RPG fire to be a complete surprise.

"Get ready!" he yelled, not caring if the police could hear. It made no difference, there was no reason to believe they were going to survive much longer. The men looked at him, their faces sweaty and unsure.

"Now!"

The fighter nearest him threw his muzzle over the wall and opened fire. The Chechen jerked his upper body above the wall and pointed the RPG at the broken window across the street. He aimed in. Then he realized only one of his men was firing.

———

Inside the auto parts showroom, Delacroix and Vickers had spent several fruitless minutes trying to find a way to the roof. The building was bare, just two floors of glass and metal display cases. There was no elevator, just an old staircase that rose from the center of the first floor, cut back and ended at the second floor. The building's alarm shrieked. Vickers couldn't hear Delacroix unless they stood inches away and shouted.

As soon as the two officers were in the building they had raced upstairs to find a spot that would let them fire onto the mosque's roof. The windows on the second floor weren't high enough. Delacroix and Vickers couldn't find anything that remotely looked like roof access on the second floor.

They were still searching when the RPG gunner fired into the street. When they spun around to look through the windows at the mosque all they saw was a huge cloud of dust. Frustrated, they ran back downstairs to search the back of the first floor for another stairwell. Vickers finally found one, a wooden door hidden behind a metal bookshelf stacked with old car manuals. They pushed the shelf over and kicked the locked door open, then charged up four flights of stairs to the roof door.

There was no way through the heavy steel door. Three sets of steel brackets were welded across the steel doorframe. Each set held a heavy steel bar secured by thick padlocks on each end. The building's owners were serious about keeping burglars out.

The two SWAT officers ran downstairs and then back up the middle stairs to the second floor, barely able to discern heavy gunfire coming from the back of mosque over the deafening noise of the alarm. Delacroix found the klaxon and destroyed it with two aimed shots. The building fell silent.

They were trying to figure out what to do when Delacroix jumped onto one of the chest-high display cases.

"Dude, get on a display case! I can see over the wall!"

Vickers was shorter than Delacroix. He struggled to climb a display case six feet to Delacroix's right. He could see over the top of the wall too. But they were completely exposed.

"This sucks," Vickers said.

"Fuck you, it was my idea and I think it's great," Delacroix responded.

"Yeah, it's wonderful," Vickers said. "Now we have the suspects, what, fifty yards away? We have a whole plate glass window to protect us from AK and RPG fire and we're standing on top of these cases. We're pretty much neon 'shoot me' signs right now."

"They can't see us, don't worry about it," Delacroix said. "The glass is mirrored on the outside."

"I guess the mirror will reflect the rounds back at them, just like laser beams in the movies."

"Quit being a bitch," Delacroix said. "We shoot as soon as they pop up. If they shoot back, get behind the display case til it's clear, then we get back up and cover the roof again. Got it?"

"Fine. But if we get killed I'm gonna beat your ass."

"Even if I was dead, you still couldn't beat my ass."

Vickers caught movement on the street, at the back corner of the mosque. He saw an officer stagger around the corner holding his face, the front of his blue shirt almost solid red. He left a blood trail as he slowly moved toward the front of the auto parts building.

"Watch the roof," Vickers said. "There's a wounded officer walking down the street between the buildings."

Delacroix mumbled, "Copy."

Vickers scanned the roof. An AK suddenly flipped over the wall in front of them. No head rose behind it, the weapon just hung over the wall, held with one hand. Flashes erupted from its muzzle. Vickers tensed to fire. Cover fire from officers on the street made the suspect jerk his weapon back behind the wall.

Vickers and Delacroix waited for another target. Vickers saw something through the small openings around the wall on the roof. A shadow moved toward the spot the AK had come from. Seconds later the AK came up again, this time with the shooter behind it.

Delacroix and Vickers opened fire as the man's torso rose over the wall. Vickers expected his shots to just put individual holes through the glass. Instead, the entire plate glass window shattered and fell to the sidewalk.

Oh, shit. Now we're completely exposed.

He kept firing. The suspect's weapon recoiled once before 5.56mm bullets punched through his chest. The man's AK dropped to the street and he disappeared behind the wall.

A man Vickers thought was dead suddenly sprinted toward the north wall. Vickers fired at him and missed. The man disappeared behind the wall. Nothing else moved on the roof.

"You wanna reload?" Delacroix asked.

"Yeah," Vickers said, quickly pulling a full magazine from his chest rig. Instead of dropping the other magazine he threw it into a dump pouch on his left hip.

"I'm up," he said.

"Loading."

Delacroix reloaded. They kept their muzzles on the roof, waiting for more movement. Vickers saw motion through the holes in the wall again. Someone moved to the corner of the roof and stopped.

"Del, someone just moved left to the corner," Vickers said. "You watch there, I'll watch the rest of the wall."

"Got it. Eyes on the corner."

They heard yelling from the roof. Vickers didn't understand what they said. But Delacroix called out, "They just said ready! Watch out!"

Vickers tensed up, more than he already was. He saw movement, and jerked his sight onto the rising form of a human head and torso. The man's AK flashed and rounds split the air between him and Delacroix.

Vickers flinched and fired back. Del yelled "RPG!" over the noise of his own weapon. Vickers heard more glass shatter as the suspect with the AK staggered backward. The man's hand came off the AK's handguard and the muzzle flipped upward. A round hit the ceiling above Vickers' head.

Vickers kept firing. The suspect shuddered and buckled from bullet impacts. He dropped face first, hit the AK's stock with his head and flipped it over the edge of the wall.

Vickers shifted left to Del's target. Delacroix was furiously dumping rounds at a head behind what looked like an enormous green rocket rising from the wall. Vickers fired, smashing out another window. The head jerked. Vickers saw its mouth drop open and shoulders jerk upward in a defensive reflex. Dark haze erupted from the back of the head, just before the RPG burst from its launcher.

The grenade smashed through huge shards of glass at the top of the window pane and penetrated thin fiberglass ceiling panels. Vickers didn't even have time to duck before it detonated on the concrete above them, no more than six feet over Delacroix's head.

Concrete shrapnel exploded downward into the display case Vickers was standing on. The case shattered. Glass slashed Vickers' calves as he tumbled to the floor. His helmet slammed onto the tile. He sucked burning air into his lungs, coughed and spit as he clutched his bloody lower legs.

The bad guys are still on the roof. Someone can fire the RPG at us again. I don't know where Del is.

Vickers opened his eyes and found himself looking the wrong way. He flipped over, pointing his carbine toward the empty space where the windows used to be. He saw nothing on the roof. He started to pull another magazine, then decided against it. He'd worry about a tactical reload later. Right now he had to find Del.

He forced himself to kneel. His calves were on fire. He looked away from blood spilling over his boots as he crawled to where Del had been. Del's display case was shattered and bloody. Above it the false ceiling was blown open. Wires, spars and insulation hung down in a tangled mess.

He stood and staggered behind the display case. Del lay on his back without his weapon, eyes closed and face black. Vickers knelt beside him. Del had a pulse and was breathing. Vickers couldn't see any blood, other than on his legs.

Vickers moved away from Del. He had to get his eyes back on the mosque. He slid out from behind the display case, thought about finding another one to stand on and immediately dismissed it. He had trouble climbing onto the display case earlier, with wounded legs there was no way in hell he could get onto another one.

He dropped to his ass and leaned against his shattered display case. His legs burned like crazy now, and the sight of blood spreading from his calves made him nauseous. He became aware of loud ringing in his ears, then pain, then noticed his head was pounding. He had his weapon in his shoulder pointed at the mosque, but after less than a minute he lowered it onto his thighs, too tired to hold it up anymore.

It occurred to him to get on the radio and tell someone what had happened. He and Delacroix had killed two suspects with AKs on the roof. He was almost positive they had also killed the RPG gunner. Del was down. That was probably important information. He reached up and keyed his radio.

He was talking to Captain English when four patrol officers rushed up the stairs to the second floor, took positions covering the roof and made Vickers lie back so they could check him out.

He mumbled, "Check on Del first."

But paramedics had already come up the stairs and were kneeling over Del. Vickers popped his helmet strap and pulled it off. Then he laid back on the floor, accepting that he'd done all he could.

———

Nunez ignored the burning on his face as he shoved a fresh magazine into his carbine, slapped the bolt release and loaded a round into the chamber. He was lying prone, ignoring the blood dripping onto the pavement under him, cursing himself and the suspect. He looked under the car and cursed again, unable to see the man at all. He took a deep breath and rose slowly to his knees.

Nunez knew he'd hit the son of a bitch when he shot back. After Nunez's first shot had hit him in the foot, the man had nearly blown Nunez's head off with a burst that tore through two cars. The rounds missed Nunez by inches. Shards of metal exploded at Nunez as bullets punctured the thin metal of the car he was behind. He felt his face burn as he emptied his entire magazine through the car in front of him, back toward the shooter.

He was positive some of his rounds had hit. He couldn't have missed. Not from that distance.

Nunez slid left, injured foot throbbing and gashed knee burning as he moved to the next car. He couldn't hear anything. No sounds of a magazine being dropped to the ground, no bolt being cycled to reload. No screaming, no crying, nothing. He dropped prone again and looked under the car. The tires on the other side of the car were flat, the car was too low for him to see under.

"Son of a bitch," he whispered, rising to his feet. He had to move to where he could see the suspect.

Nunez considered circling around, then dropped the idea. He was tired, pissed off, bleeding and in pain. Enough was enough. He was tired of chasing this asshole.

Nunez lifted his carbine to his shoulder and backed away from the vehicle slightly, just so he could get the muzzle of his weapon over the hood. Then he rose slowly, heart hammering, muzzle pointed where the suspect had been. He flicked the safety off and took up trigger slack, ready to shoot.

He couldn't see anything.

"I don't believe this shit," he whispered in frustration. "He has to be there."

The suspect might have fallen onto his back, which meant Nunez had to get up higher to see him. He kept rising.

Black hair came into view. Nunez jerked back down without thinking, then cursed himself. Now he'd have to do it again.

He forced his head up again, more tense than he had ever been in his life, looking for the black hair. He decided he was going to shoot the man in the head, as soon as he had enough of a target.

He saw the hair and froze immediately. The head hadn't moved. It looked like the man was slumped against the front bumper of a car. Nunez breathed in and blinked to clear his vision, then leaned forward as slowly as he could, getting clear of the hood. The man's entire face rose into view.

Nunez was startled to find himself looking into Rahim's eyes. His face was smeared with blood, eyes dull and heavy. He glared at Nunez with a face as hateful as the last time Nunez had seen him, in front of his apartment weeks before.

Nunez centered his dot on Rahim's face. No reaction. Rahim looked back, eyes full of undying fury. Nunez pulled the trigger.

Rahim's head rocked as a round hit him under the nose. His face went slack, but his eyes stayed fixed on Nunez. Nunez fired again. Half of Rahim's lower jaw blasted away in a spray of blood and tissue. His head snapped sideways, eyes no longer on his enemy.

Nunez fired again, shattering part of Rahim's skull. Rahim slid to the street. Nunez stood at full height and went cyclic. Rahim's body convulsed as Nunez reduced him to a butchered, shredded, nearly headless mass of smashed bone, punctured internal organs, ripped muscle and pulverized brain matter.

Nunez's magazine ran dry. He stared at the body through gunsmoke, overcome with fury at Rahim. All the innocent people murdered, all the families who'd be in agony tonight because of him and his partner. All the evil he committed, for no reason that could ever be justified to any decent human.

Reload, dumbass. And look around.

Nunez had to get his head out of his ass. Another suspect might be running loose. He dropped the empty magazine, pulled another from his bag, reloaded and realized he was nearly out of spare ammo.

He crouched low and turned around. He couldn't see anyone except a scattering of people standing around cars far to the south, holding cell phones in the air. Nunez ignored them, searched in all directions. Nothing on the highway but bodies.

He moved across the highway, looking up and down each lane. Close in he saw only the dead, but in the distance spectators clustered between vehicles, looking toward Nunez. Nunez stood and raised his carbine.

Spectators ducked. No gunfire. No screams. There were no more suspects. It was over.

Nunez lowered his carbine and leaned against a car, breathing deeply to calm himself. Then he saw three bodies inside. He moved away. At the next car he stopped again, looking at the glass to see his reflection, wondering how badly his face had been hit. Two more bodies were inside that car but he ignored them, focusing on himself.

A wave of relief spread through him. Relief that he was still alive, that he'd go home to his wife and kids. He'd beaten them. He'd gone muzzle to muzzle with two terrorists, done his best, and it was enough. He won.

Nunez looked side to side, taking in the sight of innocent, dead Americans scattered in ones and twos on the highway. Men, women and children shot in the back as they fled in panic from two heartless murderers. He never expected to see that, not in America.

He turned back to the car window, looking into his own reflected eyes. He was alive. Nobody was going to find him dead on the highway, surrounded by empty magazines and spent shells. He was still standing.

Nunez looked past his reflection, into the old, run-down car. The driver, a young Hispanic man, was slumped over a young Hispanic woman in the passenger seat. He wore blue jeans and a plaid western shirt. An old, bloody cowboy hat lay on the floorboard. He had died trying to shield the woman with his body.

Nunez took a hard look at them. Two people who had done nothing to deserve their deaths. Who would never go home to happy, smiling children. It had been Nunez's job to protect them. He had failed miserably. He had failed all of them, all the dead, and there he was, celebrating his own survival. He looked into his own reflected eyes again.

You're a selfish, sorry fuck.

He turned away from the car and walked north, ignoring pain creeping back into his legs and face, searching for a specific car. He couldn't remember where it was. He went between cars, from lane to lane, over shattered bodies, pushing open doors out of the way. There it was, one lane to his left.

He started to run toward it and tripped, barely staying on his feet. He squeezed between two cars and finally saw them, the woman's arm still outstretched, her hand where it had been when she had grabbed his pant leg.

He dropped to his knees into the pool of blood around them, reaching to the woman's throat but knowing there was no hope. She looked past him as he felt for a pulse, her eyes as dull and grey as those in every other corpse he had ever seen.

He let go and gently touched her baby's head, turning its face away from the woman's chest. The baby's eyes were closed, its mouth open and bloody. He put his hand on its back, feeling for a heartbeat and breathing, like he had with his own children when they were newborn.

Nothing.

"I'm sorry," he whispered. "I tried to help you. I swear I tried."

He ran his hand through the baby's hair, then took its mother's outstretched arm and gently placed it over the baby's back. His eyes blurred and he wiped tears away. If he had been seconds faster, maybe just one second faster, this young woman and her baby wouldn't be cold and still on the street.

He closed his eyes. Sounds he had blocked out during the fight slowly faded in from the background.

A distant explosion thumped, followed by the chatter of gunfire. His radio hissed and sputtered in his ear. It was the first time he heard it since he tried in vain to report the shooting.

His fellow officers, his brothers, were in a fight at the mosque. He still had a mission. He needed to get to the mosque.

His car was trapped in the massive jam on the southbound side of the highway. But maybe he could get the other patrol car out, the car that belonged to the older officer who had been killed. And if that car was stuck, Nunez would start checking civilian cars until he found one with keys in it. Or he would climb down to the service road and carjack someone, anything to get into the fight.

The sound of screaming reached him. He looked toward the sound. Another voice joined in, a second squeal of pain and fear. Nunez craned his neck, trying to pinpoint the sources.

A door popped open ten cars away. A man kicked himself onto the concrete, moaning and clutching his arm. Further south a voice yelled "I think they're dead, I think he killed them!"

Distant bystanders started cautiously running north. Some stopped when they reached bodies, knelt and looked for signs of life. Nunez limped to the space between the next two lanes. More people crawled from their cars crying and screaming for help. Good Samaritans ran toward them.

Nunez rubbed his face. What he had been thinking was ridiculous. He couldn't leave the highway now, he couldn't abandon people who desperately needed his help. He had been a fool to think he could. He looked southwest, where good guys who wore his uniform were locked in desperate combat with an evil, vicious enemy. He wanted to stand with them, to blast the life out of those who had attacked their country.

Nunez made the hardest decision of his life. He slung his carbine over his shoulder, searched his bag for his medical trauma kit, put the mosque out of his mind and started looking for people to help.

———

The *imam* crouched in a corner of his office, staring openmouthed at the two dead believers lying in the office doorway. He was trapped. They were all trapped.

When the police had driven into the loading bay, four brave followers fired into their SUV from close range and hit every officer inside. Two managed to drag out one of the policemen. But the two who had tried to get another officer had been shot down before the *imam*'s eyes.

Getting the officer's body was the right thing to do. In the *imam*'s country, gaining enemy bodies gave great power. If the enemy was an infidel his body could be displayed in the streets, mutilated so its soul would be unable to enter heaven as its false religion promised. If the enemy was a believer his body could be exchanged for prisoners, food, ammunition or the promise of a temporary truce used to rebuild your tribe's strength. If one of your own dead was captured it was time to negotiate, not press the attack.

The *imam* had told them to take the policeman to one of the small rooms on the lower level. Then the *imam* would begin negotiations, make demands of the police commanders. And perhaps some of the faithful would live to fight again in another place, at another time.

The police did not respond as they should have. First they killed the two believers who tried to get the second officer. Then the *imam* had been shocked to see a policeman lean into the prayer area and immediately shoot down two more of the faithful. His remaining followers had backed into the hallway and ran inside the mosque's two offices as more police flooded their sacred house of worship. Those who stood and fought were shot down within seconds.

One man in the second office had stuck a pistol out of the doorway and fired toward the police. So many enemy fired back, the man gave up and ran to the back wall. The *imam* had only two followers with him in the front office, and they were armed with only pistols. He knew another one or two were in the office across the hall, but that was all. He hoped the Chechen was still on the roof, killing the police outside.

One of the Chechen's fighters had come down from the roof earlier to pass a message. That young man was now lying dead in the doorway across the hall from where the *imam* stood. The *imam* had not seen Arredondo since he went with the Chechen to fight from the roof. He wished Arredondo hadn't gone, the man's knowledge of American police could help them now.

"*Imam!* What do we do?" one of the men with him pleaded. The *imam* had no answers, at least none the man wanted to hear. They would be martyred soon. There was no use trying to avoid it.

"We give our lives to our God, and ask that he accept us into paradise," the *imam* answered.

The man's eyes widened. He ran to the window beside the front door of the mosque, looking out to the street. Then he yelled to the other man in the office, "Come with me! We can run across the street and find a car! We can escape!"

A voice in the mosque yelled, "They're gonna make a break for it! Get on the radio and tell everyone!"

The *imam* shook his head. He put his arm on the man's shoulder and said softly, "There is no reason to run, my brother. We die here or we die in the street. We are blessed, martyrdom awaits us."

Across the hallway in the other office the *imam* heard loud, excited talking in what he recognized as Urdu, the language of Pakistan. A dark-skinned man in the office with the *imam* said quietly, "They are going to surrender."

The *imam* called across the hall, "Brothers, do not surrender! Carry out your duty to God. Be brave!"

A policeman answered, "Fuck you, you sorryass piece of shit! Shut your fucking mouth!"

"Do not surrender!" the *imam* shouted. "Do not betray your faith!"

Across the hall two young men stuck their hands from the doorway. One yelled, "We are coming out! Do not shoot!" as they stepped hesitantly into the hallway.

The *imam* was livid. He could not imagine any true believer choosing a life of humiliation in prison over everlasting paradise. Police yelled commands to the two men to walk toward them with their hands raised. The *imam* grabbed a pistol from one of the men with him. He stepped to the door, jammed the pistol around the edge of the door frame and fired blind into the hallway.

Return fire from what sounded like thirty guns exploded toward him. As the *imam* jerked his arm back he saw the two Pakistani men fall by the office door, shot in the back as they turned to run. One looked at the *imam* with wide, horrified eyes. An instant later, a bullet tore through his face.

A hand grabbed the *imam* and yanked him toward the front door. He heard door hinges creak before one of his followers pulled him into open air, down the stairs and into the front parking lot. Another follower flew past, threw his pistol to the concrete and fled toward the street.

Weapons exploded at them from the left and right. Bullets tore past their faces and smashed into cars around them. The *imam* dug his heels in to make the man pulling him stop, stand and face death like a true warrior. The man let go and ran shrieking toward the street, hands held high.

"Don't shoot! Don't shoot!"

A weapon barked ahead. A black-clothed officer sprang up from behind a tree and opened fire at the two men running toward him. The man in the lead jerked his hands to his chest and fell to the street in a fetal position, his legs kicking weakly as rounds ripped into his body. The second man, the one who had been dragging the *imam*, tried to stop, held his hands in the air and screamed like a woman.

"I surrender! Don't shoot!"

The right side of his head exploded. He flopped to the street, twitching madly and screeching the shrill cry of a wounded beast. The *imam* gasped, backed up as bullets flew close by, then turned and sprinted toward the front door. Terror and panic gripped him. He did not deserve to die like this. His holy mission was to inspire others to die as martyrs, not to be martyred himself.

As he reached the stairway a bullet pierced his lower back and exploded out of his abdomen, dropping him onto his back on the concrete. The burning pain was more than any human could possibly bear. He tried to scream. Nothing came out, he couldn't breathe. He pulled his knees up and a bullet blew his right kneecap apart. Suddenly his voice returned, his scream more piercing and inhuman than his follower's had been.

He clutched his leg and tried to block the blood spraying onto his face. Two policemen in blue shirts advanced on him from the corner of his mosque. Fire exploded from their weapons. Bullets tore through his chest, legs and stomach. He feebly raised a hand in defense. It still held a pistol. He desperately tried to yell *No, no!* to the two infidels firing on him.

His unbelievable pain and impossibly loud scream vanished as the policemen blasted his internal organs apart from less than twenty feet away.

Parker couldn't believe no officers had been killed by ricochets in the hallway. At least ten officers had fired down the hallway at the two men who were trying to surrender. Some cops probably didn't know some other asshole in one of the offices, not the men surrendering, had shot at them. Other officers probably knew, but didn't care.

The hallway was only fifty feet long, the end the officers were firing toward was just a flat concrete wall with steel framing that deflected some rounds back down the hallway. A few cops had taken either pistol bullets or ricochets from other officers' weapons. Nobody had been killed but a couple officers were out of the fight, crawling or being helped from the hallway.

After they killed the two men in the hallway Parker heard the door in one of the offices open, then gunfire and screams outside. He smiled. They hadn't heard anything since then.

A sergeant gave verbal commands for anyone in the offices to come out, but there was no response. The textbook thing to do now would be to set up a cordon on the two offices and send in a K9 or call a negotiator. But the textbook had long since been thrown away.

Someone in the mass of officers in the mosque yelled "I think we got them all!"

Patrol officers immediately rushed the two offices, ignoring SWAT's orders to stop. That maniac Calhoun immediately charged into the door a blood trail led to, then yelled behind him, "It's a stairwell! I need other people with me, fast!"

Parker followed five or six other officers into the stairwell. The blood trail led downstairs, not upstairs. That made sense. They wouldn't have dragged an unconscious body up a stairwell.

Calhoun yelled, "I'm going to the roof! Who's with me?"

Parker watched three officers rush to Calhoun. Parker and the other two SWAT officers pushed past them to get to the lower level. Moreno took lead as they crept down the stairs. The stairwell led to the short hallway of the lower level. Two rooms were on the right and three on the left. All the doors were wide open.

The SWAT officers stopped several steps from the bottom and squatted, looking into the hall. Guthrie tapped Moreno on the shoulder and pointed to the blood trail. It led to the second door on the right. They sat silently in the stairwell, trying to figure out how they were going to clear all five rooms with three people.

Parker leaned close to Moreno and whispered, "Should one of us go back up and get some patrol officers to help out?"

Moreno whispered back, "They'd fuck everything up."

Parker gave Moreno a *now what?* gesture. Moreno mouthed, *I don't know.*

From down the hallway a shaky voice said, "Hello? Is someone there?"

The SWAT officers raised their weapons. Nobody spoke. Parker took another step down the hallway, trying to get a better look. The voice spoke again, with no foreign accent.

"Hey, police? Y'all there?"

The SWAT officers looked at each other. Guthrie shrugged and whispered, "What the fuck, might as well try it."

"Houston police!" Moreno yelled back. "Come out with your hands up!"

Hands jutted from a room on the left. "Don't shoot me, alright? I can help you out. I have information."

"Get out of the room, asshole," Parker growled. "And you better keep your fucking hands up when you do it."

The man stuck his head into the hallway. "I ain't got no weapons, man. I ain't even really part of this group. They were forcing me to do stuff for them."

"Where's the cop they brought down here?" Parker asked, his red dot centered on the man's face.

The man pointed across the hall, toward the second room on the right. "He's in there! There's two guys in there with him, they got a bunch of guns and shit!"

Rifle fire exploded from the room he was pointing toward. Rounds slammed into the wall in front of the man. He screamed and disappeared from the doorway.

An AK thrust out from the door, still facing toward the man on the other side of the hallway. Screams sounded from the room the man had ducked into. More rounds blasted from the rifle toward the man, then the rifle turned toward the SWAT officers. Arms and a head appeared behind it.

All three officers opened fire. The AK fired several times toward the stairs before the man holding it dropped sideways onto the floor in the hallway, his face a bloody mess. The officers hit him with fifteen or twenty more rounds, punching the life out of him. Then they saw him slide a few inches as someone tried to pull him back into the room by his legs.

Moreno rushed down the stairs to the door the dead man was sticking out of. He stuck his head in the doorway, opened fire and lunged through the doorway. Parker sprinted in behind him.

Moreno stood a few feet from the door. A man on the floor jerked violently and clutched a pistol as Moreno's carbine rounds punched through his torso. Parker scanned for other suspects as Guthrie flipped around to cover their backs.

The second suspect was definitely dead. Moreno had hit him in the face and upper chest several times. Watson was heaped into a corner, obviously dead. Parker went through the motions of checking his pulse, then sighed and turned around.

A handful of AK-47 rifles were in the room, laid neatly in wooden racks nailed to the walls. Rifle magazines were piled in two corners of the small room. Parker couldn't imagine why the suspects hadn't used them.

Across the hallway the other man was still screaming in agony. Guthrie kept his weapon on the man as he shrieked and grabbed his stomach. Parker stepped behind him and asked, "What you got?"

Patrol officers were coming down the stairs, calling out to the officers in the hallway. The SWAT officers knew their precise procedure for clearing rooms was about to go out the window; the patrolmen would simply charge inside and flood every room. Tactically that was a bad thing, but Parker really didn't mind all that much anymore.

It had been a bad day. Several of his friends were dead, he was tired, he wouldn't complain if he never had to clear another room in his life. For all he cared, patrol officers could throw fragmentation grenades into every room, then burn the damn mosque down.

"Over here," Parker called to the patrol officers. "This room's clear. We've got one SWAT officer down in here. The other rooms still need to be cleared." Then he pointed across the hall, toward the room the screams were coming from.

"One suspect is wounded in that room, shot by his own guys. Darn the luck."

A Fox unit, from Houston's helicopter division, had finally been cleared to fly over the mosque. The pilot reported seven motionless bodies on the roof. Calhoun was hunched down just outside the roof door, with another officer squatting in the open door behind him. The door was offset from the roof, half the doorway above roof level, half below it. Four steps led from the doorway to the roof.

Calhoun kept his head below the edge of the roof. He knew officers were in the building to the north, he would have to be real careful if he fired that way. And he was worried they would mistake him for a suspect and shoot at him when he moved onto the roof.

"Patrol, I see you in the stairway," the Fox pilot said over the radio. "I don't see any movement from the suspects on the roof, there's no reason for you to go up there. Back down, we'll have officers cover them from across the street."

"1113 to Fox, screw that," Calhoun radioed back. "We're not going to take a chance on letting these guys shoot anyone else. Watch them and tell us if you see any movement."

"Fox to 1113, we think that's a bad idea, but we'll keep eyes on for you."

Calhoun turned to the officer crouching behind him. "I'm about to go onto the roof. As soon as you get up there with me, I'll take right and you take left. Cool?"

The officer behind him nodded, his eyes dark and determined. Calhoun didn't know him, but he had been right on Calhoun's ass almost since he got into the mosque and he handled his carbine well. He looked like he could be trusted.

Calhoun turned and crept up one step, straining to stay low. He breathed in, blew out, and lifted his head.

Five bodies were spread along the north wall. One was on his back with an RPG launcher across his face and part of his head beside him. Two others lay along the wall on their stomachs with their heads facing the door, their eyes closed and weapons under their bodies. None showed signs of life.

Calhoun searched to his right. Nothing. He snapped his head left, seeing another two bodies. They weren't moving.

Calhoun waved the next officer up. The small stairway was narrow, barely wide enough for one person. The officer behind Calhoun would have to scrape the wall to get past Calhoun.

As soon as Calhoun felt the other officer against his leg, he shifted right to cover the five bodies in front of him. His muzzle settled on the man with the RPG.

One of the two dead bodies parallel to the wall had its eyes open. Calhoun looked at the body, trying to remember if its eyes had been closed before. The suspect's AK lay on its left side under the man's stomach, pointed toward Calhoun. The man raised his stomach slightly. Calhoun realized the man was getting his torso clear of the charging handle, so it wouldn't catch on his clothes and jam the rifle when he fired.

Calhoun snapped his rifle left and fired as he tried to drop below the edge of the roof. The suspect's weapon kicked up a sudden dust cloud. Calhoun's head jerked as a single round just missed the top of his collarbone, blowing away the skin and muscle at the juncture of his head and shoulder.

His eyes closed against his will. He forced them back open, ignoring pain as he walked rounds upward into the suspect's chest. Another man on the roof sat up and swung his weapon toward Calhoun.

Calhoun shifted his weapon onto the other man, puncturing his body with his last ten rounds. The man stopped shuddering from the impacts as Calhoun went limp and fell down the stairs. The officer behind him backed up to let him fall, then charged past and threw his muzzle over the edge of the roof, opening fire before he could see what he was shooting at.

Someone grabbed Calhoun's collar and yanked him back through the doorway. A shadow flashed over Calhoun and he felt someone stomp on his thigh. More officers darted past.

Calhoun grabbed the base of his neck. His fingers disappeared into ripped, bleeding flesh. He looked at his hand and saw it drenched in blood. Officers on the roof blasted away. One screamed, "Shoot them all!"

Calhoun felt lightheaded. His vision started to go grey around the edges, his breath shortened. His heart raced, beating faster than ever in his life. His arms weakened and his neck throbbed in time with the pulsing of his heart.

Someone dragged him the rest of the way down the steps, onto the landing. Gunfire raged on the roof. An officer jammed his hand onto Calhoun's neck, pressing down to stop the bleeding. It didn't hurt as much as Calhoun thought it should.

Calhoun flipped his carbine safety on so nobody would accidentally fire it when they took it off his body. Two more officers ran past him. He moved his muzzle away from them as best as he could.

Hands grabbed his shoulders and jerked him a few more feet from the stairs. Officers sprinted past. One of the hands on his shoulder lost its grip. Calhoun's head bounced on the tile. And he was out.

A sergeant ran past a bleeding officer on the landing and continued to the roof, less than a minute after patrol officers fired into the heads of every suspect. SWAT and patrol had cleared the lower level and arrested one badly wounded suspect. The sergeant had personally checked both offices on the main floor, and now the roof was clear.

As far as the sergeant could tell, all the suspects in the mosque were dead or in custody. A lot of civilians and cops were down, but the bad guys had lost the fight. It was over.

The sergeant crouched below the roof's wall and waved his arms to the north, signaling to the officers in the auto parts building. Then he carefully did the same thing to the west, then south, then east. A few rounds banged over his head, but shouted orders from other officers on the street brought the shooting to a halt.

The sergeant slowly rose to full height, waving his arm and calling out on the radio, "Cease fire, we have the roof!"

Exhausted, adrenaline-hyped policemen rose from covered positions around the mosque as the sergeant broadcast again. "All units at Shepherd and Crosstimbers, the mosque is clear. I say again, the mosque is clear. Send ambulances up, we've got a lot of civilians and officers down."

The sergeant looked back at policemen handcuffing dead suspects. One met the sergeant's eyes, raised his eyebrows and shook his head. The sergeant gave him a half smile and nod, then keyed his radio again.

"It's over, guys. It's over."

EPILOGUE

Nunez's Jeep crept down the street to his house and turned slowly into the driveway. Nunez parked. Then he just sat back, letting the engine run.

He had listened to the radio for some of the drive but finally turned it off, tired of hearing news that was either being repeated incessantly or was flat out wrong. One reporter said ten police officers were killed on the highway and none at the mosque, one reported a civilian had killed the suspects on the highway, another quoted witnesses who swore police had fled from the highway and left helpless civilians to their fates. Nunez couldn't listen to it anymore.

Laura stood inside the window, looking at him through the glass. She was holding their son, and probably had been for hours. School had been cancelled throughout the city and Laura had sent their daughter to a friend's house to play, knowing Nunez badly needed sleep. But she kept their son with her, instead of waiting at home alone. Whenever she was afraid for Nunez's life, she held the kids close. She needed the reassurance they always gave her. He needed it too.

Laura didn't know he had been in the shootout on the highway. An hour after it was over he called to tell her he was okay, but he wouldn't be home for a long time. He didn't tell her what he'd done. She'd find out later.

It was three in the afternoon, the day after the attacks. Nunez was on duty for more than twenty-four hours before finally being sent home. He spent hours after the attacks aiding victims, being treated by EMS, walking investigators through the scene, and ignoring reporters when they asked him for a quote.

A lot of officers had congratulated him, slapped him on the back gently and told him what a great job he'd done. Nunez hadn't really responded. He understood in a strictly dispassionate, unemotional sense that he had done well on the highway. The death toll would have been much higher if he hadn't been there.

But anytime he thought about congratulating himself for being a hero, he saw thirty-three civilians and one police officer dead on the highway. He wasn't a hero. He hadn't rushed in and saved the day, and he damn sure hadn't been fearless. He had just been in the right place at the right time, and saved some people. That was all.

Woods had called Nunez almost in tears, apologizing for not making it in on time. He had gotten there well after everything was over. It wasn't his fault, and Nunez didn't blame him. He would have been there if he could have. Nunez wished Woods had been with him on the highway, he could have used the backup. On the other hand, if Woods had been there maybe he would have been another dead officer.

Three SWAT officers were dead, three more wounded, and one of those might not survive. The SWAT officer who had been shot on Crosstimbers lost his arm but was stable. Nunez heard conflicting accounts about what SWAT had done at the mosque, but almost everyone agreed on one crucial point. The turning point in the fight was when three SWAT cops rammed the loading bay door. Two of them had given their lives to do it, the third took a round under the helmet and was in a coma.

Patrol had suffered too. Five killed, more than twenty wounded. Most of the wounds were superficial, light shrapnel from bullet fragments, flying glass or concrete. But some were bad. Walker had been shot in the face, he'd be getting multiple plastic and dental surgeries for years.

There were psychological injuries as well. A female probationary was carried back to the station in a hysterical fit, screaming about her partner who had been killed by a sniper. A sergeant had to disarm her, and later someone found her bloody uniform shirt, body armor and duty belt in one of the station's bathrooms. She just disappeared in the general confusion at the station. As far as Nunez knew nobody had found her yet.

A young male officer who had done a good job on the south side of the mosque also disappeared. He left his badge on a sergeant's desk and walked out. Some senior officers were saying, "That's enough of this shit, I'm retiring," but Nunez doubted they meant it.

Calhoun had been hit badly. His carotid artery was almost cut, his spine missed by inches. But he'd live. Word around the station was that Calhoun led the charge into the mosque. Nunez and a lot of other officers owed him a huge apology. Calhoun might be the biggest asshole anyone ever met, but when he had been needed, he was there. Nunez would have to visit him in the hospital, as soon as they both got the rest they needed.

None of the patrol officers who were wounded were in danger of dying. Nunez tried to look on the bright side. Maybe losing "only" eight cops wasn't all that bad. The words were empty, meaningless and absolute bullshit, but they were all he could come up with.

Delisle had called to make sure he was alright and let him know that Arredondo, the lone survivor from the mosque, was at the hospital and talking. Not just talking but screaming, begging them to believe he'd been an unwilling victim, that he only went along because he was scared they'd kill him if he didn't. He was having a hard time explaining the crossed swords, crescent moon and Koranic verses tattooed all over him, but he was playing the innocent victim for all it was worth.

Delisle gave Nunez the happy news that Arredondo would be in a wheelchair and shitting into a bag for the rest of his life. Good for him, they had agreed. Nunez knew Arredondo had been in on the plot, had probably gotten the RPG from Mexico. Fuck him, he deserved whatever pain he got. All those assholes who had been part of the plot deserved the deaths they had gotten. Nunez hoped every last one of them suffered before they died.

Thirty-three innocent people had been shot down and murdered on the freeway. Twenty-seven more died around the mosque. Sixty American civilians, plus eight cops, murdered by evil, pathetic cowards. Dozens more were wounded, and some of them would certainly die.

Other officers were talking about footage of Muslim groups demonstrating in London, Kabul, and Baghdad, cheering the attacks and holding signs praising the terrorists. There hadn't been any of those demonstrations in the United States, but Nunez was sure that somewhere in his own country, people were celebrating the attacks as well. The thought sickened him.

A few commentators on TV were complaining about the use of "disproportionate force" by police, arguing that Nunez and his fellow officers should have somehow been gentler on cowards who were slaughtering innocent citizens. Fuck them. Despite his misgivings about his own performance, Nunez was proud to be a Houston cop, proud of how officers at the mosque had responded when the city desperately needed them. They hadn't sat back at a safe distance and taken time to organize, they hadn't tried to use some bullshit formula or policy to handle the fight at the mosque. They had closed as quickly as they could, made plans and decisions on the spot, and destroyed the threat. Nunez couldn't help but feel proud of the department.

And the people of Houston seemed to be proud of them as well. Just like after 9/11, Houston's streets were suddenly filled with American flags. The North police station's lobby was filled with flowers from caring citizens who wanted to honor the eight officers who died to defend them.

There had been an attempted Mosque burning in Illinois, and in Arizona an Indian postal worker had been beaten by someone who didn't know that his turban meant he was a Sikh, not a Muslim. But in Houston itself there hadn't been any reported attacks on Muslims, and Houston's Muslim community was publically denouncing any violence committed in the name of Islam.

Nunez hoped the proclamations were sincere. He didn't want to see anything like what had happened on the highway, ever again.

Nunez turned the engine off. He got out of his Jeep and locked the door, not bothering to get his carbine from the trunk. Laura was waiting at the door, and as soon as he was in the threshold she gave him a long hug, holding their son between them. He was only wearing his torn pants, duty belt and a fresh t-shirt someone had given him. His bloodstained uniform shirt and body armor were crumpled in the back of the Jeep.

Neither of them spoke as they hugged. Laura looked at her husband's face with concern, seeing the small bandages and swollen bumps on his temple and cheek. She looked down to see his right pant leg ripped and another bandage visible on the knee. She rubbed his ripped left boot with her foot.

Nunez finally broke free, kissed his son on the cheek and walked to the bedroom. Laura followed, watching him pop the keepers on his duty belt and drop it to the floor. He kicked his right boot off and gently tugged his left boot off with his hands, wincing slightly from the pain.

His foot wasn't bad, it just had a good cut. The hospitals had been so overwhelmed he hadn't wanted to burden them with such a minor injury. He let paramedics bandage it and told them he'd get it checked later. The cut in his right knee was painful, but not too deep. He'd survive it.

He pulled his pants off and carried them to the bathroom, not wanting to get blood on the carpet. Laura sat on the bed silently watching him, waiting for him to talk. When he sat back down she rubbed his back gently, then leaned against him and put her arms around his waist.

He leaned back, putting his face into her hair, trying to force himself to relax. It was over, he was home, his family was safe. He didn't have to be on guard now.

He'd eventually have to tell Laura what happened. He wanted to talk to her. He just didn't know if he could get across what he was feeling, or make her understand anything he had seen and done the day before.

He said quietly, "It was bad, Laura. Really bad."

"I know it was, honey," she said soothingly. "I've been watching the news. It must have been horrible."

"The news can't describe what it was like."

"I know," she said. "You can talk to me about it, when you're ready."

Nunez didn't know if he would ever be ready. He didn't want to picture the mother and baby he had abandoned. He hadn't said a word to anyone about it. He might take that one with him to his grave.

"I need to take a shower," Nunez said.

"Honey…lay back," Laura said. She shifted their son to one side and pulled Nunez's head back to rest on her breasts. She caressed his chest and stomach, trying to make the tension disappear.

Nunez couldn't relax. He couldn't stop thinking, couldn't stop seeing what he was seeing. Every minute since the last round was fired on the highway he had dissected everything he had done, picked his actions apart and cursed himself for every mistake he'd made.

If he had gotten out of his patrol car faster he could have caught up to the older officer and told him to get behind cover. If he had put down the younger terrorist faster, the mother and baby wouldn't have been shot. If he had made dispatch understand he needed backup, maybe Rahim would have been killed much sooner. Maybe, if only.

It didn't matter. The choices he made and actions he took couldn't be undone. He had to live with them.

Nunez looked into his wife's vanity mirror. He realized something. Since he got out of the army he had let himself get soft and out of shape. He hadn't moved as fast as he should have, he hadn't been as accurate as he should have been, had been too hesitant to move. When the people he had sworn to protect needed him the most, he'd been to slow to act. And they had paid for it with their blood.

"Jerry, what are you thinking?" Laura asked. The woman could see right through him. He didn't even have to think about an answer. The words came from his heart, not his head.

"I shouldn't have gotten out of the army. If I was still a soldier I would have done better than I did yesterday. And maybe a lot more people would still be alive. Maybe I had done my job in Iraq and Afghanistan, half those bastards at the mosque wouldn't even be in this country."

She answered quickly, struggling to keep a soothing tone. "Jerry, that doesn't make sense. If you had stayed in the army you might not even have been here yesterday. You don't need to be back in the army, you need to be here protecting us."

"I know. You're right."

"Then come lay down with me and your son."

Nunez closed his eyes. His son. His wife. His daughter. What if they had been on the highway, with nobody around to protect them? What would they do, when this happened again?

Nunez knew, or at least hoped, there would be some kind of a military response to the attacks in Houston. Nobody was talking about a connection between the mosque and any larger terrorist network, but that wasn't the point. People who wanted to carry out more attacks like this needed to be destroyed, whether or not anyone was pulling their strings. Soldiers would be at the forefront of the actions against those groups.

Nunez thought about it. There was only one conclusion he could reach. He needed to be with those soldiers.

He turned around to look at Laura. She knew what he was thinking. They'd argued about it, many times.

"Jerry, if you go back to the army, it'll ruin our marriage."

"If I join the Guard again, it doesn't mean I'm going anywhere," he replied. "It just means I'm ready to go when they need me."

Laura was angry now, not trying to be comforting anymore. "Jerry, drop it. I won't let you go back to the army."

Nunez looked back at her, his face cold. "You won't let me? It's not your choice. You didn't see what I saw yesterday, Laura. You weren't on that highway. You didn't walk through blood and look into dead peoples' eyes and ignore dying women begging you to save them and their dying babies. You didn't have some psychotic asshole trying to kill you in the name of Allah. You didn't have to hunt down mass murderers."

Laura recoiled. "*You* did those things? I thought you just helped after it was over."

"I was in the shootout on the highway. I killed both suspects. Where did you think all these cuts and crap came from?"

"Oh my god, Jerry," she gasped. "I didn't know. I thought you had hurt yourself helping people out of cars, or searching buildings or something. I didn't know you had been in the shooting."

"I was, but it wouldn't matter if I wasn't," Nunez said. "I'd feel the same no matter what. Something needs to be done, Laura. And you know me. When I say 'Something needs to be done', I have to be willing to do it myself, and if I'm not then I need to shut up. Well, something needs to be done about these people, Laura. As a cop I can't do anything until it's too late. As a soldier, I can attack them first."

"Jerry, please," she said. "You're emotional. Anyone would be after going through that. Give yourself a day or two, see how you feel tomorrow. I'll put the baby in his room, we can shower together and then I'll massage you, help you sleep. You need rest. You can't think about things like this now."

"Laura, I'm not saying this because I'm emotional," Nunez said. "And I'm not thinking about this because I don't love you. I'm thinking about it because I do love you. And our kids. I want you to be protected, that's all."

"You can protect us better if you're here, Jerry. You know that."

She was partly right. It didn't make sense for him to run off overseas if the enemy was right here. Being a soldier might do nothing but keep him away from the fight.

And yet, there hadn't been any attacks against America until the military left Iraq, and started backing away from Afghanistan. Nunez didn't know if those two things were connected, but it made sense to him. If he could fight them over there, he wouldn't have to fight them here.

"Jerry," Laura said quietly. "If you do this, our marriage is over."

Nunez looked at her. The set of her eyes showed she was serious.

He stood, walked to his closet and pulled on his running pants. Laura watched him silently until he struggled to get a running shoe over his wounded foot. Then she asked coldly, "What are you doing?"

"I have to do something," he said quietly.

"Jerry, don't do this to me," she pleaded.

He pulled his other shoe on and knelt on the bed, bending to put his face close to hers. "Laura," he said softly, "I love you. I wouldn't want to be married to anyone but you. Our marriage isn't perfect, but I wouldn't trade it. And I know it'll get better if we try harder. If I try harder. I know I need to talk to you more, to tell you what's going on my head. But you know me. I'm a cop, and I'm a soldier. And that's all I am. Being married to me means accepting that.

"I can't protect you if something like this happens again, Laura. If you've got the kids at the mall and these guys attack, I won't be there in time. I doubt anyone will. It was pure, blind luck I was on the highway yesterday, that I was right there when the attack started. And even then, thirty-four people died before I could kill the shooters. As a cop I can only respond to what they do, but as a soldier I can attack them."

Laura didn't look any less angry, her husband's explanation didn't seem to have affected her feelings one bit. Nunez touched her face tenderly, wishing he was doing a better job of explaining himself. He didn't want her to leave him. He didn't want to be away from his children. But he couldn't sit still and wait for the next attack, or trust fate to keep his family safe from the kind of people who had been on the highway and at the mosque.

"Let me do this, Laura. I need to do this."

She stared back at him, still angry, still not saying anything. He kissed her forehead and then kissed his son. The boy smiled and laughed, totally unaware of what was happening between his parents. Nunez turned away, took his cell phone off the duty belt on the floor and left the bedroom. He grabbed his keys, picked up a phone book and walked out the front door.

He found a recruiter's number and dialed it. A minute later he was setting up an appointment, deflecting the recruiter's attempts to start a conversation about the attacks. When the time and date were set, Nunez thanked the recruiter, hung up and threw his phone and phone book into his Jeep, on top of his carbine.

He locked his Jeep and looked around. His neighborhood was beautiful, with huge trees and sculptured lawns, all the comfort and safety he had yearned for when he was overseas. His mind felt clear, the decision he had just made gave him a sense of purpose he didn't know he'd been lacking.

He stepped into the street, took a breath to shake off his crushing fatigue, and started on a three mile run.

END

ACKNOWLEDGMENTS

Many men and women inspired the characters in this story. Everyone I've ever known who defended what they believe in, no matter what it was, is represented in some way in this book. I thank you all. Even the people who tried to kill me in defense of their faith.

And of course, I have to thank my family. My father is my biggest fan, my wife my soundest foundation. My mother, brothers and sisters, sons and daughter, nieces and nephews have all supported me in multiple ways.

Tactical 16 gave me a voice and support when the rest of the publishing industry turned away. I'm forever thankful to Erik and Kristen Shaw, and all the other T16 staff and writers. I owe y'all, and hope I've proven worthy of the gamble you've taken on my writing.

I'd also like to think Mike Marcon, Vietnam vet, skydiving pioneer and author of Red Beans and Ripcords. Mike gave me invaluable guidance and mentorship as I wrote this novel, and is largely responsible for the title. I am eternally in that old warrior's debt.

One final note: I'm a lucky, lucky man, living in and serving the greatest country that has ever existed. Thanks, America.

CREDITS AND CONTRIBUTORS

Publishing: Tactical 16, LLC
CEO, Tactical 16: Erik Shaw
President, Tactical 16: Jeremy Farnes
Cover Design: Bryan Dolch

ABOUT THE AUTHOR
Chris Hernandez

Chris Hernandez is a 20 year police officer, former Marine and about-to-retire National Guard Soldier with over 25 years of military service. He is a combat veteran of Iraq and Afghanistan and also served 18 months as a United Nations police officer in Kosovo. He writes for BreachBangClear.com and and has published two other military fiction novels, Proof of Our Resolve and Line in the Valley, through Tactical16 Publishing. He can be reached at chris_hernandez_author@yahoo.com or on his Facebook page: www.facebook.com/ProofofOurResolve.

ABOUT THE PUBLISHER
Tactical 16, LLC

Tactical 16 is a Veteran owned and operated publishing company based in the beautiful mountain city of Colorado Springs, Colorado. What started as an idea among like-minded people has grown into reality.

Tactical 16 believes strongly in the healing power of writing, and provides opportunities for Veterans, Police, Firefighters, and EMTs to share their stories; striving to provide accessible and affordable publishing solutions that get the works of true American Heroes out to the world. We strive to make the writing and publication process as enjoyable and stress-free as possible.

As part of the process of healing and helping true American Heroes, we are honored to hear stories from all Veterans, Police Officers, Firefighters, EMTs and their spouses. Regardless of whether it's carrying a badge, fighting in a war zone or family at home keeping everything going, we know many have a story to tell.

At Tactical 16, we truly stand behind our mission to be "The Premier Publishing Resource for Guardians of Freedom."

We are a proud supporter of Our Country and its People, without which we would not be able to make Tactical 16 a reality.

How did Tactical 16 get its name? There are two parts to the name, "Tactical" and "16". Each has a different meaning. Tactical refers to the Armed Forces, Police, Fire, and Rescue communities or any group who loves, believes in, and supports Our Country. The "16" is the number of acres of the World Trade Center complex that was destroyed on that harrowing day of September 11, 2001. That day will be forever ingrained in the memories of many generations of Americans. But that day is also a reminder of the resolve of this Country's People and the courage, dedication, honor, and integrity of our Armed Forces, Police, Fire, and Rescue communities. Without Americans willing to risk their lives to defend and protect Our Country, we would not have the opportunities we have before us today.

More works from Tactical 16 available at www.tactical16.com.

Line in the Valley

By: Chris Hernandez

Proof of Our Resolve

By: Chris Hernandez

What They Don't Teach You in Deer River

By: Julia A. Maki

Death Letter

By: David W. Peters

The Pact

By: Robert Patrick Lewis

Love Me When I'm Gone

The True Story of Life, Love, and Loss for a Green Beret in Post-9/11 War

By: Robert Patrick Lewis

And Then I Cried:

Stories of a Mortuary NCO

By: Justin Jordan

Ashley's High Five for Daddy

By: Pam Saulsby

Losing the War in Vietnam

But Winning the War to Reclaim My Soul

By: Frank DiScala

Zuzu's Petals

By: Kevin Andrew

Thank you to the following sponsor for supporting this project:

Live Fire Armory

Colorado Springs, Colorado

You dream it; we help you build it.
We get you, because we're one OF you.
Veteran owned and operated.

www.livefirearmory.com

CPSIA information can be obtained
at www.ICGtesting.com
Printed in the USA
BVOW04s0108050917
493927BV00013BA/115/P